BLOWIN' UP A STORM

Cornbread Mafia Book Two

NINIE HAMMON

STERLING & STONE

BLOWIN' UP A STORM

Chapter One

Joe-Joe came running out of the woods like his pants were on fire.

"The law's in," he cried and the four people working in the marijuana field froze in place.

No longer the twelve-year-old who'd sat on the bank of Possum Creek fishing as the lookout for Nate Hannacker's still, the gangly, six-foot-one-inch teenager had been parked in his old pickup truck, hidden from the road by a thicket of elderberry bushes, "gettin' paid to do nuthin'" as he put it, spent his time strumming on his guitar and writing country western songs while he examined every vehicle that came down Turtle Run Lane.

Riley Hannacker went from disbelief to action between one heartbeat and the next. They had talked about it, of course, knew it was bound to happen sooner rather than later, had an exit plan firmly in place — but the reality of a police raid still yanked his gut into a knot so tight it was hard to get a breath.

"Where?" Nate yelled. He was on the side of the field nearest the stretch of woods that separated the field from where the dirt track over the knob ended, the clearing where Papa'd parked his truck. The dirt track led off into the trees, up and over the knob and down to the remains of an old logging road off Turtle Run Lane.

"Three cars turned off the road. That's all I seen before I boogied. I come straight up the creek bed and they're on the road, so you maybe got two, three minutes."

Riley, his grandfather Nate, and fellow growers Willie Ray Taggart and Jessica Monaghan had topped the marijuana in this field for the third and final time three weeks ago and they were here today doing delicate pruning, removing small or dying branches or leaves — snipping a little here and a little there, enhancing the plants' final growth spurt before harvest in September.

Left to grow wild, a cannabis plant would grow *up*, focusing its energy on a single main stalk seven or eight feet tall and would produce one large cola — the flower where the bud develops — at the top. The other colas, growing vertically on the limbs below, would be small and leathery, shaded from the sunlight by the leaves above. Cutting off the tops of the plants forced them to bush *out* instead of *up*, granting sunlight to the lower branches, creating more, bigger and better colas.

This field was set to produce a bumper crop ... except not.

Now, the plants would be plowed under by the law.

This was the same isolated field where they'd planted that first crop in the spring of 1970, the disaster crop that'd grown like weeds because that's really all the plants had been. But they'd learned from their mistakes and the pot in this field last year had changed their lives, turned everything around. If it hadn't been for the money they'd made off last year's crop, none of the four of them would be living such prosperous lives, so suddenly affluent, in fact, that they'd attracted attention. Friends, neighbors … and finally the *law*.

"Go!" Papa cried. Jessie and Willie Ray Taggart hadn't moved. "Hit the woods. I got this."

Joe-Joe didn't have to be told to run. He'd delivered his warning almost without breaking stride and was already vanishing into the woods on the opposite side of the field from the trees he had come running out of. He would make his way back to his truck by a circuitous route. Knowing Joe-Joe, he'd give a big smile and wave to the police cruisers if he passed them on their way back to town, proud that the first alarm he'd ever sounded was why the backseats of those cars were empty.

He didn't know there'd be somebody in the backseat of *one* of them. That was part of an escape plan that was bare-bones simple — *run!* Scatter into the woods and put as much distance as you can between yourself and the field of weed.

Papa had picked them all up in the early afternoon, driving the pickup truck that was now sitting in a small clearing about a quarter of a mile away at the end of the road leading to the field. They'd made no attempt to conceal it. Papa had it all figured out. But right now, Papa's plan didn't seem clever. It seemed dangerous. When it came right down to it, Riley wasn't emotionally prepared to run off into the woods and leave his grandfather here alone to face the music.

"Papa, are you sure—?"

"Get out of here, *now*!" Papa called out. The others were too staggered by the warning to respond. "I can handle this!"

Still, they stood frozen.

"*Trust me*! Go!"

That broke the spell. Jessie was on the far side of the field. Riley saw her shove her pruning shears into her overalls pocket, bulldoze her way through the bushy marijuana plants and take out running for the nearby woods.

Willie Ray and Riley had been working the center of the field with Papa on the near side. Willie Ray looked a question at Riley and Riley waved him on. He turned and muscled his way down the row between the plants and raced away from the field into the trees.

His grandfather's voice carried across the field over the sound of approaching vehicles.

"I got this!"

Riley knew he'd screw up everything if he didn't leave right now. As he ran across the edge of the field toward the trees, he was tempted to stop, look back, to—

To what?

He couldn't do anything now to help his grandfather. All he could do by hanging around was get caught himself, and the domestic uproar Riley's *arrest* would cause would be cataclysmic. Looking resolutely forward, he ran into the edge of the woods as fast as he could and disappeared in the trees.

NATE RAN full-out *toward* the sounds of approaching engines, not *away* from them, watching Riley vanish into the trees on the other side of the field. Nate *had* to get to his old pickup truck before the law enforcement vehicles got to the clearing where he'd parked it.

His mind flashed back unbidden to the time he had gone running out the bay doors of a not-tobacco barn and dived into a red Corvette Sting Ray only seconds before bullets started flying. He'd had to make it to that car or get shot — and the extra rush of danger had put a spring in his step. He had to make it to his truck, now — but if he'd been granted an extra burst of energy, he wasn't aware of it. Gasping for breath, Nate bounced off the smooth trunk of a sycamore tree into the clearing, could hear cars barreling up the road, seconds away.

Flinging open the truck door, he snatched his .22 long rifle off the rack in front of the back window. There was a box of shells in the glove box, but getting them out would cost him seconds he didn't have. He'd just have to make do with the ten rounds in the magazine. Slamming the door behind him, he made a dash for the trees.

If they saw him, even caught a *glimpse* of him, he was toast.

He wasn't ten yards past the tree line when the first car roared up the end of the dirt road and skidded to a stop beside his pickup truck. The first vehicle was a Callison County Sheriff's Department cruiser, but hot on its tail was a Kentucky State Police car. It probably was a trooper who'd been pressed into service to help with the raid. But it might just be Nate's old friend, Detective Booth Graham. Given Nate's plan, that would be a stroke of exceedingly good fortune.

Nate didn't look over his shoulder again to see who was getting out of the cars, though, just ran through the trees, dodging branches intent on blinding him, sliding in slick pine needles and fallen leaves, feeling the pain in his gimp leg ramp up to something approaching unbearable — and beyond. But he kept running.

He had to get completely out of sight before he started shooting. And he only had a few rounds of ammunition. He would have to make every shot count.

Chapter Two

SHE COULD SEE the whole thing in her head. When Sherry Lynn Hannacker closed her eyes, she could see the finished house, everything about it, all the way down to the drapes, the carpet and the furniture.

Well, maybe not the furniture.

But she had drawn out a crude blueprint of the house on the back of a grocery sack the first time Riley mentioned that they might build one. There was nothing in life Sherry Lynn wanted more than to move into a house of her own with her husband and her son. Things would be better between her and Riley if his grandfather wasn't always butting in, offering his two-cents worth. And even when he wasn't doing that, even when he was silent, just sitting in that broken lawn chair on the porch, he was there.

Just *there*.

Riley would talk to her if his grandfather wasn't around to snatch all his attention. Riley would consult *her* with plans for the future, if Nate weren't the fountain of all wisdom and knowledge … so let it be written, so let it be done.

And the privacy. Oh God, what she wouldn't give for privacy. They needed to be *alone*, to bond as a couple, they needed the intimacy of privacy to seal their marriage. It wasn't too late. They could back up and *start over* in a place of their own. They could … snatch a few minutes while Drew was napping to sneak up into the bedroom and make love. She'd talked Riley into it once, had to do some serious "persuading" but it had been glorious … until they heard the screen door bang shut and knew that Nate had returned home early from town. After Riley'd dressed hurriedly and gone downstairs, Sherry Lynn had lain on the rumpled bedspread and sobbed.

If Nate weren't always around, they could make love on the kitchen table if they felt like it. If she could have that kind of alone time with Riley she was certain, *certain* she would see again in his eyes what she had seen there when they were dating. What she hadn't seen since. Oh, part of it was the whole nightmare of the national guard call-up, Vietnam, the black body bags and bandages covering the wounds you could see but not the ones you couldn't. That had put a damper on their early months as newlyweds. But the pall, the gray clouds, just never left, not with Nate around all the time. She was sure she could lose the weight she'd gained, *would* lose it as soon as they moved into their new house, where they would be alone together. There wasn't a chance of losing it now, though, with her so miserable. She could see it happening but couldn't seem to do anything about it, couldn't help drowning her sorrows in food. She had put on thirty-five pounds in her pregnancy with Drew, and she had never lost it, just kept putting it on. She stopped weighing herself after she realized she was fifty pounds heavier than she'd been when she and Riley were dating. She weighed more than that now. A lot more, couldn't get the zippers up on the clothes she'd been able to fit into then.

It would all be different when the house was done. She would make a beautiful home for Riley and her son, a place Riley couldn't wait to come home to. She would shed the extra weight, so that when she put on some skimpy nightie and pranced around the house in it — which she couldn't do now but absolutely *would* do then — she could win her husband back, his desire and his love.

"Mrs. Hannacker, Bart said you wanted to talk to me."

The words pulled her out of her fantasy, back into the reality of late afternoon on a sweltering Thursday in August, standing in the blazing sun on the construction site of the house that would one day save her marriage. The building was what they called framed-up, meaning the floor was in and there was a framework where the walls would be. You could go from one room to another, on the first floor anyway, and close your eyes and imagine what it would look like finished. That's what she'd been doing, when she realized they'd screwed up the placement of the downstairs powder room, so she demanded to see Mr. Broderick, the construction manager.

"Yes, I want to talk to you. I told you I wanted the bathroom here." She pointed to a spot blocked off with a doorway leading out into the breezeway between the kitchen and the living room. "I don't want a closet here. This is where I want the bathroom."

Mr. Broderick smiled a tight smile and went into what she called reconciliation mode.

"I talked it over with *Mr.* Hannacker," he said. He stepped through walls not yet constructed and pointed to the spot where he was installing the bathroom-to-be. "When you're building a house, you need to consider where you put bathrooms in terms of where the existing plumbing is."

He pointed to some pipes sticking out of the floor in the not-yet-walled-in room next to the bathroom he was installing in the wrong place. "You see, if you put the bathroom fixtures and the sinks and on this wall, then you can use the same plumbing for them that you use for the washing machine and hot water heater in here." He pointed to the other side of the wall to the room that had been designated the utility room.

Indicating the space on the other side of the room where she wanted the bathroom, he continued. "There ain't no plumbing over there, Mrs. Hannacker. No water or drains. You'd have to run plumbing all the way across—"

"Can you do it?"

"Can I do what, ma'am?"

"Can you run plumbing under the floor from here to over there?"

"Well, yes ma'am, I *can*, but it'll cost a lot more money. I'll have to rip up the floor we done laid—"

"You wouldn't have to rip anything out if you hadn't put it in the wrong spot to begin with. And the extra cost—" She thought about what Riley had told her.

You get to decide about the house. If it was left up to me, I'd live in a room with bare walls, a dirt floor and a lightbulb dangling down from the ceiling with a pull chain.

And he would, too.

Get what you want.

Well, the bathroom on the other side of the room was what she wanted.

"If it costs more, it costs more. I want the bathroom over there."

"Yes, ma'am," he said, pressed his lips into a thin line and nodded.

She noticed then that the other workers had stopped what they were doing to watch the conversation. And the scene somehow felt … hostile. It seemed to Sherry Lynn that these guys … didn't like her. Or thought she was bossy, or too particular.

That hurt her feelings badly, and she didn't know why—

Yes, she did. Sherry Lynn Bennett, the beautiful purple-eyed cheerleader, was used to male human beings kowtowing to her. She'd bat those long eyelashes at boys in high school and they got all tongue-tied, didn't know what to say.

Men didn't look at her that way anymore.

With a sudden shock of horror, she realized that these construction workers didn't see a beautiful young girl at all. They saw an overweight … a *fat* woman. And if that's what *they* saw, that's what Riley saw, too.

Turning on her heel, she marched with as much dignity as she could muster across the plank flooring to the front door. The porch wasn't built yet, so she had to climb down a step ladder, only a couple of steps. But it was awkward. It was hard to go down a ladder when you couldn't see your own feet.

When she made it to the ground, she threw dignity to the wind and ran to her car, leapt into the front seat and drove away. Crying. Her makeup running down her face.

She was always crying now, every day, that's all she did.

And she wouldn't if Riley'd just … just *pay attention* to her like he used to.

Chapter Three

WE COULD BE the Hole in the Wall Gang.

That's what Willie Ray had proposed the day they'd formed their marijuana-growing partnership, to which Jessica had responded, "More like the Hole in the Bucket Gang."

When Riley had told his grandfather about the meeting later, Papa suggested the better title would be "Hole in the Head Gang."

Papa had not been an immediate fan of Riley's determination to grow marijuana, and would pitch a green fit now if Riley veered from their plans and got himself into trouble for no really good reason other than not wanting his grandfather to face the music alone.

As he stopped to catch his breath beneath the boughs of a huge maple tree, it occurred to Riley that Papa might not be alone. It was entirely possible Willie Ray had gone back. Who knew? There was no telling at any given moment what Willie Ray Taggart might do.

Riley didn't like admitting it, but it was true — Willie Ray Taggart was … off. There had to be a word for it, but Riley never figured out what the word was. Unhinged? No, *unbalanced* was probably nearer reality. Willie Ray had come home from Vietnam the same guy he'd been when he left — except with no fences. There was nothing, absolutely nothing Willie Ray wouldn't do. Or say. Or try. Or fight over. There was no "balance" to his life. He partied until he passed out, took crazy chances, courting danger by climbing up into the belfry of St. Dominic's Church to see what the bell sounded like "up close." He went from one relationship to another, a frenetic hummingbird tasting nectar, laughed too loud, worked too hard … and grieved every moment of every day. There was nowhere in him anymore that recognized restraint. That part had burned away when he sat with his brother Andy's head in his lap outside a bunker in Tweety Bird, begging Riley for help. Now, he lived every moment on the outside edge.

Riley understood what was driving his friend, but could do nothing to help him. He couldn't even exorcise his own demons let alone help Willie Ray with his. But Riley'd figured out that either Willie Ray was determined, *desperate to* live enough life for two people, or he wanted to die, and not just die — but die a gruesome death.

The distance between fearless and reckless,

between brave and stupid was wide and deep and full of alligators.

An unbidden comparison often came to Riley's mind — the illumination flares the big guns shot into the sky to light up the battlefield were impossibly bright, changed midnight into noon, cast brilliance out in every direction. But the flares didn't last long, they burned out quick and then the light was gone and utter darkness rushed back in to take its place.

Might be Willie Ray was right now getting hand-cuffed alongside Riley's grandfather, about to be loaded up and hauled off to jail. That would screw up everything. His grandfather had a plan and Willie Ray wandering out of the woods showboating would ruin it all.

NATE HANNACKER finally slid to a stop, gasping for air, beside a leafy dogwood tree. He leaned against the trunk, panting. Cigarettes. It was them cigarettes. He'd quit when Sherry Lynn and the baby had moved into the house. Sherry Lynn said she was allergic to cigarette smoke and he'd tried smoking only outside for a while until he overheard her telling Riley she could smell the smoke on his clothes. He'd been quit for more than two years now — still wanted, *ached* for a cigarette every day — and still hadn't got his wind back like he'd thought he would. Just getting old, he supposed.

In what universe was fifty-six years *old* old?

His face awash in sweat, his soaked-with-sweat shirt clinging to his body, Nate struggled to slow the hammering of his heart. He had to chill out now. The plan he had in mind wouldn't work unless he could sight in on a target and take down at least *one* of them. More would be better — the more he could shoot, the better. But he had to bag at least one.

When Nate had stood in the shade long enough to cool off, so he wasn't a puddle of sweat with clothes on, he crept silently through the woods, intent on getting as close as he could to his targets before they saw him coming.

He was using a simple .22 long rifle, which was accurate up to about a hundred yards or so. Riley'd told him that was because at that point the bullet had slowed down enough for the shockwave caused by its previous speed to overtake it and disrupt its flight path. Nate didn't know about all that, just knew he couldn't guarantee a kill shot at more than about fifty yards. Certainly wasn't using a fancy scope like when he had climbed up onto the top of buildings in Brewster with Big-Un McClusky, shooting at statues. He'd clipped the head off every one he aimed at that night. But his targets today wouldn't be lined up, sitting still, waiting for him to shoot them.

He climbed quietly up onto a rock outcrop that gave him a reasonably good view of the woods below. He fit the rifle into the crook of his shoulder, settled it there. Then he began to scan his eyes through the vegetation, looking for movement. He'd get one "surprise" shot, maybe two if he got lucky, so he had to make them count.

There!

Through the tangle of leaves, he spotted movement. Just a wash of gray — the color of a Kentucky State Police trooper's uniform.

He sighted down the barrel. Grew still. Waited.

There it was again, a flash of gray. He pulled the trigger. The rifle had almost no recoil at all. The target dropped like a rock.

That was *one*.

Chapter Four

Willie Ray only ran about seventy-five yards from the marijuana field and then climbed a tree.

He'd seen the big ole tree — he thought it was an American beech — from the field. The giant towered over the other trees, the perfect spot to provide a ringside seat for the circus that was about to play out when the law come roaring into the clearing where Nate's truck was parked.

He didn't tell the others he was gonna hang out behind. They wouldn't have liked the idea, would have pointed out — and they'd have been right — that he would screw up everything if he got caught. But Willie Ray knew something they didn't — he knew he wouldn't get caught.

He just wouldn't.

Call it the power of positive thinking if you liked. He knew he wouldn't get caught because Willie Ray Taggart just never did. That's not who he was. He'd learned as a daredevil kid that he always managed somehow to skate, left before Pa caught his brothers smoking behind the shed, bailed off the sled before it hit the tree, passed the police sobriety test even though he was bombed out of his gourd. He reached up and touched the jagged line of scar tissue on his cheek. Yeah, Willie Ray always got away. But the scar was there and he was profoundly grateful that it was. It was a mark that identified who he was and dictated what he did every day since …

He struggled to control his breathing. He wasn't no track star, but he had exploded out of that field and ran as hard as he could to the tree trunk. His heart was still hammering, not because he was frightened, of course. Willie Ray wasn't afraid. Not now, not ever. When you didn't really care one way or the other whether you lived or died, what was there to be afraid of?

Settling himself on a big limb, he leaned back against the trunk and peered out through the leaves over the top canopy of shorter trees. It wasn't an ideal observation point, he couldn't see but a small portion of the clearing, so could only catch glimpses of the action. But it was enough.

He'd heard the rumble of engines while he was still climbing, and now he could see the cloud of dust the police cars had stirred up as they come roaring into the clearing, just sure as they could be they'd done busted themselves some weed growers.

He and the other three had been kinda expecting something like this ever since they seen tracks in the mud on the south side of the field, little-kid tracks.

Some boy out rabbit hunting, likely. If some kid had stumbled on the pot patch, he'd brag about it to his friends, how he seen some "marijuana growing." Kids had big mouths; word would get out.

As the dust settled out of the air, voices carried up to him in his high perch. Not clear enough that he could catch what they were saying, but the tone of the words was unmistakable even from fifty feet up in a beech tree. Them fellas was pissed off they didn't find nobody!

Willie Ray smiled a little. If they was pissed off now, wait until they "caught" Nate.

It was a shame to lose this field, though. This here was 2A, and he really did need to know how well it was gonna produce, how good the weed would be on his score sheet, where he kept track of all the hybrids he was developing.

They'd figured out after their disastrous first crop, that growing weed from the "weeds" out behind the barn was useless. So was using the seeds from the mostly-twigs-and-bark bags of pot you could buy in Louisville and Cincinnati. It was nothing like the righteous weed they'd gotten from Ace in Vietnam. That's when Willie Ray set out to make their own strain of marijuana, cross-pollinating the plants to get a hybrid that would provide a good buzz, and smoke smooth. Much of the early stuff they'd gotten from dealers in nearby cities was little better than their own. Why smoke weed if it got you stoned but you woke up with a migraine headache? You could just go out and get drunk and wake up with a hangover … and at least beer tasted good.

As soon as the four of them had banded together, Willie Ray'd dedicated his every waking moment to making them a success, looked to educate himself on the plant genetics of cannabis, though he couldn't find a lot of information on that subject.

So he'd paid a visit to Dr. Archibald Waznuski, a professor at the University of Kentucky School of Agriculture. Just walked into his office one day uninvited and unannounced.

"YOU 'MEMBER ME? Willie Ray Taggart from Callison County?"

The professor had been one of the judges for the Kentucky State Fair horticulture contests for years, and most years Willie Ray had walked away with the blue ribbons.

"Why, yes I do, son!" he proclaims, jumping to his feet and extending his hand. He isn't a guy you'd have pegged for a college professor, which is one of the reasons Willie Ray'd felt a bond right off. He talked like a college professor, but looked like a farmer. Oh, he was in a suit and tie and all, but he didn't wear it well. It didn't fit right — the coat too tight in the shoulders, the tie like a hangman's noose around his neck. It was like you could see him wiggling around inside it, desperate to shuck the costume and get into some jeans or overalls. He'd been a barrel-chested man, bald as an onion, when Willie Ray was in high school. Since then, he'd added a beer belly/paunch, which didn't do anything for the fit of his suit coat. "Callison County …" he adds and pauses, looking at the

jagged scar that traces across Willie Ray's cheek like a lightning bolt.

Willie Ray tenses for the blow. Lots of people knew about the guard unit that got called up and what'd happened to it in Vietnam, and it was always awkward when they brought it up. What can you say? "Well, yeah, I was in the unit that got massacred alright. Hate it when that happens."

Dr. Waznuski doesn't bring it up.

"To what do I owe the honor of this visit?"

"I'm fixing to raise a crop and I don't know nothing about it."

"What's the crop?"

"Marijuana."

For an instant, a mix of emotions plays across the man's broad face — surprise, shock and another couple Willie Ray can't identify. Then the man bursts out laughing, has to sit back down in his chair because he can't stand up, manages to point out in a strangled voice, "Along in here somewhere is when you're supposed to say, 'asking for a friend.'"

"I ain't asking for a friend. I need to know my own self."

That sets him off again. He finally gets control of himself and waves Willie Ray to a chair.

"Sit down, sit down," he says, wiping tears of mirth out of his eyes. "The last time I laughed that hard was at a staff luncheon when Darcy Owens, she's the chairman of the English department, coughed and spit her dentures into the punch bowl. I tore out the whole seat of my britches."

He takes a shaky breath and lets it out slowly.

"So you're going to grow pot, are you? You do know that's against the law ... right?"

Willie Ray makes a kind of humph sound in his throat.

"My family's been making moonshine for generations. You think I give a rat's ass what's legal and what ain't?"

"What is it you want to know?"

"Everything! Tell me what books I ought to go read, for starters."

"Oh, I can tell you much more than you'll find in any book. Cannabis happens to be ... a personal hobby of mine."

FROM THAT MOMENT ON, Wazzi became a de facto silent partner/technical advisor for their operation. Said he hadn't had so much fun in years.

In the beginning, of course, Willie Ray'd decided to grow weed because he'd promised his brother, Andy, he would, that he would grow enough for both of them. He'd actually *done* it, of course, because of Davie. Willie Ray had to admit, though, that his obsession with weed was fueled by his own curiosity, too. He had found something he was good at, something he could pour himself into that mattered and he gave it everything he had. He sometimes wondered now where he'd have been if not for their weed business. And knew the answer was simple. He wouldn't be anywhere. He'd be dead.

Over the next three years, Willie Ray teamed up with Wazzi to produce a hybrid strain of cannabis that was all their own. After he developed a system to trace the success of his hybrids, he bred for certain characteristics. He wanted a plant with a high THC content to produce a good buzz, a plant that smoked smooth with no after affects, that was resistant to the mold that plagued tobacco crops, and that would grow well in Kentucky. The first seeds they had to work with came from pot grown in Mexico or somewhere else in South America and Kentucky's weather was cooler, the growing season shorter.

Riley'd claimed Willie Ray loved horticulture because it was "plant sex."

In truth, he'd had to weed his mother's flower garden when he was a kid, and become fascinated by the different kinds of flowers — different shapes and colors and smells. Some that came up every year on their own and some you had to plant from the little packets of seeds his mama'd got at the feed store in Brewster. Developing a signature strain of marijuana was right up his alley.

The plants in the field they were working today are a hybrid line he had great hope for ... but the law is gonna bring a backhoe in here tomorrow and destroy the whole crop!

Unless ...

Yeah, why not. Ain't no reason they have to lose—

Bam!

The gunshot is so sudden and unexpected it startles him. His mind goes into overdrive.

And then, of course, Andy shows up.

Chapter Five

Winona McClusky picked up the framed photograph somebody'd missed when they'd cleaned out her father's desk — *her* desk, it was her desk now. She'd been unloading boxes all day, sent out for a greasy burger for lunch and worked the rest of the afternoon. She was almost finished, though, had unpacked books, lining the office shelves with volumes of law tomes, civil and criminal, plus her personal library of classics, from Homer through Dickens to novels like *To Kill a Mockingbird* and *All the King's Men*.

She'd already hung her diplomas — a Bachelor of Science degree from Bellarmine College and a law degree from the University of Louisville School of Law — on the wall and ordered business cards. The cards had the firm's name — Tanner, McClusky and Fowler, Attorneys at Law in gold on the front. That was the name the law firm had carried her whole childhood. It'd been just Tanner & Fowler, for the past four years. Her partners, Amos Tanner and Wilbur

Fowler, had heaved a collective sigh of relief when she'd agreed to come back home and join the firm. They both were nudging up against retirement age — Winona's *father,* Parker McClusky, had been the "young blood" in the office ... before he'd disappeared.

They'd said they'd give her a couple of weeks to get settled in, move the rest of her furniture into the little house she'd rented, and familiarize herself with the firm's caseload and clients. She couldn't start soon enough to suit Amos and Will — both of them aching to spend more quality time with their nine irons and putters.

Sitting down in her fa— in *her* chair, Winona studied the photograph, a family picture she couldn't recall ever seeing. It had hung on the wall somewhere, though — the faded color and blurred images testified to years in the sunlight.

It had been taken before her youngest two sisters, Karen, now fourteen and Nora eight — had been born. Mama was holding the first of the "second shift" children, Rhonda — now eighteen — in her lap.

The three older children had dubbed themselves the "first shift" and the three younger children the "second shift" because of the age gap between them. Winona and her two brothers Shep and Jody, had been born barely a year apart, and it was seven years before any more children came along.

She studied her own image — thirteen maybe. A pimpled teenager. Even at thirteen, it was clear that Winona McClusky's face would never launch a thousand ships — maybe a jon boat or two and a navy dinghy. She was … "plain" was the kindest way to put it. Her adult efforts to ameliorate her lack of natural physical loveliness had helped some. As soon as she landed the job as a clerk for a federal judge after graduation, she'd changed her hair color, and she really did look better as a blonde. Even Hank said so, and they'd been breaking up at the time so he might actually have meant it. The dark hair had accentuated the unibrow, which she now shaped into two not-so-full brows that rested on a pronounced brow ridge — which she could do nothing about. Or about her eye color. It was brown, and not some haunting dark chocolate or bright caramel shade, either. Shep had nailed it when they were kids, said if she ever got mud in her eye nobody'd notice. Her face was square, her chin and jaw too big. Even in this picture, she was the one who most resembled her father. And as it turned out later in life, she was the most like him in character, too — both strengths and weaknesses. Standing tall behind his family, Parker McClusky looked fit, her mother still thin, maybe fifty pounds ago, with dark hair that had only been the color of a tenpenny nail for a couple of years. It'd turned pure white in the months after Shep died and Pa left.

No, not *left*. Disappeared. *Vanished.* Without a single trace, didn't even leave behind a little sparkle in the air like a soap bubble when it pops. Just poof — *gone.*

She had once tried to think of the last time she'd had a meaningful conversation with her father before he'd disappeared, and that led to the unpleasant acknowledgement that she couldn't recall *ever* having a meaningful conversation with the man. Or even a meaning*less* conversation. Her father had two sons — Shep and Jody, and the fact that they had an older sister ... that part never seemed to register in the higher centers of her father's brain. He didn't mistreat her. He just ignored her. The way he could look right through her and talk to one of her brothers made her wonder sometimes when she was little if she was invisible.

No, she hadn't gone to law school in a desperate attempt to gain his approval! At least, that's what she told herself at the time and there was probably some truth in it. But she did like studying law, was fascinated by it, was an effective debater and a dynamite researcher, and had a mind that was nothing short of brilliant at sifting through mountains of minutiae to find the single salient point. She'd been a dynamite criminal lawyer, if she did say so herself, operating out of that little storefront office in the West End ... not because of some noble determination to help the unfortunate and downtrodden. It was just the only place she could go where they'd let a kid two years out of law school handle real cases — felonies, assaults, armed robbery, even murder.

She couldn't claim she'd never lost a case because the truth was she lost almost all of them. Most of her clients had been not only guilty but too stupid to cover their own tracks. She'd *loved* it, though, solving the puzzles, figuring out what her client *wasn't* telling her, reconstructing the crime in her head so she could find some little detail to trip up the prosecution, confuse the jury, or get the case thrown out altogether.

But she'd dropped the practice like a hot rock when her father's old law partners had reached out to her with an offer to come home to Callison County and take his place in the firm.

Traded defendants charged with murder for defendants charged with misdemeanor criminal mischief. Traded fighting to keep someone out of prison for fighting to keep the mayor's daughter out of the court news.

Exchanged junkie drug dealers for teenagers busted with a joint, prostitutes for truants, armed robbers for drunks shooting at stop signs.

And then there was the thrill-a-minute of probating wills and the hold-your-breath drama of conducting a title search.

The truth still in the husk was that absolutely *nothing* about a small-town law practice appealed to Winona McClusky. She'd taken the job for only one reason — to find out what'd happened to her father.

And no, she wasn't on a crusade to solve the mystery of her father's disappearance in a *final,* desperate attempt to gain his approval, either.

She'd only believed that for about a week, though. She'd never been a very good liar — not to other people and certainly not to herself. She was determined — more than determined, dedicated ... oh call it what it was — *obsessed* with finding out what had happened to her father for two reasons, and she had no idea which one was the more powerful.

The first was love. Uh huh, Winona loved her father. It was that simple and that complicated. There was no logical reason why she should, given how he'd treated her all her life. But the ways of the heart were unknowable, and seldom bowed to logic or common sense. He was her father and she loved him with relentless intensity, had ached her whole childhood to be Daddy's little girl, to sit in his lap, and have him call her "Princess" or "Precious" or "Darlin'."

Now he was gone. Now, she'd *never* get a chance to change the script of their relationship.

When Winona got the call from her hysterical mother telling her Shep had been killed in a car wreck, she'd just gotten home to her apartment from the University of Louisville's law library, where she was researching case law for an appeal she was filing on behalf of a client who was as guilty as sin. She hadn't even made it home to Callison County before her father left. She never saw him. He hadn't spoken to her mother, either — who wouldn't likely have remembered if he had, given the state of hysteria over Shep she'd been in when Winona arrived.

"My baaaaaaby boy," she'd been wailing from the bedroom when Winona came into the house that night, "I want my baaaaaaby boy!" Nobody had even *missed* her father by then, nobody was alarmed by his absence yet, anyway. He had left the house in a rage — but he was always in a rage about something. He had spoken to Jody, then leapt into his Pontiac Grand Prix and drove away.

And he was never seen again.

Nobody knew where he was going, or if he told Jody, Jody didn't say. Folks just assumed he was a father grieving, went off somewhere to work his way through his pain. It was only when he wasn't home by the next morning, wasn't there to help Mama pick out a casket or make arrangements with the funeral home. Winona had done all those things because Mama was a basket case. When he wasn't home by the next day, the family had called the sheriff and, as Sheriff Gil had said, he "sent out the hound dogs" looking for him.

Nothing.

Zip.

They put off the visitation — Mama couldn't do that all by herself. Delayed the funeral for four days. How could somebody vanish without a trace that fast?

Winona didn't know how effective the sheriff's search had been. He'd done the best he could with what he had to work with, but Sheriff Angus Gilbert was no superstar. He was competent, got the job done, kept the crime rate low and the citizenry who elected him happy and that was all that was required of him. He might have done a bang-up job looking for her father. He might have done a lousy job. She didn't know.

And she didn't know if it would matter that there was a new sheriff in town now, no pun intended. Even Winona had been surprised when County Judge Executive Wendell Blandford had appointed her Uncle Clyde to serve out the rest of Sheriff Gil's term after he got sick. Maybe her uncle'd be willing to grease the skids, if there were any skids that needed greasing. Maybe there weren't.

That was among a whole host of things Winona McClusky didn't know.

What she *did* know was that it was ludicrous to believe her father was still alive.

He might not have been a candidate for the Father of the Year Award, but he did care about his family. His home. His life. Why on earth would he voluntarily have walked out on his wife and kids like that? He'd doted on Shep, loved him more than all the rest of his progeny put together, and he must have been devastated by Shep's death. So how could he — why *would* he — vanish without going to his precious son's funeral? Leave before he even picked out a casket?

And even if he had walked away voluntarily, how had he managed it — logistically speaking? He hadn't taken any money out of his bank account, hadn't used any credit cards, didn't have anything but the clothes on his back. It took resources, *money*, to vanish.

No, her father hadn't left voluntarily. Something had happened to him. He wasn't alive somewhere, sipping mai tai's on some beach in Tahiti. He was dead.

So how'd he die?

Natural causes?

Not likely. Somebody'd killed him.

Who?

And why?

And how? How had they managed to do it without leaving a single trace, erased her father like he didn't exist? There was a body, a car … somebody'd had to dispose of both of those.

She knew she needed to start with why. To piece together the elements of a crime, you always started with motive. Why would somebody want her father dead? Once she figured out why, that would lead to *who* and she'd figure out *how* along the way.

Whenever she let herself comprehend the scope of what she was attempting, her quest reminded her of Bruno, the Hendersons' dog that had chased cars down the street in front of her house when she was a kid. She'd sit on the porch watching, wondering what the dog would do with the car if it ever caught one.

If she somehow managed to find out who had *murdered* her father — then what? What would she do with the information, the *evidence*?

Well, duh, give it to the police. She was, after all, an officer of the court, had taken the Lawyer's Oath to be admitted to the bar, had sworn to "support the Constitution of the United States, and the laws of the Commonwealth of Kentucky." Had pledged that she would discharge her duties "with absolute integrity" in obedience to those laws.

Except not.

Which brought up the second reason for her crusade. *Rage.* Winona McClusky was pissed! Never in all her twenty-seven years had she ever been so angry. Yeah, she was her father's daughter alright, with a temper every bit as fierce as his. But she'd learned what he never did. She'd learned to control it, learned to use the fiery heat of rage as fuel to power her efforts. Her anger grew every day her father was gone, filled her, threatened to consume her.

Rage and love. The piddly little attorney's oath that she'd sworn with her hand on a Bible she didn't believe in was not strong enough to restrain the twin engines that propelled her forward.

If she managed somehow to catch that car she was chasing, she knew *exactly* what she'd do with it.

If Winona McClusky discovered that somebody had killed her father, she would return the favor. She would kill him.

Chapter Six

Jessie ran until the stitch in her side forced her to stop, put her hands on her knees and gasped for breath. She was sick, nauseous, and it was all she could do not to vomit, but she gritted her teeth and forced the bile back down her throat.

"Go! Hit the woods." The words Riley's grandfather had cried had drilled down into her soul and she was as utterly terrified as she had ever been in her life.

"The law's in."

Oh, sure, she knew what they were doing was illegal, and every once in a while the realization that she was a criminal stole her breath.

No, not a criminal. That's what Riley'd said.

"We're lawbreakers. I'll own that. But we are *not criminals.*"

She agreed one hundred percent with that assessment but was certain the sheriff and the state police didn't see any significance to the distinction.

The terror of getting caught had kept her awake

at first, that first year — the first disastrous year when they grew a crop of possibly the worst marijuana that ever poked its little green head up out of the ground.

But after a while, breaking the law became … normal. She gradually relaxed, didn't spend half her time looking over her shoulder when she was working in the field, didn't find her mind racing with the fear of what would happen if she got arrested. *Arrested.*

What would happen to Davie? And to his mother?

There was a sudden sound behind her, a rattling in the dry leaves. She leapt behind a tree trunk and peered around it, ready to bolt if she saw anything suspicious. She tried to hold her breath but she was still panting from running and the best she could do was try to breathe quietly. She listened, heard her own heartbeat pounding in her ears, strained to hear again whatever had—

A squirrel darted across the ground about fifteen feet away, leapt at a tree and was up it and had vanished in the leaves in seconds.

Jessie collapsed against the tree she was hiding behind. Struggled to calm her breathing and her heartbeat. Listened as intently as she could. But there were only the normal forest sounds. Birds and cicadas and the breeze in the trees.

This was the first … but Jessica had to face the reality that it would not likely be the *last* time … they had a brush with the law. They'd worked out what Nate would do … the plan sounded solid. And she'd got away. Now she just had to figure out where she'd run to, and make it out to the road, and circle back to the designated pickup site where Willie Ray would come back for the others as soon as he got back to his truck. He'd hidden it in the trees about a mile south of the field, camouflaged it so well he was afraid he would not be able to find it when he got back.

As she made her way through the trees, her grandfather's words brought her comfort — *lost in the woods? Go downhill to find water and downstream to find a road.* She had thought she was emotionally prepared for getting caught. She wasn't. Not even close. It had … *unsettled* was the least dramatic word to describe her reaction. Her response had been much more profound than she'd ever dreamed it would be three years ago when she set out on this grand adventure.

WILLIE RAY IS LATE, *of course. Duh. Riley shows up right on time. She knew he would, knows him better, in fact, than she wishes she did, given the current circumstances. When she'd invited the two of them to dinner, she'd made sure they knew it wouldn't be anything fancy. Jessie couldn't have cooked anything fancy even if she'd had the time, and she didn't. What could she serve with a minimum of preparation? Two choices. Chili or pinto beans. She could start either of them in the morning when she went to work and let them cook all day. The cornbread she'd have to make when she got home, but it wouldn't take long. And you couldn't have either pinto beans or chili without cornbread.*

Remembering Willie Ray's hollow leg, she makes both.

She'd met Riley at the front door when he arrived, and stepped out onto the porch with him to wait for the chronically late Willie Ray.

Can you say awk-ward?

They had ... history. And she hasn't been alone with him since.

She realizes what a cataclysmically dumb idea this is as she stands in numb silence, both of them determinedly not making eye contact, scanning the road for any sign of the third guest at the party.

It's the silence ... blowing up like a water balloon, getting bigger and bigger and if she doesn't do something about it soon ... finally, she blurts out a question into the tense quiet.

"Where'd that little boy of yours get that blond hair?" It's near sundown and the warmth of the spring night has encouraged a chorus of melodious creatures — crickets, cicadas, tree frogs, and hoot owls, asking their eternal question. Who? Who-who? "I saw him in church two Sundays ago and he looks just like ..."

Oops. Stepped in it. She needed a tire iron to get her foot out of her mouth. She'd been determined not to mention anything that would send their minds to—

"Andy Taggart," Riley says, and she can almost hear a smile in his voice. Obviously, it isn't a new revelation, and it seems Riley's come to terms with it, that the boy he'd named after his dead friend was growing to look more and more like Andy every day. "Papa says my hair was a much lighter blond than it is now when I was little, but it wasn't ever like Drew's."

She likes the warmth she hears in his voice as he says his son's name.

"Of course, Papa says he looks just like I did — except for the hair." He pauses. "Sherry Lynn says he looks like her side of the family."

He doesn't say that name with any warmth at all, or maybe

she's imagining it. She's certainly not imagining the coldness in his voice when he mentions "her side of the family." The Hannacker-McClusky feud — Jessie's heard about it all her life, and she's beginning to think it's not a myth. "The blue eyes, for sure. In bright sunlight, they look almost purple."

She asks what words Drew can say. Is he crawling? Does he sleep well at night?

The conversation is forced, but it's better than standing there in silence. They both heave a sigh of relief when a plume of dust appears on the road and Willie Ray comes barreling down it. Jessie refuses to think of the day she'd watched the dust stirred up by Mama Ruth's truck approaching the tobacco barn to tell them about the guard call-up. Her memory now always changes the rising dust into the shape of a poisonous black snake, slithering across the field to bite them.

He steps out of the cab with an open beer in his hand.

"Am I late?" he asks innocently, looks at their tense faces, and drops to his knees in front of them. "Please forgive me. I won't do it again." He holds up his little finger. "Pinky swear."

Riley reaches out and snatches the beer can out of his hand and pours the remainder on the ground.

"Hey, what you pouring out a perfectly good beer for?"

"Jessie invited us here to eat, not drink, and I think I know what she wants to talk to us about." Jessie's eyes snap to his face, but he doesn't look at her. "And if it is what I think it is, you're gonna want to remember the conversation."

Willie Ray gets to his feet and they go into the house. To see Davie, of course. There's no way not to see Davie, even if that'd been Jessie's intention, because his hospital bed and the medical equipment is in the room that once was a parlor on the front of the house.

Mama Ruth and Davie's oldest sister, Sharon, rise to greet them. Sharon has agreed to sit with Davie so Jessie can have the evening to herself. Mama Ruth has already been looking after him for twelve straight hours. Jessie absolutely will not look at Riley and Willie Ray, doesn't want to see them try not to look shocked at how Davie has changed. He's skeletal, of course, the feeding tube provides basic nutrients to keep him alive, but all his weight has fallen off his frame. He's lost not just fat, but muscle mass, too. His hands have begun to draw up into claws from disuse, months of lying in a bed. Physical therapy would prevent that. A relentless regimen of the proper physical therapy could restore the muscle tone, keep them from atrophying. He would put weight back on if he could be trained again to swallow, so he could eat food instead of subsisting on the gruel that flows constantly down the tube. If something isn't done, when he finally regains his mental faculties — and he will *eventually return to the old Davie, the man she married — he will be trapped in a useless body. She can't let that happen.* She won't let that happen. *That's what tonight is all about.*

Davie's eyes are open. Jessie has grown accustomed to the vacuous look in them, the lack of focus, but she knows it must be shocking to Riley and Willie Ray to see it. She's sorry for that. But it is what it is.

"I 'member when you's all on that baseball team with the grocery store sponsor," Mama Ruth says and smiles. "You 'member them tee shirts, with 'Piggly' on the front and 'Wiggly' on the back? Davie said he'd look stupid coming and going and refused to wear it."

"We was all *gonna wear plain white tee shirts 'til coach said we wouldn't get no money for balls and bats unless we had*

a sponsor," Willie Ray says, and the forced cheeriness in his voice breaks Jessie's heart.

"The other teams laughed at us when we'd come running out onto the field in those things," Riley says. "I don't think we won a single game."

His voice is absolutely level. He's better at hiding his feelings than Willie Ray is. He's wrapped tighter.

Having to see Davie the way he is puts a damper on the evening, of course, but they all soldier through and she's proud of them for that. Willie Ray eats almost all the chili singlehandedly, and even grabs the final hunk of cornbread out of the pan to take with him when they leave for the tobacco barn.

They can't talk about what Jessie needs to talk about in the house, with Mama Ruth and Sharon to hear, so Jessie'd made up an excuse, said she wanted their help to fix a piece of farm machinery. She's picked the tobacco barn because she hopes she can draw courage there from the ghosts in the shadows.

They ride there together in silence. When they step into the shadowy barn, Jessie reaches into her pocket, pulls out the letter from Davie that she'd gotten in May, almost a year after he wrote it, and hands it to Riley. He reads it without comment and passes it to Willie Ray. As he reads, his face changes, so she doesn't have to ask either of them if they remember stacking hands — "just like in tee-ball" — agreeing to raise marijuana.

She takes the letter back when Willie Ray is finished with it.

"Davie said ... well, you read it ... he said he thought this was our way out, our ticket to ... the future, that we could make a lot of money doing it."

She keeps her voice resolutely strong. Now is no time to start crying.

"If you meant it, what you stacked hands on, then … I want to suggest that maybe we team up, do it together, and I'm here to do Davie's part."

Before either has a chance to speak, she adds, "If you weren't serious … didn't mean … I'll manage on my own." She hopes that sounds more confident than she feels. "It's just that I … I need the money."

Need the money. *She shouldn't have said that because she loses it then. She'd been certain she could hang onto her composure, but all her strength and resolve leave her and she starts to cry. Struggling to stop and to talk at the same time, her words sound strangled, her voice tear-clotted.*

"It's for Davie! He needs things I can't afford! He needs physical therapy and occupational therapy, and … you saw Mama Ruth. She can't keep this up. He needs private nurses and I … I can't make enough money to pay for it. I just can't."

Riley steps toward her then, but she draws back, determined to say it all now for fear she'll never be able to work herself up to it again.

"I've tried everything I know to do. I look after Davie at night so I could go full time at the law office, but now … with the farm … I can't take care of it all … by myself."

Riley does come to her then, and she's helpless to resist. He takes her into his arms and tells her, "You aren't by yourself."

"You ain't alone anymore," Willie Ray says, awkwardly patting her back.

Riley takes her by the shoulders and speaks into her face.

"It's illegal," he says.

"Like that ever mattered to you," Willie Ray says.

"We just need to put it out there right up front that what

we're gonna do is against the law ... and there will be legal consequences if we get caught."

We. *He said* we.

Jessie feels relief flood over her so profound she almost loses her balance. She hadn't realized how terrified she'd been that they would turn her down, tell her they didn't want to grow weed ... or maybe didn't want to do it with her. Oh, she could do it without their help — she didn't know how, but she would figure it out because she had to. She couldn't let anything stand in her way. But they didn't turn her down, didn't go back on their agreement.

But then, how could they? Davie said it himself in the letter, "If I renege, they'll kick me off the tee ball team."

IT HAD BEEN important to Willie Ray from the very beginning, that their "business enterprise" have a name. That first night, when they were all admitting their ignorance — "I've never even seen any marijuana," she'd said — Willie Ray had blown off their concern.

While she and Riley had talked about logistics — how to get seed for their first crop from what was growing wild, or perhaps buy a bag of it off the street, because there would be seeds in that, wouldn't there?

"There's big plants out along the fence rows behind the barn," Willie Ray'd said. "That ain't marijuana — it's hemp and they ain't the same. But it's a weed — how hard can it be to grow a weed?"

Then he'd turned his full attention to coming up

with a name. It was the little boy in him, playing a game, wanting an adventure.

The Righteous Weed Society? The Hole in the Wall Gang? The Hole in the Bucket Gang? The Hand-Stackers Society? Reefer Runners?

The one that stuck was what he'd suggested as they were leaving. He'd stuffed in the last of Jessie's cold cornbread and spoke with his mouth full.

"How about the Cornbread Mafia?"

That had made it official.

"So that means we're all in — right?" She'd still been a little uncertain until Willie Ray stuck out his hand. Without a moment's hesitation, she put her hand on top of his and Riley put his on top of hers. Willie Ray lifted his hand up and down once, then let go.

"There, we've stacked on it." There was no sparkle in his eyes. "A promise is a promise."

Chapter Seven

WILLIE RAY SAT on the limb of the beech tree in the woods with Andy sitting next to him.

Wasn't real, of course — at least that's what the idiot shrinks said, thought that knowing it wasn't would matter, make it all better somehow. They didn't understand that it *was* real. Not *reality* real, but real in Willie Ray's heart and his gut and his soul.

Andy really was there. Not the Andy he had grown up with — the big brother who'd shown him how to slide a fishhook through a worm, who'd laughed when Willie Ray got measles, said the additional red spots had connected his freckles. The Andy who'd let Willie Ray slip into bed with him at night whenever there was a thunderstorm. Willie Ray was like an old dog — terrified of thunder and lightning, lay trembling in his bed as rain lashed the windows, determined not to cry, not to let his father and older brothers — and certainly not his sisters! — know he was afraid.

Andy had let him snuggle up close and never told a soul.

That wasn't the Andy who showed up in the beech tree. It was the Andy who'd stalked his steps when he first got home from 'Nam, the Andy whose head had been in Willie Ray's lap when the medics had shown up at Tweety Bird after the battle.

Andy had appeared out of nowhere in Willie Ray's hospital room the first night after the battle. The corpsmen had given Willie Ray something to knock him out as he sat beside the bunker and he woke up lying in clean white sheets on a bed. Andy was standing there beside Willie Ray's bed with his chest and belly ripped open and his guts hanging out on the floor. The doctors'd had to restrain Willie Ray with straps on the bed.

He had spent some amount of time, he didn't really know how long, in Veterans Administration hospitals, where they gave him drugs, and counseling and shock treatments and therapy. Nothing they did prevented the random visitations from his brother, and when he finally came home to Callison County he brought Vietnam with him. Rumbling explosions that shook the earth, the copper stink of blood mixed with smoke and feces — and he was back there, replaying the scenes over and over, finding Andy lying face down in front of the bunker when the firing stopped.

When Willie Ray had rolled his brother over, Andy's body had fallen apart. His internal organs had come sliding out of him where his body had been sliced open from his neck, down his chest, all the way to his groin. Even with all the noise — explosions, men screaming, rattling gunfire — Willie Ray had heard the sound the guts had made, the swishy, sliding sound as they oozed out onto the ground.

And he'd tried to put them back in, of course. Tried to put Andy back together. And every time Andy visited him for months, he tried again, in vain, felt how slimy the intestines were, slippery and slick so no matter how hard he tried to stuff them back in where they belonged they came sliding out again.

Andy sat beside him now on the limb. Wasn't there, but was. Willie Ray understood what was happening, but as always was powerless to do anything about it. Andy's legs dangled off the side of the tree limb with his guts swaying in the breeze between them.

It wasn't shocking anymore, though. Willie Ray was used to the apparition, knew it would be his constant companion every day of the rest of his life. He no longer feared it, but never got over the shock/horror/revulsion of seeing it — sitting on the tree limb, or in the church pew beside him, or at the foot of his bed. Andy didn't care who was with Willie Ray, stood behind Pa at the dinner table one night and Willie Ray ran out of the room sick.

Andy meant him no harm. He was just a part of Willie Ray now. That's the way it would always be.

Bam!

Another gunshot echoed in the forest and Willie Ray jumped, looked in that direction. When he looked back, Andy was no longer sitting on the tree limb with him and he let out a strangled sob and leaned against the trunk. It was better like this, when Andy came to him privately so he didn't have to pretend he didn't see him.

If he admitted to seeing Andy, they'd put him back in a hospital bed with leather straps holding him down while he screamed. He reached trembling fingers up to his face, traced the line of the scar. He wasn't the only one of the guardsmen who returned to Vietnam from time to time. Larry Bradshaw got drunk with him one night and talked about the first time it had happened to him. Larry was squirrel hunting and suddenly he was in a jungle, with those awful creature sounds. He said he was lost, running through the tall grass with sharp edges like fields of bayonets, and a whole squad of Viet Cong was behind him, yelling awful war cries, getting closer and closer.

When Bradshaw sobered up he wouldn't talk about it, got mad at Willie Ray for bringing it up, said Willie Ray was imagining the whole thing.

Andy never came to Willie Ray when he was drunk, and so Willie Ray spent as much time as possible in some state of inebriation or stoned. If he'd had a joint, he would have lit it up right here in the tree and—

The voices from the clearing grew loud enough for him to hear and he strained to see what was going on. He thought he could hear Nate, but Riley's grandfather was a soft-spoken man. Hadn't been a whole lot of talk. Unless the lot of them was dumb as doorknobs, they'd figure out quick Nate had them. Willie Ray smiled at that, wished he could see their faces.

He wanted a cigarette and was glad he didn't have one because he'd have lit that up, too, likely. Listening to car doors slam and engines start, Willie Ray started to climb back down out of the tree. It was such a shame to lose this crop. The weed in this field was a hybrid strain, 2A. He suspected it'd be the best weed they'd ever grown, but with marijuana, the proof was in the pudding. And now the law was gonna come out here and plow under the pudding. They'd be back as soon as they could get a backhoe in here — good luck with that! — but they'd figure out something by tomorrow.

It was Willie Ray's job to go get his truck out of the thicket on the other side of the knob and pick up Jessie and Riley. The trek over the knob gave him time to think and a plan began to form in his head. By the time he made it to his truck, he was whistling.

Chapter Eight

Nate started whistling half a mile away from the
spot where he'd parked his truck. Nice and loud.
Didn't want to surprise whatever law enforcement was
gathered around it, give them an excuse to shoot him.

And it wouldn't take much excuse at all for a
McClusky to shoot a Hannacker.

That's who would be waiting out there. A
McClusky.

Nate had almost choked on his coffee when he first
heard the news.

LEROY TAGGART PULLS UP *to the front of the barn in his
pickup truck, stops, gets out and looks around.*

*"I'm up here," Nate calls down to him from the open loft
doors. "I'll be right down."*

*LeRoy has brought the extra roll of black plastic Nate needs
to wrap around his hay bales, said he had extra and it saved*

Nate a trip into town to get it. Soon's he sees Leroy's face, though, Nate knows something's wrong.

"What is it?" He dusts the hay off his trouser legs. "Either somebody pissed in your Cheerios this morning or—

"Guess you ain't heard yet."

"Guess not. What?"

"Judge Blandford announced this morning who he was appointing to serve out the rest of Sheriff Gil's term. I heard when I was at the post office."

Sheriff Gil, Angus Gilbert, had been diagnosed with cancer, a bad kind, pancreatic, and he resigned his office about three weeks ago. Since the position of sheriff is elected in Kentucky, it would be up to the County Judge Executive to appoint somebody to serve out the rest of the sheriff's term until the next election.

Judge Wendell Blandford is a smarmy little pissant who never made a decision without wetting his finger and sticking it in the air to see which way the wind was blowing. His favorite color is plaid. Nate figured he'd pick one of the deputies, probably Skeet Burkett or Lonnie Franklin. Neither of them was a particularly stellar candidate, but they were what he had to work with.

Nate sees sympathy in his friend's eyes when he delivers the news.

"He picked Clyde McClusky."

All the air whooshes out of Nate's body. He feels like he's been kicked in the belly, and he has to choke out words,

"Why in the—?"

"That's what Lonnie and Skeet is wondering. They was deputies, who you'd figure was next in line. They knew the job, knew the sheriff, was current on what was going on ... but Clyde McClusky? Ain't but one explanation. Wendell sure didn't *do it 'cause he thought Clyde was the best man for the job — so he was bribed ... or blackmailed."*

Nate can't seem to summon the air to form even a one- or two-word response, so LeRoy carries the conversational ball.

"I figure the safe money's on blackmailed. Must be some of those stories about Wendell the Stud wasn't just tall tales after all."

Rumors always washed across the county like waves up on the beach, in and out, and Nate didn't pay no attention to them. But sometimes, one of them waves coming in left something behind when it washed back out to sea. Something real, out there in the bright sun, for anybody to see who passed by.

There had been talk for years that Wendell Blandford was a womanizer. Wasn't nothing to look at — big-boned like the rest of the family but uglier than most — short and dumpy and kinda dish-faced — so Nate never gave them rumors much credence. But they never went away, same song, different verse every year. And you had to figure after a while if the pile kept stinking, maybe there was something rotten in there.

Clyde McClusky had a small accounting firm in town, did folks' income taxes and such, had a horse farm that apparently actually had at least one thoroughbred, and of course, the Hitching Post Bar & Grill out in Crawford, which didn't have enough customers to stay in business but kept chugging along year after year like the Little Engine That Could anyway. Everybody knew Clyde had something going on in the back room. A card game, for sure, but he was also running women.

"Must be Wendell couldn't keep his pants zipped up and Clyde got the goods on him for something. Incriminating pictures, maybe, that he don't want the wife and kids to see." LeRoy takes off his Allis-Chalmers hat and swipes the back of his hand

across his forehead. "Ain't no other reason I can figure. Got no qualifications, just that he fought in the South Pacific in the war."

Nate finally finds his tongue.

"Being a soldier twenty years ago ain't no qualification for being a law officer now."

"Wendell's putting it out there that law enforcement ain't the major job of the sheriff, anyway. That's what the state police is for. A sheriff ain't nothing but a glorified security guard, carting prisoners from the jail to the courthouse and back, protecting district court and the grand jury when they in session, though why they need guarding I couldn't tell you. He's saying the major responsibility of a county sheriff is collecting taxes and Clyde's qualified 'cause he's an accountant."

"The sheriff's office can hire an accountant to look after the tax rolls." Nate doesn't mean to shout, can't help it, then kicks at a rock in the dirt, sends it flying. "A McClusky as sheriff." Hard to countenance a thing like that. He shakes his head. "That's all I need ... now." He pauses and the communication passes between them. LeRoy isn't involved with his son, Willie Ray, in growing pot. Not directly, anyway. They've got crops on several small pieces of land LeRoy owns, and he'll get paid for that, but he's not a partner in the whole thing like Nate is.

"You best hope you don't get caught," LeRoy says.

NATE WHISTLED LOUDER — the theme song from *The Andy Griffith Show* — to be sure the law heard him coming a long way out. They knew he was armed, of course, had heard the gunshots. Wasn't no way for them not to. And that had been the point all along.

Chapter Nine

Nate walked out into the little clearing where he had parked his pickup truck, carrying his rifle — pointed at the ground — and the bodies of the four squirrels he'd shot. Four wasn't bad, given that he'd had only ten rounds.

He decided at the last minute not to try to act surprised that the clearing now held three other vehicles besides his own — the sheriff's car, a deputy and a Kentucky State Police cruiser — and half a dozen law enforcement officers.

Why bother? They weren't going to buy his story and he didn't care. Didn't matter what they thought. Only thing that mattered was what a judge, a prosecutor or … if it came to that … a jury thought.

"Well, hello there," he said, his eyes scanning the group of officers. They landed on Sheriff Clyde McClusky and flicked away, then settled on Kentucky State Police Detective Booth Graham. The man had been smiling — grinning, a shark grin — when Nate first walked out of the woods, but as his eyes took in Nate, the gun and the squirrels, the grin began to melt off his face and it hardened, set up like concrete.

He was way smarter than Clyde McClusky and he'd figured it out.

"What are you folks doing here?"

The sheriff stepped forward and snatched the rifle out of Nate's hand.

"We come out here to bust you for growing weed, Hannacker," said the sheriff, his face wreathed in a "gotcha" grin.

"For growing *weeds*?" He didn't even bother to sound incredulous. He didn't look at Detective Graham or he might actually have burst out laughing. "I don't grow weeds, least not if I can hep it, I grow hay and corn and—"

"*Weed* — marijuana."

"Marijuana?"

"Ain't no sense in acting like you don't know what we're talking about." The sheriff gestured toward the field on the other side of a stand of the brush, weeds and scrub trees. "You got a whole field of it not fifty yards from here. That there's a fortune … and it also constitutes a manufacturing marijuana charge, not simple possession. You're going down."

Nate glanced at the ground and was thrilled to see that the officers had been milling about in the clearing, had scuffed out any footprints he or the others might have left. It was rocky soil, wouldn't leave much of a print anyway. They had been careful not to bend down the brush and weeds between the truck and the field. Each went a different way, didn't wear a trail. You learned those kinds of tricks as a moonshiner. As far as Nate could see, the officers had at least not plowed their way from the clearing to the field. That was good. Even they would have to testify — if it came to testifying and he hoped it wouldn't — that there hadn't been no trail worn in the weeds from the clearing to the field.

"You telling me there's marijuana growing over there?" Nate pointed in the general direction of the field. "Really?"

"Really," Sheriff McClusky said sarcastically.

"Well, that's news to me. I wonder who grew it?"

"It's on your land and this is your pickup truck, ain't it?"

"Yeah … there's a field over there that's mine. And this here's my truck—"

"You musta heard us coming and run off. Finally figured out you was caught so you decided to surrender."

"I don't know what you're talking about, sheriff." Nate shot a look at the state police detective, who probably wasn't aware that a vein in his forehead swelled up and pulsed when he was upset. Nate had noticed it the day he met the man, the *first time* he'd put something over on the detective. "I came up here a couple of hours ago, parked my truck and," he held out the four squirrels he had shot, "went squirrel hunting. Only got four, but that's enough for supper. I didn't have no idea there was any marijuana in that field."

He wanted oh so badly to say sarcastically, "And there ain't no way for you to prove I did." But it wasn't usually a good idea to kick a mad dog. You could get a bad bite that way.

It was beginning to soak into the thick skull of Sheriff McClusky what was going on, but he just blundered ahead. Turning to Deputy Lonnie Franklin, he said, "Cuff him."

"Cuff me? Seriously? You got to put handcuffs on me to make sure I don't somehow overpower," he counted, "five armed law enforcement officers?"

"You're wearing handcuffs because I say you are, Hannacker. Now, you got the right to remain silent, anything you ..." He went on with the spiel. Nate dropped the squirrels in the dirt and Lonnie pulled his hands behind his back and fit handcuffs on his wrists. They were so loose he had to be careful not to let them drop off. His eyes met the deputy's for a split second and Nate acknowledged the kindness.

"... understand these rights I have explained to you?"

"Yes, sir, Mr. Sheriff, sir, I do understand my rights. I choose to exercise my right to remain silent now." He looked at Det. Graham and continued. "I've done said everything I got to say. But would you mind ...?" He cocked his chin down at the four dead squirrels lying at his feet. "Would you take care of my squirrels for me? They're big enough to make a good meal." He paused, said casually, "And besides, they're *evidence.* Wouldn't want to be tampering with evidence, now would you, officers?"

It was clear they'd all figured out they'd been outsmarted, but Sheriff McClusky'd gone too far to back down now. He grabbed Nate by the arm but didn't yank, just walked him to his vehicle, opened the door, made sure he didn't bump his head, and closed him inside. With the windows rolled up, he couldn't hear much of what the officers were saying. But by their tone, it was clear they were not happy. Deputy Burkett reached down and picked up the squirrels by their tails, held them out from his body so they wouldn't drip blood on him, and carried them to the back of his car, opened the trunk and laid them inside.

The sheriff got into the car and slammed the door, so Nate knew he'd definitely "got the joke."

He wondered if the county attorney would even bother pressing charges. What was the point? Nobody had seen him in that field. There were no tracks leading from that clearing to the field. And he had an ironclad reason to have parked his truck there. Had the four dead squirrels to prove it.

Chapter Ten

WHEN WILLIE RAY showed up to get Jessie at the "collection point" off Drury Lane, he already had Riley with him. On the way home, Willie Ray told her he'd climbed a tree in the woods and watched until the police hauled Nate off to jail in handcuffs.

Then he began to bemoan the fate of their precious pot crop.

"They gonna take a backhoe in there tomorrow and destroy all that good weed," Willie Ray said, then let out what sounded like a theatrical sigh. "Unless …"

"Unless what?"

"We get there first."

"And do what?"

"Harvest it."

"Those plants aren't ready to—"

"They've got colas," Riley said. "Small ones, but still … it's something." They had planted eight different pot fields in the spring, scattered in various locations all over the county. It was always best not to put all your eggs in one basket, and in practical terms, they were raising several strains of Willie Ray's hybrids and they needed to keep them separate. They'd gone from one field to the next setting out seedlings, and the early fields would be ready to harvest in a couple of weeks. This was one of the later fields, and it was at least a month out.

Obviously, he and Willie Ray had talked about all this on the way to pick her up.

"But the law's gonna plow the crop under tomorrow morning," she said.

The sheriff and his deputies would have destroyed the crop today if it hadn't been too late to round up a backhoe and haul it up the side of the knob — over the rutted, overgrown road that wound through the woods to the isolated field. Of course, the law didn't know about the *back way* to the field, a four-lane divided highway by comparison, the one they'd used so they wouldn't have to wrestle a tobacco setter all the way up the knob to plant the weed in the first place.

"And the key words here are 'plow it under,' and 'tomorrow morning.'" Jessie looked at the long shadow of the knobs stretching out east as the sun set behind them. "It'll be dark in a couple of hours."

"We could work all night," Willie Ray said.

"What are you talking about? One night's not enough time."

Even if the four of them could have harvested the whole field in one night, it still remained to load it up in huge piles on flatbed trailers and haul the marijuana out of there.

"Not enough time for you and me and Riley and Nate. But what if we had a whole crew of hands?"

"How could we possibly get away with it?"

"Who's gonna know?"

Then Willie Ray got it. "Oh, *that's* what you're worried about — you're afraid they posted a guard." He laughed out loud. "I watched them all drive away — everybody who come up that hill went right back down it. Why would they leave somebody to keep watch? It ain't like they're scared the weed's gonna run off. Wouldn't never occur to none of 'em that the field full of pot they busted this afternoon ain't gonna be right where they left it tomorrow morning."

"Where could we get enough workers on a moment's notice? Who'd drop whatever they're doing and come running?"

The pool of available workers was necessarily limited to the men who'd helped them raise and harvest previous crops. There were quite a few of them, though, but most weren't easy to get in touch with.

"Oh, we'd get plenty of help," Willie Ray shot a glance at Riley, "if we put it out there that anybody willing to cut the weed ... *is welcome to keep it.*"

"*Keep it?*" Her mind stumbled, trying to put it together.

"Uh huh. It's yours! All you got to do is haul it away."

Riley chimed in. "Word'll spread like a grass fire — if you got a pickup truck and want to make a year's salary overnight," he managed a reasonable imitation of Bill Cullen on *The Price is Right*, "Come on down!" Riley turned to Willie Ray. "It ain't ready to come out of the oven yet, but what do you figure a truckload of it's worth right now?"

"Depends on what kinda truck you can lay your hands on and how much you load up in it." He figured in his head. "That little dealer in Louisville, Snake Eyes, sells half an ounce of weed in dime bags. Fill up the bed of a half-ton truck with what's out there now, and you might get — what, fifty pounds of sellable weed? No, less than that, thirty-five. But that's ten, maybe fifteen thousand dollars."

"Wouldn't give it *all* away. We'd load up three or four truckloads of our own." Riley paused, always seemed to be tuned in to what Jessie was thinking. "Yeah, I know. It'd be a whole lot simpler and easier just to throw in the towel and write this patch off, let 'em have it. Other than messing with Willie Ray's hybrid schedule, it's no biggie, ain't like it's the only field we got. But ..."

Now it was Jessie who got it. "But ...you don't want the law to destroy it because you don't want them to win."

"No reason they should, if we can help it," Willie Ray said. "Wouldn't you rather give it away than have the law bush hog it? Ain't nobody I know who couldn't use that kinda easy money."

"And won't that be a fine surprise when they drag a backhoe all the way in here tomorrow and don't find anything to plow under!" Riley says, smiling.

"You in?"

"Of course I'm in."

Jessie hopped out of Willie Ray's truck and hurried into the house. She needed a shower and had to get something to eat before she returned to the field to work.

She walked into Davie's room and he turned to her and smiled.

And just for an instant, it was real. It was her Davie — with a cleft in his chin deep enough to eat pudding out of — and some wisecrack on his lips.

He'd tell her that her hair was the color of … maybe baby ducks this time. Or Big Bird on Sesame Street. And she'd tell him he'd better watch that lip or she was going to have to make him pay for disrespecting her.

And they'd look at each other, that special look that planted in her chest a wave of pure lust, and they'd both be envisioning what he would have to do to atone for that insolence — something that involved getting undressed, lots of laughter and hard breathing.

It only lasted for a moment, of course. It was a glorious moment and an agonizing moment. Glorious in the brief surge of happiness, and agonizing in the fall from there into reality. She'd learned how to keep from falling, didn't do it very often so it really hurt when she did.

Davie kept on smiling. At nothing.

"You look like you been rode hard and put up wet," said Harriet Porter, the nurse who cared for Davie and his mother during the day. She was a black woman of indeterminate age who had a soft voice and kind eyes. Her oldest son had been killed in Vietnam two years before the National Guard unit was called up. When Jessie thought about that, she was ashamed that the county had ignored his death.

Jessie looked like she had been doing exactly what she had been doing — running through the woods. Her bare arms were scratched and dirty, her whole body slathered in sweat. Exertion sweat and fear sweat. Equal portions.

"Who me?" She gestured to the briars attached with little stickers to her hair and her clothes. "I been taking a nap."

Davie stopped smiling.

Crossing the room, Jessie popped a kiss on his cheek and he turned his eyes toward her face. He didn't make eye contact, just looked at the place in space where her head was. He smiled again, or at least lifted the corners of his mouth in an expression that looked like a smile.

She turned to Harriet. "Would it be possible for you to come back after supper and spend the night?" Harriet didn't ask why. She knew exactly what Jessie and the others were doing — just like a whole lot of other people in the county knew, Jessie supposed — but never mentioned it, pretended it wasn't happening.

"Well, I guess … sure. I could arrange that."

"Thanks so much."

"Jessie?" Mama Ruth called from the next room. "Where you been, girl? I ain't decided yet what I'm gonna wear to the reception and I need you to help me pick something out." In her mind, Mama Ruth was on her way to a royal wedding. Exactly who was marrying whom, she didn't say, just talked about the preparations. The woman had no sharp edges anymore, all her cantankerous abrasiveness had been wiped away, and now she was a sweet little old lady who had absolutely no idea what was going on in the real world.

Jessie missed the abrasiveness. She missed Ruth Monaghan, the old woman who had stood with her through the worst events of both their lives. But that woman was long gone, as gone as the Davie who'd told Jessie her hair was the color of butter.

"I think the pink dress is the prettiest," Jessie said, describing a dress that didn't exist as she walked into Mama Ruth's room from Davie's. "The one with lace on it."

When Jessie started up the stairs, she could hear Mama Ruth's voice trailing after her."

"I ain't got no pearls to go with that one, though. Can't wear it 'thout no pearls."

She was still talking when Jessie closed the bathroom door and turned on the shower. Then the stinging hot water drowned out her words.

Chapter Eleven

Kentucky State Police Detective Booth Graham cursed himself for letting that stupid sheriff talk him into inviting Jim Bingham, the editor of the *Callison County Tribune*, along to take pictures of them destroying Hannacker's marijuana crop.

McClusky'd proposed the idea as they'd stood together watching Hannacker leave the courthouse late yesterday afternoon after Commonwealth's Attorney Simon Henry had "declined to press charges."

"HOW MANY THINGS can 'I won't prosecute' mean?"" says the narrow-shouldered young man who barely looks old enough to have graduated from law school. His hair is turning prematurely white around the temples, though, and there is salt sprinkled liberally through the pepper in the rest of his mop of black hair — that helps him look a little older.

"Come on, Booth." The young man gestures at the pile of

case folders on his desk. "I got better things to do than wasting it on a case I can't win. You didn't see Hannacker in the field. You didn't see any tracks through the brush from his truck into the field, no trail worn in the dirt. And he had a valid reason to be there that had nothing to do with a field full of marijuana." Henry looks at his watch, letting Graham and the sheriff know that he has stayed in the office late to hear them out. "If I took this case to court, Hannacker would sit on the stand and give the judge his favorite recipe for squirrel stew."

THAT'S when Sheriff McClusky had suggested it.

"We didn't get Hannacker, but we got his weed," he'd said. "We can make points with that, plowing under a whole field of pot. I'm gonna give Jim Bingham a heads-up."

And Graham had gone along with the idea!

Idiot!

Now the editor was scurrying around taking pictures of an *empty* field littered with pieces of marijuana plants. Tire tracks crisscrossed the dirt where pickup trucks — a lot of them — had been hurrying here and there. He could almost imagine the scene — wondered how many men it had taken to harvest the whole crop overnight and haul it away. A lone truck, older than dirt, sat broken down on the far side of the field, the back half loaded with stalks of marijuana. Booth would bet his pension that whoever owned it had already reported it stolen.

When they got back to the sheriff's office, it had taken an enormous act of will to keep from exploding.

Graham wanted to break something, and not something fragile. Something sturdy. He wanted to reach out and grab the gooseneck lamp off the sheriff's desk and wrap it around his useless neck. He didn't. A man who couldn't control his own temper was at the mercy of a world out there bent on making him mad. You want to be in charge, call the shots, you can't blow up every time things don't go your way.

But *this*.

He ground his teeth, didn't realize he had balled his hands into fists at his side.

It had been bad enough when they'd busted Hannacker.

McClusky had gotten a tip about the location of one of Hannacker's marijuana fields and it was on Hannacker's own land! Some kid out rabbit hunting had stumbled on the field, had told his older brother about it, who had gotten drunk and told his girlfriend, who told her mother, who … That was the only way you could get a tip about weed crops in this county — somebody gets drunk and spills the beans. Because there wasn't a sober man, woman or child in the whole county who would rat out a grower to the law.

Graham had found out about the tight-lipped nature of the county's residents the hard way when he was new on the job, had been hard at work on his first big bust. Then it went unexpectedly sideways. A tractor-trailer load of stolen goods was part of a sting operation to trap a woman named Mama Bert, bust her multi-faceted fencing-stolen-property ring. But the truck disappeared, and the Hannacker place was near where they'd lost sight of it. According to Sheriff Gil, the Hannacker family had been moonshiners and bootleggers for generations, everybody knew that. And there were rumors Nate Hannacker dipped his toe into other illegal enterprises now and again.

That's all it took. After all, Booth Graham understood how criminals thought! Yes, he did. He'd earned his chops busting crooks in Chicago. He'd learned there that the bottom-feeders who operated outside the law were all members of an unofficial fraternity. And the way you caught one of them was to put pressure on one of the others. Squeeze hard enough and it was like a freshman popping a zit. Crooks always rolled over on other crooks if you knew how to work them. Threaten them with a big charge and a long sentence or bribe them with immunity and a lighter one. You just had to know how to play it. Graham knew how.

So he'd demanded to be taken to meet this Hannacker fellow, though to his credit, Sheriff Gil had tried to talk him out of it. That's when Graham's education about the particular breed of criminals who inhabited Callison County, Kentucky began. Hannacker was way sharper than he had any right to be, had humiliated Graham, put him in his place. Six months later, Graham got another shot at Hannacker. An open-and-shut, ironclad case against him and a huge hillbilly called Big-Un McClusky for terroristic threatening and assault … except the two of them went on a little shooting spree that convinced the guy who'd been assaulted to drop the charges.

Fool me once, shame on you. Fool me *twice* ...

Booth had personally delivered the paperwork on the dropped charges to Hannacker's house, put him on notice that Booth Graham *would take him down*!

The opportunity had not presented itself, however.

Graham had spent the last couple of years on a special taskforce trying to stop the influx of hard drugs — heroin and cocaine — into Kentucky. Which had been like trying to catch an individual cockroach when you turned the light on and they all scattered. He'd kept his finger on the pulse in Callison County, though, biding his time. Watched as the fortunes of the Hannackers suddenly improved dramatically. Come last year, they'd had money to burn, Nate's grandson was building a fancy new house and that Taggart boy, the one who'd come home one sandwich shy of a picnic from Vietnam, was tossing money around like throwing feed to chickens.

Marijuana.

The money to be had there was like picking twenty dollar bills up off the floor. And in the past couple of years the production of the illegal weed had exploded — with everybody and his brother out putting plants in the ground on the back forty. The fox was in the chicken house and Booth Graham didn't have anything to fire but a pop gun. Kentucky had some of the most lenient marijuana laws in the country!

Any real penalty came after multiple convictions. You couldn't get multiple convictions, though, without starting somewhere. So yeah, Graham had been thrilled at the opportunity to bust Hannacker.

Then Hannacker had come waltzing out of the woods with those squirrels …

He had made eye contact, that's all. Hadn't said a word, didn't even smile. But he was gloating. Oh, my yes he was *gloating*. Knew he'd get off … wouldn't likely even face charges.

That smirky look on his face had been hard enough to swallow. And now … even the marijuana was gone! Graham felt the vein in his temple pulsing with every heartbeat.

He turned, went to the door of the sheriff's office and closed it behind him. Then he sat down in the chair in front of the sheriff's desk.

"We didn't have this conversation," he said.

McClusky lifted an eyebrow, but nodded.

"What conversation?"

"The conversation where we figure out how to take Nate Hannacker out, how to put him away."

"Now that's gonna be—"

"Not on some piddly little marijuana charge."

"What, then?"

"I'll have to figure that out. "

"You talking about … like planting eviden—?"

"If that's what it takes. Maybe more than that."

"More?"

The sheriff clearly wasn't tracking, but that was fine. He wasn't the sharpest knife in the drawer anyway, not the kind of man you could depend on to have your back. Or keep your secrets. This was between Booth Graham and Nate Hannacker. He had a badge; Hannacker didn't. He'd figure out something.

Chapter Twelve

It was just past dawn when Jessie trudged exhausted up the front porch steps and into the house. She greeted Harriet — who had to know Jessie'd been up working in a pot field all night, but acted like she didn't. Harriet just gave Jessie a report on her two charges — both Davie and Ruth had slept soundly all night — and then she left.

Jessie's bedroom was upstairs — and in the past six months she'd actually started sleeping there most of the time. Davie's condition had improved to the point that he didn't need around-the-clock care — just somebody to check on him. He slept and woke with the rest of the house, his eyes vacantly seeking something to focus on when he was awake.

As Harriet pulled out of the driveway, Jessie's eye fell on the bathtub Mary in the front yard. Just about everybody had one, a shrine with a statue of the Virgin Mary, made into a grotto by covering it with half an old clawfoot bathtub. She realized the white paint was peeling. When she'd had the house remodeled downstairs, she should have finished the job by getting the rest of the house — and the Mary — repainted. She'd do that after this year's pot crop was in the barn.

Jessie went into Davie's room and collapsed into the recliner beside his bed. When she did, a pain stabbed into her right shoulder so severe it made her gasp.

Ouch!

What was *that*? She moved again and was stabbed again. Clearly, Jessica had done something to herself, pulled a muscle or a tendon or a ... *whatever*. Lifting and hauling and straining all night would do that to a girl. The Cornbread Mafia'd made off with three pickup loads of weed from the grand giveaway. Had to cut it, load it, haul it away and then unload it in an "abandoned" tobacco barn on Round Rock Pike. Nate had used the place over the years to "store things," though Jessie wasn't sure what things. She supposed it had something to do with bootlegging. They had processed their weed crop there the last two seasons, but it wouldn't be big enough for this year's crop and they'd have to—

Davie turned his head toward her and smiled and every other thought dropped out of her mind.

The smile looked so achingly *genuine.* She'd spent a lot of time considering that, wondering about it. He wasn't smiling *at* anything. The first time he'd done it, she'd been so astounded, she had burst into tears. It was Christmastime, six months after Davie woke up.

Well, opened his eyes — which at the time was nothing more than that. He didn't look at anything, see anything. But he did open his eyes sometimes, and she and Mama Ruth had been so encouraged by that — believed he understood in some way what was going on around him — that they were determined to make whatever was going on around him good and happy and engaging.

They had put up Christmas decorations — forced themselves to be cheery. Bought a tree and decorated it in the parlor, which was Davie's room at the time. They'd sung Christmas carols — along with his sisters, who came over now and then to see him. Mama Ruth had even made a stab at Christmas dinner for the family. Wasn't the same as past Christmases, of course. But she'd made the effort, prepared a turkey and dressing and let the girls bring the rest of the dishes. They moved the table out of the dining room into the parlor — sticking out through the archway into the hall. And they'd all gathered, chatted, talked. They spoke to Davie as if he could hear them.

He *could* hear them — he'd opened his eyes and looked around, and that *proved* he could. Didn't it? He could hear them, and somewhere inside he knew what their words meant.

The Christmas of 1970 had been an aching combination of hope and despair. Since Davie had opened his eyes on Derby Day he had never focused them on anything. But he kept them open for a while before he closed them again — then opened and closed them often. And that had caused a flurry of activity, of hope and anticipation. He'd look at them soon. Wouldn't be long before he'd respond to them, maybe squeeze their hands.

And then, that day, during Christmas dinner, Davie had smiled.

Mama Ruth saw it and gasped, dropped her fork into her plate. When everybody else turned to him, they saw the smile, a big engaging smile that slowly drained off his face. Jessie had started crying, couldn't help it. The whole family spent the rest of the day trying to get him to smile again, talking about how the smile *meant* something — it really did. It meant he was responding emotionally to his surroundings, didn't it? Of course it did. After all, it'd happened on Christmas, with all of them there, he'd been connecting to their presence — the smile proved it. They'd even stood around his bed and said the Lord's Prayer together — at Mama Ruth's insistence — before the girls left. Joined hands with each other and with Davie and prayed out loud. Jessie knew Mama Ruth was hoping he'd respond to that, look at her or Jessie or his sisters, smile again maybe. He didn't.

The next summer, 1971, Mama Ruth had a stroke. Jessie had been out in the field on the double tobacco setter with Riley, placing into the ground the individual marijuana plants from the seed Ace had brought them in January. Nate had been driving the tractor and stopped in the middle of the field when Willie Ray drove up in his truck, had stopped because of the look on Willie Ray's face.

Mama Ruth had collapsed. One of her friends had

been there, helping her feed Davie. Ever since he'd opened his eyes, they had been feeding him — like feeding a baby. Mashed potatoes, soft things, that he spit out and they wiped off his chin with the spoon and put back in his mouth. The friend had called an ambulance and by the time Jessie got to the hospital, Mama Ruth had already been sent on a Stat Flight Helicopter to Jewish Hospital in Louisville.

She'd been hospitalized for a month, spent another six weeks in a rehab facility and when Jessie brought her home, there was a hospital bed that matched Davie's, set up for her in the parlor. The girls pitched in then — had to. Without their mother's caustic tongue to put them off, Davie's sisters were willing to take a hand in caring for her and Davie.

Jessie shuddered even now to think how close she'd come. How the weed money had been *barely* enough. But without it … she'd have had to put Davie in the VA Hospital. And *that* would have killed Jessie.

In the two years since, both Davie and his mother had improved. His mother's whole right side had been affected, but with three-times-weekly physical therapy — from the same therapist who'd been caring for Davie — she'd regained some use of it. She couldn't walk or anything like that, but her smile was no longer lopsided, she could mostly feed herself and she was "there." Way more "there" than Davie was.

Davie's recovery had come in fits and spurts. It was almost a year after he opened his eyes before he was able to follow an object with them. And then over the course of one winter, he began to focus his eyes on people's faces when they talked to him, smiled when they spoke, looked every now and then like he might … might … recognize Jessie. That'd been the winter of 1972/73. He remained sweet and vacant-eyed, a shell of the man she'd married. Just the outside. Unless she was deluding herself — which she frequently did — she could see nobody home. Davie Monaghan had left the building and he never returned.

Then, on New Year's Day more than eight months ago, he'd started hollering.

It was the middle of the night and Jessie was asleep in the chair beside his bed, when he suddenly started making noise. She was so surprised, she almost wet herself.

Once he began, he continued to make sounds — just sounds, loud and soft, moaning/howling/whining/keening sounds that at times so set her teeth on edge she had to leave the house and walk down the road far enough that she couldn't hear them anymore. Of course, she told his doctors about the development, but not with any real anticipation they'd know what to do to capitalize on it. The doctors' mindset was clear — research was concentrated on people they thought they could help. Davie didn't fall into that category, so the doctors had written him off and Jessie had become less and less tolerant of their eye-rolling at her descriptions of his behavior, as if she were delusional at best, a liar at worst.

"Mrs. Monaghan … the sounds your husband is making are just that. Sounds. Nothing more. They are a biological response, not a cognitive one." Whatever that meant.

So Jessie had to figure it out on her own.

You had to be able to produce sound to be able to produce language, and so she saw the hollering — *chose* to see the hollering — as a step in that direction.

How did people who couldn't speak learn how? Simple words. Easy-to-produce sounds. That was low-hanging fruit. To reproduce simple sounds, Davie would have to hear simple sounds.

She began to speak to him in short, two- and three-word sentences. Not baby talk, but not the "normal conversation" she'd been peppering him with since she brought him home from the hospital. She kept at it, day after day, month after month.

Right before Easter, Davie said, "Mama."

Well, it sounded like Mama. She told Mama Ruth about it, but sometimes his mother didn't remember who Davie was, and that day was one of those times.

Jessie decided it was a *word*. It was. Davie was talking, and she would keep on keeping on until … she'd just keep on keeping on.

Then he said "Ahhh-naaa." The sounds meant nothing, but if you put them together, it was Anna. Far as she knew he didn't know anybody named Anna, but maybe she'd been one of his nurses in the hospital.

Yeah, okay, that was a stretch. It was Ahhhhh Naaaa. Sounds, that's all.

But he had said "no" too, and that one was clear. It wasn't in response to anything, but the word was clear. And he made some sounds that might have been "uh oh," like a little kid who spilled his milk.

Last fall's weed crop had been a windfall that had made it possible for Jessie to renovate the whole front portion of Mama Ruth's house — with rehab equipment, special bathing facilities — everything necessary to make the place a pleasant, convenient environment for a crew of caregivers Jessie paid to help her look after two people whose minds were gone. That left Jessie free to take care of the farm. To grow the crop that made it all possible. The *illegal* crop. Yesterday, she'd almost gotten caught doing it.

She moved and the pain stabbed back into her shoulder. She'd pulled a muscle or something working alongside ... she didn't know how many workers total had shown up. They'd come, cut their weed, loaded it up in their trucks and left, a steady stream all night. By dawn, all the weed was gone.

Even as stinky and tired and in pain as Jessie was, she smiled at the thought of the looks on the police officers' faces when they saw it.

Chapter Thirteen

THE LAST TIME Winona McClusky had seen her father was two Christmases ago, in 1968, when the National Guard unit had just been called up, would be leaving for Vietnam a few weeks after Christmas and the whole county was bouncing off the walls in hysteria. She had come home from college for her family's Christmas and the big McClusky family shindig.

Her father had presided over the gathering. He'd been loud and boisterous, what was it called, a hail fellow well met. She thought about that Christmas often, analyzing her father's behavior, looking for some clue of mental instability. Or a glint of wanderlust in his eye, anything that would explain why he'd driven away from his home six months later and ... what? Dropped off into the Twilight Zone.

The first Christmas after her brother Shep was killed in a car wreck and her father disappeared was as bleak for their family as it was for the families who had lost sons/husbands/brothers in that massacre in Vietnam. Her cousin Jackson had been wounded in the battle where so many guardsmen had died, and she had seen him at the family gathering that'd been smaller and far more subdued than the year before. His arm was bandaged. They didn't speak, but she'd heard he'd been burned.

The next Christmas had been strange, nothing felt right, which was the way of things when a family has lost loved ones, but they were getting through. This past Christmas, Mama made Christmas dinner — with Rhonda's help. At eighteen now, it appeared to Winona that Rhonda had pretty much taken over raising their youngest sister, Nora, who was eight. Mama had not exactly fallen into a bottle after what happened, but she'd been slowly sliding down into one in the years since. Now, the wine bottles stacked up in the trash can and Mama had a glass of something within arm's reach always. But what was it they said — you aren't an alcoholic if all you drink is wine.

Riiiiight.

Jody was a mess. He had moved in with his girl-friend in a little double-wide trailer out in the hills somewhere and had been living there … doing what, Winona didn't know. She did know that he had been hurt in an accident of some kind at Bourbon Cooper-age, where he worked part time, and apparently his girlfriend didn't want to look after him because he'd come home to recuperate.

He hadn't gone back to work yet and had a big, clunky cast on his leg so at least she hadn't had to track him down to talk to him. She invited him over for supper the night after she'd moved into her father's old office. She'd spent the day getting squared away in the neat little brick house on Booker Street in Brewster that she was renting. She'd remembered how much he liked strawberry shortcake and she'd used that as bait.

Now the two of them sat in lawn chairs on the back deck of the house, which didn't present some bucolic scene of meadows and cattle and sheep. It offered a view of the neighbors' back yards, swing sets, slides and ugly plastic play houses.

She came back from the kitchen with fresh beer for the two of them — he'd already had most of a six-pack and was flying a few sheets to the wind, which she hoped would help.

"You wanna know what I think?" he said, gesturing back into the house where her muted television showed scenes of war protesters. "I think they oughta put guns in all them folks' hands and drop them in the middle of the jungle and let them see what it's like to be a soldier."

He turned up his beer and gulped down several big swallows.

"Jackson told me all 'bout it — how awful it was. He shot more than two dozen of them Cong soldiers 'fore he got hurt in that big battle."

That was her opening.

"July 5, 1969. When Shep got killed and Pa disappeared."

Jody looked pained. "I ain't never got over that."

"Mama told me you were the last person who talked to Pa before he left … what did he say?"

"Didn't say where he was going, if that's what you mean."

"Mama said he was mad. Do you know what he was mad about?"

"He was mad about Shep getting killed like he done."

"I can see *upset* … but why mad? What was he mad at?"

Jody looked at her over the top of his beer can.

"At everything. At the world. At life. You know how Pa was."

"Do you know where Shep was going that night, why he was on Hunter Lane?"

He looked uncomfortable.

"Private business. He had a … job. He'd been laid off, like. But he was going back to work."

"In the middle of the night?"

"Yeah, well …" He looked even more uncomfortable. "We wasn't all cut out to be lawyers like you and Pa. We made a living … in other ways. You wouldn't understand."

"Try me."

He was getting annoyed.

"What do you care what me and Shep was doing."

"So you were doing it *with* Shep?"

"No, not that particular job. That was his alone. But I'd kinda helped in the business, part time kinda."

"What was the job, Jody?"

"I ain't gonna tell you a thing like that. It's private—"

"And illegal. Duh. You think I give a rat's ass about illegal? Pa didn't."

Jody looked at her shrewdly.

"Yeah, well, it's true Pa got away with some things, made a little money on the side. I know. Me and Shep, we helped him sometimes."

"Were you in sales or procurement?"

"Huh?"

"Oh, come on, Jody. Pa fenced stolen property. When he wasn't playing the ponies. I hear he was in pretty deep to some not-so-nice fellow gamblers, and they wanted their money."

That was pure blue sky. Winona didn't know anything of the sort. She knew her father gambled, lost his shirt every now and then. She had put it together that perhaps his disappearance had something to do with somebody collecting a debt.

But why then … that night, the night Shep had been killed?

"He was maybe kiting a few IOUs, but they knew he was good for it."

"They who?"

"Why do you care? What you asking all these questions for?"

She probably just needed to own the truth.

"Because I'm trying to find out what happened to Pa."

"How you plan to do *that*?"

"By doing what I'm doing right now — asking questions."

"If Pa told me where he was going that night, don't you think I'd a'said something about it by now?"

"Did he?"

"*No!* I ain't got no more idea than you do."

"You said he was mad — about what?"

"I told you, about Shep getting killed."

"He ran out of here like his pants were on fire because Shep was killed in a traffic accident?"

"Might be he thought it wasn't no accident."

Winona froze, put her beer down and looked at her brother.

"If it wasn't an accident, what was it? And how did Pa know?"

"I didn't say Pa *knew* nothing."

"Okay, suspected, then. What did he suspect?"

"I done said, he didn't tell me nothing."

"I'm not asking what he told you, I'm asking what you guess, or suspect. You said you think Pa might have doubted the wreck that killed Shep was an accident. Why would you think a thing like that?"

"Him yelling and cursing, sayin' somebody *killed his boy* — that's why."

"Pa was pissed because he thought ... what? Somebody killed Shep?"

"Might be."

"You mean Pa thought somebody killed Shep, *murdered* him, then put his body in his car and ran it through a guard rail? Seriously?"

"I don't know what he thought — he didn't say. But he was yelling about somebody killing his boy — hysterical-like, not making any sense."

"So he went running out of here because he thought somebody had killed Shep and … what? Was he going after whoever it was?"

"Might be."

"Oh, stop it with the might-be's. What is it you're not telling me? What do you know you don't want to talk about? What was Shep doing out there on that road in the middle of the night?"

"Going to work, maybe … if he got his job back."

"Job doing what?"

"At a chop shop, okay? A chop shop! Taking apart stolen cars and selling the pieces."

"Shep worked at a chop shop?"

"Didn't work at — he *ran* it. He was the boss. Until he wasn't anymore."

"What does that mean?"

"I done told you, he got laid off."

"*Laid off.*" Winona couldn't help a bark of sardonic laughter. "Like … he could sign up for unemployment, maybe?" She shook her head. "So he got *fired*, didn't he?"

"I guess."

"And he was out there on that road because that's where the chop shop was? Why was he on his way to work if he'd got fired?"

"I dunno." He held up his hands, palms out before she could protest. "Me and Shep both worked at the chop shop for a while. Then me and Sally Ann got that place in Louisville — remember? Lived there about a year. She was working at GE and was gonna get me on there."

He grunted a bleat of laughter and took a big swig of beer.

"Assembly line in a factory — I didn't last a week before I was like *get me outta here*! I quit, and then me and Sally Ann split and I come back home. That was four summers ago, in June, and then in July …"

"So you and Shep talked about—"

"All's I know was he got canned and he was pissed about it. Like *royal* pissed!"

"He wasn't working at the chop shop the night of the wreck, then — right? So him being out on that road had nothing to do with—"

"I ain't saying that. Hunter Lane ain't but a couple of miles from the chop shop. That couldn't have been no coincidence."

"So … he didn't work there, but he went there that night? Why? Maybe to talk to the person who laid him off?"

Shep shrugged.

"And who was that person? Who was running that chop shop?"

Jody sat silent.

"Oh, come on. Who was it?"

"Mama Bert."

Winona managed not to gasp. Her brother was mixed up with Mama Bert? That opened up a whole new can of worms entirely. Did her father know that? Was he maybe … mixed up with Mama Bert, too?

"But she wasn't there, at the chop shop. Couldn't have been. She didn't *never* go there, hired somebody to manage it for her so's she didn't have to take the risk. That's what Shep was — her manager."

"Until she fired him." He nodded. "But you think he went to the chop shop that night … for *some reason*, right?"

"I ain't saying that."

"Then what are you saying?"

"I'm saying I don't know. I didn't know then and I don't know now." He chugged the rest of his beer, crunched the can, then threw it at the trash can by the back door. He missed, mumbled, and mumbled something else unintelligible under his breath as the can clunked away across the deck.

It was full dark now and Winona couldn't see his face in the shadows, and maybe that's why he opened up.

"It hit me hard and I ain't over it yet."

"I'm sorry. I don't mean to sound uncaring or anything, but it's hard for me to miss Pa because he wasn't ever in my life."

"Never thought about it, but I guess he ignored you, too."

"*Too?* He spent all his time and energy on you and Shep—"

"Shep, not me! The sun rose and set in Shep. A lot of times Pa looked right through me like I wasn't there."

"Pa looked right through me *all the time.* Twenty-four-seven my whole life. That's why his disappearance didn't hit me hard like it did you."

"I didn't mean it was Pa's disappearance that hit

me hard. It was *Shep* — him getting killed." He might have choked back a sob. "We done everything together when we was kids and … him running off Hunter Lane like that, it don't make sense."

"What's to make sense? Shep drove like a bat outta hell so it's no surprise that—"

"Not *there*. See, that's the thing. Me and him usta 'borrow' Grandpa's truck when we'd be over there and go joyriding, cutting up and having run. We usta open the gate on that field on Simmons Knob where the Bartons kept that bull, and we'd chase it around with the truck."

"Seriously?"

Jody made an X sign across his heart and held up two fingers. "Scout's honor."

Jody had never been a Boy Scout.

"And we'd go down to Hunter Lane on the side of the knob because it had that straightaway, see how fast we could get that old truck going."

"If you're surprised that Shep ran off the road there because he was familiar with the road, bear in mind he was probably drunk—"

"He wasn't drunk!"

"Or high, then, on something."

"If he was high — and he probably was — it was on coke or uppers, and them things don't make you dizzy and clumsy. They give you energy and clarity, so's you can do things you couldn't do if you wasn't taking them. He'd a drove *better*, been more alert."

"Yeah, with a sense of being invincible. That can get your ass into trouble when you're *not* Superman!"

"But Hunter Lane? Winnie, me and Shep used to take turns driving down that road *blindfolded*!"

Nobody'd called Winona "Winnie" since … she'd even forgotten that was her brothers' pet name for her. She shook her head. "It is a flat-out miracle either one of you ever saw your twenty-first birthday."

"It's a straightaway — don't you get it? Flat and straight as an arrow. And Shep could drive it *blind-folded*. Done it dozens of times, both of us did. I could do it right now, down the center line 'thout missing a beat. So what happened *that night*? Why'd he veer off the road that night and go crashing through the guardrail? That don't make no sense!"

It made perfect sense to her, but Winona could see it made no sense to Jody, so maybe it had made no sense to their father, too.

"Is that why Pa thought the wreck wasn't an accident — because Shep wouldn't have driven off the road like that?"

"No, it was more'n that. He didn't know about the blindfolded stuff — it wasn't about the road. He thought *somebody killed Shep on purpose*. Was hollering and carrying on about it."

"You mean … really *murdered* him? What for?"

"I ain't got no idea."

"Do you know anybody — drugs or something? — who'd want to kill Shep?"

"Naaa. Everybody liked Shep."

"But Pa knew who it was?"

"Musta thought he did."

"How'd he know?"

"I don't know nothing but what he said — cursing and screaming — that white spit on his lips he was so mad." Jody pulled the words up in his mind and quoted them verbatim.

"He's not gonna get away with killing my boy. He pulled that trick once before but it ain't gonna work this time."

"*Got away with it once* … what does *that* mean?"

Jody shrugged. "Ya got me. All I know is Pa was madder than I ever seen him, and that's sayin' a lot. He went runnin' out of here … and ain't nobody laid eyes on him since."

Chapter Fourteen

Nate reached for a cigarette, got his hand halfway to his shirt pocket before he remembered wasn't a pack in it. Still felt all wrong. Not that he'd have smoked it right then, wasn't a real good idea to smoke a cigarette in a hay loft! He'd just have held it in his mouth. He used to do that, back when he smoked. Maybe he still could, just not never light it. Naaa, that was wishful thinking.

You smoke or you don't. He didn't. That was the beginning and the end of it.

"Look, I build!" said the little boy on his knees of the loft floor with a big pile of hay bunched up in front of him.

"What's that s'posed to be?" Nate's eyes gobbled up the child in the same way he used to look at Riley when he was that age, and Riley's father John when he was. It was a look of love, sure, but also a look of pure gratitude. How was it he had managed to be blessed with such an adorable little boy in his life?

Drew Hannacker was a cherub, no doubt about it. Sure, Riley was blond, but he hadn't never been as blond as Drew. Drew took after his namesake, Andy Taggart, who'd been killed in Vietnam. Andy had been what Riley called a "Nordic" blond, meaning his hair was that kind of white blond you see in people from Norway, Nate guessed, folks from Scandinavia. His eyebrows and eyelashes was blond like that, just like Andy's had been. But the cherub-ness also sprung from Drew's little round face. At just shy of his fourth birthday, he still had chubby chipmunk cheeks that were just naturally red. Sherry Lynn was always putting lotion on them, said they was chapped, but it was just the boy's coloring. Nate didn't say that, of course, when she was smearing goo all over the boy's face. Nate didn't never say nothing to Sherry Lynn about how she done with the boy. Didn't say much of anything to her about anything else either, avoided her best as he could, which wasn't an easy thing to do with her, Drew and Riley right there in the house with him. My, but the house was going to be quiet when they got that new house they was building finished and moved in. He needed to treasure moments like now with Drew because wouldn't be long before he'd have to get in his truck and drive ten miles to see the boy.

"It's a house!" the boy cried. "A house where peoples can live and they won't get wet when it rains."

Nate was watching Drew this morning while Sherry Lynn went to a wedding shower for Mary Jean Morgan, who was getting married next Saturday to

Sherry Lynn's cousin, Wade McClusky, Big-Un's second son. He was the kid with pimples who'd followed the sewage truck from the field at the top of the knob to Louisville four years ago. That's how Nate and Big-Un figured out what was poisoning their cattle, what sent them into town on the Fourth of July to shoot the heads off statues. He could smile at that now, long's he didn't go no farther down the memory than that. Just the statues. Everything that happened after was a field of razor blades and wasn't no way to get through it without getting cut to pieces.

There wasn't nothing that Drew loved more than to "help Pop Pop" do his farm chores like feeding the chickens, gathering up the eggs, and particularly feeding Blinkin, the little lamb they were feeding with a bottle because its mama wouldn't nurse it.

Nate had wanted to get some of them miniature goats that was so cute — pets for Drew, but they wouldn't have no place for that kind of pet when they moved into their new house. Besides, Sherry Lynn wouldn't likely have let him play with them. She'd have found some reason.

With the chores done, he'd let Drew do what he knew the boy's mama would disapprove of — he let Drew play in the hay in the hayloft. The boy liked to stack it up in piles, then run and jump into the piles, even enjoyed throwing it up in the air to rain down on his head, squealing, "Wheeeeee."

Sherry Lynn wouldn't say nothing if she found out he'd took Drew to the hayloft, not to Nate, anyway.

She'd complain and carp about it to Riley, though, and Lord knows that boy didn't need to have to listen to the woman bitch about one more thing.

"He might be allergic to hay," she'd said the first time Nate let him play in the loft. "Lots of kids are allergic to hay."

"If he was allergic, chances are he would have started sneezing as soon as he got around it," Riley had said, trying to be reasonable, which was a lost cause with Sherry Lynn. They'd had the conversation sitting around the dinner table. He had to hand it to the girl. The list of that girl's shortcomings was so long he couldn't count them without taking his shoes off, but the woman could *cook*. She'd made a pot roast with potatoes and carrots and big chunks of onion that night. She'd put it all in the crock pot so it could cook all day.

"You don't know that for certain. I think it takes awhile for allergies to build up in your system. The more often he's exposed to it, the sooner he'll start sneezing, or his eyes swelling up, maybe … or *wheezing*. Allergies cause asthma, you know."

"We can't keep him away from everything because he 'might' be allergic," Riley'd said. Nate knew he was grinding his teeth. His grandson wasn't gonna have no molars left in a couple of years. "Using that logic, we really can't let him be exposed to anything."

She'd argued, of course, said hay was worse than other things — that more people was allergic to it than to other things. How she come by that information, she didn't say. But Riley'd moved the conversation on to other things — the house they was building, which always engaged Sherry Lynn. What he was going to do to keep her mind occupied once the house was done was anybody's guess.

For dessert, she'd made chocolate cake with fudge icing an inch thick. Nate'd had two pieces. Sherry Lynn had had three. Wasn't no way she was gonna lose the … thirty, forty, maybe fifty pounds she'd put on, eating three pieces of cake for supper. But that absolutely wasn't none of Nate's business. Pointing out a thing like that would cause a nuclear holocaust. He settled for being grateful she hadn't insisted Nate stop bringing Drew up into the loft to play. Nate would get all the hay off the boy before he took him inside, just to keep the peace, and maybe Drew wouldn't mention what he'd done that day.

Fat chance! That little boy talked a blue streak sunup to sundown, a running monologue, stream-of-consciousness brain-dump of what he had been doing, had seen, wanted to see, didn't do, didn't see, any ouchies he might have accumulated during the day and what he wanted to do tomorrow.

Of course, Nate stayed right beside him every second he was in the hayloft. The outside bay doors was closed, the clasp fastened tight, but the hole in the floor that led up into the loft didn't have no door, so Nate always sat on the floor there, with his feet dangling down into Daisy's old stall, to keep the boy away from it.

Drew abandoned the house he'd built of hay and was now lying on his belly on the floor near the side wall peering into the space between two floor slats, sticking pieces of hay down into the opening and watching the hay fall down into the empty stall below. You could see the floorboards where the boy'd scooted the hay away. If you looked at them boards careful, you could see a brown stain on them, but Nate wouldn't let himself think about the mark. Wouldn't let his mind get anywhere near what had happened three years ago in this barn loft. Walled it off with brick and mortar ... and put coils of razor wire on the top.

~

DREW HANNACKER TRIED to poke the piece of straw down between the floorboards so he could watch it fall into the stall below. But he couldn't. He tried, but there was something in the way. Something was stuck there. He sat up and turned to his Pop Pop to ask him to poke the stuck thing out of the way, but Pop Pop had heard a pickup pull up in front of the barn and was calling out to somebody.

"... in the barn, come on in."

The man below called out something to Pop Pop and Drew turned back to the spot where he couldn't poke straw down. His finger was so small it fit between the slats of wood that made the floor, so he jabbed at the stuck thing with his finger and it moved. He jabbed again and it moved some more. One more time and whatever was stuck there fell out onto the hay on the stall floor.

"… to go now," Pop Pop told him, and held out his hand for Drew to take. "I need to talk to the man from the gas company and I ain't leaving you up here all by yourself."

"I want to play in the hay," the little boy protested.

"There's hay in the stall you can play in."

Pop Pop held out both hands to lift him up into his arms and carry him down.

"I can do it by myself!" the boy said. "I'm a big boy." So Pop Pop backed down the ladder and held onto the back of Drew's shirt as the boy climbed down behind him.

Pointing to the stack of hay in the stall, Pop Pop said, "See, you can make a … a castle out of that. Or a fort."

"Or a spaceship," the little boy cried, and as Pop Pop walked out of the barn to talk to the man in the pickup truck, the little boy dropped to his knees in the stall and started to pile up the hay—

Something was lying on top of the hay. Something shiny. He reached out his hand and picked it up. It was small and flat — like a penny, except bigger and not round. And there was a woman on the front like that Indian's face on a nickel, with words under it.

He looked up at the ceiling. This was the stuck thing that was between the floorboards of the loft, the thing he pushed out of the way.

There was a crunch of gravel as the gas company

truck pulled away from the barn and Pop Pop appeared at the door, motioning with his hand.

"We need to go in now. I let the time get away from me and your mama will be home any minute. I need to get you cleaned up, get all the hay off you."

The little boy stood, dropped the shiny thing into his pocket and ran to catch up with his grandfather.

Chapter Fifteen

SHERRY LYNN BENNETT HANNACKER put her head in her hands and burst into tears, crying as if her heart would break. And it might, it might just do that.

She sat in her car, parked down the road from the neat brick house where the wedding shower for Mary Jean Morgan was being held. Jeanie was marrying Sherry Lynn's cousin, Wade, next Saturday. Sherry Lynn hadn't meant to burst into tears, but it all just came crashing down on her.

Jeanie was going to have the wedding Sherry Lynn had always dreamed of, always knew *she* would have. Of course she would. She would have the most beautiful white dress anybody had ever seen, and her ten best friends would be dressed in matching cherry pink gowns, and she would walk down the aisle at St. Augustine in Brewster with Riley standing there with his ten groomsmen, dressed in a suit and tie and looking so happy to see her coming down the aisle that he would tear up.

That's not what'd happened, of course. They had been married by a priest she didn't even know in the chapel at Ft. Knox, with Riley sitting in a wheelchair in hospital greens and a robe, and her wearing a dress from a bridal shop in Bardstown that her mother had picked out in her size — but her size wasn't her size by then and the dress was so tight she looked like a pale blue sausage. Pale blue. Mama wouldn't get her a white dress.

Riley had still been recovering from the wounds he'd received in the Tweety Bird Massacre — that's what the locals called it, the fire fight at Fire Station Eagle's Nest that killed seven guardsmen and wounded a dozen others.

And at the time, when they'd gotten married, Sherry Lynn hadn't been pining away for the wedding she didn't get to have. She was just so grateful that Riley had come home alive, that he was marrying her and their child would not be born "out of wedlock" that she had been nothing but grateful.

Just past their fourth anniversary, the sense of gratitude had long since evaporated. Now she lived in a state best described as "unhappiness held at bay." She was miserable, but she couldn't show it or it would just make everything worse. So she pretended everything was fine with her and Riley, that they were a happily married couple building their first house and wasn't that wonderful, just wonderful, yes sir wasn't she a lucky girl.

What had happened last night — it just kept happening again and again and she didn't know what to do about it. Riley closed up to her, shut her completely out. It almost seemed like he didn't even want to be around her!

The nightmares brought it all out in the open, where he couldn't pretend nothing was wrong.

Last night, he'd started tossing and turning, mumbling, throwing his head from side to side and she knew he was having a nightmare or flashback or whatever they called it. She only knew he was *there*, reliving what had happened, and she knew even before she woke him what his response would be.

"RILEY."

He's crying out. Mumbling.

"RPG." Sounds, groans and grunts. "Not Charlie!"

"Riley, honey, wake up." She turns on the bedside light and shakes his shoulder. "Wake up. You're dreaming. It's not real."

She shakes him hard and his eyes pop open and he looks around frantically, as if he has to find somewhere to hide, as if he is in terrible danger.

She puts her arms around him — or tries — to comfort him, but he pushes her away, scoots away from her on the bed and stares at her as if he has no idea who she is. Then she watches reality sink into his eyes. He slumps back against the headboard of the bed.

"What is it?" she asks. She knows she will be sorry, but she can't help reaching out to him. "Tell me what's wrong. Let me help you—"

"You can't—"

"If you'll just tell me about it." She tries to take his hand.

"No!" He shoves her back to her side of the bed. "What happened there stays there. Just leave me alone."

He gets up unsteadily, dressed in his underwear, and stumbles out of the room.

She knows where he's going. First he will go out to the porch, to calm down. Then he will go into Drew's room. And if Drew's there, which he often isn't, Riley will stand in the shadows, watching the boy sleep.

Drew is the light of Riley's life. He lives for that boy. And Sherry Lynn? She's just an also-ran.

HE'D LEFT the house this morning without even telling her goodbye. Just … left. Nate was looking after Drew while she came to the shower. She knew that as soon as she was gone, he'd take the boy to the barn — that was full of hay, didn't even care that Drew was allergic to hay! Maybe, probably was.

She'd started to get dressed and the zipper on her dress broke — because it was so tight she should never have tried to zip it up in the first place.

She didn't have anything to wear anymore that she could get into. So now she was sitting here in a shapeless shift, terribly underdressed for a bridal shower. The dress hid the pounds — how many? She didn't know. She never got on the scales anymore. But she had nothing else to wear.

Nothing to wear.

She cried even harder.

Tap! Tap!

Sherry Lynn almost jumped out of her skin.

"You alright in there?"

There was a face at the window.

At first she didn't recognize who — Jackson!

If she could have selected the single one of her relatives that she least wanted to have a conversation with right now it would have been her cousin Jackson, the older brother of the groom-to-be, Wade McClusky. He was Sherry Lynn's cousin. Or second cousin, or third cousin. Or whatever. Nobody ever traced such things out anymore. Well, nobody except the priests who had to figure out who could marry whom when half the people in the county had the same last name.

The term cousin was all-inclusive — meant any relative outside your immediate family. Jackson was the son of Big-Un, who was the son of Big Jake, who was the son of Rooster. Rooster McClusky'd had another son, Ike, who was Sherry Lynn's grandfather, though he had died long before she was born.

He'd been killed when Sherry Lynn's mother Agnes was just a baby ... by Nate Hannacker! Even though it had all happened so long ago nobody ever thought about it, there had been a scene when Sherry Lynn had started dating Nate's grandson, Riley.

The more serious she and Riley got, the more pissed Sherry's mother became. Sherry Lynn understood now that there would have been hell to pay if the world hadn't totally fallen apart. Riley would have proposed to her eventually, of course, and her parents would have ... what? They probably would have forbidden it, like you could have done that kind of thing in 1969.

The pregnancy cut through all the opposition, though. The bomb only went off on her that one time, when she told her parents she was pregnant. And that was such a nuclear holocaust, followed by a bleak and cold nuclear winter, that the various mean things her mother and father said to her kind of ran together in a blur.

But she did remember her mother wailing that Sherry Lynn was carrying "the git of a murderer — a murderer!" in her belly.

Sherry Lynn rolled the window down, wiping at her eyes with a tissue.

"When did you get out ... *home*?" Her face reddened and she hurried on. "I hadn't heard you were *home*."

Last she'd heard, Jackson McClusky was in prison. He hadn't been back from Vietnam six months when he'd got busted in Louisville on some drug charge, a bad one. He'd been hauling pounds of ... well, she didn't know what exactly, heroin maybe. His lawyer got him a lighter sentence in exchange for turning in his buddies — and him being a wounded veteran and all.

"A few months," he said. "Been working hard, don't get out much."

Jackson held up a bag of ice.

"I got sent to get the extra ice out of the Hendersons' freezer," he said, gesturing with his chin to the house up the road. "Mama's taken over —

you know Mama — with Jeanie's mother dead and all."

Wade's wife-to-be had lost her mother last year, and Wade and Jackson's mama, Dorothy, was a bulldozer, a git-'er-done kinda woman, probably organized this whole shower at Jeanie's house without allowing Jeanie to lift a finger.

At this point in polite chitchat, Jackson was supposed to wish her a nice day and walk on down the road to the house. He didn't, though. He just stood there beside her car door. Perfect. Now she couldn't sit here in private and get herself together. She'd have to get out and go inside. And she looked even worse than she had before because now she was not only underdressed, but her makeup was smeared.

Why was he just standing there? He cocked his head to the side, studied her.

"You ain't alright at all, are you?" he said. "You don't look good."

"Thanks a bunch," she said. "You don't look so good yourself." Which was absolutely *not* true. In fact, she had never seen Jackson look better. When she finally bothered to notice, it was hard to countenance the change that'd come over him. He had always been such a skinny runt, he might have been the last survivor of a concentration camp. But he had looked even worse after he returned from Vietnam. Oh, it wasn't about the burn scars — though they were horrific — his whole left hand and arm were covered in twisted, wrinkled and puffy scar tissue. He'd just totally let himself go, was becoming his father's son.

Not in stature, surely, but Big-Un was … his own universe. Her mother's oldest brother maybe took a bath a couple of times a month — but she doubted it was that often. He didn't socialize with the rest of the family — made it clear most of them wasn't folks he had any desire to be around.

Her mother had stopped speaking to him years ago.

After Vietnam, Jackson looked like the economy size of Big-Un — dirty, bearded, bedraggled. And he'd had a wild, crazy look in his eyes that was about way more than whatever pharmaceutical product he might have been taking.

Not anymore! He'd *changed* in the past three years. Who gets better looking in prison? Well, Jackson McClusky did. He had a golden, farmer-working-outside kind of tan, wasn't any taller, of course, but he was broader, thicker, more muscular. He had … what was it they called it? Bulked up. He'd put on weight, but not like Sherry Lynn's. His arms bulged in his shirt, which was stretched tight across his shoulders and chest. And he … carried himself differently. Not like the prancing little cock-of-the-walk he used to be. This was a man, not a boy, strong, with a determined set to his chin.

And his eyes … okay, yeah, that much hadn't changed. The meanness that'd been there when they were kids remained. But as she looked into them she became aware of a cunning that hadn't been there before, and a deadly ruthlessness. In truth, the Jackson

McClusky standing beside her car was more than a little *scary*.

"I'm sorry, I didn't mean to snap," she babbled. "I'm … just not having a good day … week … year. You best get inside before that ice melts."

"It's Riley, ain't it?" Jackson said, and Sherry Lynn almost choked.

"What's Riley? What do you mean—?"

"He ain't himself, least not the himself who left here for the grand rumpus in Vietnam."

She didn't answer.

"He's distant, ain't he? Don't connect up with people — with the people close to him, anyway."

Oh, he connects just fine with the person closest to him in all the world. Drew. He connects fine with his son, but doesn't have the time of day for the boy's mother.

"Has flashbacks, kinda, where you know he ain't there no more, know he's gone somewhere else in his mind — like if he hears a gunshot, he jumps for cover."

Jackson's description was eerily accurate. Not the jumping-for-cover part, but the rest.

"I been there." And he sounded concerned, though she did note that his concern was for Riley, not for her. It was clearly Riley he wanted to talk about. "I felt all the same things. If you let it, it'll eat you up inside. I had nightmares 'bout people getting blown up—"

"… or *burned* up."

"Burned?" Jackson's voice lost its concerned sound in just that one word.

"Yes, Riley dreams about somebody falling into a fire and then burning up — the stink of it. Over and over, the same dream."

"What else does he dream about?"

"He's all the time seeing a gun barrel, only bigger, called it … something with initials — P and G, maybe. It's pointed at him and any second …"

"Any second what? The guy with the gun is going to pull the trigger?"

"I guess."

She had wiped the makeup out from under her eyes and would have liked to redo her makeup before she went into the house, but clearly Jackson wasn't going anywhere. She'd have to sit here to put on new makeup and she did *not* want to continue this conversation.

When she tried to open the car door, Jackson was standing too close to it, and he didn't move out of the way.

"I'm going to be late—"

"That gun pointed at him, the one Riley dreams 'bout — who's holding it? Who's shooting at him?"

Now, she was annoyed.

"What difference does it make? It's just a dream. Now scoot out of the way, I need to go in."

He moved back, but kept talking.

"So you ain't never asked him to explain what he dreams?"

That made her mad.

"Of course I've asked!" She did *not* want to keep talking about this or she'd start crying again. "Over and over and over — but he won't tell me! Won't say anything about the war and what happened to him. Not a word."

Out of the car now, she smoothed her dress down and reached back in for the gift. When she closed the door, she almost tripped over Jackson. He was just standing there, too close, not moving.

"So he ain't never told you who was shooting at him?"

His eyes were riveting. The look in them was frightening. She stepped around him — because he wouldn't move — before she answered.

"Well, duh. It was a war. The Viet Cong were shooting at him. Who else would it be?"

She went down the road then and didn't look back. But she thought if she did, he might very well still be standing there.

Chapter Sixteen

JACKSON McCLUSKY STOOD with a bag of melting ice on his shoulder, watching Sherry Lynn Bennett, Sherry Lynn *Hannacker*, waddle away. She musta put on a hundred pounds since the last time he seen her. She'd still been wearing maternity clothes then and the kid had been three or four months old already. Lotsa women was like that, though, didn't lose—

He yanked his mind back, held on tight.

The cellmate named Slick had showed him how to do that. To stand still and breathe slow and make his mind behave, make it do what he wanted, instead of bouncing around like a grasshopper in a jar. He'd said your mind was like a dog, you had to train it, tell it, "sit!" — say it out loud even, worked better.

"Sit," Jackson said under his breath, closed his eyes and concentrated.

He hadn't had as much trouble with his mind being outta control after he got to Eddyville — the "Castle on the Cumberland." The Kentucky State

Penitentiary, a maximum security and supermax prison, was located on Lake Barkley on the Cumberland River, about five miles from downtown Eddyville, and during his stay there he had gotten clean. Clean and sober, his thoughts mostly behaved, didn't fly past like a train going through a station, the one he seen in a movie one time where folks was standing there beside the tracks and the train blew by them, and you could see women's skirts blowing, and men was chasing their hats—

He was doing it again.

Sit!

He squeezed his eyes shut.

"Sit!" He said it again out loud. He had to think. *Think.*

Then a wave of fear washed over him like it hadn't done in years, and suddenly he was right back there in the stinking jungle with Charlie out in the trees shooting at him and him trying to make himself so small they couldn't see him hiding behind the armored personnel carrier. The sergeant saw him crouched against the APC's tire, yanked him upright and he'd dropped his rifle. The sergeant picked it up and shoved it into his hands and threw him into a foxhole. Then it started raining and that was a good thing, oh my yes, it was a good thing because he had wet his pants and if it hadn't started raining you coulda seen the dark spot spreading—

He shook his head violently from side to side, as if to fling the images out, but he could still feel the jungle closing in around—

"Where you been with that ice?" said a little boy, must be one of his cousin George's crew, or maybe Bobby Lee's.

Jackson jumped back like he'd been stuck with a cattle prod. Liked to dropped the ice on the ground.

"Aunt Dorothy says she needs it for the punchbowl."

Jackson lifted the sack off his shoulder and handed it to the kid, who almost collapsed under the weight.

"You take it to her. I got things to do."

Then he turned and made himself *walk* back to his pickup truck, which he'd parked way behind all the other cars because he didn't want to get blocked in. He wanted to run back, but running would make it worse. Running would make his heart beat fast and his heart beating fast felt like being scared and so he *would* be scared. He made himself walk.

When he got in on the driver's side he had to bang the door shut twice before it caught. Truck was falling apart, bumper held on with Bondo and the tailgate held shut with duct tape. An image formed in his mind.

HE HAS the hood on the clap-trap truck up, leaning over the engine, trying to figure out why it'd died, just died and he'd had to coast off onto the shoulder of the road. Had to be something wrong with the fuel intake.

He hears an approaching vehicle and without getting out from under the hood, he lifts his arm and waves the vehicle on. Doesn't know who it is and doesn't care, just knows whoever it is will stop to help a stranded driver and he doesn't want help. The vehicle slows, then sees his signal, speeds back up and drives away. Jackson stands to watch it go.

It is a 1972 GMC Sierra Grande, two-tone, moss green over white. He's seen Willie Ray Taggart driving around in one just like it. Bile rises in his throat and he swallows it back down. It won't be long 'fore he has that kinda money. Them others got a head start is all. Jackson'd only got outta the iron house in February, had planted his first weed crop this spring. But 'fore he ever turned the first clod of dirt, he'd been an expert, had picked the brains of the other pot-growing cons — who was in prison for worse crimes than growing weed. He'd got good seed, was sure his very first crop would set him up for all the rest of his plans.

Jackson flips the retreating pickup the bird and sticks his head back under the hood.

WITH THE IMAGE of Willie Ray Taggart's freckled face in his mind, Jackson glanced at the gas gauge and groaned. The needle was pointing down *below* "Empty" and he didn't have money to pay for gas. He didn't have no money to pay for nothing, had barely scraped together a stake when he got out from silent partners still locked up.

He'd just have to siphon gas outta Pa's truck or Wade's or somebody's. He *couldn't* sell his little stash of coke. But if he cut it with powdered sugar he could get twice what he'd paid for it. No, he was keeping it safe for an emergency.

He *could* sell it, though. Or he could steal—

He was doing it again.

"Sit," Jackson said, out loud, concentrated on loosening his hold on the steering wheel, taking deep breaths and letting the air out slowly. It worked. He calmed. His mind stopped bouncing around all over the place. As soon as he got a grip, fear welled up in his chest again, but he choked it back, wouldn't let it take over. He knew how to do that now. Jackson McClusky wasn't a cringing coward anymore. That part was over. He'd spent most of his life as "prey," and in the joint, he'd gone over to the other side. He was a predator now.

Taking deep, slow, steady breaths, he brought his mind to bear on what had sent him spinning off center in the first place. Sherry Lynn Hannacker and what she'd said.

HE DREAMS *of somebody falling into a fire and then burning up — the stink of it. Over and over, the same dream.*

RILEY HANNACKER WAS DREAMING about what Jackson'd done in Vietnam, the civilian Jackson had killed. What he'd got away with because the soldiers who seen it wasn't around after Tweety Bird to talk about it.

The civilian's death hadn't been Jackson's fault, it'd been accidental. He'd just been joking, hadn't known there was any gasoline in that can when he turned it up and made like to pour it on the guy's hair. And it wasn't Jackson's fault the guy'd tripped and fell into the fire—

Jackson's left arm and hand suddenly began to burn, the pain so bad he felt tears well up in his eyes.

Not real.

It wasn't real.

He burped out a sound, more like a dog bark than laughter, at the way it'd turned out in the end — how he'd got a Purple Heart and an honorable medical discharge from the Army because of the burns he'd *said* he'd got in the battle at Tweety Bird, when he'd really got burned trying to put out the flaming clothes of the Jingle Bell Man.

"HE'S ALL *the time seeing a gun barrel, only bigger, called it … something with initials — P and G, maybe. It's pointed at him and any second …"*

JACKSON STOPPED BREATHING ENTIRELY as Sherry Lynn's words re-formed in his mind. *Couldn't* breathe. All the air had been knocked out of his lungs. The dark, evil thing that'd been lurking around in the back of Jackson's mind for all these years had finally slithered out into the real world. Just when everything was looking up, his life and fortunes beginning to come together for the first time … *bam!*

Riley Hannacker was dreaming about seeing the barrel of an RPG, a rocket-propelled grenade launcher — pointed at him!

Riley *had* seen. It'd all happened so fast, Jackson hadn't known for sure what Riley and the others might have gotten a look at before Jackson pulled the trigger. He'd always suspected ... but had been denying it for years. Couldn't deny it now, though. Riley *had* seen. Riley knew what Jackson had done, but Riley's mind had been so scrambled by that last battle, he didn't remember it.

If he was dreaming about it now, though ... that meant he was beginning to remember — didn't it? And what was Jackson going to do about *that*?

Chapter Seventeen

WINONA FIGURED Aunt Frannie was as good a place to start as any. Her father had had two brothers — Jerry and Greg, and two sisters, Agnes and Frances. Aunt Frannie was the most chatty of the four. Agnes was scatterbrained, Greg was a drunk and Jerry was an idiot.

It was Aunt Frannie who hosted the big family get-togethers, even organized the huge McClusky Fest, as somebody had named it, for the dozens — hundreds? — of McCluskys who had descended from Rooster and Digger. It was usually held on Labor Day Weekend when the family would descend like locusts on Brewster Park for a potluck dinner, "games for the kiddies," maybe some decent bluegrass music and beer. Lots of beer.

It usually degenerated as the day went on and by dark, it wasn't a place to shoot warm-fuzzy family pictures, unless you fancied a photo of four generations getting drunk together.

Before Winona put in an appearance at the bridal shower for Wade's fiancé — one of the Morgan girls, the oldest maybe — she had called and asked to come by Aunt Frannie's to "pick her brain." Aunt Frannie had laughed and said she wouldn't find nothing in her head but bent nails and rusty hubcaps.

Winona had chosen this particular rabbit trail in the mystery of what had happened to her father four years ago based on what Jody'd said the man was yelling the last time anybody saw him. Jody said their father believed that Shep hadn't been killed accidentally in a car wreck — that somebody'd murdered him.

It wasn't true, of course. It was ridiculous. Shep had been driving like a maniac like he always did and ran off the road. That was the beginning and the end of it. But when she stopped to think about it, she realized it wasn't surprising at all that her father had come up with that wild scenario — it was *inevitable*. In Pa's eyes, nothing was *ever* Shep's fault. He never struck out in baseball — the umpire had called the pitch wrong. He never got fired from a job — the boss had it in for him. He didn't flunk out of college his freshman year — the professors just didn't like him.

The wreck would have been no different. Her father would have refused to believe the wreck was Shep's fault, so Pa'd had come up with an alternate explanation.

The thing was, it was possible — likely — that her father *had acted* on that alternate reality. And *something* happened to him when he did. So it made sense to try to track down what it was her father had believed. Whether it was true or not didn't matter.

Pa had told Jody, "He's not gonna get away with killing my boy. He pulled that trick once before but it ain't gonna work this time."

So who did her father believe had "gotten away" with killing somebody in the family. Well, duh, the Hannackers — Nate Hannacker in particular — and his father, brothers and cousins. Something like forty years ago there had been a car wreck that left at least half a dozen people, both Hannackers and McCluskys, dead. Winona was sure the Hannacker version of what had happened that day didn't match the McClusky version. Both sides claimed the wreck had been the other side's fault. And both claimed there had been survivors, and that some of the survivors had killed some of the other survivors. *Murdered them.* Though who had been the murderer and who had been the victim depended on whose side of the families' feud you were on.

Feud. Sounded like something out of a B movie, starring an actress with big boobs, an actor with a square jaw and at least one old crone with no teeth.

The word may have been archaic, but the feelings weren't. Maybe it was the bad feelings that had caused the feud, and maybe it was the feud that had caused the bad feelings. She didn't know which. What she did know was that she had intimate, personal experience with those bad feelings and she was here to testify that they were as real today as they'd been forty years ago.

And if the old stories were also real, the only thing

that kept the two families from exacting revenge for those murders four decades ago had been some kind of agreement her grandmother had forged with the other women whose menfolk had been killed.

Winona had no idea how much — if any — of the family legends were true. And didn't care. It didn't matter one way or the other. All that mattered was what her father had *believed* was true when he went running out of the house the night Shep died four years ago.

Who was it Pa *thought* had murdered Shep and how'd Pa think they'd done it?

Did Pa go after them for it?

And was *that* why he vanished?

Aunt Frannie lived in an older home in what once had been the best part of town and now was mostly going to seed. Her husband had died years ago, and she lived there with her daughter, Judy Kaye, her daughter's husband/boyfriend and at least two and maybe more grandchildren.

When Winona'd called earlier she had been delighted to learn that her cousin Judy Kaye and her family had gone to Disneyland and wouldn't be home for a week.

Aunt Frannie got bigger every year. She was at least 150 pounds overweight and now the effort involved in moving her mighty bulk from point A to point B severely limited her activities. Aunt Frannie would not be attending the wedding shower this after-noon. She barely made it out of the house once a week to go to Mass.

When her aunt suggested they make the trek out to the gazebo in the back yard that Judy Kaye's husband/boybriend had built there in the shade of a huge persimmon tree, Winona had said she'd rather just sit in Aunt Frannie's kitchen.

They sipped coffee, ate big pieces of coffee cake and generally got caught up on each other's lives before Winona steered the conversation the way she wanted it to go.

"I'm trying to get reconnected with family now that I've moved back to town, but I confess I have an ulterior motive for coming over today."

"You knew I'd made coffee cake?"

"I'm trying to figure out … what happened to Pa."

Aunt Frannie made a dismissive sound.

"Well, good luck with that. All kinda people have been looking for my brother for the past four years and ain't none of them turned up nothing."

"All kinds of people?"

"Yeah, he'd been gone six months when some fellas come to the house asking did I know where he was or how to get in touch with him."

"The police."

"Them boys wasn't no po-lice."

"Who were—"

"They didn't never say, just said they was "business associates," which I figure means they was folks he owed money to who was looking to collect."

"Mama never said anything about any—"

"Sugar, your mama wouldn't a knowed if she'd been visited by the pope. I talked to Jerry and Agnes, and they both was paid visits. Don't know about Greg, though."

So Pa'd had gambling debts and they had come looking for him. Well, Winona could mark that off her list of suspicions. You don't go looking for somebody if you're the one who made them vanish in the first place.

"Jody told me Pa left the house that day in a rage—"

"And that surprises you?"

"What's surprising is *what* he was mad about. He didn't think Shep's death was an accident. He thought somebody had killed him."

"Shep ran his car off the road and wrecked — how do you make that out to be murder?"

Winona shrugged.

"Jody told me that Pa said whoever'd killed Shep had 'gotten away with that trick before.' Does that make any sense to you?"

"None whatsoever. What kinda trick?"

"That's what I'm trying to figure out, and I'm wondering about the wreck that killed Grandpa and the others—"

"It was the Hannackers' fault. They come gunning for the McCluskys. Wasn't no reason at all, they just started shooting into the car, trying to kill 'em. But my mama said my daddy didn't die in the wreck. She said he survived and then got kilt — that Nate Hannacker done it."

"Nate Hannacker killed Grandpa?"

"Yup, that's what Mama said. Stabbed him with a piece of glass, stuck it right in his eye."

"Seriously? Pa never said anything about that to me."

Of course, her father never said anything about anything to his oldest daughter. Maybe he'd talked about it to her mother. Shep, maybe.

"I's the youngest, just a toddler, but yore pa was the oldest, musta been eight or nine years old, knew what was going on and he was *real* tore up. When I's older, I always wondered if that's why your Pa was mad all the time, that he got mad about that when he was a kid and never got over it."

"What do you know about the wreck?"

"All's I know for certain was them cars crashed head-on, both of 'em going fifty or sixty miles an hour — like crashing into a brick wall at a hundred miles an hour. Killed a lot of people. I can't imagine how *anybody* lived through it."

"How many people—?"

"The way my mama told it, when it was all over, they was eight new graves in the church cemetery." She ticked them off with her fingers. "My grandpa, Rooster, and his brother, Digger, was kilt. And one of Digger's boys — Leo was his name. Pa, too, but he didn't die in the wreck. Nate Hannacker lived through it and he killed Pa. So they musta been four Hannackers died, too, but I don't know exactly who they was."

"How did—?"

"Everybody stopped talking about it then. My

Grandma Maude, and her sister-in-law — Digger's widow, name was Thelma — they done something, got together with the Hannacker women and swore wouldn't nobody take revenge for what happened, and nobody ever did."

"So that's not just a story, a myth? The Crows' Pledge? That's real?"

"Absolutely! Mama said it was us — the little 'uns was the reason."

"What does that mean?"

"It was something about *all* of us bein' safe or *none* of us, that was the bargain they struck."

Winona stopped and thought.

"Nate Hannacker killed Grandpa and didn't get arrested ..."

"*Arrested?* You serious?"

"Okay, but nobody did anything about it, either. There was no revenge, no *payback* because of the Crows' Pledge. That could be what Pa meant by 'got away with it.' Couldn't it? You know of any other time somebody in the family got murdered?"

"Oh, I 'spect they was all kinda times folks kilt other folks back then and wasn't no jury trial. But I don't know of nothing specific."

"Did anybody say Nate 'tricked' Grandpa somehow?"

"Wasn't no trick involved that I ever heard. They just said he kilt him. With a piece of glass, that's what Mama said."

"How'd he do that — do you know? Grandpa was a great big man, wasn't he — like Big Jake and Big-Un

— and Nate Hannacker was just a kid. He couldn't have been more than fifteen or sixteen years old."

"He was old enough to drive!"

"Nate Hannacker was *driving*?"

"That's what Mama said. My daddy was in the back seat with his cousin Leo. Grampa's brother Digger was driving and Grampa was in the front seat — and them cars hit *head on*."

Winona was halfway home before she realized the story didn't make sense. Aunt Frannie said the Hannackers had caused the wreck, had been gunning for the McCluskys, shot into their car. But then she said the cars had crashed head on. Say somebody is chasing you, shooting at you … or you're chasing them, either way … how do you crash into each other "head on"?

And besides, how could a car wreck that happened forty years ago have anything to do with her father vanishing?

Chapter Eighteen

JACKSON MADE it back to his father's farm on fumes, parked the old pickup close to Pa's. After his father went to bed, Jackson would siphon some gas into the tank on the clunker pickup. Just enough to get by. He'd carry a gas can with him to church in the morning, siphon some more out of the tanks of the cars that made the mistake of parking out of sight near the dumpsters behind the building.

When he got home after talking to Sherry Lynn Hannacker, he didn't get out of the truck right away, just sat as the sun descended the western sky and dropped slowly down behind the knob. He wasn't aware of the sunset, though. His mind was a thousand miles away, in that place he never allowed it to go. But now, he needed to remember.

CHARLIE EVERYWHERE! *Run! Hide!*

Hide where?

Rain and gunfire and explosions roar in his ears and his terror owns him. It owns him!

He races forward, going nowhere, blind panic eating his belly. The rain is so thick everything is blurred by the water. Bullets splat, splat, hammering into the mud around him.

VC everywhere! Naked. Running, shooting.

He's going to die, die here in the rain. Where can he hide?

A naked soldier appears out of the rain not ten feet in front of him, carrying an RPG, and he aims it—

Blood bursts out of the VC's back, squirts out into the rain and he collapses in the mud, and the RPG flies out of his hands. Jackson tries to leap over the fallen figure but he trips, staggers, goes down on one knee, his body tangled up with the VC and the long barrel of the RPG. He struggles frantically to get free.

There is sudden bright light, an illumination flare explodes in the air and everything is suddenly lit up like a flashbulb. The horror that is lit up steals his soul. Death everywhere.

He can see farther now, looks across the mud and blood and bodies at the doorway of a bunker. Davie Monaghan is crouched inside, firing.

"Don't shoot," cries a voice from out of the rain and a soldier races through a hail of gunfire toward the bunker and crashes into Davie, knocking him backwards. Both their helmets fly off. Blond hair. Andy Taggart.

A white face, lit up like a chalk figure in the flare. Riley Hannacker is standing back in the darkness of the bunker facing the doorway.

Jackson realizes he has the RPG in his hands. He doesn't plan what happens next, his movements are automatic. He lifts the barrel of the RPG, points it at the bunker doorway and fires. He watches as if in slow motion as Andy Taggart is thrown backward by the blast, out of the doorway into the mud in front of the bunker.

And then something falls on him, another naked VC, dead. Jackson just lies there in the rain, sandwiched between the two Cong soldiers, hearing the bullets splat into the bunkers and bodies and the mud around him, bullets so thick it's like hail falling from the sky.

He hears screaming, terror shrieking, but doesn't realize it is his own voice until it gives out and he can't scream any more. Looking out from under the dead soldier on top of him, he can see Andy Taggart's body lying in the mud, torn apart. And he keeps screaming, even though the screams are silent now because he has no voice left.

JACKSON HID under the dead body of the Cong soldier until the shooting stopped, not because it was a good place to hide but because he was too terrified to move. Then he was in shock, staggered by the enormity of what had happened, confused, wandering around until a corpsman took him to the aid tent for his burns. Outside the tent he could hear the shouting, the cheering when the legendary gunship Puff the Magic Dragon came roaring out of the sky, Gatling guns screaming, spewing out a stream of withering fire.

Before he was trundled to the waiting evacuation choppers, he saw medics carry Riley and Davie out of the bunker that'd been ripped open, the whole back wall blown out by the RPG missile he'd fired into it. No, the missile *the VC soldier* had fired. Jackson hadn't done it, the little soldier he'd been lying on top of had fired the shot, Jackson had watched him. He had tackled him when he saw where he was aiming, but it was too late and he got off the shot before Jackson could take him down.

That's what'd happened.

There was some period of time in there right after he woke up in the hospital that Jackson really believed his own version of the story, was so primed and ready to tell it to anybody who asked. But nobody asked. Nobody knew. Andy Taggart was dead. Davie Monaghan and Riley Hannacker were unconscious and when Riley woke up, his brains were scrambled. He didn't remember anymore what'd happened during that final battle. And Davie Monaghan never woke up at all.

Jackson discovered quick that word had spread about what happened *before* the battle while Jackson, Riley, Ben and Davie had been the rear guard when the company moved out of the village called Ho Sung. Other soldiers had heard about how Jackson'd set the Jingle Bell Man on fire and the other soldiers had believed it. But Sergeant Labronski had not lived to have his sit-down meeting with the captain about the "civilian incident," and there was nobody to substantiate the "rumors" about Jackson. Just Riley Hannacker, and it was Riley's word against Jackson's now. And Riley with that head wound, nobody'd believe him. Jackson didn't know if Davie Monaghan had seen him fire the RPG that night, but it didn't matter one way or the other because he couldn't tell anybody.

And soon's Jackson got home, he'd had bigger fish to fry than worrying about whether he'd have to answer for what he'd done to the civilian in Vietnam. Got in trouble, got caught selling heroin before he even knew what he was doing. He'd been an idiot, wasn't familiar with Louisville and didn't know there was a school anywhere near that alleyway, but they'd jacked up the charges because of it and next thing he knew he was facing a ten-year prison sentence. His lawyer had negotiated a plea bargain arrangement, it being his first offense and all, and him being a wounded Vietnam veteran. In exchange for Jackson's testimony against his supplier, the charge was knocked down to possession with intent to sell. Then Jackson finally caught a break. There'd been some kind of turf war — with real bullets flying, and the guy he'd been prepared to finger in court as the dude in charge got hisself kilt. Jackson still got a reduced sentence, but wasn't labeled a snitch.

And those three years in Eddyville (eight months off for good behavior) was Jackson McClusky's college education — got a Master's Degree — where he not only learned the illegal drug trade, but got his own act together, really *together*, for the first time.

Bam!

The sound was like a rifle shot, and for a moment

Jackson was transported out of the cab of the pickup truck and into a steamy jungle where …

It hadn't been a gunshot. It'd been the kitchen's screen door slamming. It'd gotten late, suppertime. He'd have more time to think on this later, plan out what he ought to do about Riley Hannacker's dreams.

Chapter Nineteen

NATE WAS SUMMONED.

Well, it felt like a summons, anyway.

Sherry Lynn had just gotten home from the wedding shower, had been pulling into the driveway, and Nate'd had to grab hold of Drew's hand to keep him from running out to the car to greet her. He'd forgotten how little kids was quick as squirrels. That's when the phone rang inside.

"You can't go running out in front of a car like that, son. You coulda got run over."

He hung onto Drew until Sherry Lynn stopped and got out, then he rushed into the house to answer the phone. The voice on the other end of the line said, "Like to see you this evening, 'bout seven o'clock. Come by the bar and they'll bring you back."

He recognized the voice, of course. Nobody on the planet had a voice like Mama Bert. But he hadn't heard the voice in almost four years, last spoke to her the night he called and told her he had a Pontiac

Grand Prix that needed to vanish. She hadn't dropped a beat, told him to take it by the shop and Brodie would be the only one there.

That was it. She'd hung up. He'd hung up. And he hadn't exchanged a word with the woman since. He wasn't such a fool as to believe she'd helped him out of that tight spot from the goodness of her heart. She worshiped the great god of self-interest, and he supposed what'd been in it for her in that transaction was an almost-new Grand Prix Pontiac to cut into pieces and sell. That wasn't just chump change. If there was any other motivation, he couldn't imagine what it was, but he hadn't tried very hard, either. He didn't like picking at that scab.

Nate could not imagine what on earth she wanted to talk to him about now. Well, maybe had a niggling itch of a suspicion, but didn't pursue the line of thought because he didn't like where it was leading. He simply managed to say, "Sure, I'll be there," without sounding too much like he was standing at attention and saluting while he spoke the words.

Just a click, no goodbye. Mama Bert wasn't big on small talk.

He hadn't been inside the tavern since he used to go there while Riley was serving with the guard unit in Vietnam. And only then because he had too much time on his hands and needed to keep his mind either occupied or inebriated. After Riley got back, there had been neither time nor motive to go there. Nate Hannacker had his hands full with the additions to his little family. On top of that, he had a new crop to plant, cultivate, harvest and take to market.

That didn't leave a whole lot of time for what Abby'd have called "cattin' around."

He parked in the crowded lot about quarter of seven, but didn't get out right away, sat there thinking and wondering. Mama Bert wouldn't have but one reason to call ole Nate Hannacker. She wanted something. He didn't know what she wanted, but did allow that his previous business arrangement with her had been mutually beneficial. He'd made a boatload of money off his partnership in the chop shop and he'd used that money to launch him, Riley and the rest of the crew into the marijuana business.

He never thought about that time now, knew Riley had similar awful, bloody experiences he'd managed to wall off out of his mind, too.

But Riley's were coming back to haunt him. Nate often heard him cry out in the middle of the night, tangled up in the grip of some nightmare with images probably too horrible to describe. Nate had thought Riley's nightmares and such would go away with time, but they didn't. He never spoke of them to the boy, but saw him on mornings after he'd been calling out, his hollow eyes with dark circles under them, and wished he could do something to help.

Walking into the darkened interior of the windowless building, Nate stepped up to the bar, leaned over and said to the bartender, "Mama Bert is—"

The man nodded before he finished and threw the rag down on the bar. "She's expecting you." Then he led Nate through the doorway in the far wall beside the hallway leading to the bathrooms, and to the room at the far end. The man didn't knock, just opened the door and pushed it farther open for Nate.

"He's here," he said, then nodded for Nate to enter and when he had done so, the bartender left and closed the door behind him.

The room hadn't changed since he'd last been there. The couch, the tables with big lamps, the over-stuffed chairs. There still was barely enough light glowing beneath the heavy shades on the big lamps to see anything beyond shadows.

"Evenin', Nate," she said and indicated for him to sit in one of the overstuffed chairs that faced the couch across the width of the coffee table. He remembered the chairs had been more comfortable than they'd looked.

Mama Bert hadn't changed either. Oh, maybe her hair was a lighter shade of gray, more white in it than there'd been before. And maybe she'd lost a little weight, didn't seem quite as gargantuan as she had before, but it was impossible to tell much in the dim light. Her voice was still as deep and gravelly-sounding, like she had pebbles in her throat.

His butt hadn't even made it down to the seat of the chair before she said, "I hear you got busted in a dope field on Thursday, that right?"

"I wasn't *in* the field when I was arrested, just *next to* it. And the commonwealth's attorney declined to prosecute."

"You had the whole thing planned from the git-go,

didn't you. How you was gonna get out of it if the law showed up."

"I did."

"Word is that state policer detective was spitting nails when he seen you come out of the woods with them squirrels." She paused. "I hear he was nigh on to apoplectic when he come back to bulldoze them plants and wasn't nothing there to plow under."

"I wasn't there for that show, but I figure he wasn't happy."

"You's mighty determined to keep the law from destroying them plants — digging a whole field of them up in the dark. I hear a lotta folks gonna have real good Christmases this year."

He didn't know how he was supposed to respond to that so he didn't say anything.

She turned up the beer in her hands and downed it, set the can on the coffee table and didn't mince words.

"I got a business proposition for you. Ain't no chop shop this time. I want us to go in partners, make ourselves a fortune raising marijuana."

Nate wasn't as surprised as he should have been. Some part of him had been contemplating that possibility as soon as she'd said she wanted to talk to him.

He thought about Jessie calling it the "Henny Penny Syndrome" but managed not to smile. Nobody'd cared that they were raising dope in 1970. Or in 1971. But when they started making some serious coin, suddenly everybody wanted in on the action. Just like nobody helped her out when Henny

Penny from the nursery rhyme was working so hard to make bread; soon's she had some, everybody showed up and wanted a bite.

"What is it you got in mind?" he asked and listened as she outlined the whole plan, simple in structure, complex in consequences.

"What you bring to the party is the marijuana. You grow it, tend it, harvest it. What I bring to the party is customers. I got me a network. Once I put it together, we gonna be selling dope all over the country." She paused. "And I'll also provide a safe place to process it, so once you get it out of the field, you got somewhere to put it where you don't have to worry about getting busted."

"And how do you figure we split—?"

"I get half, you and yours get half."

He managed not to look surprised at her brashness. But, of course, he didn't back down from it.

"So we do all the work, find the seeds, cross-pollinate to get the best possible plant, grow them, tend them and harvest them, take all the risks. You haul it off and sell it and you get half? That sound right to you?"

"It does." She didn't give an inch. "You ain't got a sales and distribution program on the scale I'm talking about. You wanna keep working your asses off to sell it on street corners in Louisville for a dime a bag?"

It was comforting to know that there were some things Mama Bert didn't know. They might have started out selling it on street corners, but they'd found dealers, who'd put them onto other dealers. Last year, there'd been some kinda shortage when a supplier didn't provide the promised product and they'd slid right in there, with better prices than the original supplier and better weed, and that'd opened up a huge sales opportunity. Ace brought with him his whole distribution network, too — and if this year's crop was the "righteous weed" he was looking for, those would become customers.

Clearly, all the negotiating was done. She'd made an offer and she wasn't going to budge from it.

He stood. "I have business partners—"

He wasn't going to elaborate, but she did. "Yeah, your grandson Riley, that wild hare Willie Ray Taggart, and Jessie Monaghan. I know."

"I'll talk to them, tell them what you're offering … and I'll let you know."

"Fair 'nough," she said and stood herself. "Come back Monday evening and we'll talk specifics."

Just like before, she bulldozed right over him and went on just like he'd already agreed. That rubbed him the wrong way, and he bristled.

"Maybe Monday. Maybe *not*. Might take longer than that. I'll call you."

He stuck out his hand and she shook it, nodding, but didn't say anything. Then he turned and left the room. By the time he got back to his truck, he'd already made up his mind what he thought about the offer. But he wouldn't prejudice the others. He'd present the offer … and see what they said.

Chapter Twenty

THE MCCLUSKY HOUSE WAS QUIET. Jackson stood outside in the dark beside his father's pickup, sliding a siphon hose down into the gas tank. He wouldn't take much, didn't want Pa to miss it. Just enough to get Jackson's truck to church in the morning where he'd get enough to fill the tank.

His father had given him the old truck to drive around when Jackson got out of prison — if he could get it to run and keep it running. And he let Jackson stay in the attic room over the tool shed. In exchange, Jackson had to do the chores his Pa needed him to do. Some days that was sunup-to-sundown work, some days wasn't nothing to do at all. Them was the days Jackson worked in his own field, raising his own crop.

When he'd got enough gas, he climbed the stairs to the tool shed's attic. Going on midnight, it might be cool enough now to go to sleep. The attic room wasn't a whole lot bigger'n a closet, hotter'n a firecracker in the summertime, but it was a roof over his head, and beggars …

Jackson McClusky would *not* be a beggar for much longer, though. He was sure his Pa knew what he was raisin', of course he did, but they didn't never talk about it and Pa didn't want to get involved in that "weed bidness." Actually, Jackson figured he was just hanging fire, seeing which way the wind blew, before he joined in.

Jackson lay down on the cot and looked at the ceiling as the night breeze through the open windows lowered the temperature out of the double digits. His mind had been churning for hours, ever since he talked to his cousin Sherry Lynn Hannacker that afternoon. He had just let thoughts bubble around, knew eventually what he needed to do would settle to the bottom.

As the oldest son of Big-un McClusky, he'd spent his whole life in the big man's shadow — literally and figuratively, the runt of the litter who never measured up. Nobody ever expected him to be any good at anything he did, so he'd lived down to those expectations. A druggie-drunk by the time he slid out of high school with a D+ grade average, he'd been sailing along going nowhere just like all the other guys when the guard unit got called up and next thing he knew he was fighting for his life in Vietnam.

What'd happened to him there had messed with him big-time. What he saw, and what he did. When he got back home, he'd staggered around, a screw-up hand grenade with the pin already pulled until he got busted in a Louisville alley on drug charges. And after that, he sat day after day in the Jefferson County Jail before the trial — wouldn't nobody post bond to get him out! — in solitary because he was supposed to testify. Went through drug withdrawal without benefit of one of them rehab programs, and once he got clean and sober, he'd had a kind of come-to-Jesus meeting with himself. He would either stay down on the bottom rung of the ladder in life, at the mercy of a world of people bigger and stronger than he was — or he could "straighten up and fly right," as his toothless granny always told him.

Through his whole life, nobody'd ever realized how smart Big-un McClusky was because he got by on intimidation to make his way. Nobody had any idea that Jackson was even smarter, definitely more clever and cunning and capable of enormous self-discipline when his mind was clear and focused.

The first six months he was in the maximum security prison in Eddyville, his life was worse than every day in Vietnam added together. He was small and weak, coming off months of inactivity in jail. That made him *prey.* His cellmate initiated him into his new life — every night for two months as he screamed and the guards ignored him. Then his cellmate had offered Jackson to his buddies. He had come very close to suicide, but was saved by meningitis. No explanation for how, when or where he'd contracted it, but he landed in the infirmary in isolation. He healed from the disease and his wounds there, and had the time and space to reinvent himself. When he was released from the infirmary, his former cellmate welcomed him back with great anticipation. Jackson almost killed him the first night. Fighting back with wild-animal ferocity, Jackson gouged out the man's right eye and bit his thumb completely off. If guards hadn't rescued his screaming cellmate from the blood-splattered cell, Jackson would have killed him with his bare hands. Sent to solitary for three months, Jackson did nothing there but work out, running in place in his cell for hours at a time, hundreds of pushups and sit-ups, and when a sympathetic guard sneaked him some free weights, he worked out nonstop from morning to night. An entirely different Jackson McClusky re-entered gen-pop, the general population, a man rumored to be more than a little insane, with a reputation for utter ruthlessness. The other cons cut a wide path around him.

After that, Jackson watched, listened, asked questions and learned. Worked out and ate right, bulked up and studied the fights that went on around him every day, studied who won, who lost and why, and figured out that to win a fight, you had to strike *first, unexpectedly,* and do *serious injury* quick. He'd tried it out on inmates clearly smaller and weaker than he was at first, but discovered the size and strength of the adversary wasn't nearly as important as the nature of the fight. You could deck the biggest, meanest con in the yard if you hit him from behind without warning, hard enough to land him in the infirmary.

Gradually, he rose up through the ranks of tough-guy wannabes, finally earned the respect of men smart enough to realize how dangerous he was when he killed a guard for no reason whatsoever. He done it in the cafeteria with a hundred witnesses, too, cut the guy open and stuffed the shiv into his guts so they couldn't find the weapon until they did an autopsy. After that, he was accepted into the inner circles of the movers and shakers, the resources he would turn to when he got out and went into business for himself.

Many of Jackson's fellow inmates were South Americans, busted for selling their own drug called cocaine in the U.S. They'd mostly started out like he did as poor farmers, working the land like their daddies and granddaddies, raising something called a coca plant. It was a little like moonshine, when Jackson come to think about it, because their ancestors had grown the plant for their own use — chewed the leaves and it made them high — and then the government got involved, telling them how much they could raise and where they could sell it. Their response had been the same as Kentucky moonshiners: *screw* that!

Jackson had come to the same conclusions in Vietnam about weed that the other Callison County boys had come to, and he set about developing a business plan to implement as soon as he was released. Jackson McClusky brought expertise and experience to the table — he knew how to farm, and not just regular farming. Jackson knew specifically how to raise tobacco. What he learned about marijuana from the "experts" inside convinced him that cannabis required the same skill and equipment. And he learned in the joint the finer points of drug wholesaling — a whole different world from selling nickel bags of weed on street corners. He had a drug distribution network lined up before he set foot outside the walls of Eddyville.

Jackson had big plans, *big* plans. He'd start a business, grow his weed on his home turf in Kentucky, get established, and then he'd take the business south! Growing marijuana wasn't the same thing as raising coca. But he believed that growing both in South America — where law enforcement could be bought off — would make it possible to build an *empire*. He intended to one day control a multi-national drug organization unlike anything that'd ever been seen before.

He'd spent the months since he got out of prison putting his operation together — finding hands willing to help him harvest the crop without money upfront, just a share of the take when it was sold. He'd talked his father out of a field that was lying fallow down by the river, wasn't nothing growing there but weeds, and Jackson'd worked his butt off to get it into shape. Borrowed Pa's tractor and tobacco setter to plant his first crop — the one that would bankroll the rest of his dreams — with seeds he got from a parolee from California. The guy swore the seeds were straight from some place called Humboldt County, California — where growing weed was already an ongoing concern.

What'd happened in 'Nam receded farther and farther into Jackson's past. He'd been working so hard on his business he never ran into anybody from the guard unit and as time went by, Jackson had relaxed and stopped worrying about it. He didn't know for sure whether Davie Monaghan had seen him before he fired the RPG into their bunker that night at Tweety Bird, but what difference did it make? Davie Monaghan didn't even remember his own name, couldn't talk or nothing, or that's what Jackson had heard. Jackson was certain Riley Hannacker *had* seen him, but again — what difference did it make? Four years after he got home and Riley Hannacker *still* wasn't dragging a full string of fish.

That's what Jackson had thought.

But now …

Sherry Lynn said Riley was dreaming about Vietnam. Dreaming about the fire. And *the gun barrel*—

That meant he was starting to remember, didn't it? That what'd happened really hadn't been wiped out of his mind — it was still there, rattling around in there. And if it was still in there, Riley could remember it eventually, couldn't he?

Yeah, he could. He *would*.

Jackson McClusky had come too far, endured too much to allow his plans to be derailed now.

Bottom line — one of these days, Riley Hannacker was going to remember that Jackson had fired an RPG into his bunker in Vietnam. And when he did remember …

Riley would come after Jackson. And Jackson had killed Willie Ray Taggart's brother, Andy. When Riley remembered, he'd tell Willie Ray and they'd *both* come after Jackson!

There was only one thing Jackson could do. He

had to silence Riley *before* he remembered. Before he told anybody. Couldn't afford to wait — one of these mornings, Riley was gonna wake up and *know* what Jackson had done.

Jackson had to keep that from happening.

And so it was settled in Jackson's mind. He knew what he had to do. Jackson had to kill Riley Hannacker as soon as possible. Now, he closed his eyes and drifted off to sleep.

Chapter Twenty-One

"Look, I got," Drew said to his mother, and she nodded her head absently.

"Uh huh, that's good, sweetheart." She was deep into her recipe book, had found a new recipe for pineapple upside-down cake she'd been dying to try. It required crushed pineapple instead of pineapple rings and they'd stopped at the grocery on their way home from church this morning and got some.

"I like the lady. She looks like the lady in church."

"What lady in church?" She didn't turn to look at him.

"The big one that's made out of rock, with the baby made out of rock."

She turned to him and flashed him a small smile.

"That's the Virgin Mary. You know, I've told you about her."

"Is dis lady the Birgin Mary?"

"Not *B*urgin Mary, *Vir*—"

Then she saw what he was holding out to her — a

dirty piece of metal, a medallion of some kind. She stopped, looked at it and took it from him.

"Where'd you get this?"

"It's a lost thing that gotted found."

"Lost where?"

"In a floor."

"Not *in* the floor, *on* the floor." The medallion was so caked with dirt she couldn't tell anything about it, so she stepped to the sink and rinsed it off. When she did, she saw that it was … well, it looked like it *might be* sterling silver. It was a saint, with her hands clasped in prayer over a book, and beneath her image were the words "Pray for Us." The words on the top were worn and harder to read.

It looked like "Saint Mary" … no "Mar*ie*." The next words might be Margaret. Saint Marie Margaret … something. The word started with a "P" and looked like Postal.

Maybe this was the patron saint of mailmen.

"Why didn't you show this to me at church this morning when you found it?"

The child shook his head.

"I not finded it at church."

Ahh … and he might not have been the one who found it at all. Drew had just discovered the game of "trading." Was always coming home from nursery school or the beginner CCD class at church or some playmate's house with a toy he'd gotten by swapping one of his own toys for it. His little plastic soldiers were often the medium of exchange.

"Did you find it, or did you swap for it?"

"It was inna floor."

"*On* the floor — where?"

"*In* the floor — where you could see from."

Turning the medallion over she saw letters on the back. They were engraved, not raised, so they were easier to read. The letter P sat alone at the top, and below it were two letter M's.

Flipping it back over, she read: "Saint Marie Margaret ..." She looked closer. Not Margaret, Magdalene. Saint Marie Magdalen Postal. She'd have to ask Father Abernathy next Sunday if he knew whose it was.

"If you'd shown this to me while we were still at church, we could have found who lost it."

Drew shook his head vigorously. "I not find it at church. It was the stuck thing, where you could see froo da cracks and poke straw except you couldn't because this was stuck there."

That made no sense at all.

She set the medallion on the window sill. "This isn't a toy you can trade. We have to give it back. It belongs to somebody, some grownup, and—"

"It b'longs to *me*. *I* keep it."

Sherry Lynn was not in the mood right now for a lesson on the vicissitudes of finders-keepers or the difference between things-that-are-toys versus things-that-are-*not*-toys. Drew's bottom lip stuck out and she knew a tantrum was not far off.

"You want a sucker?"

He held his little hand out to the window sill.

"B'longs to *me*," he repeated. "I *keep it*."

His eyes filled with crocodile tears and his bottom lip began to tremble. He was seconds away from a meltdown.

Reaching up to the window sill, she snatched the medallion off and handed it to the ramping-up-to-cry child.

"Fine, keep it."

If he showed it to his father, *Riley* would let the boy keep it. Riley let Drew have anything he wanted and smiled with amused indulgence at everything he did. About a month ago, she found the boy asleep on the floor under his bed instead of in it, and Riley'd thought it was *funny.* He just laughed it off, so now there was no telling where Drew would decide to sleep at night — she'd found him snuggled up in Pop Pop's recliner once and even in the bathtub!

She'd watched Riley the morning they found Drew in the recliner, staring down at the sleeping child, a look of contented adoration on his face. At every opportunity, Riley showered the boy with love and attention.

Riley never looked at *her* with love anymore!

She stopped.

Had he *ever* looked at her with love?

She tried to remember, but couldn't. They'd been desperately in love before Riley went to Vietnam, but after that ...

Had Riley ever *said* he loved her? That thought stole her breath. Had he?

Of course he had. This was crazy. But now it was Sherry Lynn's bottom lip that began to tremble. She sniffed hard, rubbed at her eyes with the back of her hand and stifled the sob.

She shook her head, shook off the thoughts, replaced them with images of the cake, and decided she'd make it for supper *tonight*. She hadn't planned to make dessert for tonight but why wait? And she'd put maraschino cherries all over the top. Sherry Lynn loved maraschino cherries.

Chapter Twenty-Two

THEY MET in the Cornbread Mafia Clubhouse, aka Jessie's tobacco barn. That's where they'd formed their alliance that first time and the office in the front part of the barn — a single empty room about the size of Jessie's kitchen — provided a private place to talk without fear of anybody overhearing or interrupting. And it was close to Jessie's house. Sometimes, in the beginning, she had trouble getting away for very long for private talks. Now, it was where they convened, unless it was in the dead of winter. The barn was as good a place as any. The ghosts that'd been there were gone now, but it still had a vibe Jessie liked.

A couple of years ago, Willie Ray had shown up with furniture. He'd bought the couch, some chairs, a coffee table and some battery-operated lanterns at a yard sale, loaded them up and brought them to the barn to make the clubhouse "homey." He was always doing random things like that, had purchased a regular arsenal last summer when he saw the weapons on sale at a Louisville gun store, filled the bed of his pickup with guns and ammunition as a "birthday present" for Riley. It hadn't been Riley's birthday. But when it *was* Drew's, Willie Ray'd bought him a gigantic swing set, hauled it out to the farm in pieces. It had taken Willie Ray, Riley and Nate all day to assemble it.

They usually met in the cool of the evening so they could open the door from the office into the barn, and the lone office window that looked out over the nearby fields, to allow a breeze to blow through to mitigate the heat.

It was a hot, summer Sunday afternoon now, though, and the breeze that blew through wasn't cool. You could hear the rumble from a storm gathering in the west that would come roaring across the sky like a freight train along toward sunset. Tornado season was in the spring and had been over months ago, but you never knew. Jessie'd loved storms when she was a kid, loved the grandeur and majesty of the huge clouds and the power of the wind and rain. She always wanted to stand out in the middle of an empty field and watch them coming at her ... but her mother'd had this thing about lightning — "You wanna be a french fry?" — and had dragged the girl inside.

Nate hadn't told them when he called yesterday what he wanted to talk to all of them about. Just said it was important and they needed to get together as soon as possible.

Willie Ray sat in the big overstuffed chair, his long legs out in front of him, propped up on the coffee table, a beer in one hand and a slice of cold pizza in the other. Nate and Riley sat on the couch, Jessie faced them from the "recliner" that didn't recline, as they'd found out the first time Willie Ray sat down in it, shoved back and toppled the whole thing over in the floor. Jessie perched on the edge of it like a bird on a wire. She sat very still, determined not to let the others see that she'd injured her shoulder when they'd worked all night Thursday. Some movements didn't hurt at all, others were excruciating and stabbed so suddenly it took her breath away.

She'd gone by Pizza Hut on her way home from church and bought pizza, which of course was cold now, but Willie Ray would eat anything. She also brought a cooler with soft drinks and beer. She sat now, holding a cold can of Coke to her sweaty forehead, leaning in to hear what Nate had to say.

Nate laid out the offer, short and simple. He saved the best — or the worst — for last, waited until the end to tell them *who* had made the offer to join forces with them. The two words *Mama Bert* hit the group with a distinct sizzle.

"Mama Bert!" Willie Ray started coughing. "Seriously?" He'd been swallowing when Nate said it and choked on the piece of pizza.

Willie Ray was better acquainted with the woman than any of them, since he'd become a dealer in the around-the-clock poker game in the back room of the Club Cherry when he was still in high school. He didn't work there anymore, but he still took a shift now and then to keep his skills up — "make sure I can still palm an ace when I need to." Willie Ray loved to gamble. Riley'd told Jessie about it, how he'd thought he was hot stuff until a soldier they called Scottie, an artilleryman on the Number Five gun at Tweety Bird, had cleaned his clock. He'd lost every cigarette he owned, every one he could bum from the rest of the unit, and an IOU for almost a whole carton.

When he got back from Vietnam, Willie Ray'd stopped gambling altogether. He'd deal poker hands all night, but wouldn't play. Riley had told her he didn't think it was about Scottie, though. He thought it was about Andy, as almost everything in Willie Ray's life had been when he got home. Andy didn't gamble, and if, as they all suspected, Willie Ray had some sense of "living life for two," then Willie Ray wouldn't gamble either.

"How … why? How does Mama Bert even know about *us?*" Jessie felt venerable somehow, violated that this stranger had stepped into her world and wanted to become a part of it.

"Ain't nothing goes on in this county Mama Bert don't know about," Willie Ray said.

"I have never said hi, bye or kiss-my-foot to that woman," Jessie blustered. "I can't imagine why she'd come to us—"

"Duh … we made some serious coin last fall," Riley said. "It ain't like we tried to hide it from anybody."

He looked at Willie Ray, who was driving around in that brand new GMC pickup with all the bells and whistles.

"We're building a house, Jessie renovated hers. It ain't a secret."

"We're not the only people's growing weed and making money at it," Jessie countered. It was true, of course. Small-time farmers who hadn't planted an ear of corn in five years suddenly had money. The Dawsons. Bubba Jamison and the Parker brothers. Everybody knew what was going on. People weren't stupid. Jessie suspected most of the other growers were stuck where they'd been at first — planting bad weed from bad seeds, so their crops didn't sell very well.

"She came to *us* because she and I ... had a business arrangement a few years back," Nate said, and Riley was the only one of them who didn't look surprised. Sure, Jessie knew Nate and Riley and Willie Ray were bootleggers, but clearly Nate had been involved in other shady business arrangements she didn't know about.

"Let's get back to the issue at hand," Riley said. "As I understand it ..." He looked at Nate. "Correct me if I didn't hear you right — she wants to sell the pot we raise, says she has a huge network of buyers who would gobble it up."

"Yeah, and for selling it, she gets half the profit," Willie Ray said, took a gulp of his beer, burped noisily, and continued. "We're the ones doing the work. Why should she get half?"

"And taking *the risks*," Jessie said.

"Some of the risks," Nate said. "Sounds to me like she's planning on selling all over the country. Get caught with big quantities of weed in some states and they'll put you in the iron house for a good, long stretch."

"I'm sure she can do what she says she can," Riley said. "She can get our product into the hands of buyers ... who knows where."

"We'll get to that point on our own one of these days," Willie Ray said. "This year's crop" — he lifted his chin and whistled — "we're talking some serious, serious, righteous weed."

"I got a question," Jessie said, treading lightly. "What are we doing this for?"

"Money!" Willie Ray cried, his eyes bright. "Greenbacks, sweet thing! Moola. Trash bags full of hundred-dollar bills."

"I'm serious."

Willie Ray settled down.

"We had a why in the beginning. It was a clear why and we all signed on for it. If we hadn't, I don't know what—" She suddenly found herself close to tears and she hated that. She never cried around these guys, her business partners. Never.

Riley swooped in to the rescue before she lost her composure.

"We did it for Davie, were glad to do it, proud to do it."

Though all the Cornbread Mafia's proceeds had gone to Davie's care in the beginning, last year's crop had made so much money they had split it four ways. Just her twenty-five percent was enough to renovate her house and set up special care for Davie and Mama Ruth.

"I hadn't really thought about what comes after," Riley continued. "Just on a train, going downhill—"

"Going faster and faster and faster," Willie Ray said.

"If we keep making the kind of money we've been making—"

Willie Ray tilted his head back and whistled again and cried, "*More*, baby girl. Much, much more."

"How do you feel about that?" Riley asked Jessie with a gaze so direct it made her uncomfortable. He was always looking out for what would be best for Jessie. Sherry Lynn had seen to that in the beginning. She and Jessie'd bonded on their ride home together from Texas … the last time Jessie and Davie had been together. Sherry Lynn had shown up as soon as she'd gotten on her feet after Drew was born, offering to help any way she could. She was always sending Riley over to do whatever tasks Jessie's father and brothers didn't have time to do. And Jessie was grateful … but it still had an awkward feel to it, even after all this time.

Particularly since Sherry Lynn had opened up and dumped her misery in Jessie's lap, telling Jessie way more than she wanted to know about Sherry Lynn and Riley's marriage.

"I hadn't really considered it." Jessie's voice was thoughtful. "Okay, so we're owning that we believe we're going to do better than just make good money, really good money. That we could make ridiculous money. I'll throw the question back at you guys. How do you feel about that?"

"If you asking me do I mind being rich," Willie Ray said, "the answer's no. N. O. I do not mind one bit."

"How about we circle back around to what we come here to talk about," Nate said. "We're sitting here assuming that we're gonna get rich … on our own. That ain't no lead pipe cinch certainty."

"No, it ain't," Riley said. He looked from one to the other of them. "But I do believe it. I don't know how long it'll take, maybe longer than we think, maybe not. But I think that's what's out there within our grasp."

"We throw in with Mama Bert and she gets fifty percent, but we split the other fifty percent *four* ways," Willie Ray said. "Looks to me like what we'll be doing is making *her* rich."

"Oh, I do b'lieve she can move a whole lot more product than we can," Nate said. "With her connections …"

"More than we can *right now*," Riley said. "I believe we'll get that kind of customer base on our own, without her help. Look what happened last year." They had lucked into a shortage. The product a big buyer expected didn't show up and they'd made up the difference — had done such a good job they'd gained him as a regular customer. There'd be others like that. "It'll just take longer. Is anybody in a hurry?"

"And if it's just us and we don't have to lop off the top fifty percent of profit … each of us'll become our own personal 'rich' sooner," Willie Ray said.

"The 'just us' part," Jessie said. "That's another

thing that makes me feel hinky about this whole thing. We're *us*. We can depend on each other. We got each other's back. I don't think Mama Bert is loyal to—"

"Nothing but the almighty dollar," Willie Ray finished for her.

"So, can we trust her?" Jessie asked. "I mean, would she cheat us? Or turn us in?"

"I think the only reason we can trust her is because we serve her best interests," Nate said. "She messes with us, she'd be killing the goose that laid the golden egg."

"Why doesn't she just go out on her own and raise pot?" Jessie asked. "It's not like we're the only people in the county who know how. She could hire people to plant it and harvest it. Then she could keep all the profit instead of just half."

"We're raising better weed than anybody else around," Nate said. "We all know it. Mama Bert probably does, too. But I think she also wants us because the kinds of people she runs with and does business with ... they ain't folks you can turn your back on."

"She knows she can trust us." Riley looked at Nate. "She found that out working with Papa."

"She can trust *us*, but we don't know if we can trust *her*," Jessie said. "If we're willing to be patient, we can have in a few years everything she's offering us now, and we won't have to share it with anybody."

"Yeah ..." Willie Ray said, "... but it's hard to turn down somebody who can make you rich *right now*."

"Maybe I don't want to be rich," Jessie countered. "I've never thought about it one way or the other."

"We can keep wrangling about this all night," Nate said, "but I think each of us has had a chance to say what we think about it. I believe it's time to decide."

"So we vote?" Willie Ray asks. "This is America — majority rules."

"No, not majority," Riley said, and he was looking at Jessie again in that way that made her uncomfortable. "We started this agreeing on everything. Everybody on board. I think we need to go forward the same way — we need to all be on the same page."

"Riley's right," Nate said. "It needs to be unanimous. If we can't agree one hundred percent to take Mama Bert's offer, then I say we need to leave things alone and keep on keeping on."

"Rocks in a box, rocks in a box," Willie Ray suddenly cried, leapt up and headed out to his truck, trailing "I'll be right back" in the air behind him like a balloon attached to his shoe. They saw him get something out from under the front seat, then bend over and pick something up off the ground, several different somethings. When he'd found whatever he was looking for, he came back into the office.

He held out a wooden box, about the size of a box of tissues. It was handmade, but Jessie could see no nail holes. The surface was smooth and flawless, a dark ebony color, and there was a hole in the lid about the size of a fifty-cent piece.

"This here's the box Andy gave me to keep my

baseball cards in," he said, in a voice so hollow it about broke Jessie's heart. "He made it in shop class in junior high."

The lid was hinged and he opened the box and they saw inside what he'd been picking up. Rocks. They were small, different sizes, some light colors, others dark.

He tried to smile then, but couldn't quite pull it off. "I found a horned toad in the woods one summer and wanted to keep it as a pet, so I made a hole in the top of the box to let it breathe." He paused. "Mama found the box in the back of Andy's closet when she was cleaning out ... when I got home. She thought I'd want it. I use it now, keep joints in it."

He tried again to smile and got fairly close.

"That danged toad died anyway." He held out the box. "Everybody get yourself a white rock and a black rock." Jessie looked at him questioningly. "Okay, I know they ain't *white* and *black* — light and dark, work with me, people."

He passed the box around and when everyone had two rocks, he poured the rest of the rocks out on the floor and closed the lid of the box.

"I'm gonna pass the box around. If you think we ought to throw in with Mama Bert, put a light rock in the box. If you think we shouldn't, put in a dark rock." He handed the box to Jessie. "Turn your back."

She did, put a rock in the box and then handed the box to Nate, who did the same thing.

When the box made it back around to Willie Ray,

he turned his back, inserted his own rock, and turned around to face them again.

"Let's see what we got here."

He slowly lifted the lid so everyone could see the rocks in the box. They looked up and grinned at each other. All the rocks were the same — dark.

"Guess I get to bear the glad tidings to Mama Bert tomorrow that we have 'declined her gracious offer,'" Nate said.

"Think she's gonna be mad?" Riley asked.

"I s'pect she's likely to say so if she is," Nate said.

There was a rumble in the distance, thunder from a coming storm.

Chapter Twenty-Three

RAIN HAMMERED the window panes of Winona McClusky's office so hard it sounded like somebody was throwing rocks. She'd been almost ready to leave when the storm struck. In this downpour, she'd get soaked on the way to her car. She had an umbrella. Of course she did. It was in the car. She'd wait. She'd come to the office after church and had been puttering around the whole rest of the afternoon and early evening, trying to get things squared away in case she actually had to do some work when the office opened for business tomorrow morning.

She turned the gooseneck lamp back on, the only light in the room, while she waited for the rain to ease off. Wouldn't take long. Leaning against the edge of the desk, she picked up two pads of Post-it Notes off the desktop, and began arranging them on the wide cherry surface, like dealing out cards. Slowly, she became engrossed in the activity, moved everything off the desk to accommodate them all, lit up in the glow of the gooseneck lamp like actors on a stage in a spotlight.

Half an hour later she became aware that the rainfall had been reduced to a gentle patter against the windows.

Sitting back in her office chair, she reached into her purse and drew out the unopened package of cigarettes. The temptation to rip off the top, pull one of the cigarettes out of the pack, put it in her mouth and light up was almost overwhelming.

Almost. Good.

That's what the package of cigarettes was for. It was there to tempt her. Winona McClusky was a firm believer that you didn't get stronger by avoiding temptation. You got stronger by confronting it, by beating it. Holding the package under her nose, she inhaled the sweet cigarette smell through the paper and cellophane, and then she made something of a grand gesture out of putting the package back into her purse.

She hadn't had a cigarette in three months, two weeks, four days — she looked at the clock — nine hours, eleven minutes and pocket change in seconds ago. Not that she was counting or anything. And oh my, wouldn't one be fine right now.

Focus!

The Post-it Notes she had arranged on the desk were color-coded — orange on the left side of the desk, blue on the right. She was using them to create a McClusky family tree as it'd been in 1933, lining up the descendants of the brothers who'd been killed in that long-ago car wreck. Rooster McClusky's were orange, the descendants of his brother, Digger, were blue.

Rooster and Digger.

If there was a single relative who knew where their ancestral progenitors had gotten the nicknames, she didn't know who it was. And she had asked! Their real names were recorded in family Bibles, of course, but those ridiculous nicknames had actually been inscribed on their headstones in the cemetery.

She stared at the orange notes.

Rooster'd had two sons and three daughters. She moved her fingers down the orange stairs of her lineage. Rooster's oldest son, Ike, was Winona's grandfather. Ike had left behind a house full of kids when he was killed, small children. The oldest was Winona's father, Parker, followed by her uncles Jerry and Greg, and her aunts, Agnes and Frances. All of her uncles and aunts had had children, too, of course. Hey, these were upstanding Catholic families and they all reproduced like rabbits.

The sheer number of Post-it Notes was impressive and somewhat surprising. It was one thing to stand around making small talk with a herd of acquaintance-relatives — first, second, third and whatever cousins — at a family reunion, but it was another thing entirely to look at the family laid out like this before her. Rooster's other son, big Jake, had had four sons and three daughters. His three daughters had had … she paused and counted fourteen children altogether.

And those children had had children of their own.

She picked up a pad of purple Post-it Notes, reached out and swapped out some of the blue and orange ones. She put purple Post-it Notes in the spaces occupied by the people who'd been killed in that long-ago wreck — or killed shortly after the wreck by means unknown. Rooster and Digger. Her grandfather Ike, and Digger's son Leo.

She replaced her father's Post-it with a purple one, and her brother Shep's, too.

Thunder rattled the window panes and she realized the rain had ramped back up and she might have missed her opportunity to make it to her car without getting drenched.

All those people — all those relatives, and yet her father had vanished from among them like a soap bubble had popped … and none of them had any idea what had happened to him.

The telephone on her desk jangled and she jumped in surprise. Who'd be calling at this time of night?

"Hello, Tanner, McClusky and Fowler. We're closed right now—"

"This Winona?" She didn't recognize the man's voice.

"Who wants to know?"

"You don't need to get persnickety, baby girl. I'm just calling 'cause I talked to Frannie and she said you was looking to find out about the wreck that killed all them McCluskys back in the day."

She finally recognized the voice. It was her Uncle

Greg. He was drunk, of course, or on his way there. She couldn't remember a time she'd ever talked to him when he wasn't in some state of inebriation. His brain had to be pickled.

"The man you need to talk to is Skeeter. He told me one time that he was *there*, just a little bitty kid at the time. Uncle Jonah was one of them that come on the wreck when the dust was still settling out of the air, I think. But maybe that wasn't the way of it. Anyway, Skeeter was with him."

Winona's eyes went to the Post-it Notes. Not the orange ones, the blue ones, the descendants of *Digger* McClusky. His son, Leo, had a purple Post-It Note, had died with his father in the wreck. But his other son was Jonah. He was a little younger than Leo, she thought, both had been in their mid-twenties.

In his mid-sixties now, Jonah was in a nursing home somewhere, she thought, early-onset Alzheimer's.

Running her fingers down through blue Post-it Notes, she found Jonah's children. There were six of them. Josiah was the oldest, but they called him Skeeter.

Rooster.

Digger.

Skeeter.

What happened to the other four dwarves?

"You want to know what happened, you best talk to Skeeter quick, though. I heard he was in the hospital up in Lexington. Bad cancer, but I ain't sure what kind."

"What hospital?"

"How would I know?"

He banged the receiver down so hard the clunk sound hurt her ear.

Was rudeness an inherited trait? If it was, it was definitely *not* a recessive gene in the McClusky family.

Chapter Twenty-Four

It was still raining. It had started late Sunday afternoon and had rained all night. Wasn't pouring anymore, though, thunder rumbling in the sky like being inside a bowling alley. Even to this day, Willie Ray Taggart didn't like storms, wasn't afraid of them like he'd been as a kid, they just creeped him out, made him edgy.

As he drove through the rainy pre-dawn hours to get to Louisville early Monday morning, he watched the view through the windshield of his truck appear and disappear with the wipers' zipping trips across his windshield, blurring everything until they got all the smeared bug guts off.

Snake Eyes had his own corner where he made penny-ante drug deals with local customers. If you wanted to buy more product than he had, or wanted to sell it, he could put you in touch with people higher up the food chain, but he stayed resolutely "small time."

In this downpour, Snake Eyes probably set up shop somewhere else, and Willie Ray didn't know where that might be, so when he got near the dealer's regular spot, he drove slowly along, searching alleyway openings, recessed doorways, and under awnings and overhangs for the little man whose nickname didn't have nothing to do with rolling dice. The scrawny little black man had eyes so dark there wasn't no way to see the pupils in 'em. Even when he wasn't stoned, with his pupils dilated, his eyes were *black* and *white*, that's all — white with a solitary dot on top that meant, "You lose, sucker."

As he drove slowly along, block after block, and found nobody, Willie Ray figured he ought to just turn around and go back to Callison County. Wasn't like this was some big important sale or nothing. You didn't do business on street corners for sales like that. Oh, they'd started out that way — selling weed by the baggie. He smiled when he thought about selling off the crop they'd grown last year in sandwich bags! He'd made one sale on that crop where he'd handed over fifty *pounds* of weed in exchange for a grocery sack full of twenty, fifty and hundred-dollar bills. Nate had established an etiquette for handing "bulk sales." It was all based on trust, and the growers Willie Ray knew was trustworthy — had to be. Just like back during Prohibition, there was a built-in quality control system. Sell to people you know and you won't cheat them and they won't cheat you.

A routine had been established for Away-From-Here's who came to Callison County to do business.

The man who was buying would show up with the money and hand it over to the grower. The grower would leave with the cash, drop it off somewhere, and go to wherever he'd stashed the product, and return with it. That way the weed and the money wasn't never in the same place at the same time. Yeah, the grower could run off with the buyer's money and not deliver the product the guy'd paid for, but that never happened. Not in *Callison County*! Everybody knew they had to play by the rules.

Willie Ray saw himself as the Product Development Department of the Cornbread Mafia. Nate handled Sales and Marketing. Nate had connections all over the state — who had their own connections all over the country — folks who operated on the south side of the law who put him in touch with bigger-better folks who were engaged in a different kind of enterprise than buying and selling stolen property. It hadn't taken long at all to find a market clamoring to buy what they were growing.

Willie Ray hadn't come to Snake Eyes to sell him weed! He'd come because the little dealer came across all kinda different strains of cannabis through his connections in South America. Willie Ray's "silent partner in crime" had sent him out in search of something exotic. Wazzi told him to buy a couple of different kinds to see what they might be able to grow from the seeds in the baggies.

Snake Eyes suddenly stepped out of a recessed doorway and hurried across the street in the rain, his collar turned up and his hat pulled down over his eyes.

Willie Ray pulled up right in front of him, told him to "get in 'fore you float away," and Snake Eyes hopped into the truck.

Willie Ray's smile of greeting drained off his face when the little dealer cried, "Get out of here! Now!"

He floored the accelerator and the pickup's big tires spun on the wet asphalt before they grabbed hold and propelled it forward down the street.

"What in the—?"

"Turn in here," Snake Eyes said, pointing to a short, dead-end alley next to an abandoned building.

Willie Ray pulled to a stop in the alley.

"You wanna tell me what we're running from?"

"I can't be seen doin' business with you. They looking for you and they ain't happy."

"They who? The law?"

"The Colombians, Los Asesinos." He paused. "Translated, that means 'the killers, assassins, *butchers*.' They started out as a street gang in Bogotá, in a place called El Paraiso — a ghetto up on a mountainside. They killed off all the other gangs and took over the drug trade, smuggling coke and weed into the United States."

"How'd I piss in their Cheerios?"

"You stole one of their biggest customers." *That's* what this was about, the huge weed deal that'd literally fallen into their laps last year. "Long as you was just some local farmer selling nickel and dime bags of rangy weed on the street corners, the big dealers didn't care. You was a pesky mosquito to them. But after what you pulled last year — you not a bug anymore, you're *competition!*"

"Competing with who? Them assassin dudes?"

Snake Eyes sat back and eyed him critically.

"Tell me something — did you not know who you was elbowing away from the table last year or did you just not care?"

"Both, I guess. Or neither. Look, if them fellas can't grow enough weed to satisfy their customers—"

"They don't *grow* it, they ain't farmers. They *dealers.* Only reason they was short last year was they had transport issues."

"And that means?"

"Border Patrol spotted them crossing the Rio Grande west of Ciudad Juárez." He caught Willie Ray's look. "El Paso, Texas. Two big trucks and they had to run off and leave the whole load."

"What the angels took."

"Huh?"

"An old bootlegging phrase, means the part of the brew that evaporates. Sounds like their weed got to the border and evaporated. It ain't our fault they can't deliver."

Snake Eyes rolled his eyes.

"You got any idea how powerful some of them South Americans are? A couple of 'em's got friggin' armies."

Willie Ray lost his breath for a moment.

"These guys got they own … *army?*"

"Not yet. Los Asesinos ain't the big time. But they's working on it. They got where they are by eliminating the competition. And now their competition is *you.*"

"They's plenty of folks looking to buy weed. They'll find customers."

Snake Eyes shook his head in wonder.

"You not getting it, man. Them big operators, the ones with armies … when they was starting out, if somebody got in their way, they didn't just kill him. They'd gun him down in the street — his wife and kids, too — in front of two dozen witnesses. They wanted people to see, to know who they was dealing with, to know there wasn't *nothing* they wouldn't do. Them dealers stay off each other's turf, and once you got that kind of *reputation* don't nobody mess with you no more."

"And you sayin' Los Asesinos is looking to make a reputation by gunning us down in the street?"

"They'd shoot you down like dogs if they could get away with it! Where they come from, you can buy off the law, or scare 'em off. They know they'd get locked up if they tried that kinda thing here. But you got in their way, and they ain't gonna just let that slide."

"If they mad now, they gonna be plum apoplectic when they find out we gonna be selling twice as much to 'their customer' this year as they was supposed to deliver last year.

"You walking out on thin ice, my friend. These ain't guys I wanna get crossways with. You and me, we quits. I told them the Cornbread Mafia was just a handful of dumb hillbillies that I don't do business with no more."

"I didn't come here to *sell* you weed — so you ain't in trouble. I come to *buy* some. I's hoping for something from somewhere besides Mexico or Colombia. A nickel bag's all I need."

"You growing *acres* of weed and you want—?"

"Just call it breeding stock." Then Willie Ray realized Snake Eyes didn't have no idea what that meant. "I's wantin' to try something different, that's all."

"I might be able to lay my hands on … how about Honduras, maybe, or Nicaragua?"

Willie Ray had only the vaguest idea where in Central America those places might be located.

"That'd be great."

"Go get yourself something to eat and meet me in two hours in the alley behind Saint Louis Bertrand Church on Sixth Street."

Willie Ray had a runaway case of the munchies so he was more than willing to kill a couple of hours smoking weed and chowing down. He found a convenience store that sold hotdogs, bought a dozen of them and parked his truck in the back lot behind the store to eat. Then smoked more weed, filling the truck cab with that unmistakable odor. Once it got in your clothes and hair, you had to shower and change or you'd smell like weed all day. And it had so saturated the tattered upholstery of Willie Ray's old truck that he'd had to yank the seat out and hose it down to get rid of the smell. The seat in his new truck was leather, black leather, and the pot stink didn't penetrate it.

He should have realized he might have trouble finding the meeting site. Willie Ray was a country boy and the labyrinth of one-way streets in Louisville confused him, got him all turned around. And smoking all that weed probably didn't help. He was half an hour late to the meeting and by the time he showed up behind the big church on Sixth Street, Snake Eyes was nowhere to be seen.

Chapter Twenty-Five

WINONA MCCLUSKY GOT UP EARLY Monday morning and discovered it was still raining. She didn't like driving in the rain, but the parkway to Lexington didn't have much traffic on it. The Bluegrass Parkway — from nowhere to nowhere through nowhere. Yeah, that was about right.

She could not remember the last time she had spoken to her cousin Skeeter. Correction: she couldn't remember if she had *ever* spoken to him as an adult, save the obligatory, hi-how-ya-doin'? at family reunions. She hadn't seen him at Aunt Frannie's Christmas bash last year, and now she knew why. He'd obviously been sick even then.

She had some difficulty locating Skeeter. Aunt Frannie'd said Skeeter's father, Jonah, was in a nursing home somewhere, suffering from Alzheimer's. Skeeter had been married and divorced two — three? — times and was currently between wives. His brother Kenneth was in his early thirties, closer to Winona's age, and unmarried. The unmarrieds hung out together at family gigs, away from the rowdy children of their siblings so the two of them had chatted amiably at Christmas. She called Kenny, who said his brother'd yo-yoed in and out of several hospitals, but he wasn't sure exactly where he was at the moment. Their sister Elizabeth would know, Kenny'd said, and so Winona had called her. Lizzie gave Winona all the information she needed. It had been a little awkward trying to explain to Skeeter's sister why his long-lost cousin Winona suddenly wanted to have a sit-down conversation with him, but she'd made up something about an interest in genealogy and that she was putting together a "family tree." Lizzie said she'd call Skeeter and give him a heads-up that Winona would be coming for a visit.

When Winona finally located his room in the rabbit warren of hospital rooms in the gigantic Albert B. Chandler Hospital on Rose Street in Lexington, she found him there alone. Hooked to a spaghetti mass of tubes and monitors, he was sitting on the side of his bed with his feet dangling off, licking an ice cream cone. She checked the room number again to be sure before she knocked on the door frame. The man sitting on the side of the bed didn't look even remotely familiar. The Skeeter she remembered had been in his mid-forties, a big man with red hair and a ruddy complexion. This man could have been anywhere between twenty and a hundred years old. He had no hair at all, on his head or anywhere else — not even eyebrows. He was emaciated, with burnt-cigarette-hole eyes in a sallow face.

"Skeeter?" she asked tentatively as she knocked. He looked up at her, surprised.

"Do I know you?"

"Yes. Well, no. Actually yes, but just barely. I'm Winona — your cousin — Parker's oldest. Last time I saw you was …"

"Yeah, Lizzie called and said you wanted to come talk to me—"

A nurse built like the front end of a Mack truck rumbled into the room, spewing admonitions before she even crossed the threshold.

"… can't sit up on the edge of the bed like that!" She lifted his legs and swung them up onto the bed and yanked up the side rail. "You're trying to get me fired, aren't you?" She reached for the ice cream cone and he held it away from her. "You know that's gonna make you sick."

"I'll buzz when I start puking so you can be the one who gets to clean it up."

The nurse stormed back out of the room and Skeeter offered the scraps of a smile.

"I got an aide who sneaks me ice cream. It makes me God-awful sick — the milk in it — takes about half an hour, though, so we got a few minutes to talk before I start barfing." He indicated a chair beside the bed. "Have a seat. I won't throw up on you. I'm a pretty good shot."

She sat down in the straight-backed chair beside the bed. "I could come back some other …"

"Right now is all I got."

"That's what Uncle Greg said, told me if I needed to talk to you I'd better do it soon because …"

Oops. Stepped in it. She wanted to bite off her tongue.

"I mean … uh," he just looked at her, "… you might be, you know, *busy* later."

"Busy dying."

Winona owned it. "Uh, you think maybe there's one of those Jaws of Life things down in the emergency room that I could use to pry open my mouth and extricate my foot."

He burst out laughing so abruptly, he spit ice cream on the sheet and began to cough. It was a little while before he got his breathing under control enough to continue.

"I like you. Me and you mighta been friends if we'd got a chance. Greg's right. They won't tell me how long I got, but they did say probably wasn't a good idea to buy green bananas."

It was Winona's turn to snort out an unattractive laugh.

"Did your sister tell you why I wanted to talk to you?"

He shook his head.

"Good. What I told her wasn't the real reason."

"What is the real reason?"

"I'm trying to find out what happened to my father."

"He disappeared, didn't he? A few years back.

Wasn't it about the same time your brother got killed in that wreck?"

"It was the day after Shep died."

"Why would you think I'd know something about it? I ain't completely sure I'd recognize yore daddy if he was hiding under the bed."

"I want to ask you about the wreck that happened forty years ago." His pale face turned white. "The one that killed my grandfather, Ike, and great-grandfather Rooster —"

"And my Grandfather Digger and Uncle Leo and maybe some others," he finished for her. "Why in the Sam Hill ...? Now there's one from left field." He started coughing again and she had to wait until he caught his breath to continue.

"You were there that day, weren't you — just a little kid, maybe five years old? Uncle Greg said your father took you with him when he went there ... after."

"Yeah, I's there." There were warring emotions in his voice, but Winona couldn't tell what they were. "Why do you want to know about *that*?"

"It's a long story," she said and drew a breath. "It'll take a bit of explaining—"

"Never mind, then. I ain't got but a little while 'fore I start throwing up that ice cream. How about I tell you what I know — and it might not be what you're looking for at all — then if I still care why you want to know it when I'm done, I'll ask."

"Fair enough."

Skeeter drew in a shaky breath, not deep or he'd have started coughing.

"I ain't got no idea why Pa took me with him that day. Why would anybody let a little kid see a thing like that? Course, he didn't know how bad it was gonna be 'til he got there and then he parked and told me to stay in the car. I didn't, though. I sneaked out for a better look."

He paused, asked her to hand him the water glass on the side table. After he took a drink he lay back on the pillows and let out a whoosh of air that ended in coughing, but he choked it back before it could take over.

"It was night and spitting rain. I didn't see a whole lot because they was grownups close up, blocking my view, and I was hiding behind stuff so Pa wouldn't see I'd got out of the car."

"Were there any witnesses to the wreck?"

"Naaa, I don't see how there could have been. It was the middle of the night out on a lonely old road. But they was folks come up on it right after. It was a bad one, both the cars was all tore up — the engine of Grampa Digger's car got knocked plumb out of it and it was laying in the grass ... with my Uncle Leo under it, smashed him." He paused, was looking at images only he could see. "I seen that part ... well, I seen the engine and an arm and leg sticking out from under it."

"When you got there, was everybody already dead?"

"Them cars hit head-on, so—"

"That's what Aunt Frannie said, but if nobody witnessed the wreck, how did they know that?"

"I ain't rightly sure. Might be 'cause the cars was so tore up, but I think there was some McCluskys there that knew which ways the cars was going before they hit. All I know is didn't nobody ever dispute that was the way it happened. Everybody said the same thing."

"Who was 'everybody'?"

"Don't know that either. I just remember they was a lot of people had already showed up before we did. Somebody called and woke my daddy up. I remember wasn't nobody else at home — Mama and the other kids was gone somewhere. That musta been the reason he took me with him."

"So it was dark and raining … how could anybody see—?"

"They was lots of car headlights, and one of the Hannakers or Taggarts had a lantern. The wrecked cars landed on different sides of the road and I could see lantern light over there on their side. When the fighting broke out, all's I could see was shadows."

"Fighting?"

"Yeah — they was both Hannackers and McCluskys there at the same time so you know they was fighting."

"Gunfire kind of fighting?"

"Naaa, fistfights. I think the Taggarts and maybe some Jamisons showed up and kept everybody from killing each other. But both sides was mad as hornets shook up in a Mason jar."

"About the wreck?"

"Well, that too, I guess. But mostly they's furious 'bout what happened *after.* I couldn't see much of nothing, but I could hear the yelling. Nate Hannacker survived the wreck and so did your grandfather, Ike. And then Nate killed Ike."

Winona's heart kicked into a gallop. This was the part she wanted to find out about.

"I'd heard that story—"

"Weren't no *story.* It's what happened. Nate stuck a piece of glass in Uncle Ike's eye and killed him."

"Did you *see* … you know, the body with a piece of glass—?"

"Naaa, they was too many people in the way. But the ones who could see was all yelling about it."

"So how'd Nate Hannacker do that, do you know? He was hurt pretty bad—"

"Not just hurt, he was pinned in the wreckage, so they had to work to get him out. Probably the only reason didn't nobody else get killed — the Hannakers and their bunch was so busy getting Nate out of the car."

"But if Nate was pinned in a wrecked car, how'd he kill—?"

"When Pa told Mama about it later, he said Nate was trapped, and they was broken glass all around him and he picked up a piece and used it."

Winona shook her head.

"That still doesn't add up. If he was lying there, couldn't get out of the wrecked car, how'd he get to Grampa to kill him?"

"Musta been yore grandfather got to him, got close enough that Nate was able to stab him."

"Why would he do that?"

"I can't tell you that for sure. Everybody was yelling, and I sneaked closer, hiding behind a car. That's when I saw the part I 'member best. It was just for a couple of seconds, everybody moved out of the way and I seen they was picking up somebody who'd been laying in the middle of the road. I *seen* that part my own self. Won't never forget it. That fella had a big ole bullet hole" — he put his finger to his forehead — "right there, smack in the middle of his forehead."

"He was shot?"

"He weren't the only one, but I didn't see the other. Just heard them talking about a boy in the weeds, shot the same way."

"Who were they?"

"I ain't completely sure how many people was in them cars, so I can't be sure. They coulda been McCluskys, I guess. But I think they was Hannackers. I b'lieve the one I saw was Nate's older brother. I think his name was Johnny."

"Who killed them?"

Skeeter shrugged.

"If they was Hannackers, musta been a McClusky. If they was McCluskys, musta been a Hannacker. But I don't know any of that for sure."

"The only McClusky who lived through the wreck was Grandpa Ike — right?"

"And at least one Hannacker — Nate. In the end, he was the only one of all them people who walked away alive … and he wasn't walking real good his own self. But he did survive the wreck. Might be he shot them fellas."

"But the Hannackers were just getting Nate out of the wreckage when you and your pa got there — which means he was stuck in that wreck until then."

Winona's analytical mind wasn't having any of it. After Skeeter spoke, all the expression left his face, but Winona blew by it, thinking out loud. "So … what? Nate got out, killed a bunch of people with a gun … and then chucked the gun and crawled back into the wreckage so he could use a broken piece of glass to kill Grandpa — that make sense to you?"

Skeeter put his hand over his mouth.

"You need to go now. I ain't feeling real good."

"Just one other thing … maybe you know. Aunt Frannie said the Hannackers ambushed the McCluskys, were chasing them, shooting into their car. Is that what you heard?"

He didn't speak, maybe couldn't, just nodded yes.

"Then how did the cars crash into each other *head-on*? If one was chasing the other—?"

Skeeter struggled, whispered, "One of them cars musta turned around." Then his chest began to hitch and he started making retching sounds. Winona leapt up and ran to the door, called to the Mack-truck nurse who was walking by, "I think he's—"

Then you could hear him heaving. The nurse hurried into the room as Winona hurried out, riding a whiff of vomit in the air.

Chapter Twenty-Six

NATE WAS DETERMINED NOT to appear apprehensive about telling Mama Bert that he and the others had "declined her gracious offer" to go into business together. In truth, he certainly wasn't looking forward to it, but if you had bad news to deliver, it was best to get the task over with, so he'd called and arranged to see her Monday night. He knew she wouldn't like what he was going to tell her, but he figured she'd just write it off as nothing ventured, nothing gained.

And he got *one* of those right — the she-didn't-like-it part. The rest of it … not so much.

Nate had never liked the arrangement of her office, the dark shadows, her seated on the couch while you had to stand before her … a peon before the queen. The more he thought about it, the more he realized the whole thing was calculated, the atmosphere designed to intimidate. He managed to keep that from distracting him as he delivered the words he'd rehearsed in his truck. Told her they appreciated the offer, but "regrettably" had to decline.

He didn't give her a reason. You tell somebody you ain't gonna do what they want, you're best to shut up after that. Give them a reason and they'll see that as a chance to change your mind, an opportunity to talk you out of your decision. They figure if they can make a better argument than the reason you give, they'll win.

"You gonna tell me why not?" she said when he finished talking. He didn't like her tone.

"It just ain't in our best interests right now."

"You 'fraid you can't trust me, is that it? That I won't hold up my end of the bargain?"

He wasn't going to be badgered into defending the decision. It was what it was.

"Trust isn't an issue. Need is. Right now, we don't need another partner."

She made a dismissing sound.

"I don't 'need' a gold-plated spittoon, neither, but if somebody was to plop one down in front of me, I'd be a fool to walk away from it."

He nodded. Wasn't no response to a remark like that. When he started to turn for the door, she said, "That trust thing. It matters. Got to be able to count on the people you work with to keep your ... *secrets*."

Just the one word, the way she said it, felt like she had kicked him in the belly. He turned back and looked at her. Her face was as impassive as them plaster faces him and Big-un had blown off them statutes three years ago.

"You got any particular secrets in mind?"

She seemed to make her mind up about something because she sat forward and picked up a small bowl he hadn't noticed on the coffee table. Turning it over, she dumped out the contents. It took a moment for him to figure out what he was looking at.

Bullets. Bullets that'd been fired.

"These here was dug out of a Corvette Stingray. Ever hole in that car hurt Brodie's soul. He was as careful as a dentist pulling teeth. Didn't scratch up the bullets and patched the holes so's you'd never know they'd been there."

Dumfounded, Nate stood staring at the little pieces of metal on the table, his mind spinning.

What point was she trying to make with them bullets? And why'd she have 'em dug out in the first place? Because she thought she might have a use for them someday, that's why.

He didn't like where his mind was going.

What kind of use? What did smashed bullets *prove*? He s'posed they could be traced to Shep McClusky's gun. And if they were … it'd prove that Shep McClusky shot holes in that Corvette. So what? Brodie'd have to roll over, finger Nate for driving that car that night for Nate to be implicated at all, and even then it'd be Brodie's word against Nate's. And what did it prove if Shep was shooting at the car? Shep died in a car wreck, end of story. Everybody believed it. Nobody knew what'd happened on Hunter Lane that night but him and Shep McClusky and Shep wasn't gonna tell anybody.

"Them as know-how can change the VIN number on an engine block so you can't hardly tell it's been altered, else the law could trace a stolen car right back to the real owner, slicker'n snot. Of course, they's some cars you's better off not to fool with, hard to make it look right." A beat. "Pontiacs is like that."

He was proud of himself that his voice was firm.

"Are you threatening me? If you are, just come right on out and say it."

She looked him square in the eye.

"All I'm saying is I know the whereabouts of a 1967 Pontiac Grand Prix, black over silver, that's still got the *original* VIN number on the engine block."

He couldn't help the snarl that crept into his voice.

"So you was planning all along to *blackmail*—"

"I wasn't planning no such thing!" she shot back, fire in her eyes. "All's I was doing was taking out an insurance policy. You always got to make sure it costs somebody as much as it costs you if they was to decide one day to roll over, like them idiots that write tell-all books — "My Days in a Chop Shop." Only a fool runs a business th'out no insurance on it."

It would take a considerable hunk outta Mama Bert's hide to make good on some kind of threat to implicate Nate in the deaths of Shep and Parker McClusky. She'd have to out her own illegal enterprise. And go to the law. That last part. Go to the law. Nobody did a thing like that, not even Mama Bert.

Maybe she read his mind.

"I wouldn't never roll over for the po-lice! But you

see, this here's a kinda unusual circumstance. If somebody was to whisper secrets into ears that'd be eager to hear 'em … ain't my fault the McCluskys got a sheriff in the family."

He'd be better off if she did turn him over to the law. He'd have a chance there. Circumstantial evidence. Hearsay testimony. Self-defense. That kind of thing. None of that would mean beans if the McClusky family was convinced he'd killed two of their kin.

"It's like this." She spread out her hands before her. "I got … business connections who want weed, good weed, a lot of it. The demand's far exceedin' the supply. And they want it soon's it comes out of the field in a coupla weeks. I said I'd provide it and Mama Bert don't never go back on her word."

He wanted to say, unless she's promising to help you out of a jam. But in truth, she hadn't never promised nothing about that. He was just counting on her … good character.

Riiiight.

He'd known going in that getting mixed up with Mama Bert was dangerous bidness. Did he really have any right to complain when she turned out to be a snake?

"I ain't gonna play some kinda idiotic cat-and-mouse game with you, Nate, and that's 'cause I like you. Here's the deal, plain and simple. I intend to get into the marijuana business in a big way, a way bigger'n you can likely even imagine. Looked around, and the best on-ramp to that particular superhighway is you and yours … what is it you call yourselves, the Cornbread Mafia."

Nate didn't move because he couldn't, was frozen to the spot. He would have bet his soul the only people who knew that name was the four of them.

"Mine's one of them offers you can't refuse. So don't. You'll be a whole lot better off if you just roll with it."

"We voted that we ain't taking in no partners."

"Fine, then, don't call me a partner if that's what's got your panties all in a wad. I'm a 'business associate.' You run your show and I run mine. You grow the weed and I sell it. You fill my orders and whatever weed you got beyond that, do whatever in the world you want with it. Sell it to whoever you want for whatever price suits you."

When you didn't know what to say, most times you's better off to say nothing at all.

Maybe she saw he was off balance, because she hit him again while he was still reeling.

"You know Winona McClusky, Parker's oldest?"

He said nothing.

"Well, a little bird told me she's out sniffing around, bound and determined to find out what happened to her daddy."

Nate's knees felt like bags of water.

"You ain't looking at this right, Nate. You need to see this as opportunity's come knocking on your door. I could just grow it myself, but I'm letting you in on the action and you'd ought to be grateful for that." She paused, looked at him keenly. "Okay, and this here is the best offer I'm gonna make so you'd better leap at it like you's a bass jumping up out of the creek at a June bug. You grow, I sell, we split … sixty-forty. That's as good as it gets." And he understood then she'd been planning this all along. Made him a ridiculous fifty-fifty offer he'd turn down so she could seem magnanimous with a counter offer.

The whole show might have been all about getting a good cut.

Or she might have been dead serious, would have set him out as a sheep for the slaughter without blinking an eye.

With a woman like Mama Bert, there just flat out wasn't no telling.

Then she dropped the final bombshell on him, what she called "honey to sweeten the pot."

Nate sat for a while in his car in the parking lot after he left the meeting, trying to figure out his next move. But he didn't have one. He'd go back to the others with the new deal and see what they said. Her offer to take a smaller cut, and the honey she'd offered at the end — those might actually be enough to change their minds.

He sighed. How had Mama Bert managed it? The guarantee of a completely safe place to do all the processing at the end of the season. No more fear of getting busted, losing the crop and getting caught with so much weed it'd jack up the criminal charges.

When she told him *where* she had in mind … he wasn't completely sure his mouth hadn't dropped open. Seriously?

If she could pull *that* off, it was a big deal. A very big deal.

Chapter Twenty-Seven

W HEN R ILEY WENT OUT to the mailbox Tuesday morning and opened up the *Callison County Tribune* that'd come in the mail, he took one look at the picture on the front page and burst out laughing.

Wait'll Papa sees this!

He turned and headed for the barn with Drew in tow.

"I fought we was goin' to town."

"I have to show something to Papa first."

"But you said I could have a Sugar Daddy."

"If …?"

"If I don't tell Mommy," he said in a familiar sing-song chant. And he wouldn't. Even at four, he had kept every one of their "secrets" from his mother.

Sherry Lynn didn't like for Drew to eat the sticky bar of almost-solid caramel, said it was bad for his teeth, but Riley had eaten Sugar Daddies when he was a little boy and he still had all his choppers so he figured they were safe.

As he hurried across the lot to where Nate was working on the tractor's engine in the barn, he thought to wonder if it was damaging Drew in some way to allow — *encourage* — him to keep things from his mother. But if it were left up to Sherry Lynn, she would put Drew in a vacuum-sealed jar, never let him go anywhere or do anything. And to confront her every time he allowed the boy to be normal would mean a tangled-up argument that was always about way more than a candy bar — or swimming naked in the creek, or making mud pies — that would culminate in three days of pouting, awkward, silent meals and bouts of sobbing. There wasn't much in life worth going through that.

The seminal moment in those ever-escalating brawls had occurred almost a year ago. It was no different from the ones preceding it, just louder and uglier, maybe the biggest ever. Papa had come home from Louisville with a GI Joe for Drew, a twelve-inch doll dressed in a combat uniform, that boasted "21 moving parts."

Sherry Lynn had come into the kitchen to find the child playing happily with it and she had exploded. She marched up to Drew, snatched it out of his hand, and fixed Riley and Papa with a glare brutal enough to cause internal organ damage.

"My little boy is *not* going to play with a ... a *war* toy. How could you dare give him something like that after what we've all been through?"

Papa had done what he always did when Sherry Lynn went on one of her tirades. He was apologetic and agreeable and got out of the room as quick as he could. It was impossible to miss the sympathy on his face when he looked at Riley, how sad it made him that Riley's wife wasn't like Papa's beloved Abby. And the look on his face that day had lit a fire of anger under Riley. This time, Riley met Sherry Lynn head-on, the two colliding like two charging rhinos.

"It isn't a war toy. It's a soldier doll. You think there's something wrong with soldiers, do you?"

"Is that it? You want him to play with a soldier toy so he'll grow up and be a soldier and come home in a black—"

"Sherry Lynn!"

By that time, Drew was engaged in his own melt-down, reaching up to grab the doll out of Sherry Lynn's hands and wailing.

The row had lasted all day and into the next, until Riley finally negotiated a surrender — because at some point during the whole thing Drew had totally lost interest in the doll and didn't seem to care one way or the other.

It was weeks later before Riley found out why Drew had given up — discovered that Papa must have told him to, must have promised him he'd get what he wanted in the end. It happened when Riley went into the small storage room behind the tack room in the barn, seemed to remember an extra set of Allen wrenches on the shelf there, and discovered that Papa had made a GI Joe *world* there for Drew. There were a couple of GI Joe dolls, a toy tank and an entire army of small, green plastic soldiers about two inches tall that stood upright on flat plastic bases, plastic cannons along with a set of blocks to build forts with. The toy trove was safe there. Sherry Lynn never even ventured into the barn, let alone the tack room inside it.

Riley had never told Drew that he'd discovered the secret playroom and when he mentioned it to Papa, Papa'd said he had made Drew "pinky-swear, hope-to-die" that he'd never reveal its existence.

After that, Riley'd thrown in the towel. He would no longer fight Sherry Lynn, he would just go around her. It was the only way to keep the peace. And on Drew's part, he was remarkably disciplined for a small child. He knew how to keep his lip zipped.

Papa was up to his elbows in the guts of the tractor when Riley and Drew approached.

"Check *this* out," Riley said and held out the newspaper to his grandfather. Papa wiped the grease off his hands on a shop rag, reading the headline as he reached for it.

"Whooo eee!" he cried, grinning so wide his gums showed above his teeth.

The headline all the way across the top of the front page of the Monday, August 20 issue of the *Callison County Tribune* said: *Now You See It, Now You Don't*. The sub-head asked the question: *What happened to the marijuana crop that mysteriously disappeared?*

But the picture! The whole story was captured in that one shot, and Tribune editor/owner Jim Bingham had played it big.

"Remember how you said you wished you could

see the look on their faces when they saw the weed was gone?" Riley said, laughing. "Well … there it is."

And it was!

It had most certainly been the sheriff — newly appointed to the position and being a McClusky "all hat and no cattle" kind of guy — who'd invited the newspaper editor Jim Bingham to ride along to the marijuana field where Papa had been arrested. The crop that an endless convoy of pickup trucks had hauled away during the night.

The biggest picture, four newspaper columns wide, was focused on Sheriff McClusky and State Police Detective Booth Graham. A smaller picture below it showed what they were looking at — an empty field crisscrossed with tire tracks among scattered pieces of foliage.

Graham's picture was truly cringe-worthy — one of those momentary images photographers rarely catch — a frozen moment in time, like a baseball hanging in the air before the batter hits it, or the Junior Miss contestant's face an instant after it's announced that she had won. His eyes were large, his face a study in confusion, his mouth in a perfect "O" shape. McClusky just appeared monumentally stupid, a man who'd benefit from immediate placement in a first-grade special education class.

The story below described how police had received an anonymous tip about a marijuana crop growing in the back of a field on the farm of Nathaniel Hannacker, how they'd rushed to the scene and found the field, various farm tools and a pickup truck, but no workers.

The story did not name the owner of the truck. The newspaper editor was an honorable man. Riley'd always liked him because he played fair with everybody. If the daughter of the governor of Kentucky had been busted for Driving Under the Influence of Intoxicants in Callison County, her name would have been listed right alongside the other DUI arrests in the newspaper's Court News section. Position or money or power got nowhere with Jim Bingham.

Oh, the story gave a glorious blow-by-blow description, provided by a deputy, of the arrest of "a suspect" who'd come walking out of the woods with four dead squirrels, claimed he'd parked his truck there to go squirrel hunting and had no idea a field of marijuana was growing nearby.

If the commonwealth's attorney had charged Papa with any one of half a dozen different marijuana crimes, Papa's name would have been listed. Since the prosecutor had declined to prosecute, he was "innocent until proven guilty" and therefore not identified.

Of course, there wasn't a Callison County citizen above the age of ten who couldn't read between the lines of the story. The crop was on Papa's farm … duh, he'd been the man who'd claimed he'd been squirrel hunting. And the squirrel-hunting dodge was pure brilliance — anybody could see that — left the police with egg on their faces and no charges to file that the prosecutor was willing to pursue.

What …? "Possession of a dead squirrel?" That'd

be a misdemeanor. Or, the felony version of that charge, "possession with the intent to sell a dead squirrel?"

Then, to add insult to injury, the police didn't even get to gloat over destroying a marijuana crop. Riley was sure Jim Bingham had been invited to accompany the officers so he could take pictures of the backhoe destroying the weed, with Graham and McClusky standing beside it, grinning like hunters with a foot on the neck of a dead deer.

It was a perfect storm of awful for law enforcement. Not only did the embarrassing squirrel-hunting story get out, but the growers had made off with their crop, leaving police with a heaping handful of nothing.

After they'd read the story through a couple of times, Papa took the paper from Riley and ripped off the front-page picture. "I'm hangin' this up," he said, walked to the wall just inside the barn door and affixed the piece of paper to a protruding nail.

With the afterglow of the enormous *gotcha* still warm in the air, Riley pointed out, "You do know that you have kicked a tiger … in front of the whole county."

"Ain't the first time, neither. Only this time, I kicked him in the mouth, likely broke out some teeth, and bloodied his nose. I'm sure my name has been permanently removed from Booth Graham's Christmas card list."

Chapter Twenty-Eight

Booth Graham marched through the front office of Callison County Sheriff Clyde McClusky, his eyes focused on the door, not looking to either side. He made eye contact with none of the deputies or the dispatcher. He entered without knocking and slammed the door so hard behind him it was miraculous that the frosted-glass window didn't shatter from the impact.

He threw the newspaper on the sheriff's desk, though McClusky obviously didn't need Graham's newspaper because he was reading his own. Graham ground out a string of obscenities. Growled them, barely raised his voice, didn't want others outside to hear his rage, carry it back to Hannacker how upset he'd been by the story.

It was possible he had never been this angry before in his life. No, not "possible" — he was sure he hadn't. He knew for certain he had never been *this kind* of angry, this blend of rage and humiliation and helplessness. With a side order of scarlet-faced embarrassment.

No one, *no one* had ever made a fool of Booth Graham and gotten away with it. Until Nate Hannacker came along. He'd done it over and over.

Graham had grown up in an abusive home in Fuller Park, on the South Side of Chicago, where his mother had run off and his father took out his rage on any kid who got in his way when he got home drunk from Topsy's Tavern. The middle child of five, two older brothers and a younger brother and sister, Graham'd been pretty adept at staying out of his father's reach most of the time. In that household, it was every man for himself. He came home one day when he was going on nine and found the police surrounding the apartment building where he and his family lived. Elbowing his way through the crowd, he made it to the steps leading up to his building as the ambulance crew was carrying a stretcher down them. Lying on it was his younger brother Billy, five, and he looked like he'd been kicked by a mule. Graham could hear his father yelling at the police officers who were trying to handcuff him, that he hadn't touched the boy, that the kid was so stupid and clumsy he'd fallen down the stairs.

Billy died. His father should have been arrested and put away, but he wasn't. Graham never found out why not. He lived in hell until he was eleven and discovered that his father had been molesting his younger sister her whole life. The next day, when his father came home, Graham beat the man to death with a pipe wrench. He'd just walked into the kitchen where his father was sitting at the table drinking a beer and started wailing on him, clipped him in the back of the head and when the chair tipped over backwards, he hammered his face until he was unrecognizable.

He'd been sent to some kind of juvenile home because he was only eleven years old. He'd managed to get the arrest and all traces of it expunged from his record so he could join the Marines, and later became a Chicago police officer. It hadn't really mattered in the end, of course. His sister was already too damaged for his rescue to matter. She'd started working the streets before he joined the military, and while he was stationed in Germany, he was notified that she had died of an overdose. He could picture her lying in an alley somewhere with a needle in her arm. Her death was his father's fault, too.

As Booth had grown older, he had struggled to contain the rage he felt in his chest every moment of every day. He'd joined the military just so he'd have somewhere to vent it, imagined going to some war somewhere and killing indiscriminately. Instead of allowing him to vent his rage, the Marine Corps had given him the self-discipline to harness it, to use its energy, to control it like a very dangerous dog you had to keep on a tight leash or it would hurt people, hurt them bad.

Oh, he'd been written up time and time again for excessive use of force as a police officer, but none of the reprimands earned him more than a few days off without pay. He'd bailed out before the last one could catch up with him. He'd gotten into a fight with a smarmy little drug dealer, hit him too hard and he died. There had been a crowd of witnesses, and rather than fight all the legal battles on the horizon, he'd turned in his papers and took early retirement at age fifty — searched professional journals until he found the opening he was looking for and took a job with the Kentucky State Police, hired on as a sergeant and got lucky when a detective retired. He took the test and was promoted.

And after that, he and Nate Hannacker had collided head-on again and again. So far, Graham had gotten the short end of the stick every time.

Just a couple of days ago, he and the sheriff had conspired to find some way to put Hannacker behind bars. Manufacture evidence. Plant evidence. Whatever it took. That plan was forgotten now. Behind bars wasn't good enough. Nate Hannacker had to die.

Booth Graham would put a gun to his forehead and blow his brains out.

Which meant that Graham had to control his reaction now, so there would be no reason to suspect him when Hannacker turned up dead. The first step was to suck it up and live with the humiliation of that newspaper picture and story. Maybe even … try to be a good sport about it. The newspaper came out once a week, which meant he would have to keep his facade in place for the next six days. Once another edition came out, folks would stop talking about this one.

When he turned back to the sheriff, his face was

solid granite, didn't have a single emotion of any kind showing on it.

"You believe he got that picture?" Graham said. Oh, he couldn't manage a laugh at it, not even the scraps of a smile, but he could muster something that sounded like amusement.

"We look like idiots, morons," McClusky roared. "I oughta go shove that newspaper down Jim Bingham's throat." When Graham didn't join in, McClusky continued his rant. "You got a job where it don't matter, but sheriff is an elected position and I'm planning to run. I *was* planning to run. Shoot, with that picture floating around out there, I couldn't get elected to clean the tanks at the sewage treatment plant."

"Roll with it," Graham said, his voice even. "It is what it is. Let's go get some breakfast at Donavan's."

"Donavan's?" The sheriff was incredulous. "Everybody in the whole place will be taking about the picture and the story."

Which would make it a good place to begin establishing that Booth Graham wasn't upset, didn't hold a grudge or anything like that against Hannacker.

"Might as well face it head-on," he said. "Folks will get tired of talking about it eventually."

McClusky opened his mouth to protest and Graham growled, "You want Hannacker to find out how pissed off you are, give him the satisfaction?"

Without waiting for his response, Graham turned and headed for the door he had slammed only a couple of minutes ago, found that his hand was still shaking with rage when he reached for the knob, but nobody'd see that.

"I'm hungry," he called out over his shoulder as he began to put together a plan. He hadn't ever plotted out a murder, and it was interesting to view it from the other side, use his expertise in following clues to a killer to be certain he didn't leave any clues himself.

Chapter Twenty-Nine

Winona had spent most of Monday evening after she met with Skeeter wallowing what he'd said around in her mind in an effort to make sense out of it. She finally gave up and went to bed. She needed a fresh, rested mind to figure it out.

But Tuesday morning, there was no grand epiphany, so she sat glumly at her kitchen table, drowning her sorrows in multiple cups of black coffee, trying out various explanations.

There was only one deduction you could make for lead-pipe certain about the whole event. For two cars to crash head-on they had to be going in opposite directions. One or the other of those cars *turned around*.

Hypothesis Number One: The Hannackers ambushed the McCluskys, chased them and the McCluskys got away. Then later, the McCluskys went gunning for the Hannackers and the two cars crashed into each other.

Number Two: The McCluskys were the ones doing the ambushing and the chasing and the Hannackers were the ones who turned around.

Three: Nate Hannacker was trapped in the car … and the only way he could have killed Grampa was if Grampa got out of the wrecked McClusky car and went to where Nate was stuck in the wreckage of the Hannacker car, laying there with broken glass all around him.

So who shot the man lying in the middle of the road? And the kid in the weeds?

It couldn't have been Nate Hannacker … unless he got out, killed the guy, and then got back into the wrecked car in time to greet Grampa when Grampa got within stabbing range so he could stick a spike of glass in Grampa's eye.

Considering every conceivable option, Winona was only able to come up with one that fit all the known facts. She didn't like it, but there it was. She argued with herself, tried to jam the reality of what happened into her pre-conceived notion of what must have happened. It didn't fit.

Nate was trapped, which meant Grampa got out of the wrecked car and went to him. So Grampa lived through the wreck, and was mobile enough to go to Nate Hannacker.

Why?

And who killed the two men who were shot?

Unless some unknown subject ran out of the woods, shot some people and then ran away, it *had* to be Grampa. That was the only answer that made sense. He got out of the car and killed the guy in the road — who must have been a Hannacker. Duh. Probably Nate's older brother.

Well, it was possible the guy was shooting at Grampa, wasn't it, and Grampa was just defending himself? The Hannackers had, after all, ambushed the McCluskys.

Right. And when Grandpa returned fire he landed a center-of-the-forehead shot at night … in the rain.

And what about the guy in the weeds … who had a bullet hole in the center of his forehead *just like the guy in the road?* Was he shooting at Grampa, too?

Not likely. An uglier explanation made more sense.

It was obvious Grampa went to Nate Hannacker. Had to have gotten close enough to be stabbed, and the only reason Winona could come up with for why he would have gotten that close was that he went to shoot Nate Hannacker … *just like he'd already shot the other two Hannackers.* But Nate got him with a shard of glass before he had a chance.

That was the only scenario that fit.

And in that scenario, Nate was acting in self-defense.

That absolutely flew in the face of everything she knew and believed about the Hannackers.

So the Hannackers ambushed the McCluskys. The McCluskys got away, then turned around and went back after the Hannackers — and the cars collided head-on. Grampa and Nate survived. Grampa shot

Nate's brother and the other Hannacker and Nate killed Grampa.

It all fit.

So, okay, fine. Nate was defending himself. She didn't like it, but there it was. So what? She wasn't here to pass judgement on the right or wrong of the McClusky/Hannacker killings forty years ago. It didn't matter who was at fault — the point was that Nate Hannacker killed her grandfather ...

And got away with it. The Crows' Pledge stopped the inevitable revenge and payback.

Fine. That worked.

Except ... what was the trick?

How did Nate *trick* Grampa? What — he played dead so Grandpa would get close enough for him to stab him?

She could find no trickery involved in any of it — pretty straightforward stuff. You shoot at me, I shoot back. I get away and go back to continue the fight and we crash into each other going fifty miles an hour down a dark road in the rain.

Even if all that was right, none of it fit into any scenario where forty years later, Nate was somehow responsible for Shep's death. What ... he *tricked* Shep into crashing through a guardrail? Why would he do a thing like that? And how? Then Pa went after Nate for revenge and ... what? Nate killed Papa? Magically got rid of his body and his car without leaving so much as a piece of lint behind?

That stretched the bounds of reasonable possibility far too thin.

Sitting in her kitchen drinking her fourth … maybe fifth cup of coffee before heading into the office, it occurred to her that maybe she was chasing down the wrong rabbit trail altogether. Maybe she ought to back up and punt.

Perhaps she really ought to try to find out why Shep had gone out to the chop shop that night in the first place. He didn't work there anymore. He'd been fired. Perhaps Papa thought somebody there had "tricked" Shep and got him killed.

It would make slightly more sense in a different way than the rabbits she'd been chasing so far. Maybe she'd been wrong about the whole "got away with it" part, assumed it had to refer to the only time she knew about when somebody'd killed a McClusky and got away with it. But maybe it was referring to something else entirely. Some incident she didn't even know had happened.

The chop shop was an illegal operation, run by criminals. If Pa thought Shep had gotten crossways with those people somehow, maybe that's who Pa went looking for. And maybe those criminals had killed Pa — shoot, if Pa went gunning for them, it might even have been self-defense for them, too. Then they got rid of the body and the car. A chop shop would certainly be equipped to make a car vanish.

So, should Winona abandon the rabbit trail that led to Nate Hannacker and go chasing down an entirely different one that led to — gulp — Mama Bert? Winona was as awed by that woman as everybody else in Callison County. Well, awed by the stories that circulated around about her, which might not even be true. But even if only twenty percent of what Winona'd heard about the owner of The Tavern was true, Mama Bert was a dangerous woman you didn't want to get mixed up with.

One you absolutely did *not* want to cross.

Chapter Thirty

THE OTHERS WERE ALREADY THERE in what Willie Ray'd dubbed the Cornbread Mafia Clubhouse before Nate arrived. He could hear their voices as he approached. Willie Ray laughed, and if Nate let himself, he could ease into a fantasy about them, that he was just overhearing Riley and Willie Ray cutting up before they went to work in the tobacco field as they had done every summer since they were old enough to drive a tractor. And that Jessie'd come over to hang out with Riley.

There had been a summer when Riley and Jessie were dating that she came around some. He had always liked her more than any of the other girls Riley'd dated because she was real, down to earth. He hadn't never spent any time around teenage girls other than his sisters, and that'd been a so long ago he didn't remember what it was like. Nowadays, teenage girls seemed unutterably silly to him, flouncing around in their football-helmet hairdos, chewing gum and singing about something called Shamala, whatever that was. Least they didn't seem interested anymore in putting on peace crosses, getting stoned and chanting "make love, not war." Them folks had won. The only time Nate'd seen the television news this whole year was in March when folks was climbing up on rooftops, trying to catch the last helicopter out of Saigon. He didn't like thinking about all them boys who'd got wounded or died over there … for nothing.

Jessie'd been different from any girl Riley'd ever gone out with, totally unpretentious, her pretty face so wholesome it belonged on a box of Kellogg's Corn Flakes. Nate let out a sigh, dismissing the fantasy world as he reached the door.

Riley had adored Jessica Harrington. Nathaniel could tell he still did.

They'd agreed to meet after supper tonight to hear from Nate how Mama Bert had taken their refusal to go into business with her. He had not come to tell them that.

"Was she pissed?" Riley asked as soon as he walked into the room.

Wasn't no sense it beating around the bush.

"No, she wasn't pissed off … because she got what she wanted. Least she thinks she did. Depends on what you say."

The three of them shot looks at each other but didn't say anything. Nate had already decided he wasn't going to tell them the whole story.

"I told her that we'd voted no, thanked her for her kind offer and meant to be on my way."

"But ..." Riley coaxed.

"But she told me if we were unwilling to take her up on her offer, she would ... make life very difficult for me."

"Difficult how?" Willie Ray asked.

"If she decided to, she *might* be able to get me arrested and put away for a long time." He paused. "Don't b'lieve she'd do that, though ... but I do believe she'd be willing to put out a word on me that'd get me killed."

They were so surprised nobody spoke and he filled up the silence before they had a chance.

"You know Mama Bert and I was involved in a little business deal the summer," a breath of a pause, "while you boys was in Vietnam — right?"

They nodded. Just saying the word "Vietnam" seemed to suck all the oxygen out of the room.

"I'll tell you this much and only this much. It was a chop shop." He wasn't sure that Jessie knew what that meant, so he added, "where stolen vehicles are taken apart, 'chopped' up into pieces and the pieces sold off."

She nodded. Either she already knew that or she didn't want to look like she didn't.

"We parted on good terms, except ..." He ran out of air then. He'd planned out what he was going to say, but now that it was time to say it the words evaporated from his mind.

"I'm not going to get into specifics. You're way better off if you don't know. I will just say that I did something seriously illegal."

"If you were partners in the chop shop, she was an accessory ..." Jessie began.

He held up his hand.

"She was a silent partner, I was the front man. She couldn't possibly be connected to the chop shop. But the crime I'm talking about didn't have nothing to do with the chop shop." He let out a breath. "She wasn't in on it, but she helped me cover it up, and now she's threatening to uncover it. If we don't go into business with her ..."

Before they could speak he held up his hand again.

"I made it clear — absolutely *clear*, that the decision about what we do or don't do is a group decision and I ain't got but one vote same's the rest of you. If you're still opposed to the offer, I will ... what would it be ... *resign* from the Cornbread Mafia. I'll step down, get totally out of the business. I am the only leverage she has, and without me she ain't got no hold on you whatsoever."

He had screwed himself up to being okay with whatever the others decided. One part of him hoped they stuck to their guns and continued to turn her down, but if they did ... Mama Bert wasn't a woman who issued idle threats. She'd see it as a weakness if she didn't do exactly what she'd threatened to do.

Into the silence, he added the rest of what he had come to say.

"She did come down some on the split of the take — we'd get sixty percent to her forty. And then she added what she called 'honey to sweeten the pot.'"

He shook his head, still dumfounded by it.

"And it's the danged-est thing I ever heard of. She said she could provide us a place to process the weed where we wouldn't never have to worry about getting busted ... you ain't gonna b'lieve where she's talking about."

You coulda heard a mouse trotting across a cotton ball in the silence that followed.

"Hold onto your shorts, Mildred ... she says she has already set up a marijuana processing area ... in the largest barn at Land's End."

"*Land's End!*" Willie Ray had been taking a swig of beer when Nate said it and he spewed the beer all over the room, coughing and sputtering.

"You don't really mean ..." Jessie began, her eyes the size of dinner plates.

"If I'm lyin', I'm dyin'," Nate said and made an X across his heart.

"*The* Land's End?" Riley asked.

"Unless there's another one somewhere in the county that I don't know about."

The breeding farm was home to who-knew-how-many thoroughbred mares and stallions that wandered around in pastures enclosed by white fences, dotted with horse barns that cost more than most whole farms in the county. Looked like something right off the cover of that fancy magazine *Southern Living*, and it was owned by none other than the City of Brewster's Mayor-for-Life Malcolm Murdock.

"Malcolm Murdock is in the weed business?" Jessie was incredulous.

"I didn't say that. I ain't got no idea why he's

doing this ... and it might be Mama Bert's black-mailing him over something same's she is me. All I know is she said this was a 'safe zone,' that wouldn't no law ever bother us there."

Willie Ray didn't even give Nate time to draw another breath.

"Well ... I figure that right there is worth the price of admission." He spoke with conviction. His glance crossed Nate's face but didn't linger, and Nate knew before he spoke that the words would come from the little freckle-faced boy who'd practically grown up at Nate's house. "Where else you gonna get a deal like that? It ain't the kind of thing you can put a price tag on."

Whether Willie Ray really believed that or not was a matter of debate, but the other two lined up right beside him like crows on a telephone wire. Nate knew before he looked into the box that there'd be only white stones there. They told Nate to go back and tell Mama Bert they'd changed their minds, that they couldn't wait to go in partners with her — give her *forty percent* of their take on their crop.

Nate didn't say nothing after they all started talking about it, had a lump in his throat too big to talk around.

Chapter Thirty-One

THE MORNING after the Cornbread Mafia had voted officially — rocks in the box — to go into business with Mama Bert, Riley was in his front yard washing his car. Okay, he wasn't really washing his car. It was just an excuse to use the water hose. It was easier all around to say he'd been washing his car than to talk Sherry Lynn into letting Drew be a normal little boy. It could be, "Oops, I accidentally squirted him, and since he was already wet, I just let him play in it."

Riley *hated* that, the fact that even the smallest thing — letting Drew play in the water hose — meant tiptoeing though a minefield with Sherry Lynn. Nothing was easy, simple, straightforward. He didn't understand any of it. All that was clear was that Sherry Lynn was profoundly unhappy. And he didn't know why. She had what she'd said she wanted. She wanted them to get married, and they had. She wanted a big fancy house and he'd spent a fortune already getting the foundation and the framing up on her "mansion." It would likely cost everything he made on this year's crop to finish it. No, not everything. This year … there was no telling what they might make this year. So let her build a castle. That's what it'd be, if he left it to her. And he would. He didn't give a rat's ass about the house, and if it kept her occupied and contented, he'd build her ten houses.

She wanted "a houseful of kids," too, and they had only Drew. Whether or not there would be more … Riley doubted it. He didn't want more children. Drew was already old enough to pick up on the tension and stress in the air. Why bring more kids into that kind of home? And he didn't like admitting it, but the thought of having sex with Sherry Lynn … She had gotten so fat. He'd never have dreamed she'd do a thing like that, either. She always cared so much about how she looked, was beautiful and knew it and liked strutting her stuff. Now she wore only shapeless dresses that hid the pounds she kept piling on. She didn't put on makeup unless she was going out somewhere, wore her hair in a ponytail.

It was almost like she was … punishing him for something. Whatever he said, she wanted the opposite and so everything became a battle of wills.

Even something as simple as this.

"Eeeeeech," Drew squealed, when he darted out from behind the car and Drew aimed the hose at his chest. "You gotted me, Daddy!" he cried, and darted back away from the spray.

Daddy.

That single word turned Riley's heart to mush.

He had never thought about fatherhood, what it meant, never gave any thought to how much his grandfather loved him and had loved his father. Until Drew came along. And Riley would die for that child. He was the absolute delight of his existence. Drew was what made it bearable to live every day with Sherry Lynn.

"Riley Hannacker, what do you think you're doing?"

Sherry Lynn had come out onto the front porch and saw him squirt Drew. She had no idea how much she sounded like the Wicked Witch of the West or East or whatever in *The Wizard of Oz*.

"I didn't mean to get him wet, but since he was already—"

"Squirt me, Daddy!"

"You know he had that ear infection …"

Here we go again.

But she didn't finish. She was looking down the road at the car approaching. Then she stepped back inside quickly, clearly didn't want whoever it was to see her "without her face on" as she called it. Riley squinted into the sunshine, but didn't recognize the car. It was a nice one, big and wide, like a yacht sailing down the road, and as soon as he got a look at the driver's face, he burst out laughing.

Then he walked out to greet the man who got out of the car and limped toward him.

"Where did you get *that* car?" Riley asked.

"Bought it with the proceeds of some illegal endeavors in which I am engaged at the present moment," Ace said, smiling, his teeth as white as ever they'd been. Riley shoved aside the offered hand and hugged his friend, who hugged him back just as tight.

"What'd that thing cost, anyway?"

"In the words of a cornpone friend of mine from years back," Ace launched into a credible imitation of a Kentucky accent, "it'll run ye! Might be more'n a buck two ninety-eight."

"Even Willie Ray doesn't have wheels *that* fancy." The GMC truck he'd bought with all the doodads on it was so posh he didn't want to take it into the field. Didn't want to get it muddy.

"Unka Ace!" Drew squealed, raced around the car and launched himself at Ace, almost toppled him. Ace had mastered a prosthetic limb, had a pronounced limp but it didn't stop him from doing whatever he wanted. His balance was off, though, and the impact of Drew crashing into him almost knocked him over.

"Drew, be careful!" Riley cried.

Ace didn't mind. Reaching down, he picked up the little boy — sopping wet — and hugged him. That image — Ace so black, Drew so pale blond — sent Riley back to the day at Tweety Bird when Ace had joined the unit, and told Willie Ray it wouldn't take him more than a day or two to get a tan in Vietnam's tropical sun.

"When I got here" — *he'd pointed to Andy, the Nordic blond* — *"me and him coulda passed for twins."*

"You's thinking 'bout Andy, wasn't you?" Ace said quietly.

"What, you're reading minds now as well as selling

weed?" But Riley didn't pull back, didn't throw up emotional walls like he did whenever Sherry Lynn spoke about the war or the guys who didn't come back.

Ace had earned the right to talk about it.

"I think about him a lot, too," Ace said. Then he tickled Drew and sent him into a gale of giggles. "My but this boy sure do favor him!"

"He does, doesn't he. Isn't that amazing. And Andy's own little girl has dark hair like her mother." He paused. "You know Emily got married a couple of weeks ago."

"Nice guy?"

"Yeah, he's good people." Riley took a deep breath. "Life goes on."

Clapping Ace on the back, he turned toward the house. "Get your stuff and come on in. Sherry Lynn is making her legendary meatloaf tonight. I'll call Jessie and Willie Ray, tell them you're here, though Willie Ray can be kinda hard to track down."

"Just tell him I got some 'specially righteous weed! That'll build a fire under him."

Ace always had the best weed. He'd had it in 'Nam, when they'd toked their first joint together, and he'd had it two years ago, when he'd shown up in response to Riley's desperate plea, standing in Riley's front yard, grinning, patting his pocket.

"You Kentucky boys is gonna love your ole pal Ace," he'd said that day, 'cause I got more'n righteous weed to smoke. I got *seed*."

Chapter Thirty-Two

As soon as the law office closed its doors Tuesday afternoon, Winona drove out to Hunter Lane where Shep had died. Somewhere near that road there had been a chop shop four years ago. At least, that's what Jody'd said.

Her grandparents lived on the side of Simmons Knob near there and she and her brothers had visited often … she'd never have dreamed that the two of them had used Grandpa's old farm truck to chase the Bartons' bull. No wonder that animal was so mean! Or that they had driven the truck as fast as it would go on the Hunter Lane straightaway. She also couldn't imagine driving down the road blindfolded! Seriously. It was a flat-out miracle teenage boys ever lived to adulthood to repopulate the world.

Winona had never liked the custom of putting up crosses on the roadside when somebody was killed there in a wreck. There were many reasons, foremost among them that the people who put the cross up almost always failed to maintain it. Oh, sure, somebody you love "dies" right in this spot, it'd certainly be a natural inclination to commemorate that spot somehow.

But that's only in those first ragged sliced-open days of grief. A year later, two years later, five … the crosses fall into disrepair. Nobody repaints them, or even sets them back up after a storm. Plastic flowers left there fade in the sun, fall out on the ground or blow away.

Pretty soon, a spot where you intended to commemorate the memory of a loved one becomes not a tribute but an insult, a symbol of the decay of the memory.

She also didn't like driving down the road and seeing a white cross beside it. She couldn't help her mind conjuring up images of the accident, the cars crashing into each other with screams of ripping metal, breaking glass and terrified, dying people.

Maybe they did it right in Bogotá. She'd been there once and noticed crosses painted right on the streets themselves, right on the asphalt. It was disconcerting to see how many there were, maybe cautioned drivers to slow down, but at least nobody was aware of the memory of the deceased sliding down into oblivion.

She wasn't exactly sure why she had come out here to the spot where Shep had wrecked, what she hoped to find. It'd just been an impulse. What she did find surprised her, though — a white cross by the road near the guardrail her brother Shep had gone flying through that summer night in 1969. This guardrail didn't look new. She supposed guardrails must age quickly because she understood Shep took out the whole thing when he went flying off the road.

Who had put the cross there? And who'd been looking after it for the past four years, doing all the things nobody ever did — setting it back upright after snowplows knocked it over in the wintertime or chasing down the plastic flowers after a storm. She pulled her car off the road at the guardrail and walked slowly up to the cross.

There was no name on it. Either that part had worn away or there'd never been one. She supposed it was possible this wasn't even a cross for Shep, that some other unfortunate soul had bought the farm here in the past four years.

She looked out over the drop-off that lay beyond the guardrail, then stepped to the edge and looked down. She was grateful to see that nothing remained to mark the explosion and fire that had killed her brother, no blackened rock or piece of wreckage.

A vehicle approached, and the pickup truck slowed down as it got nearer. The old truck pulled to a stop behind her little blue Ford Maverick, and a grizzled old man got out and walked up to her.

"I ain't never seen nobody here before," he said.

"This is where my brother Shep ... died. He was in a wreck—"

"Oh, I know all about that wreck. I did hate it so because I told myself that night that something bad was gonna happen and sure enough it did."

The old man stuck out his hand. She shook it, leathered from the elements and the grip was firm.

"I'm Oscar Hanks," he said, and she introduced herself.

Either the old man had a really scraggly beard or he just hadn't shaved in a week. Gray stubble stuck out in bristled tufts on his wrinkled face. His hair was white, his eyes a pale blue.

Then it occurred to her — "Did *you* put up this cross?"

"I did. I tend to it now and again when I come past it and see it's fallen over. I live in Tucker Hollow." He pointed vaguely west, on the other side of Simmons Knob.

"May I ask you … why'd you put the cross up?"

"Oh, I just always felt bad 'bout what happened that night, because I knew it was gonna, soon's them cars blew by me, going so fast they was just a blur, I knowed wasn't nobody could keep a car on these roads going that fast. I said to myself, 'One or the other of them boys is gonna git kilt.' And sure enough, one of 'em did."

Two cars.

It took Winona a moment to process that.

"You saw *two cars* on the road that night?"

"Shore did. They was racing each other, both of 'em roaring down the road like rocket ships."

"So you were … *here* that night?"

"No, not on this road. When I seen 'em, they hadn't got this far yet. I come off Willis Lane, on my way home. My brother had a cow was tryin' to birth a breech calf and I went to help. Took all afternoon and most of the night and in the end, we lost 'em both, the calf and the cow. I's plum wore out, just puttering along, trying to think if they was something me and him coulda done that we didn't, or something we did do that we shouldn't a'done. I seen headlights ahead. And 'fore I could take two breaths, this car blew by going the other way, so fast it startled me and I jerked the wheel like, almost run off into a ditch my own self. I couldn't imagine who was … and next thing I know, here comes another one, going just as fast. I was prepared this time and it just went on by.

"And I says to myself, Oscar, I says, they's gonna be a wreck. One or t'other of them boys is gonna crash. And I hadn't even got all the way home 'fore I heard this little rumble, like thunder a long way off. Next mornin', I found out that was the sound of your brother's car exploding."

Winona stumbled mentally, trying to jam this new piece into a puzzle she thought was already complete.

"I'm surprised … nobody mentioned to me that there was more than one car. I just figured Shep lost control and crashed through the guardrail."

"Didn't nobody ever ask me nothing about the wreck so I went in to the sheriff's office a couple of days later, told him what I seen. He said your brother was driving a white car, some fancy I-talian sports car I ain't never heard of. The other car I seen was red, a sports car like, too."

"If there was somebody else there that night, why didn't they say so, come forward?"

"And admit they was racing? I wouldn't a'done that if I's them. It might be that red car never knew the white one had crashed, though I don't know how it coulda missed the sound of the explosion. I guess it's possible, though, that the driver didn't know. The red car was the one winning the race, way out in front of your brother."

"Do you know who was driving the red car?"

"Ain't got no idea. That's what the sheriff asked, but it was going so fast I couldn't see nothing but a red blur. I didn't even know it was your brother in the other car until later, when it come out about him getting killed and all."

He paused, wrinkled up his brow.

"I looked for it, the other car, though. After that, I kinda kept my eye open for the little red sports car I seen that night. But I ain't seen it since. Must be whoever was driving it was from Away-From-Here."

All the way home, Winona tried to fit the new information into her understanding of the events of that night. She had always assumed ... so had everybody else, apparently ... that Shep had been out there by himself in the wee hours of the morning. She hadn't ever asked for the official accident report, didn't know if the police had done a blood test on her brother — and according to Jody, they would have found a whole pharmacy of illegal substances if they did. Everybody just figured he was an impaired driver, going too fast, who ran through a guardrail.

Her father apparently believed somebody'd murdered him, believed somebody'd deliberately killed

Shep … somehow. Now that she knew Shep hadn't been alone … that somebody else had been here … what did that prove? Who was the other person? Did her father maybe know who it was, thought he was a murderer?

Okay, that part was delusional. Ridiculous. But the simple traffic accident explanation of her brother's death did have more moving parts than she'd known. When she got home, she told Jody what she'd found out, and he'd poo-pooed the whole thing.

"That whole story's bogus," Jody said. "Couldn't possibly have happened the way that old guy described."

"And you know that how?"

"He said they was racing and the red car was winning. There ain't no way on earth that coulda been the way of it. Shep was driving a Ferrari 365 GT. You know what that means?"

"No, what?"

"He was driving the fastest car they make!"

"His car was faster than *every*—?"

"Okay, I don't know about that. But I guarantee it was the fastest car on any road in Callison County, Kentucky. If he was racing somebody, *he* was the one winning. Ain't no vehicle anywhere around coulda even kept up with Shep, let alone *outrun* him."

It was the next morning before Winona had figured it out in her head and called Jody at her mother's house.

"That chop shop where Shep worked, you said it was—?"

"Shhhh!" he hissed. "Don't go talking 'bout stuff like that over the phone."

"Whose phone is it you think's tapped, mine or Mama's?"

"You can't go around saying I *told* you where that—"

"My lips are sealed. You said Shep was on his way to the chop shop when he was in the wreck, didn't you?"

"No, I did not. I didn't say nothing of the kind. I said the chop shop was out that way. He was going *south* on Hunter Lane. So he wasn't on his way *to* the chop shop, he'd done left there and was on his way back to town."

Chapter Thirty-Three

THE FIRST TIME Riley had seen Ace since Vietnam —
the day he'd brought them the seeds that saved their
floundering enterprise — Riley had been sitting alone
on his front porch in the rocking chair he'd purchased
a few weeks before at a new restaurant near Lebanon,
Tennessee, called Cracker Barrel Country Store.

A CAR PULLS UP *in front of the house, a big, long car, a
black and silver Lincoln Continental that totally dwarfs Riley's
red Mustang, that's sitting in the front yard with a "for sale"
sign on the windshield. Riley can't make out the driver until he
pulls to a stop and gets out, squints in the bright sunlight at
Riley and asks, "Don't you rednecks b'lieve in addresses —
streets and numbers, stuff like that? And road signs would be
nice, too — ones without bullet holes in 'em. Them holes was
bullet holes, wasn't they, but I can't figure out what a poor old
street sign done to deserve getting shot at."*

Riley sits where he is, too shocked to move, and says one word: "Ace."

Ace comes around the car and Riley nearly bowls him over before he gets to the front sidewalk. Ace is moving good for a man with a prosthetic leg from the knee down. The rest of his leg had been blown off at Tweety Bird a two-year lifetime ago.

He hugs his friend tight, fiercely, holds the hug a beat too long before letting go and stepping back.

"When I said I needed help, I never dreamed you'd … you'd show up."

"What'd you expect me to do — ain't like I'd entrust my babies to the United States Postal Service." Ace pats the pocket of his shirt. "You Kentucky boys is gonna love your ole pal Ace 'cause I got more'n righteous weed to smoke. I got seed."

Riley ushers Ace into the house. He can hear Drew crying from upstairs, so he doesn't call up to Sherry Lynn to come down and meet his friend. Papa is out on the tractor, so Riley pulls Ace into the kitchen and offers him a beer and a piece of Sherry Lynn's hot-from-the-oven apple pie. Can't stop gobbling up the sight of his friend, a man who'd saved his life more than once in Vietnam.

"Would you stop fussing over me like an old maid aunt," Ace says. "Just let me sit here. Feels good to get off the road — if I'd figured out how long it'd take to get here I might not have come. The last hour and a half was the worst. I don't know why you boys wasn't right at home in 'Nam, all these trees."

"That was a jungle."

"Trees is trees, and you got a pot load of them out there. But I figure, dirt that'd grow something as big as all them trees shouldn't have any trouble growing a little bitty weed plant."

"Our problem isn't the dirt. It's the plant. And it's …

awful."

"I have come to the rescue."

"Well, it's about time."

As soon as they'd formed the Cornbread Mafia, they'd started trying to track down Ace. But their friend was not to be found. Half a dozen, maybe a dozen letters to the address the military gave them of an apartment house in East Harlem either came back marked Return to Sender or never came back at all. Maybe they'd been forwarded — by somebody … to somewhere. They had no idea. They wrangled a phone number from a soldier at Ft. Knox, but the line had been disconnected. And it wasn't like they could hop in a car, drive to New York City and track him down. So they'd set out on their own.

"… and them peanut butter ambushes going off in the fire, like incoming mortar shells," Ace was saying when Sherry Lynn sweeps into the room with the baby on her hip and stops cold when she sees Ace sitting at her kitchen table. She recovers reasonably fast.

"I was wondering who you were taking to."

Riley introduces them, and when he says the baby is his "son," Drew, Ace smiles broadly and holds his arms out to the baby. Sherry Lynn looks like she doesn't want to give him up, but she hands him over. Ace examines him and says "Looks just like his mama — thank God!"

When Ace excuses himself to go to the bathroom, the smile drops off Sherry Lynn's face.

"You didn't tell me that your friend Ace was—"

She hesitated.

"Black?"

"Well, yes. You might have mentioned it."

"What difference does it make?" Riley feels himself being

needlessly belligerent but can't help it. "That man is the reason I'm alive. He saved my life more than once and—"

"Whoa, did you hear me say it mattered to me that he's black? That I care? I just would have … liked to have known, that's all."

And he has to admit that from that point on Sherry Lynn is a gracious hostess to the houseguest Riley insists stay with them, though the lumpy fold-out bed on the living room couch is probably not a whole lot more comfortable than sleeping in his car.

The next evening after supper, Ace makes something of an official "presentation" to Riley, Willie Ray, Jessie and Papa, hands over the seeds he's brought with him — in response to a single letter that had somehow followed him all over New York City.

"These here seeds will grow you some righteous weed … in Ecuador — least that's where the fellow said this weed come from. Will it grow at all here? That, my Kentucky friends, is for you to figure out. You're the farmers."

"It's gonna take some trial and error," Willie Ray says and Riley marvels at the change that comes over him when he has something to focus on besides his own demons, and some task to perform that he's good at. "Most important part is getting high, so it's got to have a high THC content."

Willie Ray has been learning from a master, taking "Cannabis 101" from Dr. Archibald Waznuski, a professor at the University of Kentucky School of Agriculture whose hobby is raising marijuana.

He hauls out a crude, hand-drawn chart and shows it to Ace.

"This here's the checklist. Is the THC high enough that you get a good buzz? Does it smoke smooth? How do you feel after?

And for us, we also got to develop plants that will grow in a climate that's colder than South America—"

"And that are resistant to mold," Jessie says, the first contribution she's made all night. Ace had been surprised, but hid it well, that there was a woman involved — even if she was Davie Monaghan's wife, but he discovers quick that she isn't a useless ornamentation.

"Tobacco mold ruins the leaves, and black shank will kill the whole plant outright," she tells Ace. "I don't know if weed molds the same as tobacco, but it's something we need to consider."

They stay up into the wee hours of the morning, talking, planning, toking on joints — and devouring all of Sherry Lynn's apple pie, plus all the chips and dip in the cabinets.

When Ace leaves the next morning, they all feel more confident about being able to raise a crop that's worth selling.

THE HARVEST of the 1971 crop had actually made a profit. Not much of one, but a profit was a profit.

And the crop they harvested last year …

Willie Ray had gone right out and bought a fancy truck.

Jessie'd set about turning her mother-in-law's home into a care facility for the two adults she looked after — David and Ruth Monaghan.

Riley had sat down with Sherry Lynn and started planning a house.

That first time Ace came, after Willie Ray and Jessie'd left, and Papa'd gone to bed, Ace and Riley sat on the front porch together. In companionable silence, they smoked weed and watched fireflies light up the trees like blinking Christmas lights.

"Not much like 'Nam, is it," Riley said, gesturing out into the darkness.

"You planning on doing anything about it?" Ace asked. "Or you just gonna let it lie?"

Riley exhaled a lungful of smoke and felt the mellow flow over him. *This* was what he wanted. He wanted their weed to be this good.

"About what?"

"About your feelings for Jessie."

Riley froze, but his face was obscured in shadow.

"I don't know what you're—"

"It's me, hoss. Remember ole Ace? It's wrote all over your face. Go on ahead and deny it if you want to, but it don't make it any less true. I's just wondering what it means … now, you know, with Davie like he is."

"It doesn't mean anything," Riley said with much more assurance than he felt. "Not now. Not ever. It can't."

"Oh, I see all kinda reasons why it can't." He took another long drag on the joint he was holding. "And I also see you're gonna eat yourself alive with the wanting of it. I'm sorry, man. You in a bad spot. No matter what you do, or don't do, somebody's gonna get hurt."

"Just so long as it's me who gets hurt, I'm okay with it."

"Yeah, but who gets hurt ain't a decision it's up to you to make."

Chapter Thirty-Four

Wazzi was itching for new seeds, so Willie Ray decided to make a quick trip to Louisville Thursday afternoon to see if he could hook up with Snake Eyes. He parked down the street from Snake Eyes's corner next to a streetlight that was inexplicably on in the middle of the afternoon. Streetlights annoyed Willie Ray, one of the many reasons you wouldn't ever get him to live in a city. If he wanted light, he'd flip a switch and get some, thank you very much. What must it be like to live in a house where a light came on out in your front yard at a certain time whether you liked it or not, and would shine in your window all night and you couldn't do nothing about it.

Snake Eyes had his back turned as Willie Ray approached, talking to someone. Must be a customer — a Hispanic guy who looked like a professional wrestler with a barrel chest, powerful arms, and shoulders so muscled it looked like he didn't have no neck at all. Willie Ray slowed, hung back. He didn't never see no product change hands, but Snake Eyes was probably an expert at slipping his customers their product without anybody seeing him because the customer turned away and walked down the street in the other direction. When Snake Eyes turned around and saw Willie Ray, he froze, his eyes huge. He was a black man, so you couldn't rightly say he turned pale, but his face was the color of ashes in ice.

"I ain't interested in nothing you got," he called out before Willie Ray even got close. Then he cut his eyes to the man he'd been talking to, back to Willie Ray, back to the man again.

Willie Ray Taggart didn't fall off a hay truck yesterday. Shrugging, he turned casually around and walked back to where he'd parked his truck on the street. He didn't hurry, made sure he didn't look like he was runnin' off or nothing like that. When he got behind the wheel, he saw that the man had returned to where Snake Eyes was standing and was yelling at him.

Not wanting to drive past the pair, Willie Ray cut a U-turn in the middle of the street and went back the other way. He'd have gotten out of there fast but for the dad-gum traffic light — another reason Willie Ray wouldn't live in a city. He'd have run the light, but there was a car stopped in front of him. So he had to sit through it, fidgeting, drumming his fingers on the steering wheel — come on, *come on*! He kept his eye on his rearview mirror, watching Snake Eyes and the man beside him. By the time Willie Ray pulled away from the intersection, the man had turned toward his truck and was full-on watching him drive away.

Goody.

Willie Ray would *not* be doing business with Snake Eyes again. He'd find some other dealer with exotic weed. Gratefully, Ace had brought seed with him from some place in California called Humboldt and that was about as exotic as Wazzi was going to get until Willie Ray managed to score.

Ace would be leaving in the morning. Riley'd said he was going to take him on a tour of the fields this afternoon, then they were all to get together again tonight — more of Sherry Lynn's home cooking — to talk about the future. About how the partnership with Mama Bert would affect them and what they were trying to build. Ace had some interesting plans of his own he wanted to share with them before he left. Jessie couldn't come, though — and they hated to meet without her. The Cornbread Mafia was a team and they all needed to be in on key discussions. But Davie'd been running a slight fever today and she didn't want to leave him.

When Jessie talked about Davie, it liked to broke your heart the yearning you could hear in her voice. She acted like the sounds he was making now was the beginning of him starting to talk, but Willie Ray knew there wasn't no way Davie Monaghan was ever gonna carry on a conversation. Everybody else knew it, too. Well, except Jessie. Davie never even made eye contact and Willie Ray believed — though he'd never say as much to Jessie — that Davie had no idea what was going on around him, didn't hear people talking to him, or if he did, he didn't know what they were saying.

The image of Davie flashed through his mind, the real Davie, not the one who was trapped now in a motionless body staring at the ceiling. That day in 'Nam when Willie Ray'd got him convinced there was a bug in the jungle that'd crawl in your ears and eat your brains — how he'd leapt up dusting the salt off his shoulder that Willie Ray'd put there to look like bug crap — whooping and hollering and carryin' on. Willie Ray smiled, but it was a sad smile.

He hoped Andy wouldn't decide to come to dinner tonight.

Chapter Thirty-Five

"What do you know about the wreck that killed Shep?" Winona asked the newly appointed sheriff of Callison County. Uncle Clyde was the oldest son of Leo McClusky, who was killed along with his father, uncle, cousin and a bunch of Hannackers in *the wreck* all those years ago.

Winona got right to the point because she didn't want to spend any more time than was absolutely necessary with her Uncle Clyde. He made her skin crawl.

Oh, she had nothing concrete to base it on, nothing that'd "hold up in court" anyway, but her older cousins had warned her about being alone with Uncle Clyde.

"He gets kinda touchy-feely," said Loretta, who was the oldest of Jonah McClusky's six children one Easter Sunday when they were at Aunt Frannie's for a family get-together. At the time, Winona was too young to know what touchy-feely meant, but she was a watcher. When you're invisible, you learn to look after yourself.

So she watched. She saw how he looked at Loretta's sisters, Opal and Lizzy, how he was always hugging them, or wanting the little girls to sit in his lap. She had never been extended an invitation into his lap — such were the rewards of being an ugly little girl — but her cousins often had to squirm out of his grasp to get away.

Nobody ever accused him of anything, but he was a predator and Winona kept her distance. Actually, her most vivid memory of Uncle Clyde from childhood was the fact that he left a trail of ugly brown spittle in the dirt at outside events, spitting tobacco juice everywhere he went. She'd stepped in it once while barefoot and could still remember how it had grossed her out.

Now, the man sat across from her behind the wide expanse of the ancient desk in the sheriff's office. She thought of him as an old man, though he was probably in his early fifties. He hadn't aged well, had a big gut that stretched out the shirt of the sheriff's uniform he wore. And, of course, he'd been blessed with the blunt, square features common to Digger McClusky's limbs on the family tree.

He had no lechery in his eyes when the deputy showed her into his office. Uncle Clyde's tastes ran to little girls, not women.

"I don't know a whole lot about it," he admitted. "Why you want to know?"

She could tell him the truth, that she was looking

for her father, but she really didn't think that was any of his business.

"I had an odd encounter yesterday and it got me to thinking. I was out on Hunter Lane, where Shep ran off the road, and there's one of those white roadside crosses there. An old man named Oscar Hanks came by, saw me there, stopped. He's the one put the cross there, and he told me he had seen Shep the night of the wreck, that Shep blew by him so fast he almost ran off the road."

"Yeah, I heard they figure he was going eighty, maybe ninety miles an hour when he hit that guardrail, tore the metal off the posts and tore the posts right out of the ground."

"Mr. Hanks said he saw another car that night on that road, that he thought the other car and Shep were racing."

Uncle Clyde looked interested.

"Well, that's news to me. I ain't never looked at the accident report, but I don't recall anybody ever talking about another car."

"Could I please have a copy of the accident report?"

He looked annoyed.

"I'd have to dig it out of the files, it'd take awhile."

"I'm not in a hurry."

That annoyed him more, but he called in a deputy and dispatched her to go find the report, probably in the basement files.

"And radio Lonnie. Tell him to come in to the station, I want to talk to him."

Lonnie Franklin was the officer who'd investigated the accident.

He tried to make small talk with Winona while they waited, and she realized that even though he was no longer predatory — not to her, anyway — he still made her skin crawl. When the deputy returned, she carried a folder, rather than a single report.

Uncle Clyde took the folder and opened it, displaying the contents to Winona.

There was an accident report, a toxicology report — so they *had* done a blood test on Shep — and an inventory sheet of the car's contents.

She scanned down the accident report and saw nothing out of the ordinary.

Lonnie Franklin came into the office then. He was the senior deputy, had been with the department the longest, was surely the man who was in line to take Sheriff's Gil's job when he got sick. But the job had been given instead to her Uncle Clyde, who had zero experience in law enforcement. It was clear it had been a political appointment. Most folks believed that Uncle Clyde had something over on the county judge and the sheriff's job had been payback.

"Winona here is wanting information about the wreck in 1969 that killed her brother."

The deputy pointed to the folder. "Everything I know is in that folder. I don't know what else I could tell you."

"Did anybody tell you there was another car out there on that road that night, that the other car and Shep were racing?"

"No, never heard that. Maybe somebody told Gus but he never told me." She heard warmth in his voice, as he called his former boss by his first name now. She was sorry he hadn't gotten the promotion he'd likely earned. He smiled then. "I don't know who'd have bothered to race Shep. He had the hottest rod in the county, could outrun anybody."

Something on the inventory sheet caught Winona's eye.

"There was a gun, a pistol in the car?"

She wasn't surprised by that and smiled, thinking of the pistol she carried in her own glove box. It was a Smith & Wesson .38 snub nose revolver and before it came into her possession it had belonged to Roberto Giovani Marino, aka Bobby G, aka The Weasel. May he rest in peace. Weasel had been one of the revolving door of petty criminals she'd represented in the storefront law firm in the West End of Louisville.

Wease — that's what his friends called him — was a drug addict with a rap sheet so long it needed to be divided into chapters. She'd already gotten him off on three different misdemeanor possession charges but he had been charged with a biggie this time, assault with a deadly weapon. Seems his ex-girlfriend had been shot in the arm from a passing car and the slug had come from a .38 revolver and Wease owned a .38 revolver.

Some paperwork snafu had landed him back on the street after his arraignment and he'd bailed. He was on the run when he'd called Winona and she'd agreed to meet him privately in her office one Saturday morning.

"I didn't shoot that whore!" he'd told her as he sat on a folding chair in front of her ratty little desk in the phone booth-sized office off Second Street. And he was probably telling the truth. A junkie, yes, dumb as a box of doorknobs, absolutely, but violent, not so much. "I can prove it." He'd pulled out the pistol he had pushed down in the waistband of his jeans, and dropped it on her desk. "They can test them things, can't they, tell this ain't the gun that fired the shot."

Yes, they could do that, she told him. And if the bullet didn't match his gun, he'd be free and clear. She'd convinced him to turn himself in on Monday morning, but thought it probably wasn't a good idea to give him back the gun. So she'd said she'd keep it over the weekend, and surrender it as evidence for him in court.

But Wease didn't make it to court Monday. He overdosed and died on Sunday night. Winona hung onto the gun, figured he owed her way more than the gun was worth in unpaid legal fees.

"What kind of gun was it? The report doesn't say."

"It looked like a Browning Hi-Power nine millimeter, but it was pretty charred. The holster was in a little better shape because it was in the glove box." He glanced at the sheriff before he continued. "There was a little metal box in there with it. The kind of little box where … users carry their coke. But, of course, there wasn't anything left of the contents, and wasn't no reason to test it—"

She knew he was on coke. That didn't interest her. The gun did.

"Are you saying the holster and the little coke box were in the glove compartment, but the gun wasn't?"

"Uh huh."

"The gun came out of the holster during the wreck?"

"No, the glove box was smashed shut. We had to pry it open."

"If it wasn't in the holster at the time of the wreck, then where was it?"

The deputy shrugged.

"Coulda been anywhere — on the floorboard, under the seat, on the seat, in the trunk …"

That didn't strike either officer as particularly odd.

"Am I the only one here who's wondering why my brother had a gun out — like within arm's reach — while he was racing down the road at four o'clock in the morning?"

The officers looked at each other.

"You don't know it was 'out,'" Uncle Clyde said, in that dismissive tone stupid men always took with women smarter than they were. "It coulda been in a cardboard box taped shut with duct tape in the trunk. Or in a gun case instead of the holster."

"Did you find a gun case?"

"No, but we wasn't looking for one."

"What difference does it make?" Uncle Clyde

wanted to know. "That gun didn't have nothing to do with the wreck. It was just in the car."

Right, Winona thought. It was in the car but not in the holster. Which said to her, though obviously she was the only one who'd connected the dots, that Shep had taken the gun out of the holster for a reason. If their father had taught his children anything in their growing-up years it was the proper care of a firearm. It was a macho thing to say but it was also good firearms advice. *"Don't you never take out a gun unless you intend to use it."*

Did Shep intend to use it? What for?

"Had it been fired recently?"

The two men looked at each other but it was Lonnie who spoke. "In the movies, they make it look like they can just pick a gun up, sniff the barrel and know right away. It don't work that way in real life. And even if it did, that gun got burned pretty bad. Wouldn't have been no way to tell."

"Was it so damaged you couldn't have traced a bullet fired from it?"

"Tracing bullets is done by examining the inside of the barrel, the marks it leaves on a bullet." Like Winona didn't know that. "I s'pose it'd be possible." The sheriff looked at her quizzically. "Are you going somewhere with all of this?"

She ignored the question.

"Where's the gun now?"

"I give it to your brother, Jody."

Chapter Thirty-Six

THEY HAD JUST FINISHED DINNER. Sherry Lynn had put on a feast — pot roast with potatoes and carrots, fresh corn on the cob, fried okra, homemade yeast rolls and gravy and hot cherry pie. The woman could cook! One look at her and you could tell that!

Riley was instantly sorry for the thought, though he couldn't help wondering just how big she was going to get. Every week it seemed like she weighed more than she did the week before. She had taken to wearing shapeless shifts — moo-moos, they were called — colorful and flowing, looked like flowered drapes to Riley, but they did hide her ever-expanding figure from prying eyes.

She'd been sweet and charming during dinner, making sure everybody's tea had fresh ice, that there was plenty of butter on the table for the rolls, and plopped a dollop of vanilla ice cream on each piece of cherry pie, which was served in the kitchen instead of at the big table in the dining room

"I wanna hear more about this place in California where they grow weed," Willie Ray told Ace.

Willie Ray was amazing. He had suffered from perpetual hunger when he and Riley were kids. No matter how much he ate, he was always sneaking cookies out of his mother's cookie jar. And with so many kids running in and out of the house, she was never the wiser. When Willie Ray started smoking weed, the continuous munchies turned his craving for food into an obsession, and he could eat anybody Riley knew under the table. He had already finished the first piece of pie and was handing Sherry Lynn his plate for a second when the phone rang and she went to answer it.

"Oh, Humboldt County ain't the only place that's got good weed," Ace said. "It's just that don't nobody there care one way or the other, so they's pretty much free to raise it almost right out in the open."

"Seriously?" Riley said. Ace nodded.

"You fellas don't realize it, but you got it pretty good right where you are. The marijuana laws in Kentucky ain't near as strict as they are in most other states."

A first offense of possession of marijuana was a Class C misdemeanor, carrying a $500 fine and up to thirty days in jail. Jail time, not prison. You had to get caught with truckloads of the stuff — more than once — before you were in any real danger from the police. And even then, it didn't much matter, not in Callison County, anyway.

"Oh, we realize it, alright," Riley said and grinned at his grandfather. Ace had been given a blow-by-blow of Nate's arrest and subsequent release. "Even if you do get caught, they's ways out of it and if by some miracle the bust holds up, you ain't gonna get convicted, not by a Callison County jury."

Sherry Lynn stepped back into the kitchen.

"The phone's for you, Willie Ray."

That was a bit of a conversation stopper. Weren't many people who knew to call him here, that the old shack on the back of the Hannacker place was where he lived — well, one of the places he lived — even though he showed up often enough at home to eat his Ma Taggart's famous beef stew to claim domicile there.

Willie Ray hadn't cared about much of anything when he got back from 'Nam. Growing weed and creating hybrids was the first thing he'd taken any interest in. There was a shed next to an old shack at the back of the Hannacker property. They'd run electricity from the shack to the shed and Willie Ray'd set up shop there, cross-pollinating different strains of pot. He'd grow the plants the mix produced into seedlings that they'd plant with the tobacco setter in specific fields, so he and his college professor friend could keep track of which hybrids produced the best yield. He spent so much time in the shed that he'd kinda sorta moved into the shack next door, at least that's where you'd be most likely to find him if you went looking.

"Is it Mama?" he asked as he rose to go to the

phone. His mama wouldn't call him here unless something was wrong.

"No, some guy. I didn't recognize the voice and he didn't tell me his name. I could tell he was—" She stopped and looked at Ace, then blushed.

"Of the darker-skin persuasion? We easy to pick out of a crowd even when you can't see us."

Didn't bother Ace one bit. Or did it? He always laughed, joked whenever something came up about him being black. But at that moment Riley thought to wonder if maybe that was an act. If maybe Ace did care, maybe it did bother him. Maybe there were a lot of things that happened to Ace because he was black that bothered him.

Willie Ray went to take the call and Riley picked Drew up out of his booster seat and set his feet on the floor, taking a napkin to mop the cherry pie drippings off his chin. "It is past your bedtime, young man." He looked at Sherry Lynn. "I bet you could talk your mama into reading you a bedtime story."

Sherry Lynn wouldn't want to hang around after supper while the others talked business.

"How about that one you like about the Wild Things—" She stopped talking and Riley followed her eyes to the doorway where Willie Ray stood.

She'd stopped talking when she saw the look on Willie Ray's face. He actually appeared to be at a loss for words, which was not good.

"What is it?" Ace asked.

Everybody was looking at Willie Ray now.

Willie Ray shook his head, like he hadn't yet completely figured it out his own self.

"Remember what I told you was goin' on between me and that pusher, Snake Eyes? How he acted this afternoon in Louisville, how he yelled at me 'fore I ever got close, cut his eyes to some fella who was walking away ..."

"Do I have to tell you you aren't making any sense, or do you already know it and you just don't care?" Riley said.

"That was him, Snake Eyes."

"How'd he get my phone number?"

"From Information, I guess."

Information? How'd the operator—?

"What'd he call for?" Nate asked.

"Them Colombians, the ones who were pissed off at us for selling weed to *their* customer ..." He paused, took a breath, looked like he'd run out of air before he finished what he had to say. "They're on their way here."

"Here?" Sherry Lynn had heard the story. He'd told the saga of his meetings with Snake Eyes when they were all sitting around the kitchen table while she was rolling out the dough for the rolls. She knew the men were dangerous, even though Willie Ray hadn't elaborated on that part. She didn't know how dangerous, but she didn't need to know a thing like that. The rest of them knew, though.

"You didn't give that pusher your *real* name, didja?" Ace demanded.

"Of course not!" Willie Ray replied, indignant.

Then he looked at the floor in front of Riley's feet, sounded like a little kid when he spoke. "I give him … yours."

"*Mine?*"

"He was the first one, remember? The very first time I *ever* done anything like that, back three years ago. I didn't have no idea what I's doing."

He'd been drunk, of course. Or maybe stoned. One or the other. Willie Ray Taggart didn't draw more than a handful of sober breaths the whole first year after he got back from 'Nam.

"And when the fella said, 'They call me Snake Eyes,' I wasn't 'xpecting it. I couldn't come up with a fake name quick enough so I just blurted out the first one that come to mind." He hung his head. "I wasn't thinkin' too clear at the time …"

They got it. He'd been both — drunk *and* stoned. They understood — didn't like it, but it was water under the bridge now.

"So they know your name," Ace said to Riley — *that* was how Snake Eyes got this phone number from Information. "How they gonna find you?"

"*You* found me."

Ace had complained when he arrived the first time about the winding roads and signs full of bullet holes, said he'd got hopelessly lost, finally had to stop and ask a fellow hoeing in his garden how to get to the Hannacker place.

"He knew right where to send me," Ace had said in awe.

"What's going on here?" Sherry Lynn finally cried,

terror in her eyes. "Who are you talking about? What do they want?"

"My guess is it ain't to give us Team Colombia tee shirts," Willie Ray said. He took a breath, tried to smile, couldn't pull it off so he gave up. "Snake Eyes figures we got half an hour to get ready."

Chapter Thirty-Seven

NATE WATCHED THE TRANSFORMATION, and it was hard to countenance the change. Seemed like between one breath and the next, Ace, Riley and Willie Ray changed from three friends eating cherry pie after supper into soldiers. He supposed it was what Riley'd told him about, how his sergeant had said "nobody rises to the occasion." When the guano comes in contact with the air conditioning, everybody ... *everybody* reverts to the level of their training. These three young men were veterans of bloody, deadly combat.

"Sherry Lynn," Riley said. "Get Drew into the truck and go to your mother's."

"She could run into 'em on the road," Willie Ray countered. Riley nodded.

"Then take him to the tobacco barn." The tobacco barn was separated from the house by the ten-acre cornfield, and the road leading to it went around the back side of the field. "Stay there, don't come back *no matter what.* I'll come get you."

"Riley, what's going on?" Her voice was high-pitched and frightened. "I'm not going any—"

He took hold of her shoulders. "Yes, you are! Right now. No questions, just go!" And he shoved her in the direction of the back door. She immediately burst into tears and Riley stepped close, growled into her ear as he nodded toward Drew.

"*You're* the grownup here, act like it! Straighten up and take care of your son. His safety depends on *you*! Go!"

She drew in a ragged, sobbing breath and ran to where Drew stood terrified, looking from his mother to his father and back to his mother.

"Mommy, whaaat …?" Drew was coiling up to launch into a full bore meltdown. Sherry Lynn took his hand.

"It's a *game*, sweetheart. Hide-and-seek. It's our turn to hide."

Nate was proud of her, she'd grabbed hold of herself quick and done what she'd ought to do.

Turning with Drew in tow — who wasn't buying what she was selling, but was confused enough to go along — Sherry Lynn headed out the back door toward the truck.

"… going to hide where nobody will *ever* find us …"

The door banged shut behind her, the pickup truck engine rumbled to life and Nate saw her roar down the road toward the barn. Didn't turn her headlights on, though. Good girl!

"What kinda hardware we got?" Ace asked.

Willie Ray and Riley exchanged a look.

"I's in a gun store in Louisville last summer, seen a whole wall of M1 carbines they'd just got in from the Civilian Marksmanship Program," Willie Ray said. He shrugged. "So I bought me some."

"Bought *me* some," Riley corrected, "for my 'birthday,' remember?"

"I got two Inlands, a couple of Saginaws, an IBM, and two … no three National Postal Meters. They all got 30-round magazines."

Ace's face broke into a grim smile. "As you hillbillies would say, I b'lieve we in bidness."

Nate had helped Riley and Willie Ray unload the weapons out of Willie Ray's truck and into the storage room in Nate's garage. "These was standard issue for soldiers during World War II," Willie Ray had told him, then added defensively, "Hey, when I was in 'Nam, I ate K-rations older than I was. Didn't kill me."

The rifles were in pristine condition, didn't look like they'd ever been used or if they had, they'd been cleaned up real good after. When Nate and Riley tried them out later, they'd fired true. Nate wouldn't use one tonight, though. He had his own weapon — the .308 Winchester he'd used with a 3-9x40 Simmons scope to blow the heads off Oliver Morris's statues four years ago.

Five minutes later, after Riley'd passed out the rifles, Nate stood on the front porch beside the ancient swing as the three soldiers plotted out a defense, using words like "flanking maneuver" and "natural cover" that he didn't understand — but they did and that's what counted.

Nate watched the others defer to Ace because he was the most senior of the group, had years more experience than Willie Ray or Riley. It was more than that, though. Riley had told him that behind his gregarious facade, Ace was a certified badass. He had already been in 'Nam two years before he became a replacement in the guard unit. And during those two years, he'd … done things. Riley wasn't sure exactly what, but there were whispers that Ace had once got vital information about an attack plan out of some Cong prisoners after all the other interrogators had given up … and those prisoners wasn't in very good shape after. Like maybe they was "missing non-essential body parts."

"You think we ought to try to talk to 'em, reason …" Riley didn't even finish when he saw the look on Willie Ray's face.

"Let's figure where we're at," Ace said. "Sound off."

"Secure position," Riley replied, clipped and precise. "High ground."

"Surprise," Willie Ray said. "They don't know we been warned so they ain't expecting us to be waiting for 'em. It's possible they think we won't even fight back. I bet ain't many folks in their world who'll take 'em on."

"What *are* they expecting?" Ace asked.

"Me — and maybe two or three others like me."

Ace raised an eyebrow. "You did your dumb hillbilly song and dance?"

Willie Ray nodded. He could dial up an impressive "good ole boy" accent and the kind of toe-in-the-sand persona that outsiders found charming and disarming — oh, definitely not the sharpest knife in the drawer, but a really nice guy. He figured it was best to convince his business associates that they were smarter than he was.

"What size force we up against?"

"Snake Eyes said some of them South Americans got *armies*, but these guys don't. Los Asesinos ain't that big. Might be they'll send out a couple of guys." He paused. "Might be they'll send a dozen."

Nate swallowed hard. This wouldn't be the first time these three young men had faced an army of killers. They knew what it felt like to get shot at. Nate had no idea.

Riley must have read his face.

"It don't matter how many times you done it, every battle's like the first one — dries up all the spit in your mouth and makes it hard to get a deep breath."

"I s'pose it's possible they'll try a sneak attack," Willie Ray considered. "But 'cording to Snake Eyes, all the South Americans is used to goin' balls out, blasting away 'thout a whole lot of planning."

Ace put the tips of his fingers together to make a peaked roof over his head and said, "Umbrella of mercy."

Nate knew what that meant — you was about to

say something others wasn't gonna like, but they had to listen all the way to the end 'thout arguing.

"We could call the law, you know. Even in Kentucky it's illegal to come roaring in here shooting at people." It seemed like everyone else was drawing in a breath at the same time to respond, but Ace cut them off. "I get it that you don't play things that way and I'll hang with you — just putting it out there as an option."

"Calling the law ain't *never* an option," Nate said. It was the first time he'd spoken and they all turned to him. "Even if it was, seems to me we got to beat these guys our own selves or they'll just wait 'til the law leaves and try it again. And next time, we won't likely get a warning."

"Right," Ace said and they all nodded. A little smile flitted across Riley's face, like maybe he was proud his grandpa had been both courageous and the voice of wisdom.

"… so we talkin' deadly force here," Ace said. It wasn't a question.

No one spoke.

"I don't figure *they's* worried 'bout that, do you?" Riley said. "We'll give as good as we get."

"Strategy's simple, then," Ace said and gestured out into the front yard. "We stop them right here, on my signal."

It was a good-sized front yard, roughly square, seventy-five feet on each side. The road from the highway ended in front of the house and the driveway curved around the yard on the left to the garage and went on around the house to the out buildings, the tool shed, chicken house and barn in the back. There was a thick hedge of hydrangea bushes in the front part of the yard with an opening where the sidewalk began and led to the porch. A huge sycamore tree stood on the left of the sidewalk with a picnic table in its shade, and there was a woodpile on the right of the sidewalk. The woods snuggled up to the road and the yard on all sides.

"If they try a sneak attack, protect your flank. Take out anybody comes at you."

"If they don't, if they just storm the beachhead, we just — what? Mow 'em down?" Willie Ray asked. His voice sounded haunted and Nate understood that this whole thing had catapulted these young men back into a time and space none of them *ever* visited voluntarily.

"Depends on how many of them there are and what they do. Getting a surrender's best case, but if they ain't in a white-flag mood ..."

Willie Ray's eyes darted away, focused on one of the front porch rocking chairs. His face paled, making his freckles stick out like red sequins on his face.

Ace was still talking. "Leave the lights on in the kitchen, the TV on in the living room — *loud*. Upstairs dark. Make it look like it's a normal old Thursday night and you's just hanging out."

"Front porch light on," Riley said, "like company's welcome."

Ace pointed to Nate and Willie Ray. "Spread out in the woods on the right side of the yard." To Riley,

"Up in that big tree. I figure you climbed it a time or two as a kid."

He pointed to the hydrangea hedge in the front of the yard. "I'll be in them bushes. I hide better than you white boys. Soon's they pass by my position, I'll move in on their rear flank and take up a position behind the bathtub Mary. We all open fire at the same time, on my signal."

He looked at Nate. "You got an empty wine bottle I can put on that picnic table?"

"I got a *jug.*" He went into the house to get it and heard Riley asking as he returned.

"… we do with them if they do surrender?"

"You know well's I do battle plans fall apart soon's the first shot's fired," Ace said. "We gonna be dancing before we even know the music. If they come here like they's determined to take scalps, then yeah, we mow 'em down. If they just come to kick ass and take names, then we make 'em sorry they got out of bed this morning."

He paused.

"Ain't no sense in letting this turn into some kinda shootout, neither. We got the advantage, so we hit first, *hard,* take all the fight outta 'em. Lay down a blistering line of fire into the ground all around 'em. The guys nearest your position are your targets. Once we've pumped enough lead, I'll holler for them to surrender. If they throw down their guns, we take 'em prisoner. If they keep comin', we" — there was only a brief pause — "take 'em out."

Willie Ray looked at his watch.

"Our half hour's 'bout up."

"Take your positions," Ace said. And for the first and only time in his life, Nate Hannacker felt like a soldier.

He and Willie Ray crossed the yard and went into the woods. He took up a position behind the trunk of an oak tree that'd probably been an acorn when his daddy was a little boy. His bum knee made it hard for him to crouch down, but he done all right hunkering back out of sight behind the tree. Willie Ray had found hisself a place behind a big elderberry bush and had poked his rifle barrel out through the limbs. Riley hopped off the porch and ran to the sycamore tree and shinnied up it like a squirrel. Ace went to the hedge of hydrangeas and vanished into it.

Nate had turned on the porch light as well as the big light on the porch roof that lit up the front yard when he went in for the moonshine jug. He'd switched on all the lamps in the living room and kitchen but left the upstairs rooms dark. He'd stopped to turn on the television, volume high, and as he stood behind the oak tree in the darkness, he could hear the theme music from that new show they'd all been watching, *All in the Family*, found himself quietly singing along with Edith Bunker's chicken-squawk voice.

"... those were the days!"

As an advertisement for Colgate toothpaste come on, he seen the headlights of a car turning off the main road and up the winding lane to the house. 'Parently they wasn't trying to sneak up on nobody 'cause they come driving up the road like they owned it.

Unless, of course, it wasn't them South American drug dealers at all but some neighbor lady — "Avon calling" — who was about to get the shock of her life.

The car didn't pull on into the driveway proper, just stopped in front of the house and killed the engine and the headlights. Five men got out, two from the front and three out of the back seat. All of them were carrying what looked like machine guns — AK-47's if Nate was to guess, though he'd never actually seen one.

Appeared these fellas hadn't come to sell lipstick.

Chapter Thirty-Eight

THE FIVE MEN held their guns at the ready, fanned out across the front yard and walked slowly forward, lined up like crows on a clothesline. An image flashed like a comet through Nate's mind — a painting of a Revolutionary War battle he'd seen somewhere, where the Redcoats advanced in orderly rows while the American frontiersmen in coonskin caps crouched behind bushes and trees.

These guys probably hadn't studied American history.

The one on the far left who'd pass under Riley's position in the tree looked like the guy Willie Ray had described talking to Snake Eyes. A professional wrestler with a barrel chest and powerful arms, and no neck at all. His head just rested on the lumps of muscles in his huge shoulders. Probably spent a lot of time behind bars. Nate'd heard that every guy in prison looked like that, didn't have nothing else to do but lift weights. That coulda been a myth, though.

Nate's nervousness sent his thoughts ping-ponging around in his head.

The guy next to him had a full, black beard. Coulda used some of that hair on his head, which was completely bare. Maybe he hadn't gone bald, though. He looked young so maybe he'd just shaved it off for effect. His head shone, literally reflected the porch light.

The fellow beside him was the tallest, long skinny arms and legs. He didn't look South American, and the lighter skin on his arms displayed full sleeves of tattoos.

The guy beside him didn't just appear short by comparison. He *was* short, smaller than Jackson McClusky, maybe five feet two inches. Fat, though, looked like a stereotypical "Mexican," even though he apparently hailed from farther south.

The guy on the end closest to where Nate crouched behind the oak tree in the woods had a handlebar mustache that drooped far below his chin, looked like that Poncho Villa fella, except he wasn't wearing a stupid sombrero. His belly hung out over the belt of his jeans and jiggled with every step.

Though this was shooting ducks in a washtub — targets wouldn't be more'n forty or fifty feet away, Nate put his eye to the sight on his rifle and focused on Poncho's right hand, holding the machine gun out in front of him. The scope's magnification made it possible for Nate to see the black hairs on the tops of his fingers and the showy ring with a huge stone on his pinky. Coulda put a bullet right through it.

Ace had planned to signal "open fire" by shooting the jug off the picnic table.

He never got a chance.

With a sudden thunderous roar, all five machine guns sprang to life.

Rat-tat-tat-tat!

You could hear the sound of the bullets hitting home beneath the gunfire.

Thunk. Thunk. Thud. Plunk. Thud-thud.

Pieces of wood on the house and porch flew away in splintered chunks. The porch swing suddenly hung lopsided after a bullet clipped one of the chains that affixed it to the ceiling. Flower pots disintegrated into broken pottery, sending clods flying and clouds of dirt into the air.

All the front windows exploded in a shriek of breaking glass. The door, riddled with holes, flew open.

With a glance up over his sight, Nate could see the men standing with feet spread wide, spraying the front of the house like firemen pointing water hoses on a blaze.

The shooting stopped as abruptly as it'd started, so there musta been some kinda signal. Lasted maybe thirty seconds. The men stood where they were, chuckling in the sudden silence, as dust settled out of the air.

"Hey, hillbilly," cried the tall, skinny man in a Spanish accent. Maybe he was in charge. "You come out and maybe we don't shoot your wife and kids, too."

"You got a pretty wife, huh, hillbilly?" called the short, fat one. There was bawdy laughter.

"Even if she's ugly, we all get a piece," called Poncho Villa.

"We show her what a *real man* is like." That was the big guy on the end.

The jug on the table exploded, Nate put his eye back to the scope and squeezed the trigger, put a bullet through the ring on Poncho Villa's finger. The guy shrieked and Nate figured he musta took off the finger and the one next to it, too, and at this range there wasn't likely nothing left of either one of them.

The roar of gunfire that followed was not the rat-tat-tat of machine guns. It was the rumble of multiple M1's fired in unison. With his vision shrunk to a few square inches visible through his scope, Nate dragged the magnified image to the ground in front of the men and put three quick rounds in the grass half an inch from the skinny man's shoe. Dirt and grass sprigs kicked up in tufts all around them, like the ground itself was exploding in a circle 360 degrees.

Nate lifted his eye from the sight just for a second to get a view of the whole scene.

Three of the advancing tough guys were dancing around like they were walking on hot coals, crying out in dismay. Poncho Villa had dropped to his knees, cradling his bleeding hand, shrieking. Only the pro-wrestler wannabe on the far end had the cajones to stand still. He began to turn, lifting his gun up toward Riley's sycamore tree. Before he could get the barrel chest high, Nate sighted in and put a bullet in his left ear. His head snapped to the side. Nonstop gunfire roared then, so many bullets it sounded like a single gun. Nate looked up from the scope to see the man he'd shot dancing in jerky impact-movements, his body held upright by the hail of bullets that riddled him from all sides. When the gunfire ceased, he collapsed in the dirt, looked like he had two dozen bullet holes in him, and the three men in the middle threw their weapons down on the ground, put their hands high in the air, and cried, "Don shoot, don shoot."

The whole gunfight — attack and ambush — hadn't taken a full minute.

Nate sat back and thought — now what?

Riley'd put that question out there earlier — what will we do with them if they do surrender? Nobody'd had an answer for him then. Maybe Ace had a plan. Nate didn't know, he only knew he wasn't going to move from the position Ace had assigned him behind the oak tree until he was "ordered to."

The bald, bearded guy had his hands in the air, but he was looking down at the gun he'd dropped right at his feet and anybody could see the gears turning.

A bullet suddenly slammed into the ground in front of him. From the sound, it was Riley in the tree. If he'd been aiming at the gun, he'd missed by maybe half an inch, but he wasn't looking through a fancy scope like Nate, and he might not have been aiming at the gun at all.

Riley fired into the ground in front of each one of them in turn.

Bam! Bam! Bam! Bam!

After the first couple of rounds, they looked up into the tree where the gunfire was coming from, but Nate was sure Riley was hidden so they couldn't see him.

Nate dropped shots in front of them, too, and their heads jerked toward the woods. Willie Ray did the same so they could tell they were surrounded.

Ace's voice suddenly rang out from the lush profusion of hydrangea blossoms behind the statue of the Virgin Mary in her grotto made out of a bathtub.

"Willie Ray, why don't you relieve these here gentlemen of they firearms."

Ace sounded ridiculously twangy, like he did when he was making fun of the Kentuckians' accents.

Willie Ray came out of hiding in the woods down from Nate and advanced on them slowly, his rifle fit snug to his shoulder.

"Twitch and you done lost a leg," he called out and the men froze. "Twitch twice and you gone wake up in the mornin' on the wrong side of dirt."

As Willie Ray came around in front of the men where their guns lay in the dirt, Ace called out, "Aw, come on now, twitch for ole Willie Ray. 'Cept for your dead friend there, he ain't got to put a hole in nobody for nigh onto a week."

The accent was credible, Nate supposed — for a black man from Brooklyn. But why was Ace trying to sound like a Georgia cracker?

"Now I'm gonna ask you gentlemen once, all polite like, for the rest of your weapons. You got a pistol in a shoulder holster, you pull it out with your fingertips so slow they wouldn't outrun molasses."

Riley suddenly called out from the tree.

"If'n I catch any one of you with anythin' more dangerous than toenail clippers, I'm gonna poke an icepick in yore eye and pop your eyeball out like squeezin' a grape." He paused. "I'll let you pick which eye."

The light was beginning to dawn on Nate.

"Gotta knife strapped to yore leg?" Willie Ray asked as he approached. "That blade best be shining in the dirt in five seconds. I'll make it easy, case you ain't learnt to count that high. One. Two."

Before he made it to four, two of the remaining men had divested themselves of their blades. Poncho Villa had rolled over onto his side, cradling his hand, which was missing the pinky finger that'd sported the diamond-stud ring and the finger next to it. Willie Ray leveled the rifle at him.

"You got to the count of one to hush up that caterwauling."

The man choked on his own sobs but stopped hollering, holding his hand tight to his chest as blood gushed out between his fingers.

Willie Ray gestured with his rifle to the bald guy.

"You shore you bein' total honest with ole Willie Ray?" He lowered the rifle barrel to point it at the man's groin. "Miss one, and you gonna lose your cajo-nies."

He didn't pronounce the j as an h, totally mangled the word, with his own twang dialed up to a hundred. Then he let out a maniacal laugh.

"Whooo-eee! I ain't had this much fun since I drowned them puppies."

That was definitely a bridge too far, but that was Willie Ray for you.

"Go get some rope," Ace ordered, "and let's truss up some Christmas turkeys, get 'em ready for roasting."

Chapter Thirty-Nine

As soon as the dust had settled, the prisoners gagged
and tied securely, Riley went to the tobacco barn to
get Sherry Lynn and Drew and take them to her
mother's house to spend the night. Sherry Lynn was
holding onto her composure with her fingernails —
and he didn't blame her. The only thing keeping her
from dissolving into hopeless hysterics was Drew, who
was in better emotional shape than he had any right to
be. Sherry Lynn had told him his Daddy and friends
were having a party — and the gunfire was fireworks.

The woman deserved a medal for how she'd held
it together.

"I'll explain what happened *later*," Riley had told
her in a tone that brooked no argument. Then he'd
driven around the back side of the cornfield to the
road so's not to pass the bullet-riddled house and the
four prisoners, who lay tied up in the dirt next to their
car. Their dead comrade's body had been dumped
into the trunk.

By the time he returned from the Bennetts' house, the others had cleaned up as much of the mess as they could. Couldn't do anything about the bullet holes until tomorrow, of course, but the broken glass, pieces of chipped wood and busted flower pots were all gone.

Now, Riley sat on the front porch in one of the two handmade wooden rockers he'd purchased from that Tennessee store called Cracker Barrel to replace his grandfather's lawn chair. Nate sat in the other. Ace had fixed the broken link in the porch swing chain with two plastic zip ties he'd found in the kitchen junk drawer and sat in it now, moving it slowly back and forth. Willy Ray sat on the porch steps.

Riley'd brought out a cold six pack of beer and Willie Ray had downed one in a single long swallow, but gratefully didn't reach for another one. Riley had almost gotten himself a glass of tea, but realized the ice would clink against the sides of the glass in his shaking hands and he didn't want to make a spectacle of that.

The adrenaline rush of battle had done to all of them what it always did — sapped every bit of their strength until they felt so exhausted it was a huge effort to look like they felt fine — just dandy. The three soldiers put forth that effort ... because that's what you did. Papa didn't bother, sat rocking slowly back and forth, looking as worn out as he felt.

Riley gestured toward the prisoners, who couldn't see them on the porch because Willie Ray had put brown paper grocery sacks over their heads, with the explanation: "It's hard on your nerves when you can't see."

"The deranged hillbillies shtick, that was because ...?" Nate asked.

"Willie Ray said they was expecting hillbillies," Ace answered. "Might as well seem crazy, too."

"Do you really think those guys were buying it?" Riley asked.

"As the lone Away-From-Here in attendance, I am here to testify that the rest of the world has no idea how people like you live," Ace said. "The first time I came here, it took me half an hour to work up the nerve to stop and ask for directions. All those stories about the hillbillies in the mountains, shooting outsiders on sight. I believed every word of it and I bet these guys do, too." He paused. "They also believe you're going to kill them."

"Well ... are we?" Willie Ray asked.

"We got two options and that's one of them," Riley said. "We kill them, or we let them go."

"They're illegals, not American citizens," Ace pointed out. "They're not supposed to be here in the first place and if they vanish, nobody's gonna report 'em missing."

Riley fit his finger into one of the bullet holes in the chair and said quietly, "If your friend hadn't warned us ..." His face grew hard, his voice cold. "My wife and son were in there!"

"Is that what you guys want to do, then?" Ace asked, his voice emotionless. "Put a gun to their heads and blow their brains out?"

Silence.

"You know, a thing like that could ruin your whole day," Willie Ray said, and in spite of themselves they smiled.

More silence.

The crickets and tree frogs were performing their nightly concert and it seemed overloud — jarring.

Then the men found themselves looking into the faces of the others, each of them searching. What they found was confirmation of an understanding that didn't need words. *That's not who we are.*

Nate spoke out of the darkness, his voice deliberate. "If you's to send out five guys to do a job like this and they never come back … what would you do?"

Riley felt the gut punch of the obvious answer, but saw the truth in it. "I'd send out five more to see what happened to the first five."

"Uh huh. We kill these, we gonna have to kill the next five and the next five and …"

"So we gotta turn 'em loose … and then what?" Willie Ray asked. "That's it? We're done? We plow up our weed and go back to corn and tobacco?"

"I don't think murdering five strangers or picking up our marbles and going home are the only choices we got," Nate said, and probably didn't notice that the younger men leaned closer when he spoke. "You ever watched a peacock when it's threatened? It lifts the tail dragging along behind it and spreads out them feathers and suddenly it looks four or five times bigger than it really is. That's what we gotta do. The Cornbread Mafia's gotta be peacocks."

"Okay," Riley said. "Peacocks."

"It's two parts," Nate said. "First, we gotta convince these guys that there are a whole lot more of us than there really are."

Riley picked up the ball and ran with it. "They got to think the four of us, we're … *just the guards*—"

"Not even *all* the guards," Willie Ray said. "And the big, badass boss ain't even here, that's why we ain't done nothing with them. We gotta wait for him to tell us."

"How do we do that?" Ace asked. "How do we look like more people?"

"I been thinking …" Nate said. "Maybe I know a way."

"Okay, I understand the first part," Riley said. "What's the second?"

Nate sat very still, then he spoke softly.

"Think what coulda happened to Drew if we hadn't got that phone call from Snake Eyes."

Riley felt like he'd been kicked in the belly.

"We'd have been sitting at the table eating cherry pie when them bullets started flying. They probably put a hundred rounds in this house and it wouldn't have taken but one of them to kill that little boy."

It didn't feel like there was enough air in the universe for Riley to get a whole breath.

"This kinda thing … we can't *ever* let it happen again. It's got to stop. *Right now*. We can't be worried what's gonna happen if we step on some drug dealer's toes. This right here — we got to make this 'one and done.'"

"And by that you mean …?" Riley said.

"What Snake Eyes told Willie Ray about the big operations — that they had *reputations*. They's respected and nobody messes with 'em. Seems to me we been given this chance to make the whole drug-dealing world b'lieve we the meanest dogs in the junkyard."

He took a breath.

"So we ain't just talking *big*. We ain't just talking convincing them they's out-gunned. We're talking 'bout convincing them we're … *ruthless*, that there ain't nothing we won't do. "

"When you get your ass thoroughly kicked, the usual response is to exaggerate the force you was up against," Willie Ray pointed out. "You don't want the boys back in the hood to think you got whipped by the Little Sisters of the Poor."

"Whatever happens to these guys, they're gonna tell the world it was a whole lot worse than it really was," Riley said.

There was a pause.

"If you serious, if you really wanna convince them we're hillbilly savages …" Ace paused and looked them each in the face, and Riley saw in his eyes a hint of what had been whispered about him in 'Nam. "Then we gonna have to take the gloves off."

"We done killed one of them," Willie Ray said.

"That ain't enough."

"What *is* enough?"

"We got to hurt 'em … so bad they won't never forget."

"How?" Willie Ray's voice was hollow. Nobody spoke.

"I got some thoughts on how we can scare the bejesus out of 'em," Nate said. "But for now, let's dump 'em in the barn. Keep them gags on 'em so they can't talk nothing over. If they have to piss and crap their pants, they'll be pretty demoralized by morning."

Chapter Forty

Papa was burning up the phone lines by morning. Rounding up an army.

"When it comes right down to it, all they gotta see is a whole bunch of men with guns. That ain't hard to arrange."

Papa called the field hands they'd hired to help them harvest their marijuana crop the last couple of years — many of them men who'd made off with the bed of their pickup full of marijuana a week ago. Altogether, maybe two dozen men. Then he called some Hannackers, cousins, nephews. Willie Ray called some Taggarts.

Nate made a simple request of all of them. "Come by my place between eleven o'clock and noon — and bring a rifle. Won't need but half an hour or so of your time and then you can go on about your day."

He'd commandeered the five loaves of pumpkin bread Sherry Lynn had made for the Saint Dominic bake sale on Saturday, and he promised strong coffee to go along with it. Sweetened the pot with a promise to host a cookout on Derby Day next year, a bring-your-whole-family, blow-out-the-stops whoop-de-do, with a cow roasting on a spit and a covered-dish social, complete with a bluegrass band, if he could convince Elmer, Joe Dan and Clarence to pull out their fiddles and Dobros and come make music.

Nate offered only a simple explanation for his request: "I need to put on a show of force for some Away-From-Here's been giving me a hard time." That was all they needed.

The prisoners had spent the night up against the back wall of the barn, with their hands bound behind them, their feet tied together, and tape over their mouths to keep them silent. Ace, Riley and Willie Ray had taken shifts guarding them. Nate had left the front bay door of the barn open about a foot. The view out that door from the back barn wall was all the reality the prisoners would be able to see. Figures, shapes, men a hundred feet away.

When the men Nate had summoned started showing up, they parked all along the lane leading to the house and in the driveway. And they couldn't miss seeing the bullet holes that riddled the front of the house and porch and the busted-out windows. That set their jaws. Nate ushered them through the kitchen for coffee and pumpkin bread then out through the back yard to the space in front of the barn that would be visible through the crack between the doors.

They'd brought shotguns, deer rifles, .22's, .30-06's and every other imaginable kind of firearm.

"You can hang out in groups, but I need each of you to get close enough to the barn at least once so they can get a better look at you and your guns. Don't want them to figure we're just parading the same half-dozen men back and forth in front of the barn door."

He told them the men inside the barn would be able to hear voices, but wouldn't be able to make out what they were saying. "Talk about whatever you like — the weather, the crops, who'll fall asleep in church Sunday — just no laughing." He needn't have worried about *that*. Once the men got a look at the bullet holes in the front of the house, any gregarious spirit they might have brought along drained away.

Riley knew that it was only respect for his grandfather's privacy that kept the men from peppering him with questions, and he was sure that rumors of unimaginable proportions were brewing within the knots of men as they stood together, rifles in the crook of their arms. It wasn't rocket science to figure out that the men in Nate Hannacker's barn were the ones who'd fired those rounds into his house. Men from Away-From-Here. Outsiders.

Riley was on "guard duty," inside the barn with the prisoners, watching their faces as they viewed his grandfather's dog-and-pony show. From their point of view — sitting or lying on their sides, hands and feet tied, mouths taped shut — it was an impressive sight. What they saw was a crowd of hillbillies. How many? Fifty? A hundred? No way to tell, but one thing was abundantly clear — every one of them was armed.

When the crowd was just about cleared out, it was

time for the dog-and-pony show Willie Ray'd come up with. A couple of years ago, Willie Ray'd purchased a set of walkie-talkies at an Army Surplus store. He'd been proud as punch of himself for getting them. Why, they'd be handy as a pocket on a shirt. Somebody in the house could use them to communicate with somebody on the tractor plowing. Or a lookout could warn hands working in a field. It'd all sounded pretty good, in fact, until they discovered the range of reception. Separate the two walkie-talkie units by more than 150 feet and all you could hear was static.

But they would do just fine today.

The tack room/office, with Drew's GI Joe World in the storage room beyond, was close enough to the tied-up prisoners that they could hear what was said there. Willie Ray and Ace went into the tack room through the door from outside and proceeded to have an argument. Willie Ray said they needed new walkie-talkie units because their ten-mile range wasn't reliable in the hills and hollows. Ace contended the ones they had were just fine. Nobody won the argument, and when Ace left, a disgruntled Willie Ray thumbed the "send" switch on one of the walkie-talkie units and spoke into it: "Command here, guard station roll call, sound off with your call signs."

There was a bleat of static and nothing else.

Willie Ray cursed, then repeated, "Sound off with your call signs!"

More static and then a raspy voice replied.

"Guard Station One, ten-four."

That had been Papa, who was standing on the

back porch with a group of half a dozen men who'd stopped for a second cup of coffee and whatever was left over of the pumpkin bread.

"Command here, One," Willie Ray replied. "Ten-four."

Papa handed the walkie-talkie to Ace.

"Guard Station Two, ten-four," Ace said in a deep voice and after Willie Ray acknowledged, he handed the walkie-talkie to the man standing beside him. That man thumbed the send switch and said, "Guard Station Three, ten-four."

After they'd passed the walkie-talkie all the way around once, they started over with Riley, who lowered his voice and said, "Guard Station Nine, ten-four."

Sometimes it took a while for Willie Ray to make contact, during which time he cursed the walkie-talkie. They stopped at twenty guard stations, figured beyond that was overkill.

The grand finale Nate had arranged even shocked Riley, who was still "standing guard" over the prisoners in the barn when the six-inch space between the two bay doors suddenly went dark. Then somebody grabbed both the doors and flung them open, walked in with the light behind him. A terrifying giant, who looked to be at least ten feet tall.

When he lumbered out of the glare and approached the prisoners, Riley sucked in a gasp.

It was Big-un McClusky.

~

UNTIL HE SAW Big-un's pickup truck pull into his driveway, Nate had been sure the big man wouldn't come. Nate had swallowed his pride only because he was desperate. The fate of the Cornbread Mafia and the safety of its members was riding on putting on a good show for the prisoners.

"It's like when me and you shot them statues," he'd said on the phone a couple of hours ago. "Intimidation. A warning. I need to send a message like that."

"What you want from me?"

"You walk into my barn, look at these fellas that's gonna be tied up there, turn around and walk out. Don't got to say or do nothing. Won't take five minutes."

The silence on the other end began to drag out toward uncomfortable. Nate was sorry he'd asked, wished he hadn't given a McClusky an excuse to snub a Hannacker, had his mouth open to take back the request—

"My boy Wade's getting married Saturday. Dotty's making me go to the barber today. Might be I can stop by your place on my way into town."

He hung up. No goodbye, just a click.

Nate went to Big-un's truck when he pulled to a stop. The man who got out — the suspension springs on his truck sighing in relief — was …

If Nate had been a director casting a movie, he'd have said this guy was over the top. At six-foot-six, he'd weighed three hundred pounds four years ago when the two of them had gone on a statue safari on Main Street in Brewster. Looked like he had put on another fifty pounds since. Smelled like maybe he hadn't taken a bath since then, either. His enormous belly swelled the front of his dirty overalls, his arms bulged out of his equally filthy tee shirt — muscle overlaid with fat. Black hair stuck out at odd angles from under the big straw hat he wore and his beard looked like it always had — a pelican's nest knocked out onto the pier by a hurricane.

"Big-un," was all Nate said by way of a greeting. It had been his experience that the big man was not particularly chatty. He cocked his head toward the back of the house. "Barn's back there."

Big-un said nothing at all, just stomped off in that direction. But Nate saw him take note of the bullet holes in the front walls, porch and door of the house. When he got to the barn doors, he flung them both open and went inside. Nate saw the look of astonishment and horror that flashed across Riley's face when Riley saw him, figured if the man's presence upset the prisoners even half as much, he'd accomplished what he set out to do.

Stopping in front of the four men tied up on the floor of the barn, Big-un spoke, his voice the sound of thunder. "These here the ones?"

Nate managed a strangled, "Yeah, it's them."

Big-un spit a huge squirt of tobacco juice on the floor beside the man on the end, the skinny one with full-sleeve tattoos.

"Kill 'em," he rumbled, turned and lumbered out. Nate could do nothing but follow along behind like the tail on a kite. Big-un walked back around the house to his truck, opened the door and crunched the tortured suspension system when he got back in. He hadn't been there five minutes.

"That oughta scare 'em," Nate said. "It scared *me*."

Big-un actually smiled — not with a mouth full of blackened teeth like the stumps in a forest after a fire. They were white and mostly straight. One of the McCluskys — Rosie, Nate thought — was a dentist.

He flicked a glance at the front of Nate's bullet-riddled house and said, "Figgered the 'kill 'em'd be a nice touch."

Nate nodded, choked back a "Thank you" because he knew Big-un didn't go in for that kind of thing.

He merely nodded. "Big-un."

"Nate," Big-un replied and did the same. Then he started his truck and drove away, leaving Nate to wonder how on earth the man's wife was going to get that behemoth cleaned up and presentable enough for a wedding.

Chapter Forty-One

NATE DIDN'T RAISE PIGS, but a neighbor, Rufus Gant, did. Even though he lived about four miles away, when the wind was just right … Gant was one of the people Nate had called this morning, but he hadn't asked him to come to the house packing a rifle.

"Why sure, Nate," Gant had said. "You got Away-From-Here visitors wanna see pigs, you're welcome to show 'em mine. I ain't gonna be home, but you know where to find them."

They'd done all they could on the first part of Nate's plan, the peacock part. Either the prisoners had bought it, thought they had an army, so well organized they'd set out guard stations with walkie-talkies. Or they hadn't bought it. What came next was the part about earning a reputation. Big-un had teed the ball up for that one. Nate would have to take it from there.

He outlined what he intended to do for the others after Big-un left. He could tell by the looks on their faces they were surprised, but Willie Ray'd started smiling before Nate even got to the end of the story.

"You ain't got to say nothing if you don't want to. But you're welcome to join in. I got it planned out in my head what I'm gonna say — if I don't forget half of it." He paused. "This here's all we got left. We gotta take our best shot."

Nate sent Riley into the house with a grocery sack to get the things he needed. Riley about filled the whole sack. The last thing was the hardest to find. Riley'd had to dig around in the attic, in the boxes behind the stored Christmas decorations to locate it.

Nate noticed that Ace went to his car and got something out of it, before he joined them to load up the prisoners. Willie Ray drove his pickup truck into the barn, and they hauled the prisoners upright one at a time and set them side by side in the truck bed, then threw a tarp over them. Ace went from one to the next, making sure the pieces of duct tape over their mouths was secure. The tall, skinny fellow was clean shaven, and the tape stuck down, but the bald guy with the black beard — the tape didn't stick real good and they'd had to wrap the tape around and around the back of his head. Poncho Villa's mustache had presented the same problem.

The men was rank — stunk of urine and feces. When they started loading them into the pickup, the prisoners had to believe the end was coming.

Ace and Riley rode in the back with the prisoners. Nate drove the Colombians' car, left about ten minutes before Willie Ray, taking the sack Riley'd filled with him. He was waiting when Willie Ray pulled his truck to a stop in front of Gant's pig pen. It held probably two dozen pigs and hogs in various sizes. Most lay in mud under a tin awning that extended out from a lean-to where there were three big troughs, each extending in a different direction to keep the animals as separate as possible during feeding time.

Nate stood beside the gate as the other three unloaded the prisoners and lined them up on their knees on the ground in front of him.

"You fellas is smart enough to know what's 'bout to happen. You heard the boss say 'kill 'em,' and he's the judge and jury around here." The short, fat guy was crying. Not making any sound, but his shoulders was shaking and tears ran down his face. Nate looked away.

"I understand you ain't farmers. You're city boys so you likely don't know a whole lot about livestock — probably think hogs and pigs is two different animals." He gestured to the hogs grunting inside the pen. "These here is hogs. The big one over there," he pointed to a beast that stood at least three feet tall at the shoulder, "probably weighs eight hundred pounds. Hogs get a bad rap, folks thinking they're filthy and all. Truth is, pigs wallow in the mud to keep cool. They ain't got sweat glands and they can't pant like a dog."

Nate turned and picked up an almost empty slop bucket hanging on a hook on a fence post. He climbed up a couple of rungs on the wooden fence and tossed the contents into the pen. Though there was little to eat — some watermelon rinds and rotted vegetables

— the pigs went into a feeding frenzy, grunting and squealing, pushing to get to the food. He let them go at it for a while, then hopped down off the fence.

"Another thing people don't know about hogs is what they eat. They's like goats — fruit, vegetables, rotted food, whole chickens. A good-sized hog can eat two pounds of raw meat in a minute. A hog will eat anything."

Riley interrupted. "Not *anything*." He pointed to the tall weeds growing beside the pen.

"Well, that's right," Nate said. "They ain't partial to shoes and boots. Don't like belt buckles much, neither."

There was stunned silence as realization dawned. Lying in the weeds were two old shoes and a work boot, and a belt with a big metal buckle only barely attached to the leather.

The prisoners reacted viscerally — cried out with voices muffled by the tape over their mouths, made sounds that had to be pleading. Nate ignored them and went on.

"Takes them awhile sometimes to get every last bit." He reached down and picked up a rock and chucked it at something lying beside the wallow in the pen. It was a human skull. A *plastic* skull, but you couldn't tell that after Nate smeared mud on it. Riley'd had to dig it out of the box of Halloween decorations in the attic.

The skinny Mexican used his shoulder on the tape on his face, ripping it free to dangle off one side of his mouth.

"You goinna to do that to us, jes?" he cried, his voice a strangled sob. "You gonna kill us and feed our bodies to the pigs!"

"No." Nate's voice was void of emotion. "When we bring folks here, we don't kill them and throw their bodies in the pigsty." He paused for effect. "At least that ain't the *order* of it."

He watched the sense of what he was saying soak in, waited until it had dawned on all of them before he continued.

"We shoot 'em — get 'em bloody — and *then* throw 'em in."

Willie Ray appeared to freak out.

"I ain't staying!" he cried. "I ain't watching them pigs eat live people ever again. I had nightmares for months."

He deserved an Oscar.

The prisoners became instantly hysterical. Two of them fell from their knees to the ground sobbing, wailing, crying "Moooo," which was "no" with taped-together lips. The bald, bearded guy just leaned his head back and made some kind of cry, garbled and muffled, a wail with words tangled in it, feral and desolate.

It chilled Nate's bones.

Ace suddenly pulled out a pistol that'd been stuck down in the waistband of his jeans in the back. It was a small gun, a .22, looked like a Smith & Wesson revolver, one that fired them .22 shorts — hollow-point rounds used on small animals like raccoons.

He pointed it at the sky, fired three quick rounds, and cried, "Quiet!"

The wailing men instantly silenced, their cries reduced to sniffling and snuffling.

"Nate ain't done talking," Ace spoke into the silence. "Shut up your caterwauling and listen to what he's got to say."

That pistol musta been what Ace went back to his car to get. Nate didn't have no idea he was gonna do a thing like that and wasn't real sure why he'd done it, but rolled with it like it'd been the plan all along.

"That there's the way we deal with them that crosses us," Nate continued, gesturing at the snorting, grunting hogs. "That's what Big-un meant when he said, 'kill 'em.' He meant we was to bring you here, cut you good, and let the pigs eat you while you's screaming."

He let that lie in the terror silence that had stolen the prisoners' voices.

Then he continued slowly. "But … I ain't gonna do what the boss said, and there'll be hell to pay if he ever finds out. See … the thing is, Big-un sometimes don't think things all the way through to the end. First bullet you fired into what b'longed to him, you was dead men in his eyes and that there was the beginning and the end of it.

"But me … I try to look out there into tomorrow. So I said to my man here," and he indicated Willie Ray, "I said, 'If you's to send out five men to do a job and they didn't never come back … what would you do?' And he said, 'I'd send out five more, or maybe ten.' And that there's the rub. I'm the foreman of this here operation. I'm the one's got to get the work done, running crews on fifty acres of pot." Nate almost choked when he said 'fifty acres," but he kept moving. "I flat-out ain't got time to fool with you people! I done lost dang near two days of work dealing with you idiots. If I's to look up two weeks from now and here come more of you ... that's harvest time!"

Only one of the four men, the bald, bearded one, was still on his knees and Nate walked up behind him, put his boot in the man's back and shoved, sent him sprawling face down in the dirt. The man rolled over and looked at Nate and when all the men were looking at him, Nate continued.

"So here's what I figured. I figured if I's to send you men back with a message, might be there wouldn't be no five more men next week. Might be you could tell 'em what's waiting for 'em here, maybe keep 'em from coming so I could get my work done."

He got down on one knee and looked down at the men sprawled on their backs in front of him.

"So this here's the message." He spoke quietly, soft so they had to listen intent to hear. "If you decide to come back, we'll know you're here soon's you cross the county line. Just like we done this time. Don't matter how many people you bring, none of their kin will ever see hide nor hair of 'em again. I'll have the fattest pigs in the county and a pile of shoes and belt buckles to donate to the Goodwill."

Nate shook his head. "Them fellas you seen today at my place — they was the hired help, some of it, not all. But what you need to know is … if you's to come against us, we'd put out the word and every farmer in this county would grab his shotgun and come running. How do you think your fellas would fare against a thousand men so hidden in the trees you won't even see them when they kill you?"

He stood then, looking down at them, and ground out the next words in a gravelly voice: "Know this. If you don't remember a single lesson we been trying to teach you, hold onto this truth. *We take care of our own.* Outsiders come against *one* of us, you come against *all* of us. And won't a one of you live to see another sunrise if you do."

Sometime during Nate's little sermon it had begun to dawn on the prisoners that they weren't going to die a horrible death, eaten alive by pigs. They probably thought the worst was over. Nate did, too, actually, but they was both wrong.

Without any warning, Ace stepped forward and started making his own speech. It wasn't near as long as Nate's.

"We ain't done yet. We got a going-away present for each of you, to make sure you don't never forget us or what happened here in Callison County."

He stepped to the nearest man, the short, fat one, and asked, "Knee or ankle? Pick." The man had no idea what he was talking about, so Ace said, "Fine, then. I'll pick for you. Knee."

And he put the barrel of the little .22 pistol to the man's kneecap and pulled the trigger.

The man shrieked and rolled away. Before Nate

could grab another breath, Ace had the pistol pointed at the bald man with a beard.

"He got knee," Ace said, indicating the first man. "So you get ankle."

He put the barrel of the pistol to the man's right ankle and pulled the trigger.

The third man was Poncho Villa and he knew what was coming, and was trying to scoot away. He had a crude bandage that Willie Ray had wound around his right hand where Nate had shot off two fingers. Ace grabbed his left hand and put the gun to it, pulled the trigger and shot off the little finger on that hand.

"Now they match," Ace said.

That left one man, the tall, skinny one with sleeves of tattoos. He sat frozen in terror.

Ace stuffed the pistol back into his pants and pulled out a knife. He grabbed a handful of the man's hair and yanked his head back and put the blade up to the man's cheek an inch below his eye.

Nate sucked in a breath. Surely Ace wasn't going to …

"Somebody's gotta drive back to Louisville. You got the long straw."

Then he pointed to Willie Ray, to the jagged scar on his face.

"You get one of those to remember us by." He jabbed the point of the blade down into a cow patty at his feet. "That's to make sure there's an infection." Then he sliced down the man's cheek from his eye to the corner of his mouth."

Nate knew this must be what a battlefield sounded like — men moaning and groaning, crying out in pain. Ace, Riley and Willie Ray had heard those sounds before.

"Let's get 'em in the car," Ace said. He was the only one who didn't appear to be in shock.

Knee and ankle were loaded in the back seat. Missing fingers and slashed face were in front. The fifth man had been stuffed in the trunk after he was shot dead last night.

"Key's in the ignition." Nate found himself telling the man behind the wheel. "You got fifteen minutes to get out of Callison County before we come after you and feed you to the pigs."

The man reached down with a hand covered in blood and started the engine, managed to turn the wheel and get the car on the road, and drove away.

Nate, Ace, Willie Ray and Riley stood beside the pigsty until the car was out of sight. Then Ace answered the unasked question, his face still turned toward where the car had disappeared. "Used a small gun, short round — maximum pain, minimum damage."

Then he turned to look at them.

"I didn't tell you about it because it had to be me. Just me. I done," he paused for a beat, "stuff like that before, but you boys is virgins. I didn't want you to bust your cherries."

Then he ground his teeth together. "What you done wasn't enough. Like I said, if we want a reputation, there's gotta be blood. We got to hurt 'em. What

I done," he took a breath and continued quietly, "that was for Drew. To keep him safe."

No one spoke, just stood in silence.

Nate knew he had to do it, that he was the one who had to tack words on what'd happened.

"They woulda killed ever last one of us if we hadn't got them first. They come here to *kill* us. We sent them home *alive.* Don't know about you fellas, but I ain't gonna get cut shaving in the morning — I'll be able to look myself in the eye in the mirror. I don't figure them guys for the kind who'd have wives and kids. But if they did, we didn't make no widows nor orphans today. I'll stand by that."

Chapter Forty-Two

BURCHEL MULLINS, Burch to the world, was not a typical used-car salesman. He was a small man with narrow shoulders and long, thin fingers that made Winona think of a tree frog. Always impeccably dressed, he wore coke-bottle-thick glasses — and even then, he squinted — and as he aged and lost his hair, he bore more and more resemblance to Mr. Magoo. Quiet and soft-spoken, polite to a fault, he'd show you a car, could tell you about every nut, bolt and screw used to build it, and if you wanted to buy it, he'd sell it to you. If you didn't, he was fine with that, too. He didn't dicker over prices, either. He offered his cars as cheap as he could and still stay in business, so there was no wiggle room.

Winona had always liked him, particularly liked the way he'd refused to allow her father's bluster to rattle him the day Pa had purchased the Grand Prix Pontiac that'd disappeared with him. It'd been Pa's gift to himself the last Christmas he was alive, and she'd been home from school so she'd tagged along. She had watched Pa try to bully Burch into lowering the price, enjoyed watching the little man stick to his guns. Most people crumbled under her father's bluster, particularly when he started raising his voice, and got little specks of white spittle all over you if you got too close.

She found Burch in the service area of the car dealership, with his sleeves rolled up, his head under the hood of a car. She was surprised he was into the grease-under-the-fingernails mechanical side of the business.

"How can I help you, Miss Winona?" he asked, wiping off his arms and hands with a towel. "You got a right fine car in that Maverick. You looking to trade it in so soon?"

"No, I just need some information. I'm wondering about the car my brother Shep was driving the night he died."

"Oh … well, I couldn't tell you much about it. I didn't sell it to him."

"I didn't think you did. I just figured if anybody in town could tell me about the car, it's you."

He smiled with small, perfect teeth and pushed his glasses back up onto his nose with the edge of his finger so's not to get grease on the lens.

"Well, it was a Ferrari 365 GT, five-speed. With a net horsepower of 315, it could go from zero to sixty in under seven seconds. And I'm sure your brother had one with lots of …"

"Bells and whistles?"

"Upgrades."

"Shep usually wasn't happy with the standard issue of anything. Tell me, was it a fast car?"

Burch's face spit with a wide smile.

"Do you think your brother would have wanted it, if it weren't?"

"Was it the fastest car in the county?"

"Well, I don't know every car—"

"Did you know anybody whose car was faster?"

"No, I can't say I did."

"Say a red sports car of some kind."

"Not that I know of. Why would you ask?"

"Oscar Hanks told me that the night Shep died, Shep was racing a red sports car on Hunter Lane."

Burch's eyebrows shot up.

"Racing with who?"

"Somebody driving a red sports car … and the red car was winning."

"I can't imagine who *that* could have been. Had to be somebody from Away-From-Here, some boy from Bardstown or Campbellsville."

"What kind of car would it have taken to beat Shep's Ferrari in a race?"

"Not many — the boys nowadays soup their cars up, put all kinda gadgets on 'em, I suppose some kind of souped-up car could run faster. The only car right off the assembly line I can think of that you wouldn't have to soup up to outrun Shep's Ferrari is a Corvette Stingray L88. But I don't know anybody around here who's got one of those. They're rare — they only built a couple hundred of them — and they cost more'n my house." He paused. "Would you like to see a picture of one?"

Burch had shown more interest in the conversation than Winona'd ever seen him display about anything. She supposed there was a special language car lovers spoke that the rest of humanity didn't, and if you spoke it, that whole world opened up for you.

"You have a picture?"

He smiled a conspiratorial smile.

"Do I have pictures of cars …?"

He led her to his office, where he'd sat across the desk from two generations of car buyers, trying to get just the right fit. Like old Mr. Pettis at the shoe store, who measured her foot with the metal thing that you stood on, with metal appendages that slid up and down it.

But Burch didn't stop in his office, continued through it and out a door into a small windowless room the size of a big walk-in closet it. When he flipped on the lights, the walls came alive with cars.

Cars, cars and more cars. The walls were literally wallpapered with car pictures, from the floor to the ceiling. There were framed pictures here and there, showing men with big trophies standing beside bright-colored race cars.

"I've been a NASCAR fan since I was a kid. Wanted to be a race car driver when I grew up." He gestured out to the car showroom. "I figured out quick that selling them was more my speed than driving them."

He walked across the room and pointed to the

picture of a sports car — it was a Stingray, candy-apple red.

"That right there might just be the most beautiful automobile ever manufactured," he said in awe. "I've never seen one, just pictures, but those lines and—"

She watched him catch himself. Always polite, he'd realized his listener wasn't nearly as interested in the vehicle as he was. She wondered for a moment if she could take that picture to Oscar Hanks and ask if it was the car he saw that night, but discarded the idea as soon as it formed. Oscar was an old man. It'd been a dark night three years ago. And the car was going so fast he might not have been able to tell what it was in broad daylight.

"You did know the heritage of NASCAR is bootleggers?"

"I did *not* know that."

"Oh, my yes. Particularly in Georgia. The first thing a bootlegger needed was a car fast enough to outrun the law. Automobiles with six-cylinder engines were the preferred choice, so much so that they earned the moniker 'Whiskey Six.' They modified those cars with secret compartments for liquor, put special shocks on them to carry heavy loads, and, of course, they modified the engines — blew everything off the road in the mountains. Government cars didn't have a chance. Bootleggers left them in the dust."

Sensing Winona's interest, Burch went on.

"The most famous of them was a fella named Lloyd Seay, kinda the father of NASCAR. There's a wonderful story about him … but I don't want to take up your time, you have other things—"

"I would love to hear the story."

He warmed so to the telling of the tale that Winona saw a side of Burch she would never have dreamed existed.

"Seems there was a police chief of a town north of Atlanta who took off after a black 1939 coupe that came roaring through the town square at noon. It was Lloyd Seay headed home to Dawsonville to pick up another load of moonshine to take back to Atlanta. Seay pulled over and when the officer approached the car, Seay stuck two five-dollar bills out the window.

"'Dammit, Lloyd, you know the fine for speedin' ain't but five dollars,' says the chief."

"'Yeah,' says Seay, 'but I'm likely to be runnin' from somebody comin' back, so I'm payin' in advance.'"

Winona laughed with Burch, as much at the joy he took in telling it as at the humor in the story.

"It was Seay who come up with the bootlegger's turn. At least he gets the credit for it."

"And that is?"

"Say it's night and you're traveling a hundred miles an hour down Georgia State Highway 9 toward Atlanta with fifty gallons of corn liquor sloshing around in the trunk and you spot the lights of a road-block flashing up ahead. What you gonna do?"

"Get arrested?"

"What Seay did was slow down to about fifty—"

"Slow *down* to fifty!"

"Then he'd take his foot off the gas and yank on the emergency brake, which locks the rear wheels—"

"At fifty miles an hour?"

Burch nodded.

"That fella could *drive*. As he locked the brakes, he'd spin the steering wheel and the car'd spin all the way around,180 degrees, and switch from fifty miles an hour forward to fifty miles an hour backward."

"Seriously?"

Burch grinned like a little kid.

"That's what they say. Then he'd release the emergency brake and jam the accelerator and the car'd stop sliding backwards and start going forward in the opposite direction."

"You believe that?"

Burch smiled.

"Well … it's a neat trick if you could pull it off, one of those stories that if it's not true it should be."

Winona was driving away from the car dealership, thinking about the red Corvette, when it occurred to her that a car "worth a fortune" would be the kind of car a thief would steal, right? And out past Hunter Lane where Shep was driving, was a chop shop — a place where *stolen* vehicles were reduced to salable parts, or modified so they'd be unidentifiable. Could it be that a Corvette Stingray had passed through that shop?

But who could have been driving it?

And why would the driver be out racing Shep at four o'clock in the morning?

Chapter Forty-Three

WHEN RILEY PICKED Sherry Lynn up at her mother's she gave him the silent treatment. He was sure she hadn't told her mother what had been going on last night, when she'd shown up with Drew in tow and said she needed to spend the night. The way her mother looked at Riley when she opened the door, it was clear Sherry Lynn had characterized her night-time visitation as "going home to Mama" after a married couple's fight.

Well, she'd had to tell them something, he supposed. Probably better that than the truth.

Sherry Lynn's father gave Riley an evil eye the whole time he was there waiting for Sherry Lynn to get hers and Drew's things gathered up. But he'd expected no less. He was grateful for the silent treatment from Sherry Lynn, too, though it was like having his neck on the slot, waiting for the guillotine to fall.

She'd told him on the phone that Drew'd been invited to a birthday party for a little boy in his nursery school class that afternoon. Sherry Lynn would surely unload on him as soon as their son was out of the car.

She looked awful. Her eyes were puffy, from lack of sleep and crying, and she had put on no makeup, so her face was washed out and sallow. He had noticed some time ago, and realized it was true across the board, when people got fat, their features … *went away.* Just went away. The pretty face of the high school cheerleader had been about planes and angles, and her face now had none. It was just soft and rounded, with jowls that hid what had been a pretty, slender neck.

She was wearing what she'd had on yesterday. He'd assumed she still had some clothing at her mother's, then realized that was a foolish assumption. Whatever clothing Sherry Lynn had left at her mother's wouldn't fit now. She'd been a size eight in high school. He didn't know her size now, suspected she'd passed by sizes some time ago and just wore all things marked "one size fits all."

On Drew's part, he was on the verge of a meltdown from the moment he saw his daddy. He was tired from getting to bed so late, and he did not wear grumpy well. He wanted to go see Pop Pop and burst into tears when Sherry Lynn reminded him he was going to the birthday party instead.

No! He wanted to see his Pop Pop … and why had Daddy made him and Mommy hide in the tobacco barn … and he didn't want to go see grandma last night and … It continued in a wailing meltdown until they arrived at the party. The sight of children playing happily outside had silenced his tantrum and he'd been smiling when he hopped out to join the fun.

They drove home in silence, but the heat of anger pulsing off Sherry Lynn was like standing too close to a potbellied stove.

Looked like that, too.

Stop that! He understood that how he thought about her affected how he treated her. And she deserved a good husband. She didn't know he'd been preparing to break up with her when the guard had suddenly been called to active duty, that he never in a million years would have married her if it weren't for Drew. Riley had thought he'd reconciled himself to spending the rest of his life with a woman he didn't love.

When the one he did was so achingly close.

He tried to slam the door on those thoughts but they got a foot past the jamb and wouldn't let him seal it. He would be seeing Jessie this afternoon. Willie Ray had told her a bit about the night's adventure, but she had, of course, wanted the whole blow-by-blow account. And knowing he would see Jessie in a few hours made spending time with Sherry Lynn until then immeasurably harder.

He drove the truck into the driveway in front of the house, turned off the key and sat beside her in silence. He watched her take in the damage, the bullet holes and broken windows. He planned to have those holes patched and the whole thing painted over by noon tomorrow, wished he could have spared her the sight of it but it was what it was.

"You want to talk about this now?"

She turned and fixed him with a look of such startling rage that if he'd been standing up he'd have taken a step back.

"Tell me what happened," she said, grinding the words out between clenched teeth. "All of it. No sugar-coating. I have a right to know what's happening in my own home!"

She spit the words at him like they burned her mouth, and she was right. She did have a right to know what had happened last night that sent her running off with their four-year-old child to cower in a tobacco barn listening to gunfire.

So he told her. Short, simple sentences. All of it. Started with the phone call and ended with standing with the others in front of Rufus Gant's pigsty watching the Colombians drive away.

Her eyes grew huge, her breathing ragged. Tears ran down her cheeks but she didn't cry, just jabbed at them with a tissue she had wadded up in her fist. He watched her clench and unclench her jaw. He didn't pull any punches, though, gave her the facts just as they'd happened.

When he talked about the Colombians firing their machine guns at the house, she whispered, "I heard the gunshots. I wondered if … you were dead."

And it hit him hard then that Sherry Lynn had suffered greatly from what had gone on, that she was entitled to all the anger and hurt she was feeling. When he'd finished the tale, he told her so.

"You have every right to be furious. It was horrible for you and for Drew and I never would have put either one of you in such a position if I'd ever imagined … I never meant for anything like that to happen."

"It did happen." She spoke softly.

"It won't ever happen again."

"And you know that how?"

"I know." And he did. He felt an unreasoning certainty in his gut that they were safe now.

"I want you out of the marijuana business."

She said it like she really believed all she had to do was snap her fingers and he'd give it all up.

"Sherry Lynn …" He stopped. He felt all his arguments formulating, backing up in his head, all the reasons why.

But he didn't say it.

What he did say was, "If you want me to quit, I will quit. We will stay here, living with Papa, save up for a place of our own someday." He turned to face her square on. She was staring ahead, but eventually his silence forced her to turn and look at him. "I mean it, Sherry Lynn. It's up to you. You decide."

She said nothing, didn't make eye contact, just stared.

"The marijuana business is paying for our new house. It pays for all the new clothes you buy." Had to keep buying since the size constantly changed. "It pays for the furniture we're going to put into the house, the drapes and appliances, carpet and tile. And it will pay for the new cars we will buy at the end of harvest this year. Whatever kind of car you want, you can have. And I was thinking we ought to just go ahead now and build a swimming pool in the back yard, not an above-ground pool, a real one, a big one so you can invite your friends over and Drew can have pool parties—"

"Money!" She spit out the word like it tasted bad in her mouth. "That's all you care about. It's more important to you than your wife and child."

"I'm not trying to convince you of anything. I'm saying this because you need to give full consideration to what you're giving up. What happens next is *your* choice, not mine … but whatever you decide, *it's from now on*. I will not have this conversation over and over and over again. If you want me out, I'm out. Decide now." He thought about what his grandfather had said about their altercation with the drug dealers. "It has to be one and done."

Emotions washed over her face he couldn't begin to fathom. He realized he didn't know her anymore. The girl he'd dated, the one he'd intended to break up with as soon as the war was over … didn't exist. The boy he'd been when he left was gone, too.

This new person, encased in what might well be a suit of armor she'd built around herself for protection, was a stranger. He could get to know her, but it would take an effort. He would have to try. And sad as it was to say, he just flat-out didn't have the energy.

"Fine, then. Stay in. But—"

"No buts. From now on, whatever is is and we just have to make a way through it."

She didn't argue, lifted eyes he'd once believed were the most beautiful eyes in the world and locked her gaze on his. Wordless communication passed between them. It was like some kind of gear had shifted. Like maybe the two of them had struck an unspoken bargain. He would make lots of money for her to spend — and that would be enough.

She nodded her head slowly.

He did the same.

Then she got out of the truck wordlessly, crossed the yard and went into the house. She never looked back.

Chapter Forty-Four

DREW HANNACKER LOOKED up at his mother with those almost-purple eyes that were the same color as her own and asked, "Why are you crying, Mommy?"

Sherry Lynn heard that question a lot from the little boy, because he'd walked in on her sobbing more times than she could remember. At least this time she had a reasonable explanation.

"It's a wedding. Lots of women cry at weddings." She gestured with her chin toward her best friend Gloria, sitting on the other side of the aisle on the end, tears ruining her makeup as they ran down her cheeks. "See?"

And they hadn't even played "Here comes the bride" yet. Gloria always tuned up the instant she heard it and bawled her way through every wedding Sherry Lynn had ever attended with her. And there were tons of those. Weren't very many weekends in the spring and summer when there wasn't at least one big wedding somewhere in the county, and often more than that.

She was glad she wasn't sitting with Gloria now because Jeanie, the girl Wade McClusky was marrying, had been the maid of honor at Gloria's wedding two years ago. Sherry Lynn had been the matron of honor. Gloria was pregnant now so her emotions were all over the place.

"Why?"

"Shhhhh. We're in church. You're not supposed to talk in church, remember."

"Do dey cry 'cause they're sad?" He whispered this time.

"Yeah, they're sad. Now hush."

"Why are they sad?"

She shouldn't have brought Drew. Big mistake. But Nate, Riley and Willie Ray were working on the house this afternoon, patching the … *bullet holes* — she shuddered — putting new glass in the windows and repainting. Drew would get in the way.

She reached into her purse and brought out Drew's GI Joe doll. She'd been furious with Nate for buying it for Drew — didn't want to glorify war in the child's mind. There'd been a big row over it … and she'd *lost*, naturally. After that, the doll sort of appeared now and then, and then disappeared again. She'd found it this morning on the floor in the playroom and stuck it into her purse.

"Here, play with this and be quiet."

She'd sat down in the back row at the end of the pew so she could take Drew out if he started acting up and she figured she wasn't likely to make it through the "I-do's."

He stood up on the seat and turned around like everyone else looking at the doorway through which the wedding party, bridesmaids, groomsmen and bride would enter any minute.

"You can't say hi," she told him quietly. "Remember, we talked about that."

A figure appeared in the aisle beside where he stood in the pew.

"Can I scoot in here?"

It was Sherry Lynn's cousin Winona, out of breath and sweaty. Sherry Lynn moved over and dragged Drew out of the way so Winona could sit down, though that jammed Sherry Lynn up against the Thompsons, who were seated on the other side of her.

"Flat tire," Winona whispered, and sat back in the pew, wiping the sweat off her brow with the back of her hand.

Drew was dancing his doll around and he bounced it onto her shoulder. Winona gave a tight-lipped smile and the kind of fish-eye people who didn't have kids always give to parents trying to control theirs, like you ought to be able to take out their batteries or something.

"Don't do that," Sherry Lynn whispered and took the doll away. Drew's face melted downward, a sure sign he was about have a fit. Sherry Lynn prepared to get up and slip out into the vestibule before he could make a scene.

"It's okay, I don't mind," Winona said quietly. Clearly, she did mind, but she was being polite.

"I got one of dose!" Drew said to Winona suddenly and pointed to the necklace she was wearing with a pendant on a chain so long it hung down almost into her cleavage. Standing on the seat beside her, he could see it clearly.

"One of these?"

Winona held it out where he could look at it.

"Uh huh. Wanna see?"

He began to dig around in his pocket. Sherry Lynn didn't know he had brought it with him. She'd forgotten all about it. Drew pulled his hand out of his pocket and held the pendant out to Winona on his palm.

Suddenly, the organ began to drum out some kind of processional. Winona didn't know the name of it, but it signaled the imminent approach of the parade of bridesmaids and groomsmen. Sherry Lynn leaned around Winona so she could get a clear view of the six bridesmaids, in matching pale pink gowns, march in with the groomsmen. Seated on the groom's side of the church, Sherry Lynn had watched in astonished wonder earlier as Big-un McClusky, Wade's father, lumbered down the aisle with his wife, Dorothy, Aunt Dotty, on his arm. Big-un was wearing a suit and tie! He'd gotten a very recent haircut, too — obvious because of the white line on his neck above his collar, and his beard had been trimmed, still hung halfway down his chest, but he no longer appeared to be looking out at the world through a bird's nest.

Down front, Wade and the best man, his brother Jackson, had entered the sanctuary and were looking up the aisle.

When the last of the bridesmaids had filed past, the music changed. The first notes of "Here comes the bride," issued from the organ and there was a rumble in the sanctuary as the members of the congregation got to their feet and turned toward the back entryway where Jeanie stood resplendent in a white dress. It was gorgeous, must have cost a fortune, had little sequins shimmering in the skirt and tiny white pearls covered the bodice. She held a bouquet of pink and white roses. Jeanie was an average-looking girl, but it really was true that there are no ugly brides because she looked movie-star gorgeous now. Her father, whose arm she held, was fighting tears. The tenderness in his face touched Sherry Lynn — she'd never see that look on her own father's face as he walked her down the aisle — and her own eyes filled with tears at the thought.

Jeanie moved majestically along, trailing a train that went on and on and on! Must have been fifteen feet long. Marian and Melissa, Wade's twin sisters, carried the end of the train. At eight, they were a little old for that task, but their cookie-cutter resemblance — the exact same face on two little girls — made a lovely impression.

When the last of the bridesmaids had filed past and took up positions beside the bride, the priest asked, "Who gives this woman in marriage?" and everybody sucked in a little breath when Jeanie's father replied "*I* do" instead of "*we* do" since her mother had recently died.

Then the congregation sat down, and that's when Sherry Lynn noticed that Drew was playing with a tiny metal pony, the fob off the end of a keychain.

He held it out to her and whispered.

"She *traded* me!"

Sherry Lynn looked at Winona. Her face was a mask totally devoid of emotion. She stared forward, but it didn't appear that she was looking at anything at all, just staring.

Drew made it another five minutes or so before he became unmanageable and Sherry Lynn had to take him out. Winona had stepped out into the aisle to let them pass and when Sherry Lynn got to the vestibule she saw that Winona had followed them.

As soon as they were out of earshot of the congregation, Winona asked, "Where did Drew get this?" and she held out the medallion.

"We swapped," Drew said, and held up the keychain fob.

"Maybe *that's* where," Sherry Lynn said.

"Huh?"

"He showed up with it one day and he's just gotten into trading, quite the little bargainer. 'I'll give you this if you give me that.'" Sherry Lynn nodded toward the metal pony. "Drew could have swapped one of his plastic soldiers for the medallion with some other child."

"Who? Did he say what other child?"

"No, he just said it was 'a lost thing that gotted found.'"

"If he *found* it, where? At church? Or nursery school maybe? At somebody's house?"

This was an odd conversation. Sherry Lynn felt like she was being cross-examined, but that might be an occupational hazard for attorneys.

"He'd been playing in the back yard, around the barn and with his blocks in the playroom. I was making a cake in the kitchen and he came walking in with it, said it was 'the stuck thing.'"

"Stuck thing?"

"Stuck between some boards so you couldn't poke a straw through."

"That's all he said? That it was stuck?" Sherry Lynn nodded and shrugged.

"I showed it to Father Abernathy. The print is so worn on the front it's hard to read. He said it was a Saint Marie Magdalen of Postal medal. You can make out the letters on the back, P for Postal — the father said that was somewhere in France — and then M.M. under it."

Sherry Lynn pointed to the medallion at the end of the necklace around Winona's neck, which was far enough down in her considerable cleavage that Sherry Lynn couldn't get as good a look at it as Drew had gotten up close.

"Is that what yours is, a Marie Magdalen medal?"

Winona looked totally rattled, like she didn't know, or didn't want to answer the question.

"No," she said, but didn't pull the medal out so Sherry Lynn could see it. "It's … Saint … Vincent de Paul. You know, just a plain old Saint Vincent de Paul medal."

Sherry Lynn had never met a soul who wore a Saint Vincent de Paul medal.

Winona closed her hand over the medallion in her palm.

"You don't mind if I keep this, do you?" Before Sherry Lynn could answer one way or the other, Winona pointed to Drew. "He likes the pony better anyway, don't you, Drew?"

He looked up long enough to nod his head and say, "We traded," then went back to galloping the small horse across the tiles.

"Well, sure …" This was decidedly weird. "Why do you want it?"

"Because …" It seemed to Sherry Lynn that Winona didn't have a "because" and was scratching around in her head trying to come up with one. "Marie Magdalen is the patron saint of Christian schools."

How in the world would she happen to know a thing like that when Father Abernathy didn't even know? And why would she care?

"I went to Saint Augustine, you know, in elementary school."

So did Sherry Lynn and everybody she knew, but that hadn't made all of them feel warm and fuzzy about the patron saint of Christian schools.

Then Winona said, "Good seeing you. I need to go."

But she didn't go back into the wedding! She went down the wide front steps of the church and out into the parking lot to her car.

What was *that* all about?

Chapter Forty-Five

UNTIL TWO MINUTES AGO, Jackson McClusky's chief concern had been getting back home before he ripped out the seams in the severely too-tight tuxedo he'd worn all day for his younger brother Wade's wedding. His mother had rented the smallest size she could get, which would have been too big for Jackson before he went to prison. Now, with broad shoulders and muscular arms, he could barely get the coat on, couldn't button it at all, and had spent the whole day trying not to move for fear the fabric would tear.

It'd been worth spending the day uncomfortable, though, he figured. Jackson had been sincerely touched when Wade asked him to be best man. Never woulda happened before Jackson went to prison, but he'd come home a different man, and working with his brother doing chores for Pa the last few months, the two had gotten close for the first time in their lives.

Jackson had stopped at the Buy-Low Grocery Store on his way home to pick up a six-pack, got in the long checkout line, and that's when it'd happened. Though his whole world was tumbling down around him, he didn't show a thing on his face, just inched closer to Phyllis Carter so he could be sure he was hearing her right.

Phyllis Carter and her husband Earl owned and operated the Sunnyview Motel on the edge of town, a shoebox-shaped building with eight rooms facing the parking lot on each side. Jackson hadn't never seen more than two or three cars parked there — either traveling salesmen or couples from some other county shacking up for the night. Wasn't like Callison County, Kentucky, was a tour bus destination.

Phyllis had pink sponge curlers in her bottle-blond hair, with a blue-and-white checked scarf tied around them. The house dress she was wearing had a big, ugly flower pattern, like upholstery fabric. Standing next to Edna McGuire, in her own flower-design dress, the two looked like a couch and matching loveseat.

"It's the most amazing thing" Phyllis said to Edna. "I wouldn't never have believed it would happen — but Jessie Monaghan says her Davie is trying to talk."

"Seriously?" Edna was a grumpy old lady with gray hair in a bun who lived alone in a big house in Bear Claw. Edna'd had sixteen children total, with three different husbands, but refused to move in with any of her kids, just complained nonstop that the whole lot of them had abandoned her. Jackson figured she musta had seventy or eighty grandchildren she likely wouldn't recognize without name tags.

"Absolutely," Phyllis replied. "That's what Jessie said."

"I was over at the Monaghans the other day to talk to Ruth." Erlene Phelps was in line in front of Phyllis and turned to join the conversation. "You seen her lately?"

"I stopped by after church a couple of Sundays ago," Edna said.

"Ruth got down thin as a rail when her and Jessie was trying to look after Davie all by their-selves, without no hired help," Erlene said. She'd recently retired from the post office after working there for fifteen years with the postmistress, Selma Witherspoon. Erlene's high, squeaky voice was worse than fingernails on a blackboard. Folks put off going to get stamps 'cause they didn't want to hear it. "I got real worried 'bout her. And then she had that stroke and—"

"Seemed like after that her health got better, didn't it," Phyllis said.

"It was probably getting out from under all that stress is what done it," Edna said.

"Guess they's something to be said for losing your mind," Erlene said.

Jackson saw Phyllis flinch and Erlene knew she'd stepped in it, started back-pedaling.

"Well, you gotta admit it don't wear on you if you don't know how bad things are."

"I mentioned Davie to her once a couple of months ago and she asked me who Davie was," Phyllis said. "Can you b'lieve that?"

"She's right well acquainted with them folks she thinks is 'bout to get married, though," Edna said.

"It's a *royal* wedding," Erlene said.

"Harriet Porter works days now, but she usta look after Ruth and Davie at night and she told me if Ruth wakes up, she babbles for hours 'bout that imaginary wedding."

Jackson was grinding his teeth. Erlene had had a grocery basket full of groceries, stacked up high as she could, and a handful of coupons to go with each one, but she was just about checked out. When she left, the conversation would likely end.

He didn't want to intrude, but he had to know.

"Excuse me, Mrs. Carter," he said. "I couldn't help overhearing you ladies talking about the Monaghans. I was in the guard with Davie. How's he doing?"

Phyllis knew who Jackson was, he thought. Edna didn't — well, knew he was one of the McCluskys but not which one. The way Erlene was looking at him, she knew who he was and didn't like it, maybe knew he was that oldest McClusky boy who had been in prison.

"My but aren't you all dressed up," Phyllis said, eyeing his tux.

"My brother Wade got married today. Now, about the Monaghans …?"

"Oh, they both doing fine, just fine," she said.

"You was saying Davie has started to talk?"

"That's what Jessie told me last time I was there."

"Talk how? About what? Can he like … carry on a conversation, something like that?"

"Oh, I couldn't tell you that. I didn't talk to Davie, just to Jessie."

"And you got to remember, sometimes Jessie … sees things through rose-colored glasses, if you know what I mean."

Erlene hadn't wanted to speak to Jackson, but she couldn't stand to let Phyllis take over the whole tale. Gossip was only entertaining if you's the one telling it.

"Rose-colored glasses?" he feigned ignorance.

"Oh, you know. I think she sees what she wants to see sometimes. Maybe believes he's doing better than he really is."

"So maybe he really can't talk, then?"

"Oh, he can talk alright," Phyllis said, elbowing her way back into the limelight. "That much is sure. Ain't just Jessie saying it, neither. Thelma Riddle stays with them some, and she told me that on New Year's Day Davie started to hollering and carryin' on. Liked to scared Jessie to death."

"Hollerin' about what?"

Phyllis shrugged. "Couldn't tell ya, but he musta been right upset about somethin'. He calls out for his mama sometimes, too."

"And somebody named Anna." Edna put in, "but Jessie said he don't know nobody by that name."

"Maybe he's calling somebody else, then," Erlene said. "Like … Jana or Hannah. Annie, maybe."

"Or Andy," Phyllis said.

Jackson stopped breathing. Davie was calling for Andy.

"Well … I surely would like to pay Davie a visit, now that he's getting better and all. You saying there's somebody stays with him nights as well as days?"

"There usta be, but not no more. In the beginning, he wasn't never left alone. And now Jessie can afford to *hire* folks to help her care for him …" Phyllis cast knowing sideways glances at the other two women.

"Put that addition on the front of the house … musta cost—" Edna picked up the ball and ran with it.

"A whole boatload of money," Erlene finished for her.

"Musta had a real good … *tobacco crop*," Phyllis said, lowering her voice slightly.

"Or some *other* crop," Erlene said, and wasn't no way to keep that squeaky voice of hers from carrying all over the store. "I seen she had a new pickup truck the other day. Not nothing fancy, but not that old one of Ruth's neither."

Erlene set the last of her bags into the basket to roll it away so the checker could start on what Phyllis had been setting on the conveyor belt behind that little separating bar while she talked.

"I'd like to see Jessie, too," Jackson asked before the conversation could break apart. "Any of you ladies know when she might be home?"

"During the day, I reckon you can catch her out on the farm somewheres," Erlene said, then turned and began to push her cart toward the door.

"You know Jessie sat up in a chair beside him

every night for going on three years!" Phyllis leaned around Edna to tell Jackson.

"Not no more," Edna countered. "He sleeps by his self — oh, it ain't like he's all alone or nothing like that. Jessie's right there in the house."

"I s'pose he could call her if he's to need something," Phyllis said. "Must feel real good that he's finally starting to communicate again."

Jackson carried the six-pack of beer he'd purchased back to his truck, got in carefully so he wouldn't tear his coat, and then sat there, fuming.

Davie was talking. Well, wasn't that just great! Jackson banged his fist on the steering wheel. The last he had heard, Davie was a vegetable or near about. 'Parently, all that'd changed.

So if David Monaghan was talking, what was he talking *about*? What was he so upset about that he was *hollering* in the middle of the night? What was he telling Jessie?

Jackson was certain Riley had seen him that day, leveling the RPG at the bunker doorway. He was certain Andy *hadn't* seen him. His back had been turned. But Davie? He might have seen, he might not. Jackson didn't know.

He did know it probably wasn't a good idea to let it ride and just hope. Shoot, wouldn't be hard at all to silence Davie! Him lying there in the bed helpless and all, put a pillow over his face and smother him. Wouldn't even look like murder. They'd just come in the next morning and see he'd stopped breathing sometime during the night, and wasn't that really the best thing in the end — they'd think that, even if they didn't say it. Him not even being Davie anymore, it was better for him just to die and let Jessie go on with her life.

Why, if Jackson put an end to Davie, he'd be doing his poor trapped wife a favor.

He smiled at that, but then the smile drained off his face. He could end Davie easy … except for the dog!

Jackson had seen Jessie in town with the beast now and then, a great big black thing looked like it could rip your leg off. Jackson had always been afraid of dogs.

He shook his head. Yeah, it'd be a good idea to take Davie out — easy to do, too — but that big ole dog would rip Jackson apart if he tried.

Chapter Forty-Six

WINONA'S HANDS had started to tremble as soon as she took the pendant from the little boy and got a look at it. Gratefully, she got enough grip on herself not to shake and babble when she talked to that idiot cousin of hers, Sherry Lynn Hannacker.

Hannacker. Hard to imagine a McClusky'd do a thing like that, marry into the family of the enemy. And *Nate* Hannacker's grandson! A wave of revulsion washed over her. But it was 1973, after all, and the whole idea of a feud sounded preposterous. Even as she said the words, loathing made her cringe, actually cringe. The concept might be dated, but the emotions were as strong now as—

Stop it.

Winona was sitting in her car in the Saint Augustine Church parking lot, clutching in her fist the pendant a little boy had gotten "out of a crack." Her fingers were curled around it so tightly she could feel her fingernails digging four half-moon holes into the palm of her hand. Her mind was bouncing off one thing and colliding with another, thoughts flying around like balls in a pinball machine. She hadn't been prepared emotionally to have her whole world turned wrong side out over the space of a few minutes of casual conversation.

She'd come to her cousin Wade's wedding because she was trying to fit into the community, re-engage with her big extended family again. Even though that wasn't the main reason she'd come back, she did have to make a life for herself here. The main reason, of course, had been the preposterous idea that if she did, she could find her father. At least find out what'd happened to him. Ever since she got here, she'd been chasing that elusive butterfly, just outside her grasp. She'd traipsed hither and yon, from one relative to another, from the roadside where her brother had died to the car dealership where he hadn't purchased the car he had died in.

She'd slowly been putting a puzzle together, piece by piece. Then Bam! A piece she hadn't even known existed appeared and everything else fit into it. The whole mystery had opened up, the petals of a flower in sunlight, and inside lay a silver pendant.

It was a "lost thing that gotted found," Drew Hannacker'd said.

His idiot mother didn't know where he'd found it, but the kid was what, three, four years old? It wasn't like he had some kind of life of his own, went out after nursery school to have a little milk with the boys. He had obviously found the pendant at home because he hadn't been anywhere else!

Unless maybe some other kid found it and now was the proud owner of a plastic toy soldier instead.

Winona had glanced at the pendant when she first saw it and the sight had so totally knocked the wind out of her she had not been able to force herself to look at it again. She couldn't seem to now, either, just held it clutched tight in her fist.

Reaching down, she dragged out her own pendant, the *matching* one. It hung from a beautiful thin chain with alternating silver and gold links.

Pa had given all the kids saint medals the Christmas when her youngest sister, Nora, was two years old. They were all the same, just different saints. Shep's had been a Saint Anthony's medal. Figured. Her father would entrust the care of his favorite child to no less than Saint Anthony, the patron saint of miracles. Jody's had been a St. Christopher's medal. Hers was Saint Vincent de Paul, the patron saint of kindness. Must have figured that homely girls should at least be nice … right? One of the nuns who taught her father's first grade class had given to every child a medal of Saint Marie Magdalen of Postal — the patron saint of Christian schools. He was probably the only grownup who'd kept up with his.

Winona turned the silver medallion over in her trembling fingers and looked on the back. Engraved there was a large P at the top, and beneath it MM. Sherry Lynn had thought the letters stood for Postel,

Marie Magdalen. They stood for Parker Michael McClusky.

She looked at the back of her own medallion. Engraved there in the same style was a W at the top and GM below it. Winona Gail McClusky.

She couldn't seem to get her mind to stop spinning! Around and around in circles it went, going faster and faster until she feared the friction might set her hair on fire.

Drew Hannacker had *somehow* come into possession of the medallion her father had been wearing when he disappeared. Well, she supposed he was wearing it that day, he wore it every other day. But she would ask Mama, make sure it wasn't in some jewelry box somewhere.

She didn't believe that, though. She believed Pa'd had it on when he left the house in a rage the day he disappeared, threatening to kill whoever it was who'd killed Shep.

Did that mean he thought Nate Hannacker had done it? Had killed Shep? What for?

How would Nate Hannacker even know Shep, other than he was the kid who drove around town in the fast car? What dealings could the two of them have possibly had with each other?

If her mind would only stop spinning, maybe she could figure it out. She shook her head fiercely, looked around for somewhere … finally settled on the now clean and empty cigarette ashtray in the car dashboard, and laid the pendant carefully in it. She flipped the lid closed, turned on the ignition, and drove slowly home, trying to make some sense of it all.

Her father had believed Shep's wreck hadn't been accidental, that somebody'd murdered him.

He had left the house on a mission to make that person pay for the crime.

So did he find the person? Was the person Nate Hannacker? Did he find Nate Hannacker and Nate killed him?

All of that sounded so totally preposterous she couldn't make herself take it seriously.

When she got to the corner of Proctor Knott and Main streets, she didn't turn north toward her new rental house. She turned south toward Mama's house. She'd seen Mama at the wedding, seated up in one of the front pews. So she wouldn't be home for a while, which suited Winona fine. She wanted to talk privately to Jody.

She found him snoring loudly in the recliner in front of the television set where the re-run of some basketball game was on the screen. The floor around the recliner was littered with empty beer cans. She reached down and shook his shoulder.

"Jody, wake up, I need to talk to you."

His head lolled on his shoulders, but he opened one eye and appeared to see her.

"Leave me alone. Takin' a nap."

"You're not napping, you're drunk. It's not even dark yet. You need to sober up because I want to talk to you."

"Go away."

Winona went into the kitchen and got a glass, ran cold water into it out of the tap, and returned to the living room. She'd intended to splash it into his face, but that was a little harsh, so she just held it above his head and let a small stream of water drip onto the top of his head. He didn't notice at first, but when it began to run down his neck into the collar of his tee shirt, he squirmed away. His squirming jostled her hand and she accidentally spilled the rest of the water, not in his face, but on his chest. It was still enough to send him scrambling, batting at her and the glass, cursing and squalling.

"What'd you do a thing like that for? Wasn't for this broke leg, I'd be up out of this chair and kicking your—"

"You're too drunk to fight anybody, but I'll fix that. I'll get you sober so you can beat the crap out of me."

She went into the kitchen and made a pot of strong coffee and returned with a steaming cup so black and thick you could trot a mouse across the surface. While she was gone, he'd removed his wet tee shirt, reached over and dragged the afghan off the back of the couch and covered himself with it and was already back asleep.

"Jody!" she yelled. He sat up and the motion released the footrest where his leg was lying and dropped both feet painfully on the floor. He let out a yowl, fixed her with a murderous glare and opened his mouth to eviscerate her with profanity.

"I think I know what happened to Pa, but I need to know something first."

Understanding lagged behind her words. "I don't care what you … what did you just say?"

He fired an angry glance that meant to challenge, tell her this was nothing to joke about, but the look on her face told him she was serious.

She held out her hand to him and when he offered his palm, she dropped the medallion into it. He sucked in a gasp. His eyes shot from the medallion to her and back to the medallion.

"Is this what I think it—?"

"Look at the back. Pa's initials are on it, just like on mine and yours." She held out her own medallion on a chain around her neck.

"What I need to know is — was Pa wearing this when he left the house that day?"

"He musta been. He wore it everywhere."

"Did you see it on him?"

"I don't know … I wouldn't have noticed it if I did. But I do know it ain't around here nowhere."

"How do you know that?"

"About a year ago, Ma had a little too much wine one night and decided to give me a bunch of Pa's stuff. She dragged me into her bedroom, half-bawling, saying I was 'the only son left,' that I'd 'carry on the family name,' like I'm the lone surviving McClusky in the world. So she gave me some monogrammed cufflinks and tie pins that was in a jewelry box — like I wear shirts that use cufflinks and tie pins. If his medallion had been in that box, she'd have given me that, too."

Winona stood very still, then said quietly, "I know

who killed Pa."

"*Killed* him? What are you sayin' — Pa's dead? How do you know that?"

"What … you think he's still alive? Out there somewhere? Forgot the way home, maybe? Stopped off to have a four-year beer with a friend? If he were alive, he'd have come home. No use pretending otherwise."

Jody didn't argue.

"Where did you get this?"

"At church. I sat down beside Sherry Lynn Hannacker and her little boy had it, said it was a 'lost thing' that'd been found."

"Found where?"

"Sherry Lynn didn't know exactly where, said he might even have gotten it from another child. She said he'd called it the 'stuck thing' and told her it was in a crack. The kid's four years old, probably doesn't get out much, so if he's the one who found it, the safe money's on he found it *at home*."

"How'd you get it?"

"I traded him Secretariat."

The Big Red horse had cracked the two-minute mile in the Kentucky Derby in May, and she'd gotten a miniature as a souvenir. "Off my keychain." She knew she needed to bring Jody along with her slowly, but the minutiae were annoying. "Look, none of that matters. What matters is that Pa was wearing this when he left the house and nobody's seen him since. And four years later, it winds up in the hands of a kid whose last name is Hannacker."

Chapter Forty-Seven

WINONA SAT with her head in her hands, the throbbing like the tolling of a gong on some high Himalayan mountain.

Bong. Bong. Bong.

Whatever had possessed her to get drunk last night?

Correction. She had not gotten drunk. But she had consumed a considerable amount of alcohol and that wasn't like her. She figured Jody was an alcoholic, and most assuredly Shep had been. And Mama?

You're not an alcoholic if all you drink is wine.

Riiiiight.

With that much family history, it'd seemed prudent to steer clear of booze.

She had come home from talking to Jody, and from her brief conversation with Mama, more confused than she'd been when she went there.

Her emotions were stirring the pot, fueling the pounding ache in her head. Seeing Pa's medallion had hit her like a wrecking ball. Love and longing and grief … and rage. Trying to solve the mystery of what'd happened to Pa had been winding a spring inside her tighter and tighter.

The medallion had tightened the final turn on that spring — it was ready to blow.

Booooong.

She made the sound aloud, then grimaced at the renewed pain it stabbed into her skull.

She had come home to her house from Mama's, and plopped down on her bed, telling herself she would get up and get ready for bed later, just wanted to take a little nap.

She had awakened at dawn, when the first shaft of sunlight slid under the blinds and right into her left eye. Her mouth felt like a week's worth of bread mold was growing inside, her eyes felt like a truckload of gravel had been dumped into them, and she smelled like a goat.

A thorough teeth scrubbing, a shower, and several cups of black coffee had solved her physical problems … well, except for the gong-bonging headache, but she had earned that.

Rising carefully, she took her fourth cup of coffee out onto the deck and sat down in the Adirondack chair, remembering too late that sitting there involved a considerable commitment because getting up out of the chair might require a winch.

She wished she had some pastoral view to gaze out into as the sun lifted above the knobs. She didn't. Just her neighbors' backyard gym sets, pools and sandboxes, but at least it was early Sunday morning so nobody was outside yet.

Sequential thinking.

In the final analysis, that's all the study of law was.

To get her client off, she had to figure out what had really happened at the crime scene, out there somewhere beyond the officers who'd built the case.

So what was her case?

Fact: Her father believed someone murdered Shep and ran out of the house to make that person pay for the crime. He was never seen again.

Fact: Shep had not been alone on that road the night he died, as everyone had believed. There had been a red car on the road with him. They were racing and the red car was winning.

Fact: Her father had been wearing his St. Marie medallion necklace when he'd gone running out into the night and three years later, that medallion had turned up ... where? Somewhere in the environs of a small boy named *Hannacker*.

Subsidiary Fact (not as significant as a first-class fact): Her father had claimed that someone had "gotten away with" ... something, apparently killing a McClusky, had "tricked" them. It would appear her father believed somebody had tricked Shep and killed him, too, which didn't jive with a traffic accident but had slightly more credence given that Shep had not been alone on that road.

Subsidiary Fact Number Two: Nate Hannacker had killed a McClusky and gotten away with it in the

1930s. But there hadn't been any kind of trick involved. It'd been a traffic accident.

Traffic accident.

She stopped and tried to push her stodgy mind forward.

The traffic accident years ago had involved one car chasing another ... which made no sense because the cars had collided head-on.

Skeeter's words came back to her. *One of them cars musta turned around.*

And then she set her cup down very carefully on the table.

"SAY you're traveling one hundred miles an hour down Georgia State Highway 9 toward Atlanta, with a hundred gallons of corn liquor sloshing around in the trunk and the lights of a road-block flashing up ahead. What do you do?"

"Get arrested?"

"What Seay did was slow down to about fifty—"

"Slow down to fifty?"

"Then he took his foot off the gas and yanked on the emergency brake, which locked the rear wheels."

"At fifty miles an hour?"

"Then he'd spin the wheel and the car'd spin all the way around, 180 degrees, and switch from fifty miles an hour forward to fifty miles an hour backward."

"Seriously?"

Burch grinned like a little kid.

"That's what they say. Then he'd release the emergency

brake and jam the accelerator and the car'd stop sliding back-wards and start going forward in the opposite direction."

WAS it possible that one of the vehicles in the legendary McClusky/Hannacker wreck had done that? Used a bootlegger's turn to turn around?

The bootlegger's turn … *it's a neat trick if you can pull it off.*

What if Nate Hannacker, who had been driving that day decades ago, had used a bootlegger's turn to go roaring back at the McClusky's car — which had caused the head-on collision?

And what if he'd used the *same trick* on Shep the night Shep was killed? What if Shep's gun had been out because he was chasing Nate Hannacker — *the red car was winning* — shooting at him? What if Nate had used the bootlegger's turn trick to come roaring back at Shep out of the darkness … running him off the road?

That left a pot-load of unanswered questions. Chief among them — why was Shep trying to kill Nate Hannacker in the first place? Nobody she'd talked to had mentioned the two of them being at odds. The red Stingray must have come from the chop shop — what other explanation could there be for the presence of a car that cost more than a house zipping up and down lonely roads in Callison County in the middle of the night? So if Nate was driving the Stingray, he must have been mixed up with the chop shop, too. Jody said Shep was *coming back to town* from the chop shop. So they'd *both* been there that night ... and *something* happened between them. She'd probably never know what it was, but she didn't need to know. Obviously, Papa knew, or thought he did. Papa figured it out and he went after Nate Hannacker.

And Nate Hannacker ... had killed him.

Had killed him somewhere that Pa's necklace came off, and the medallion got jammed down between some boards.

Or not.

"Drew could have swapped one of his plastic soldiers for the medallion with some other child."

And *that* kid, whose last name was *not* Hannacker at all, had been trying to "poke a straw" through a crack and found a "stuck thing" there.

How could she figure out which? Was it Drew Hannacker who found the pendant or—

The pendant had hung on a necklace, on a unique chain that had both gold and silver links. If the kid who'd found the medallion had found the chain, too, he'd have dug it out of the stuck place, too, and put it around his neck, wouldn't he? Sure he would. No, the kid who found the medallion *didn't* find the chain that went with it. Why not? It could have remained around Pa's neck. Or the kid just didn't see the chain, saw the medallion and took it, but didn't notice the little chain it'd dangled from.

Which meant ... maybe the chain was still there, stuck where the pendant had been.

Chapter Forty-Eight

Winona decided quickly that attorneys made lousy criminals. It did not help your concentration, to say nothing of your manual dexterity, to know the name of the crime you were committing, right down to its number in the Kentucky Revised Statutes.

Oh, and not just the name of the crime. Its classification — misdemeanor or felony. And its severity. Class A, B, C, D. The penalty, too — "not less than one year nor more than five years in prison."

That was the penalty for first offenders who committed the crime of trespassing.

In just a few minutes, if she could keep her hands from shaking long enough to get the door open, she would be committing the crime of breaking and entering in the first degree. Though it didn't seem quite fair to her, the "breaking" part. She'd heard criminals complain about that and blew them off. Made sense now. Oh, sure, if the door were locked and she had to break out a window or something, then yeah, she could see it. But nobody locked their doors in Callison County … *do a dang fool thing like 'at and then you'd hav-ta dig 'round in your overalls pocket and find the dad-gum key ever time you had to go back in the house to take a dump.*

But the law didn't make a distinction, break in or walk in, it was still a Class D felony. And the punishment for a Class D felony was "not less than five years nor more than twenty years" in prison. She felt the weight of that hit her in the belly as soon as she got to the house.

What if she got caught?

She wouldn't get caught.

That's what they all say.

She had at least an hour, more than that if Father Abernathy gave a long-winded homily. She'd calculated it like a bazillion times.

The Hannackers — Nate, Riley, Sherry Lynn and Drew — had left five minutes ago. She'd pulled off the road onto an overgrown track — tractor turnaround, or logging road — driven down it to a stand of bushes and left her car behind them. She had been hiding behind a tree on the lane that connected their house to the road, and she'd watched them go by. It took fifteen minutes to drive into town, add another five to find a parking place, walk to the church and get situated in a pew. The Mass would take about forty-five minutes, not counting the homily. And then if they got up and walked out without saying hi, bye or kiss my foot to anybody — which they wouldn't, nobody ever did that — they would be back here twenty minutes later. That totaled an hour and thirty to forty-five minutes. It was ten-thirty now and she would be done and gone from this place by eleven-thirty. She'd stay no longer than *one* hour.

No chance of getting caught.

That's what they all say.

The strong Grand Magistrate of the High Court of Common Sense reared his ugly head in her mind for the umpteen billionth time since she'd made the decision to do this. He spoke into her head three words in the melodious tones of James Earl Jones.

"This. Is. *Crazy.*"

She'd stopped arguing with him hours ago. Gave in, surrendered, ran up the white flag. Yes, this is crazy, she'd shouted at him, out loud, "but I'm going to do it anyway."

She didn't bother to argue with him now. She didn't have time to waste precious seconds of her self-imposed sixty-minute deadline arguing with herself.

Winona Gail McClusky had decided to look for the chain of her father's medallion. He'd been wearing it *and* the medallion the day he disappeared. So she meant to look for the chain in the place where the medallion had been found — the Hannacker farm.

It was an insane task, ten blocks south of ridiculous. The possibility that she'd stumble over something the Hannackers hadn't noticed in four years was … but they hadn't noticed the medallion either! It'd been there all along, too. The medallion and the chain had both been "hidden in a crack." The little boy had found the medallion … which meant the chain could still be there, too, "a stuck thing" in a crack. Crazy notion? You betcha. But she had to at least try. The wanting to know of it itched in her mind and there was no other way to scratch that itch than to try. She'd come too far to give up now.

She raced down the edge of the lane toward the house, wishing she hadn't stopped working out on the treadmill six months ago. She hadn't gone fifty yards before she "got into an oxygen deficit" — fancy words for running out of breath. By the time she got to the house she was slathered in sweat — exertion sweat and fear sweat — and gasping for air. She knew nobody was home now, she'd watched them drive away. But it was possible there might be somebody else in the house besides the Hannackers.

Who?

Who knew? But there might be somebody. Besides, she'd already thought out her defense if she got caught on the property before she could make a getaway and she needed to practice it from the very beginning. Wouldn't hold up five seconds in court but it was what it was — she would act *normal*. She had gone for a jog on Gallagher Station Road — she was wearing the jogging clothes and shoes to prove it — and decided to stop by and talk to her favorite cousin Sherry Lynn Hannacker. Nothing wrong with that, was there?

Riiiiight. Even Winona didn't believe it and it was her alibi.

She could embellish it with half a dozen reasons *why* she had stopped to see Sherry Lynn …

That wonderful pineapple upside-down cake that Sherry Lynn had described at some family gathering sometime ... would she give Winona the recipe?

That hair color Sherry Lynn used to make her hair look so naturally chestnut brown, would she tell Sherry Lynn the name ... oh, she didn't color her hair? It was that color naturally? Well, how about that.

Or even ... she'd come to give Drew the medallion back. He had, after all, been the one who found it — finders keepers.

In her heart, she knew she'd never be able to pull off any kind of defense whatsoever. Bottom line — don't get caught! Do what she'd come here to do and get the hell outta Dodge.

Still panting, she knocked on the screen door, ready with an answer on the tip of her tongue in the unlikely event somebody answered her knock. Nobody did. She knocked a couple more times, opened the screen door and knocked another couple of times on the door. Then she turned the knob — it was unlocked, of course — and stuck her head in, calling out, "Anybody home? Yoo-hoo, Sherry Lynn. You here?"

No response.

She was seized by an almost overpowering urge to run, turn around and bolt down the steps, run all the way to her car, full out and—

No, she had come this far. She would see it through.

Her game plan, such as it was, was to try to look at the world from the perspective of a four-year-old child, a being only about three feet tall. He had noticed from that perspective what the adults had not, saw what they didn't see.

She hauled what little she knew about the finding of the medallion into her mind, the conversation she'd had with Sherry Lynn at the wedding—

"WE WERE AT HOME. *He'd been playing — in the back yard, around the barn — and with his blocks in the playroom. I was making a cake in the kitchen and he came walking in with it, said it was "the stuck thing."*

"Stuck thing?"

"Stuck between some boards where he was trying to poke a straw."

THE MOST LIKELY place to look was on the floor. Kids spent all their time on the floor, playing with toys, driving little toy trucks or blocks or whatever. They got closer to the floor on eye level than grownups ever did. He was playing with a straw. The plastic straw from a milkshake or malt was about a quarter of an inch wide, but the space he was poking it into could have been slightly more narrow because the straw would flatten out if he pushed it into a tight space. So she was looking for a place between boards, about a quarter of an inch wide … on the floor, or the baseboards, nothing higher than a yardstick.

Sherry Lynn had been working in the kitchen, so it wasn't there. She said he'd been playing in the playroom, so Winona moved silently to the hallway — she didn't have to be quiet, there was nobody home, but she couldn't help it. Glancing in first one room and then the next, she found a small room next to the bedroom that might once have been a sewing room. Her mother'd had one like it, with a big window for lots of light. There were toys strewn all over the floor — trucks and cars and tractors and balls.

But the floor wasn't a hardwood floor, where small spaces could have formed between the boards over the years. It was linoleum, like in the kitchen, such a small room that it'd only taken a single seamless sheet. She bent low and flipped on the beam of her flashlight — and knew she looked like every detective in every cop show she'd ever seen. She only now appreciated why all those police officers had flashlights, because even in the brightly lit room there were shadows and she needed the extra brightness to see details. Moving slowly, she searched for some space between the linoleum and the molding at the base of the wall.

Nothing.

She looked for any kind of crack on the wall, between the wall and the door jamb, anywhere — up to a height of about three feet, which was as high as Drew could see.

Nothing.

She went out into the hallway, which had hardwood flooring, and searched along the slats with the flashlight beam. It was well built and tight, no spaces. It took twenty minutes — she knew because she looked at her watch about every thirty seconds — to examine the whole house that way, room by room. The living room and both the upstairs bathrooms were carpeted so that eliminated all but the area around the floor molding. There were rugs in the hall-way, the parlor, the entrance hall and she didn't move them to look under them. Drew would have been playing on top of the rug.

Forty minutes left before her self-imposed deadline of eleven-thirty. She'd given herself a comfortable half-hour buffer, so she'd be out and miles away before they got back home.

She went out onto the front porch — a likely spot because the floorboards were old and weathered. But they were still solid and the old porch steps had been replaced by concrete. Returning through the house, she examined the back porch, which was older and still had the original wooden steps. Lotsa cracks and holes where only the fingers of a four-year-old would fit, but she couldn't see anything stuck down in them but dirt.

Nothing.

She stood and looked again at her watch. Eleven o'clock. Thirty minutes left to search. Her eye scanned the backyard play equipment, and the picket fence, the outbuildings and the barn. She shook her head. That kid could have been playing on the floor in any of them trying to poke a straw between the boards — three small out buildings, a tool shed and she didn't know what the other two were for. The barn wall had lots of spaces between boards, but it had a dirt floor.

She looked at her watch again. Time was moving

like a hurricane. She imagined she could hear the seconds ticking off a timer — tick, tick, tick — counting down toward the moment when the Hannackers' car turned off the road onto the lane toward the house.

Hurry!

She left the yard — the outbuildings with wood floors made more sense — and ran across the dirt area in front of the barn to the first of them. It had looked like a storage shed and was. She opened the door and the fertilizer stink hit her in her first breath. The kid wouldn't play in there. She closed the door and went to the next building.

It was eleven-ten. She had twenty minutes left.

She didn't know what was in the second of the outbuildings, set behind the barn in overgrown weeds, because the door had a padlock on it.

The third outbuilding was a tool shed, the dark, cool interior crisscrossed with flaming arrows of sunlight shining through the boards of the wall. She probably ought to investigate those, because this was a place where a kid would play, around the lawn mowers, rakes, hoes, and garden implements, step ladder and wheel barrow and sawhorses.

But she stepped back outside and closed the door behind her. The building had a dirt floor and the something-fell-on-the-floor-and-got-stuck-in-the-slats logic made more sense than something getting stuck between boards in a wall.

Now what? Time was running out. She looked around. All that was left was the barn. It was ancient, with big bay doors on the front to open it wide enough to fit farm equipment. And a side door that maybe opened into the tack room from the outside. Perhaps a door on the back wall, too, but she couldn't see it from here. The two big doors that opened up the hayloft were both standing ajar. One of the barn's bay doors was standing open and she could see a tractor in the shadows inside beyond the puddle of sunlight and one of the animal stalls, but nothing else was visible. There were likely half a dozen stalls, an area for farm equipment, probably an area with tools where equipment repairs were made.

But the barn floor was dirt.

Then she froze.

Her heart stopped dead in her chest when she heard the distinctive crunch of tires on gravel. A car was coming down the driveway.

___

Chapter Forty-Nine

Winona had never in all her twenty-seven years of living felt the kind of raw, naked panic she felt now.

She'd been caught!

No, not yet she hadn't.

The survival instinct was a powerful drive, stronger than any other force she had ever experienced. When it kicked in, she was running before she had time to form the intent to do so. Couldn't go back in the direction of the lane and her car. She had to hide!

She ran through the open bay door of the barn and looked around frantically for somewhere to hide, something she could crouch behind in case somebody came into the building.

The tractor.

What if that's why they'd come into the barn — to use the tractor. There was a mower attached to the side of it — she could see the empty spot along the wall where the mower was missing from the row of machinery. So either the mower had recently been used and they hadn't gotten around to taking it off or they'd hooked it up and were getting ready to use it.

Her head was on a swivel, eyes darting back and forth, trying to look everywhere at once and consequently not really seeing anything at all. Farm equipment offered no large surfaces to hide behind. Hay rake. Harrow, manure spreader.

Where—?

The hayloft.

She was climbing the ladder when the Hannackers' car came into view, driving fast, and stopped abruptly, kicking up a small cloud of dirt.

The back passenger door flew open and Sherry Lynn jumped out with Drew in tow, got him only a couple of feet beyond the car door before he stopped, leaned over and vomited. Sherry Lynn stood beside him, holding his forehead and patting his back.

Nate and Riley got out more slowly, stood around looking helpless while the little boy heaved.

Climbing the final few feet into the hay loft, Winona crawled quickly to the far side, out of sight, could hear their voices.

"… that sausage he had for breakfast …" Nate said.

"… some kind of stomach bug …" Riley said.

"… clean up the back seat …" Nate said and his voice got louder and she could hear him approaching the barn.

No, please, oh please, oh please no. *No!* Winona cried out desperately in her head, hunkering down as far back out of sight as she could get. She could have hidden in the hay if she'd opted to leap off the side of the ladder where there was a big pile by the bay doors. She'd dived the other direction, though, and there was only a few inches of it on the floor boards.

But you couldn't see into the hayloft from the ground below. You had to climb up the ladder.

"… some rags in the barn." Nate's voice carried up to where Winona crouched in terror.

She could hear Riley and Sherry Lynn talking, but she couldn't quite make out their words. Listening in terror as Nate rummaged around, she heard a lid or door of some kind open with a squeak and then close, then she heard what sounded like his retreating footsteps as he left the barn. She could see what was going on if she crept to the open hayloft doors and peeked out but she didn't dare move, could barely breathe, remained as perfectly still as she could.

There were retreating voices — Sherry Lynn and Riley. The screen door squalled open and then slammed shut. A few minutes later, the car door closed, and the screen door did an encore.

Then silence.

Well, silence punctuated with the thundering hammer blows of her heart which surely could be heard for a hundred yards in every direction.

She gradually stopped panting, and her heartbeat slowed. Didn't return to normal, but slowed. She was able to think.

What should she do?

She supposed she could stay where she was, hidden in the barn loft all day, wait for the whole family to go to bed and then sneak out and escape. She didn't want to stay here all day! But right now, anything less than that was too terrifying to contemplate. The barn had an outside door on the side. At least, she thought she'd seen one when her eyes were raking the walls looking for somewhere to hide. A door on the back wall, too … she thought. She could climb down, leave by one of those doors and run into the cornfield behind the barn, find her way through it to the road and her car.

She could do that. She *should* do that. Couldn't, though. Could not make herself move. She did finally relax out of the crouch that had cut off the circulation to her left leg and foot, managed to get down on her knees and then slowly to a sitting position in the shadows. She looked at her watch.

It wasn't even eleven-thirty yet.

Seriously?

She would have sworn, would have bet her life that it was noon, maybe one o'clock.

Then, time dragged by on leaded feet. Now that she could look at her watch, keep track of it, every second was the longest second of her life. Until the next one. And the next one.

She needed to pee. As soon as the sensation struck her, it was all she could think about, and it consumed her, the urgency growing and growing. Did she really need to go that bad or did it just seem like it because she couldn't go? She supposed somewhere there was an account of somebody who'd died when they waited so long their bladder burst. Three cups of coffee – and part of a fourth. What had she been thinking?

The sun crested noon and started down the western sky. She tracked its progress as sunlight grew, shining through the west-facing hayloft doors chasing the shadows across the floor. It was two o'clock when she heard sounds and froze. The squawk of the spring on the screen door. Voices, words.

"… feel better …"

"… not get dehydrated …"

"… fluids in him …"

Riley and Sherry Lynn. The bang of the door swinging shut.

She had inched … literally *inched* her way to a position where she could look out through the one-inch crack between the loft door and the wall. The view revealed a slice of the back yard and she watched Riley and Sherry Lynn cross it. Riley was carrying Drew. There was no sign of Nate.

She heard the car doors open and close, the engine start, and the car make a circling turn and head down the lane to the road.

Riley and Sherry Lynn were taking Drew some-where. Where? The hospital? The kid hadn't been *that* sick! Come on, he was throwing up for crying out loud. Well, he'd been at it for a couple of hours and maybe that was a big deal with a little kid. Or maybe they were taking him to Sherry Lynn's mother's house, or to some other relative who could help in some way. Didn't Sherry Lynn's younger sister just graduate from nursing school? Or was that another one of Winona's cousins? She didn't know, didn't care. They were gone!

But Nate was still home.

The surge of hope she'd felt when she heard the movements died in her chest. Didn't matter who was home. As long as anybody was, Winona was not going to budge out of her hidey-hole.

She did need to pee, though. Didn't think she'd ever needed to pee so bad in her life. She didn't have to look at her watch to know it was mid-afternoon now, the sunlight and the accompanying heat filled the loft and she was slathered in a full body sweat. Finally, she made a decision — she'd wait another half hour, and if Nate didn't leave by then, she'd find a spot in the far corner and pee on the floor.

Couldn't you smell it, though? How long would it take to dry?

And it would drip through. There were spaces between the floor slats. All she needed was for Nate to come into the barn and feel piss dripping on his head from the hayloft.

She wiped off a piece of straw stuck with sweat to her forehead.

And froze.

From the moment she heard the sound of tires on gravel, she hadn't devoted so much as a millisecond of thought to the *reason* she'd come here in the first place. Every molecule of her body had been consumed by the fear of getting caught.

. . .

"IT WAS STUCK *between some boards where he was trying to poke a straw.*"

MAYBE NOT *A* STRAW — just straw. *Hay!*

Poking hay through the floor slats in the hayloft.

Now, her heart took up that jackhammer thingy again, but it wasn't fear this time. She turned and did a serious survey of the hayloft, for the first time viewing it not as a hidey-hole but as a place where a four-year-old would play. But surely they wouldn't let the kid come up here to play — with the big hole in the floor for the ladder on the far right side — there was no trap door above to close, just a hole. And the bay doors opened up to a thirty-foot drop to the ground outside.

You wouldn't let a kid play in a place like that, would you?

Still … this would be the perfect spot to poke straw through floor slats. There was a huge pile of hay on one side, but you could get to the boards in the rest of the loft by dusting the thin layer of hay away. So she would look. If nothing else, it would take her mind off how bad she needed to pee.

It took an hour to travel the length of every floor board with her nose an inch off the floor. There were spots where things were stuck — but just pieces of hay, or maybe a hunk of dirt or manure. Unless the kid had been playing under the big pile—

There was a sound from the house. The spring on the screen door squealed, then the door banged. She crawled quickly to the slice of the world she could see through the crack beside the hinges of the loft doors and watched Nate walk through it.

Was he coming to the barn?

Oh, please no. She couldn't breathe. No!

She needed to get under the pile of hay, bury herself in—

A vehicle door opened. His pickup truck was parked along the fence row. The door closed, the engine started and she caught sight of a swatch of the truck as it passed through her viewing area and she listened as it crunched on gravel all the way out to the end of the lane.

And then there was silence.

She bleated out a single sound. A strangled sob, relief flooding over her in such a warm flow she almost released her bladder and peed her pants.

Out. Now. *Run!*

She leapt to her feet and raced to the hayloft ladder, when she turned and placed her foot on the top rung. She could see the whole hayloft floor, where she'd scooted the hay aside to peer down between the slats. The floor was lit up, the bright late-afternoon sun firing a yellow spotlight through the open bay doors.

She paused. Stopped. Looked at the floor.

All the old boards had been weathered gray with age. But there was a dark spot on the gray. She fought against her near-panicked need to flee, forced herself to remain still. The dark spot was about two feet by three feet, a place where something brown had spilled on the wooden slats.

She stepped back up into the loft and got down on her hands and knees. Took out the flashlight and shined it between the boards in that area. The boards were stained in between, where something liquid had dripped down between them. But with her flashlight she could see the stain clearly — where years of sunlight had not faded it away. Between the boards, the color was still visible. What had been spilled there hadn't been dull brown. It'd been red, bright red.

The color of blood.

She stood slowly, looking at the bloodstain on the boards for a moment, before she let go her restraint and gave in to the terror in her chest. Leaping onto the ladder, she climbed down it, jumped the final couple of feet to the floor, ran across the barn and out the back door and into the cornfield behind it. She ran heedlessly, through the scratchy leaves, burying herself in the foliage, as far as she could run before she had to stop. Yanking down her jogging pants she squatted, felt tears of relief flow down her cheeks as the stinky yellow liquid splattered up onto her shoes.

The relief was so profound she squatted for a few moments afterward, savoring it. Then she stood up, pulled up her pants and looked around. The rows of corn ran west away from the farm and she followed them to the end of the field and into the woods. Her car was on the other side of the farm. She'd have to cut a wide berth through the trees around it and back out to the road.

She turned north and headed out, her mind churning.

Well, she hadn't found what she'd come here looking for, but she had found out what she needed to know.

There was a bloodstain on the floorboards in the hayloft of Nate Hannacker's barn. Oh, it coulda been something else besides blood — a Big Red Cola, maybe. And if it was blood, it coulda been anybody's. And the boy coulda found Pa's medallion stuck between the boards of an old outhouse somewhere, where her father had stopped to take a dump before he vanished in a puff of smoke.

That wasn't the truth of it, though.

In that place inside where you just know things, the soul connection place, Winona knew Pa's blood had been spilled on those boards. He'd died in that barn, bled on the floor of the hayloft, lost his medallion — in the violence of a struggle, maybe, and it stuck between the floor slats until a little boy spotted it and pulled it out.

Pa had died here. Nate Hannacker had killed him.

And what exactly was Winona McClusky going to do about that?

Chapter Fifty

Winona held the Smith & Wesson .38 snub nose pistol she'd gotten from a junkie named Weasel four years ago. It was a revolver, a smaller six-round pistol, the kind you could cock before you pulled the trigger if you wanted to.

She wished she could use her father's gun to do the job, liked the symmetry of that. Her father's murderer killed with her father's gun. That had a comforting closed-loop feel to it.

But she couldn't do that, of course. She needed an untraceable weapon, and there was none more untraceable than the firearm a long-dead junkie had given her to keep for him until the arraignment he didn't live to see.

Sitting on her deck as the sun sent out its first pink rays to light the day, Winona looked out over her glorious view in the first glow of morning.

Her neighbors' kids' swing sets.

Their overturned riding toys.

And an ever-ugly plastic playhouse.

She passed the pistol back and forth, right hand to left. It fit comfortably in her hand, almost like it'd been made for it, and she let herself enjoy the feel of the cold metal against her skin. Winona had been shooting some kind of weapon for as long as she could remember. Pa had gotten Shep a BB gun for his ninth birthday and he'd gone stalking birds with it that very day, with tag-along older sister one step behind him.

Shep was a lousy shot. She always wondered why that was because he did everything else well, but he couldn't hit the broad side of a barn with a firearm. In the beginning, she'd supposed there was something defective about his vision to explain it, had to be. Anybody could learn to be a reasonably good shot if they put their mind to it. Just took practice, basic hand-eye coordination. But Shep spent most of his childhood and teenage years shooting at things and missing. She figured then that he'd been bad at it for so long he had the yips, would miss every time because he had missed the last time and the time before that.

Winona, on the other hand, became something of a crack shot with her brother's BB gun. Well, as proficient as it was possible to get with a weapon designed for kids. When they were older, Pa had gotten her and her brothers hunting rifles for Christmas, an egalitarian move that had warmed her heart at the time, before she realized she couldn't use the firearm unless she went hunting with her father — you didn't go out and shoot cans off the back fence with a .30-06 — and her father always took Shep with him *alone*. After a while, he took Jody, too. She'd sucked it up like she did every other such injustice, and it was years before she figured out why her father wouldn't take her. It was because she was a better shot than Shep and that wouldn't do — oh my, no, that wouldn't do at all. In fact, she suspected she was a better shot than any of the three male hunters.

When she moved out of the house, one of her first purchases was a pistol that she kept in the glove box of her car because there was a rule against firearms in the girls' dormitory at Bellarmine College, where she'd done her undergraduate work. It lived in the bedside table when she got her own apartment. Of course, she took shooting lessons at a range in Louisville, and true to form, she was still a crack shot. That's mostly why she'd kept it up, kept the gun. It wasn't that she was terrified and needed the gun for comfort to secure her own protection. It was just a skill she was good at, and life didn't afford the Winona McCluskys of this world very many of those.

She'd sold her own pistol to a young law student after she came into possession of Weasel's .38. She didn't need two pistols and she'd liked the idea of owning a gun that could never be connected to her. That'd been a good decision. Now she could use the gun a dead junkie had left with her for safe-keeping, to kill Nate Hannacker.

Kill Nate Hannacker.

She felt a chill run down her backbone, as if ice water were trickling off an icicle and down her back, slowly dripping from one vertebra to the next. Drip. Drip. Drip.

She'd been so shaken when she got home last night from her adventure in the Hannackers' barn that her hands were still trembling as she stood in a hot shower, the water attacking her skin like hailstones. Shaken and scattered. Sounded like the way you'd order a martini — make mine dry, shaken and scattered, please. The shaken part subsided by the time she was dried off, but the scattered had hung on, some kind of whirlwind in her mind where thoughts chased each other around and around in circles.

Her stomach was still a little queasy from her drinking binge with Jody on Saturday night — she really needed to just foreswear alcohol altogether — so she'd eaten a light supper, got ready for bed, and then took out her happy pills. They were in an aspirin bottle that she'd emptied into the toilet so she could put her handful of illicit pills into it.

Jody'd had a prescription for pain pills when he injured his leg. She'd noticed the empty bottle amid the trash on the table beside his chair the first time she'd spoken to him more than a week ago. And she'd snatched it up. It was just an impulse, some part of her aware that there might be a time somewhere down the line when she'd be glad for some "happy pills." The next day, she'd gone to Mr. Freeman, the pharmacist at the drugstore, with a cock-and-bull story about how Jody'd accidentally spilled his pills, knocked the bottle off into the toilet and could he give her a replacement, please? Arthur Freeman would never have bought that story from Jody, but she was Winona McClusky, after all, recently come home from law school to take over her father's law practice. She could be trusted.

Last night she'd popped two of the pain pills into her mouth — some kind of narcotic — and slept like the dead. Yeah, she'd felt the buzz before she dozed off, but didn't find it the least bit pleasant. Winona was clearly safe from junky-hood.

When she awoke this morning, her mind was clear and rested, her purpose clear before her.

And now, finally, she could let out the caged lion of her rage, she could glory in the power of her anger, suck all the sweetness out of her hatred.

Nate Hannacker had killed her father! Killed him. Murdered him in the hayloft of his barn and did God knows what with his body. She would ask that. Before she put a bullet in Nate's brain, she'd get him to tell her where he'd buried her father.

An unexpected spasm of grief seized her and she choked out a strangled sob. *Buried her father.* Oh, yeah, sure, she'd been telling herself for years that her father was dead. That if he were alive, he'd come home. She thought she had accepted the fact of his death. But it was *real* now. Final. He would *never* come home. She would *never* see him again. She'd never get a chance to build the father-daughter relationship with him that she had ached for every day of her life. Nate Hannacker had stolen that chance. Had stolen the future she could have had with her father. And Nate would pay for that. He would pay with his life!

All that remained was *planning* the execution of the

deed — execution being an appropriate word — and the doing of it. Winona would use Weasel's .38, and then toss it off a bridge into the muddy Rolling Fork River.

And that would be that.

Yes, sir-ee, Nate Hannacker would be dead inside a week.

Chapter Fifty-One

Nate Hannacker would be dead inside a week.

Booth Graham liked the sound of the thought in his head so much he spoke out loud.

"Gonna be one cooked goose."

He looked at his watch as he drank his second cup of coffee, seated in his kitchen in his underwear before he got ready for work. Yep, they were working on it right now, the August 27, 1973 issue of the *Callison County Tribune*. Finally, his week-long sentence in hell was about to end.

The Tribune staff came in on Monday mornings first thing and put the final touches on that week's issue, then the newspaper page flats would be transported by van to Elizabethtown where they would be turned into page negatives, and those negatives turned into plates and those plates fastened onto printing presses so newsprint on big rollers could be passed between them to make the newspaper. He'd gone with editor Jim Bingham once to see the process.

Then those newspapers would be loaded into the back of the newspaper van and delivered to the post office, usually around midnight, to be bulk-mailed to subscribers and then delivered to different outlets all over the county — newspaper racks in front of businesses, convenience stores, outside the library, the lobby of the courthouse, even to the jail.

When Callison County woke up on Tuesday morning, *this week's issue* of the Tribune would be in their mailboxes and stacked on newspaper racks. With the front page on top, of course! Shouting some story or another to the world. Graham didn't know what the lead story in the newspaper might be and didn't care. What mattered was that as soon as this week's issue was out, *last week's issue* would disappear! It'd be collected from all the racks, stacked up in the storage room of the newspaper office and eventually hauled out to the city dump.

Graham knew the newspaper's schedule because he had become friendly with Jim Bingham over the years. Bingham was a good man who respected law and order, but still had that quirky Callison County sense of morality that baffled Booth Graham more and more the longer he was around it.

Oh, the newspaper editor was a straight arrow when it came to the integrity of the newspaper, paid much greater homage to the First Amendment of the Constitution about freedom of the press than any of the reporters Graham had dealt with in Chicago. Those guys just wanted a story, the best story, the one that would make those newspapers fly off the racks and keep their circulation figures high. To that end, they were perfectly willing to bend the law when they needed to, and by and large were a heartless bunch. If getting the story meant jumping out of the bushes and snapping a picture of a grieving mother as she knelt over the body of her murdered son, not a one of them would bat an eye.

Bingham wasn't like that. Jim was a native and there was something … must be in the water … about how these people viewed themselves, their community and outsiders. Oh, and law enforcement. Bingham had explained to Graham once over a beer the difference between man's law and God's law. And Graham had finally understood why everybody in the county — not just the criminals, but the little old grandmothers planting daisies in their front yards — made a distinction between *lawbreakers* and *criminals*. They passed no moral judgement whatsoever on the former … and not nearly enough, in Graham's opinion, on the latter. And Jim Bingham had way more respect for the sensibilities of his readers than any of the ignorant hillbillies deserved.

But there had been no malice on Jim's part when he put the picture of Graham and the sheriff on the front page. Objectively speaking, it was a really good photograph, captured the essence of the story without words. Jim had just been doing his job. But by tomorrow morning, the newspaper where the humiliating picture of Booth Graham dominated the front page, *screamed* off the front page, seemed to Graham to *glow in horrid neon colors* on the page, would be gone.

Old news.

Forgotten.

Another newspaper would be there in its place and the world would march on without a blip.

In Graham's own mind, he would never, *never* be able to live down the humiliation of that picture. He couldn't catch his breath sometimes when he thought about it. His whole jaw ached from clenching his teeth. It was the single worst thing that'd ever happened to him as a law enforcement officer and he couldn't do a thing about it!

But he would get even for it.

Graham had to wait until the newspaper transition was complete to carry out what he thought of in his head now as the *assassination of Nathaniel Hannacker*. It would be good judgement, of course, for him to wait even longer than that. If he wanted to ensure nobody connected that picture to Hannacker's death, he really ought to wait another week, two, a month … six.

But he was doing well to hold his temper for seven days!

He'd thought it would get easier after a couple of days. It didn't. His rage had grown, blown up in his chest like pulling that cord on a Navy dinghy. He had forced himself to face it head on, pretend he wasn't embarrassed at all, smile and laugh about it, take all the ribbing, the joking, the jabs with a "good-sport attitude."

"Hey, it's what happened. I think Jim captured my good side, don't you?"

Everywhere he turned the picture was waiting

there to slap him in the face. Again and again. The teasing spread beyond Callison County to his fellow officers when the newspaper made its way to the Columbia State Police Post. He even got a call from an officer in his old Chicago precinct — said somebody'd thumb-tacked the whole newspaper page to the dayshift bulletin board.

Yeah, it might be prudent to wait longer before he exacted his revenge, but Graham just couldn't do it. Wound tighter and tighter every day, growing angrier and angrier, he might actually have a stroke if he didn't release the pressure soon. He hated Nathaniel Hannacker with every cell in his body and every second the man drew breath eviscerated Graham's very soul.

He had never exercised more self-discipline than he had in the past week. Not a living soul had any idea Graham was upset about the picture. So nobody'd give a second's thought to making him a suspect in Hannacker's murder.

Hannacker's *murder.* Growling the word aloud between clenched teeth, Graham picked up his "throw down," the pistol he'd carried for years in Chicago to "throw down" if he got in a tight spot and needed to make it appear a suspect had been armed. It was a Smith & Wesson .38 snub nose revolver. He'd "borrowed" it from an evidence locker after his first brush with an Internal Affairs Division investigation of his role in a fatal shooting. It'd been used in some crime, but he didn't know what. All he knew was it couldn't be traced back to him.

He took a sip of cold coffee and rose to get dressed, looking at his watch, imagining the newspaper staff busily putting together his get-out-of-jail-free card. Only a few more hours.

He had already baited his trap.

Chapter Fifty-Two

IT WAS Monday morning and Jackson McClusky had been trying to get a shot at Riley Hannacker for more than a week now. He'd picked this sniper spot today because Nate had been out mowing weeds around the edges of this field late Sunday afternoon and didn't finish. Maybe Riley'd take over today.

Jackson had been stalking around in the woods surrounding the Hannacker farm every chance he could sneak away since he'd talked to Sherry Lynn the day of Jeanie Morgan's wedding shower. Wasn't hard to sneak off since the Hannackers and the McCluskys were as-the-crow-flies neighbors. Their land bumped up against each other's deep in the woods on the side of Bald Knob. Though you'd have to drive all the way around the knob — go into town and out the other side to go from Big-un McClusky's house to Nate Hannacker's house, if you climbed up to the top of the knob and went down the other side, fought your way through the tangled brush and woods, you'd come out at the bottom on Hannacker land in Hickory Stump Hollow.

Every time Jackson'd had a few hours to himself when he wasn't doing chores for Pa, he'd made the journey, hid in the woods around the Hannacker place, waiting for a chance to take his shot. Eventually, he'd catch Riley out alone. Mending a fence, or working in the garden or out on the tractor. He'd had a great shot two days ago, but before he could line it up, Nate had joined Riley and they'd worked together for the rest of the afternoon.

Every day that passed Jackson got more anxious — a clock was ticking. Every hour he spent hiding in the woods waiting was an hour he *didn't* spend working on his own pot crop. He needed to top the plants one more time, let them bush out some more before he cut them. They was fine weed! Woulda growed eight or nine feet tall if he'd let 'em. He remembered the lessons he'd learned in prison about that, though, how you didn't want 'em to grow *up*, you wanted 'em to grow *out*. The tall plant shaded the limbs below and they needed the sunlight. He'd tried to hire hands to help him with the work, but they wasn't real dependable, since he wasn't paying them nothing and they was just gambling he'd make good money on the crop to settle up.

And every night that passed, the tension built. Would this be the night the dreams haunting Riley Hannacker suddenly made sense to him. Would he wake in the middle of a nightmare about an RPG pointed at his bunker and remember Jackson had fired it?

Though it was still early, the cicadas were already squalling in the woods around him. The first time Jackson had noticed cicadas was when they wasn't there. In the Vietnamese jungle, the insects' cries were so foreign they set his teeth on edge, and he found himself imagining what kind of horrible *thing* was out there in the dense undergrowth could make such a sound, some creature with hairy legs and fangs and antennae, that would come crawling down into his foxhole and eat him alive.

When he'd first got back home, he'd gone out into the back yard and sat near the woods, just listening to the different creatures' sounds, feeling comforted in a way he couldn't explain by their familiarity. Their cries still comforted him somehow, still spoke of home and real. There had been no bug cries in prison.

The sound of a tractor's engine, elbowed through the cicadas' cries. It was coming this way, getting louder and louder. Nate, returning to finish yesterday's job, or maybe … *maybe* Riley taking over today.

Jackson had set up at the end of the last row, so the tractor would be coming at him. Lateral shots were hard to make. You had to track the target with the barrel, put the shot out a little ahead of it. With the tractor traveling toward him, the target would get bigger and bigger as it approached, the shot easier and easier to make. The tractor's path down the outside edge of the field would bring it in a couple of minutes to within fifty yards of where Jackson lay in wait.

Jackson had "borrowed" his father's .22 long rifle and it was *not* his weapon of choice. But it was either the .22 or nothing. Jackson didn't have the cash money right now to go buy himself a rifle, and this was the only rifle in his father's considerable arsenal that Jackson could take, use and return without his father knowing about it. The rest were in the house, locked up behind the glass in his gun cases, but Pa kept this one in the barn so he could get to it quick if he needed it to kill snakes and varmints. Wasn't nothing to look at, weathered like it was from being in the barn for years. The wood on the stock was starting to splinter. His Pa kept it loaded with rat-shot so Jackson'd had to buy a box of .22 hollow-point shells to load into it to use on Riley. A whole box full, but he only needed one.

He hadn't wasted time trying to figure out how to kill Riley so that it would look like an accident. Might be it would look like an accident. Might be it'd look like just what it was — an execution murder. It didn't matter what it looked like so long as there was no reason to connect Jackson McClusky to the crime. Jackson had taken a big risk offing that prison guard in the cafeteria at Eddyville. The guy was standing in a big group of cons and Jackson struck without warning, shoving the shiv into his fat belly, burying it in the wound so they wouldn't be able to find the weapon at the scene.

Jackson'd even grabbed the guard when he fell — so, of course he had the guard's blood all over him, then laid him on the floor and hollered for help. Jackson's defense was that he had *no motive* for the murder. Several other cons held grudges against the guard, would have killed him in a heartbeat, but Jackson was never even a suspect.

The rumble of the tractor's engine grew louder and Jackson fit the stock of the rifle to his shoulder and sighted along the barrel out through the branches of the bush he was hiding behind, squinting to see who was driving it.

A huge rush of adrenaline flooded his veins when he saw that it was Riley.

Yes!

As the tractor drew closer, he could see Riley clearly, no shirt on, sweating out in the hot sun, bumping along the edge of his field, using a side flail mower attached to the right side of the tractor to cut the weeds and brush reaching out for his tobacco crop from the woods.

Jackson's heart pounded with fear and excitement, but his hands were steady. After all, there was absolutely nothing to connect Jackson to the shooting. He hadn't exchanged so much as a hidey-do with Riley since the two of them got back from 'Nam, hadn't been anywhere near him in almost four years.

What possible motive could Jackson have to kill him?

A body shot was easier, of course, but Jackson didn't have the luxury of the easy shot. Not with a .22. You could shoot a man in the belly with a .22, and he could keep coming at you, take the gun away from you and beat you to death with it … and then die from internal bleeding an hour later. For a kill shot, he had to sight in on the head. He'd wait until Riley was less than fifty yards away. It was a bolt-action long rifle and he'd already racked a shell into the chamber. Putting the sight on Riley's forehead beneath the bill of his John Deere cap, Jackson drew in a breath and let it out slowly.

The rumble of the tractor grew louder and louder.

It drew closer and closer.

His target got bigger and bigger.

Jackson began to *squeeze* the trigger, didn't *pull* it.

The tractor lurched suddenly and the target blurred just as he fired.

Bam!

There was no loud crack, like from a .30-06 hunting rifle. That was the sound of the bullet breaking the sound barrier as it flew toward the target. The hollow point he was firing from a .22 wasn't going that fast. But the normal sound of the exploding gunpowder was unmistakably a gunshot. And Riley disappeared off the back of the tractor.

There was no kill switch on the tractor so it chugged along the direction Riley'd been traveling — right toward Jackson in the bush in the woods. It was slowing down, of course, because Riley's foot was no longer exerting pressure on the accelerator, but it was coming. Jackson stood up out of the concealing bush, but the tractor coming toward him blocked his view. He couldn't see where Riley'd fallen off behind it, couldn't see his body. He almost took a step in that direction before he thought better of it. No, he had to get out of here — now! He might have no motive, but he still couldn't risk being seen anywhere near the spot where Riley'd got killed.

Killed. Jackson had *killed* him … right? Of course he had — Riley'd pitched backward off the back of the tractor. And he'd been aiming at his forehead. He'd killed him, alright.

Now, Jackson had to concentrate on getting home, into his truck and into town. Drive into Brewster from the opposite direction of the Hannacker farm. Then he'd just hang around somewhere until he heard the news — which would flash fire all over the county — that Riley Hannacker was dead.

Soon's he got back home later tonight, he'd put the rifle back in the barn before Pa missed it. Couldn't clean it or Pa'd know right away it'd been fired. It'd needed a good cleaning before he used it and it had to need a good cleaning when he put it back.

No one saw him come running out of the woods and leap into his truck. Then he roared down the lane to the road, firing up a rooster tail of dirt after him. After that, he forced himself to drive slowly into Brewster, just another old pickup putt-putting along. As he drove, he picked the briars off the pants legs of his jeans, cleaned the cockle burrs off the front of his shirt. He rolled down his sleeves so you couldn't see the fresh scratches on his arms he'd gotten running through the brush. He had both windows down and the breeze would dry his sweat.

By the time he got to town, wouldn't be no indication at all he'd been out in the woods all morning.

Chapter Fifty-Three

POP!

It all happened at the same time. Riley's hat flew off just as he saw the solid mass of kudzu vines that had grown out across the weedy ground at the edge of the field. He saw the kudzu, but he'd been distracted by his hat, and hadn't been quick enough to miss the hole beneath them.

Even though he'd reminded himself when he'd gotten on the tractor this morning to remember the huge hole — probably three feet across and easily two deep, where the roots of a fallen oak tree had ripped out of the ground. He and Papa had long since cut up the tree branches and stump for firewood, but the hole in the dirt remained. And in the summertime when the kudzu vines struggled to eat up the whole world, they covered it in a leafy mat. It was as well concealed as any booby trap—

. . .

THE SOLDIER *at the front of the line on the jungle trail suddenly vanishes and starts screaming. Riley gets to the edge of the trap first, looks down into the hole where the man has fallen to see that he's impaled on half a dozen punji sticks, pieces of sharpened bamboo stuck upright in the ground, always smeared with feces to ensure that the wounds inflicted by them got infected. One stick has come all the way through his thigh, another sticks out of his shoulder. The side of his face is stuck on another—*

RILEY'D YANKED his mind away from the images like he'd touched his finger to a hot stove. But they'd clawed their way into his consciousness farther than most such horror did and he imagined he could still hear the screams.

He had a label for such times — when he was slammed back into hell in an instant. He called the event "a body surfaced."

The phrase came from an awful outing as a teenager to nearby Green River Lake in Taylor County. He and Sherry Lynn, Willie Ray and Gloria, and Ben Higgs and Shannon Phillips had borrowed a ski boat and spent most of the afternoon getting delightedly sunburned.

Then a Kentucky State Water Patrol boat had approached theirs, and the green-uniformed officer asked if they'd "seen anything unusual."

"Unusual how?" Willie Ray'd asked.

"A man drowned in this area of the lake a couple of days ago and the body's due up today."

The officer left them contemplating the awful implications of "due up today." Apparently, the body of drowning victims stayed submerged for a certain amount of time and then …

Their outing ended five minutes later after Willie Ray had cried out, "Look, the body surfaced" and pointed to a floating log. Even when he showed them it was just a log, the girls refused to get back into the water.

The image of a body surfacing … coming up out of the black depths, rotting and decayed, a horror too awful to contemplate, had stayed with Riley. When he got home from 'Nam, the phrase was a word picture of the images that stalked him constantly for a couple of years. Now, they just haunted his sleep.

Maybe it was his deliberate effort not to think about a booby trap that had caused him to forget all about the hole on the edge of the field. He'd been what Grandma Abby used to call "wool-gathering," thinking about his son as he rode along, performing the monotonous task of battling the weeds and encroaching forest, fighting for the cleared land.

Drew'd had some kind of stomach virus yesterday — had lost his breakfast all over their pew at church — and Sherry Lynn had freaked, demanded they haul the boy over to the house of her sister, who was a nurse, so she could make sure he was okay. By suppertime, he'd been able to keep down the 7-Up his mother gave him, and this morning they'd found him sleeping soundly on the floor of his closet! Riley shook his head and smiled. That boy—

Riley was caught totally off guard. With a more narrow wheel span, the front two tires missed it. But the right back tire on the tractor suddenly slammed down into the gigantic hole in the dirt and then bounced upward as it came up the other side.

The down-and-up motion literally catapulted Riley into the air and he flew backwards out of the metal seat. If he'd been pulling any piece of farm machinery *behind* the tractor — tillage equipment like a disc harrow or ripper, a hay rake, a hay baler or a cultivator — he'd have become the latest statistic in the state's listing of farm-related fatalities, which was always in double digits every year.

But he was using a *side* flail mower, attached to a power take-off on the right side of the tractor. So instead of being cut into small pieces by the slicing blades of a harrow, or impaled on the tines of a disc ripper, Riley merely landed with a bone-jarring thump in the dirt, like he'd been thrown from a horse.

He banged his head painfully and the world swirled in a tangled mish-mash of sounds, feelings and images as it grew fuzzy and gray, insubstantial.

The rumble of the tractor engine came from inside an echoing drum, getting fainter and fainter.

The sun was a bright flare that lit up the sky.

FLARE.

The rumble of thunder.

A blurry figure seen through water ... a round black hole in the world.

· · ·

RILEY BLINKED in the glaring sun, totally disoriented. The back of his head hurt where he'd banged it. His butt hurt. Where was he …?

The sound of the tractor dragged reality back into the world. The motor was slowing.

Riley blinked. Blur. He blinked again. The world righted itself and though he had to struggle to get his thoughts un-jumbled, he realized he'd been thrown off the back of the tractor when he hit that big hole. The tractor had continued chugging along, but without his foot on the accelerator, it slowed. It was beginning to veer off course on the edge of the field into the tangle of weeds and grass beside it.

Struggling to stand, Riley staggered after it, grateful it had veered right instead of left or it would right now be smashing a trail through his tobacco crop.

Running made the back of his head throb.

DARKNESS.
A flare.

IT WAS GONE.

What in the world …?

Then he got to the back of the tractor and clambered up onto it, yanked the steering wheel left to avoid clocking a good-sized sapling, reached his hand down and switched off the ignition. The roar of the engine ceased, filling the world with silence that was, itself, rumbling *whum-whum-whum* in his temples.

He sat where he was, suddenly winded, grabbing huge lungfuls of air as the reality of what'd just happened settled over him. Leaning his forehead on the steering wheel, he closed his eyes, but that made the whumming inside his head worse so he opened them again, looking down through the steering wheel at his muddy work boots.

His hat.

Reaching up to his head, he felt its absence, turned around and saw it lying in the dirt about twenty feet behind the tractor. He sat for maybe another minute until the throbbing sound faded out of his temple, then climbed down off the tractor and trudged back to his hat lying in the dirt.

He picked it up. The world started doing that crazy graying-whirling-dizzy thing again as he looked at it.

There was a hole in the bill of the hat. A bullet hole.

He remembered now — the pop sound right before he hit the hole. Was that a gunshot? That thought would never have occurred to him if he weren't holding a cap in his hands with a bullet hole in it.

Suddenly, he felt terribly exposed. He was just standing there out in the open, holding his hat in his hands. Anybody, anywhere could—

He ran back to the tractor and ducked down behind the big rear tire, flattened himself against it panting. With his mind whirling around in denial, he forced himself to stick his finger through the hole in his hat to make himself believe it.

It was a small hole, a .22 maybe, a rifle that wasn't much use for anything except squirrels and other small animal game. The wild shot of some hunter in the woods? That was crazy. These were Hannacker woods, stretched out over hundreds of acres. Who would suddenly decide to come here to shoot squirrels? Wasn't like they were any more plentiful here than anywhere else in the county.

But what other explanation was there? That ... somebody'd been *shooting* at him?

Now, that was certifiably crazy. If somebody'd been shooting at him, why use a .22? If you wanted to kill a man, you packed a bigger gun than that!

And besides, who had a motive to kill him?

He staggered over a breath at the thought — the Colombians! Had they come back?

No way. Those dudes hadn't been packing .22s. If they'd wanted him dead, they sure wouldn't have come after him with a pop gun. And *ambush* him from the woods? It was almost a mile through the trees to the nearest road. How would they have found the tobacco field? And how would they have known he was out here anyway?

And fire a single shot?

It took a full fifteen minutes for Riley to convince

himself he was an idiot, that he'd been hit by a random shot from some squirrel hunter. It'd been an accident. That's all. An accident.

Chapter Fifty-Four

When Jackson got to Brewster, he went immediately to the post office because it was the one place with a guarantee there'd be folks standing around. He made sure to pass right in front of the mayors — the old men who sat in the shade of the big maple tree in front of the courthouse every day, chewing tobacco and telling lies.

"You doin' alright?" he'd said casually to J.W. Williams. His grandson, Travis, had been in the first squad of the Whiskey Run Platoon with Jackson. Travis had come home without a scratch.

"Can't complain. Woke up on the right side of dirt this mornin'. You?"

"If I's any better, I'd be twins."

J.W. flashed a toothless smile and Jackson walked on, certain that all of them had noticed him.

Wouldn't be long before word got out about Riley Hannacker and he wanted people to remember he'd been in town at the time. He didn't need an alibi, of course, because he'd never be a suspect, but you couldn't be too careful.

He'd stood in line to buy stamps, made small talk with the people around him, real friendly like, the whole time his ear cocked to hear the siren of the ambulance screaming out of the Rescue Squad headquarters headed in a hopeless flight to save Riley Hannacker. He looked at his watch. What was taking so long? It'd been forty-five minutes. But if wasn't nobody home, Sherry Lynn and Nate out and about somewhere, they might not discover what'd happened to Riley for … *hours*. All the better for Jackson 'cause then nobody's know for certain what time Riley'd got shot.

But Jackson couldn't hang around in town all afternoon. He needed to get home, put that .22 back in the barn before Pa missed it. Be Jackson's luck, a big ole rattler would curl up on the seat of the tractor and Pa'd go looking for his varmint rifle.

Jackson had done what he intended to do, established his whereabouts at the time Riley was shot. More or less. They never could tell time of death any closer than a couple of hours either way. Folks would recall they'd seen Jackson in town somewhere around that time frame. That'd be enough.

Heading back to his truck, he made sure to pass by Mrs. Pettigrew's Pretty Paws Dog Salon. Blanche Pettigrew was a flighty little woman with wispy gray hair and a constant look of concerned sympathy on her face, whether there was anything to be sympathetic about or not. She had an annoying toy poodle, a yappy little mutt that went with her everywhere. She'd 'a took it in church with her if the Father hadn't laid down the law. And nothing happened in Brewster that she didn't know about. With that big picture window of her shop looking out on Main Street, nothing escaped her notice, and there existed nowhere on the planet a more resolute gossip than Blanche Pettigrew.

She was coming out the shop door as he passed by.

"Afternoon, Mrs. Pettigrew," he said as he stepped around her. "You doin' alright?"

"I most certainly am *not*!"

That stopped him and he noticed that the yappy little dog in her arms had a bandage on its hind leg.

"What happened to—?" He scratched around in his mind but couldn't locate the mutt's name.

"Name's Pebbles, and he got bit, that's what happened!"

Jackson wasn't surprised. The pooch was a sour-tempered little dog that snapped at just about every-thing that got near it.

"A fox bite him? Those carry rabies, you know."

Mrs. Pettigrew was both horrified and offended.

"Oh, I wouldn't ever let Pebbles out where he could get bit by a fox! He isn't vaccinated, you know, got so sick from the distemper vaccination I'm sure he must be allergic to vaccines. But it ain't just foxes that carry rabies. That's why I *insisted* she turn that dog over to Mitch to be tested."

Dr. Mitchell Garrison was Callison County's only veterinarian.

"Pebbles got bit by a dog? Whose dog?"

"Jessie Monaghan's. Great big black thing. Pebbles wasn't doin' nothing, just playing, nipping at him and that beast bit him!"

Jackson didn't appear more than politely interested.

"And does her dog have rabies?"

"Won't know until the test results come in."

Jackson's mind spun.

"What does Mitch think? Does he think the dog's rabid?"

"Well, no," she admitted reluctantly. "He said the dog didn't have any rabies symptoms. And Jessie said she'd got him vaccinated when the state health department was doing free vaccinations a couple of years ago, but she couldn't find the certificate and Mitch didn't have no record of it. And I just couldn't take the chance, you know." She nuzzled the dog in her arms. "Not with my sweet Pebbles."

"When will you know the test results?"

"Tomorrow. Until then, Mitch has her dog penned up in quarantine so he can't bite anybody else."

Jackson pasted a smile on his lips.

"Well, I sure do hope everything turns out alright."

He continued to his truck, his mind flying off in a dozen different directions at once.

Jessie's dog wasn't home, and wouldn't be back until tomorrow.

Jackson drove home slowly, made sure nobody was around and carefully returned the varmint gun to its spot in the tack room of the barn. When he walked out of the barn, his father growled, "Where you been? I been looking all over for you."

"I been … around, went into town for a little while is all, to …" It was lame, but it was the truth, so he dug in his jeans pocket and pulled out the book of stamps. "To get some stamps." His father looked like he'd swallowed his wad of chewing tobacco. Jackson went on, kept talking. "What was you looking for me for?"

His father gave him the look he always did, the you're-such-a-loser look, and shook his head.

"Cows got out on the road again. Gonna have to get ridda that dang bull." One of his father's bulls was Houdini, could get out of any enclosure, and usually took the rest of the herd with him when he made a break for it. "Go on out there and help your brothers round 'em up, 'less you's too busy with your correspondence."

Jackson helped gather up the cattle, came in and ate supper with the family, thinking any minute somebody'd call Mama or Pa and tell them that they'd heard about Riley Hannacker. Nobody called. Wasn't just 'cause they was McCluskys, neither, and didn't hang out with the folks who hung out with the Hannackers. A shooting — a *murder,* word of that woulda spread like a fire through dry wheat. When there was no word by early evening, Jackson knew something had gone terribly, terribly wrong.

Claiming he had a headache, he begged off watching *Gunsmoke* with the family and went on out to his little attic room over the tool shed, where he paced back and forth, back and forth. What had happened? Had he *missed?* That was impossible. How could you miss from that distance? The tractor'd hit a big bump just as he was squeezing off the shot, but he allowed for that, aimed lower. And Riley'd gone flying off the back of the tractor.

What had happened?

And perhaps more important, what was Jackson going to do now — about Riley, and *about Davie Monaghan?* Jessie's big, black monster dog wouldn't be there tonight. A single window of opportunity. He visualized himself slipping into the house, into Davie's room, putting a pillow over his face. Would he fight back? Maybe not, maybe he was such a vegetable-head he wouldn't know he was supposed to. Jackson would be out of there inside five minutes.

Could he do it ... *tonight?*

Why not tonight?

Well, because ... Riley and all ... just because ...

If he didn't do it tonight, the door of opportunity would slam shut and who knew when it'd open again, if it *ever* did?

Chapter Fifty-Five

OF COURSE RILEY said nothing about what'd happened to him when he got back to the house, though Sherry Lynn'd grilled him about why it'd taken such a long time to finish mowing the weeds around the tobacco field.

"I was about to come out there looking for you. What took so long?"

What had taken him an extra forty-five minutes was making himself get back up onto the tractor and finish the mowing, sitting up there like a target in a penny arcade.

By the time he got back to the barn and was taking the mower off the side of the tractor, he had convinced himself it meant nothing.

Sherry Lynn had made chicken-and-rice casserole for supper, with fresh corn on the cob and sliced tomatoes still warm from the garden. And she was in a reasonably good mood, though she hovered over Drew as he ate. Still mindful of the stomach virus that had caused an embarrassing vomiting episode during church yesterday, she had watched every bite of food that went into his mouth at breakfast this morning and at lunch, too. After Riley skillfully steered the conversation away from finding Drew asleep in his closet this morning, she was content to babble on about the new house, the flower garden she wanted to plant there, and the big trees she wanted in the front yard.

During supper wasn't the time to point out that any trees they planted now wouldn't provide shade until Drew was out of high school.

After supper, Sherry Lynn put Drew to bed and then joined Riley and Papa on the porch, where they lounged over beer and talked about the weed crop that Willie Ray would any day now pronounce ready for harvest.

The conversation quickly bored Sherry Lynn and she told Riley she was going up to bed.

He caught the tone of the words. The unspoken invitation implicit in them. It was married-people-speak, unmistakable. Obviously, she wanted to get romantic. But try as he might, Riley couldn't work himself up to desire for her. Oh, now and then, when he got … desperate.

In the beginning, their sex life had been almost nonexistent. Sherry Lynn was pregnant and miserable and was perfectly happy to inflict her misery on others. And Riley didn't even understand for the better part of a year, that he'd been shell-shocked himself ever since he got home.

Then there was a new baby in the house. With a

new mother. Given how many younger siblings she had, it was a mystery to Riley how Sherry Lynn could be so inept with her own baby. She spent all her time on the phone to her mother, asking her if something was wrong every time Drew hiccupped. Her mother couldn't come to stay with her daughter after the birth — that was customary, expected, but the unspoken feud would have made that far too uncomfortable. Wasn't no McClusky gonna spend the night under Nate Hannacker's roof. End of discussion.

With Riley recovering from wounds both physical and mental ...

And Sherry Lynn struggling to figure out a new baby and motherhood ...

And Papa. Riley didn't know what was wrong with Papa during that first year, chalked it up to the nightmare the whole county'd been through. But his grandfather had taken a long time to come back to himself, seemed to be dealing with demons of his own that Riley didn't know about.

When you mixed all that up in a house without the normal kind of newlywed privacy, Riley and Sherry Lynn's marriage had gotten off to a rocky start sexually. When Drew was finally sleeping through the night and Riley's nightmares had tapered off to something less than a nightly ordeal, he had struggled to be a good husband. The sheer novelty of being able to have sex, going to bed beside a woman, not sneaking around in the back seat of a car, was enough to keep him aroused.

That part was short-lived. Sherry Lynn made no

effort to take care of herself after Drew was born, was too frazzled and fragile. By the time she finally relaxed, she'd put on twenty-five pounds, on top of the twenty-five she gained while she was pregnant that she didn't lose afterward.

It wasn't long before she went from "overweight" … to "fat" … to … well, whatever came after that when you couldn't fit into anything with a shape to it.

That had killed what little desire Riley could muster for her. He tried, and every now and then succeeded, but he feared sex was going to become more and more infrequent as long as Sherry Lynn stayed …

He sat alone on the porch after Sherry Lynn and Papa went to bed, wanted to be sure she was asleep. After undressing in the bathroom, he tiptoed into the bedroom so as not to wake her. She slept soundly, didn't rouse when he slid between the sheets next to her. But Riley couldn't get his mind to settle enough to go to sleep. He'd wanted to talk to Papa about the bullet hole in his hat and all that'd preceded it, but Sherry Lynn had hung around on the porch for so long that when he and Papa were finally alone, Papa was tired and went on to bed.

"DON'T SHOOT," comes a cry from out in the rain and Andy Taggart dives into the bunker, a bowling ball that knocks Davie Monaghan off his feet.

Riley looks out past them through the doorway into the monsoon, the solid wall of water that hides and distorts every-

thing in it. The rumble of explosions is deafening. Clearly the VC had set off the ammunition storage for the guns and the cacophony is ear-splitting.

Then a flare torches the night sky beyond the tangle of Davie and Andy in the doorway, lights up the world beyond them.

Davie is struggling to get to his feet, has turned toward the door. His helmet has been knocked off.

The rain doesn't let up, but for a brief instant of frozen time, images are clear in the brilliant flare light. That's when Riley sees the RPG launcher. The barrel is pointed at the doorway, a black hole of death that seems to swell up bigger and blacker, seems to eat up the world.

His eye takes in the dead VC soldier in the mud, naked and bleeding, and then travels the length of the rocket launcher to the VC holding it.

The little guy is pointing the barrel right at the door of their bunker.

But the little guy isn't naked.

That guy has clothes on, is fully dressed. Camouflage combat fatigues.

For a frozen instant, their eyes meet and lock.

Riley looks into the crazed face of Jackson McClusky. And then the world goes black.

RILEY SAT bolt upright in the bed, didn't cry out, just sat there with his eyes bugging out of their sockets, looking into what his mind could see that was not there in the darkened bedroom.

"You okay, sweetie," Sherry Lynn said in a groggy voice beside him. "Was the nightmare bad?"

"No," he said. "The nightmare wasn't bad."

And that was absolutely true because it hadn't been a nightmare. It had been a *memory.*

Jackson McClusky!

Jackson!

It hadn't been the Cong. It'd been Jackson who'd killed Andy and destroyed Davie's brain.

Jackson.

The name rumbled like a huge boulder crashing through his mind, knocking everything askew, crushing whatever it touched, destroying all the pieces of what Riley *thought* was reality, fragments he had been unable to put into some kind of order.

Riley leapt up out of the bed and staggered out of the room, down the hallway, almost tripped and fell down the stairs but somehow made it out to the front porch where he hung up like a piece of driftwood on the porch railing.

He leaned over and heaved.

His dinner spewed out into the roses beside the porch, the stench of it wafting up to him as he continued to vomit.

When he got control of his breathing, he turned away from the stench and stumbled down the porch steps and out into the front yard, passed the swing set Willie Ray had gotten Drew for his birthday, the one he, Papa and Willie Ray took all day to put together. He almost tripped over the tricycle in the driveway.

Across the driveway and into the woods, he staggered, realized at some point that he was crying and fell to his knees in the fallen leaves on the forest floor as great wrenching sobs swept over his body in waves.

The little Asian doctors in the Japanese hospital who made Riley's flesh crawl every time they touched him had said it could happen.

"With a concussive blow like that ... it often happens that the force wipes out the memories of what happened right before the injury," said the one who'd come in every day and scolded him for being stoic, said if he didn't admit what hurt they might end up sending him home before his wounds were healed.

"So that's it. I'll just never remember what happened?"

"Maybe that is so. Maybe it is not. Sometimes those memories come back in a week, a month, a year." He paused. "And sometimes they never come back."

Riley had long since resigned himself to the fact that he never would remember the last moments of the battle at Tweety Bird. And he found after a while, that he was grateful for that. He was grateful for the images he'd been spared. Just that one glance at Andy's body, torn up like it had been, had fire-branded a hole in his soul. He was grateful he hadn't gotten a better look.

And the rest of it. Robbie Benson ... maybe it was Robbie ... so badly burned ... Ace with one boot on and the other leg ending in a jagged bone.

Kneeling in the dark woods in his underwear,

rocking back and forth, Riley cried, bawled, great heaving sobs that went to the core of his being.

Then he stopped.

He stopped crying so abruptly that he got strangled, got to his feet coughing to catch his breath.

There wasn't a tear left in him. The tears had been burned away like chaff in front of a blow torch. And the fire of the rage in his chest threatened to burst through the skin and consume him.

Jackson McClusky had killed Andy Taggart.

And suddenly Riley was running through the dark woods, stumbling, falling, getting back up, ricocheting off trees, getting tangled in vines.

Running and running until he broke out of the woods on the dirt road that led to the shack Willie Ray Taggart called home. His truck was parked outside but the house was dark.

Riley staggered up onto the wooden porch and banged on the door with his fists.

Bang!

Bang!

Bang!

"Willie Ray," he cried and discovered that his voice was hoarse, though he didn't know what he'd done that had made it so.

"Willie Ra——"

The door flew open and Willie Ray stood in the deeper darkness beyond the shadow of the porch roof that held at bay the glare of the full moon.

"What in the——?"

"Willie Ray, I know ... I *remembered*."

"Remembered what? What are you talking—?"

"Tweety Bird!" He screamed the word in a hoarse voice and Willie Ray took a step back.

And in that instant, Riley understood *why* he knew now what he hadn't known since it happened. It'd been the blow to the head. When he flew backward off the seat of the tractor and banged his head on the ground, something about that "concussive force" had shaken the memories loose.

"I know what happened."

"So do I," Willie Ray moaned, like the pain of instant remembering had punched a hole in his belly.

And then Riley was suddenly calm. The white-hot rage that had propelled him through the woods banked back, like the fire in the blast furnace of a locomotive that powers it, that moves the train down the track.

Riley felt a wave of sympathy for his friend, knowing what it would do to him to hear the truth. It would open the wound in Willie Ray's soul that had finally begun to scab over, but never healed enough to form a scar.

Reaching out, he put his hand on Willie Ray's shoulder, saw the fear in his eyes. Willie Ray knew something catastrophically horrible was about to the knock him down and stab into his being.

How did Riley tack words on it? Just spit it out.

"Willie Ray, the Cong didn't kill Andy. Jackson McClusky did."

Chapter Fifty-Six

THE HOT SHOWER after Jessie came in out of the field had felt especially soothing, easing the ache in her shoulders. But she still had that pesky "pulled muscle" or whatever it was, the jabbing pain under her right shoulder blade she'd been feeling for more than a week, ever since she'd worked the night through with Riley, Willie Ray, Nate and the other field hands to rescue the weed crop before the sheriff could plow it under.

They'd gotten finished just as the sun was beginning to turn the eastern sky pink, and Riley had wanted to hang around in the trees to see the look on the sheriff's face when the crop he'd come to destroy wasn't there. He probably would have, too, if he hadn't had too much work to do to waste a whole morning waiting for the sheriff to show up with a backhoe.

And as it'd turned out, he didn't have to hang around to see it. When last Monday's issue of the

Callison County Tribune came out, there was a picture of it on the front page. Served up for Riley, the others in the Cornbread Mafia, and every other man, woman and child in Callison County to see. The picture of Sheriff McClusky and State Police Detective Booth Graham had been absolutely priceless. Graham had been caught with his mouth open, literally, gaping at the empty field where there was supposed to be a pot crop.

Jessie still smiled when she thought about it, though she was sure the state police detective would view it as the day that would live in infamy. He'd be glad to see a new issue of the newspaper, with a different front-page picture, on the racks in a couple of hours.

She was certainly ready to fall into bed exhausted tonight, which was just the way she liked it. If she got tired enough, she fell asleep instantly and that was always preferable to lying awake thinking the thoughts you could keep yourself from thinking during the day when you were busy.

Dressed in sweatpants and a tee shirt, her definition of pajamas, Jessie went down the wide front stairs to what she thought of as the "assisted living" quarters below where Davie and Ruth lived with all the equipment they needed — paid for, of course, by weed.

That still staggered her sometimes. She'd grown up on a farm, watched the prices of different crops rise and fall, and the fortunes of her family along with them. Tobacco was the cash cow, of course, but it was so heavily regulated to keep the price stable, you could only raise a certain amount of it, your allotment, and usually it was just enough to make ends meet for most of the farm families she knew.

But weed.

An image flashed through her mind like a comet and was gone, Davie describing the magic carpet ride out into the future. He'd said they would have a long life together. And as his physical condition had progressed, that looked more and more like it would be the case. He and Jessie would be together. With Davie locked inside himself … somewhere.

The stairs ended in the front entryway that opened through an archway into Mama Ruth's room. The old woman lay on her side, snoring softly. Jessie stepped to her, moved a strand of her hair off her cheek and she stirred so Jessie stepped back, flipping off the wall switch that turned off the table lamps and floor lamp, just leaving a small nightlight glowing in an outlet. She did not want to wake Mama Ruth. It was easy for her to get her nights and days confused and Jessie did *not* want to stay up all night tonight to provide company, listening to the old woman talking about a mix of reality and fantasy, woven together as masterfully as a folk tale.

From Mama Ruth's room, she went into the kitchen, switching off the light there. She glanced out the window into a back yard, lit bright by a full moon earlier. Now the moon was high in the black velvet sky, glowing there amid stars as big and shiny as chunks of ice.

From the kitchen, she went into Davie's room,

stood looking at his still-handsome face in the soft light. She wouldn't let herself imagine … anything. He made a soft, moan-like sound and she watched an expression take over his face. She froze. That'd been happening a lot lately. He would look … frightened.

Which had to indicate some kind of higher-order thinking, didn't it? You had to have some level of awareness to be afraid. After a few moments, his face became serene again. She kissed him tenderly on the cheek and turned to go, very aware of Magic's absence. Jessie didn't realize how much she had come to depend on Magic until he wasn't there. The whole house seemed empty without the big lumbering black dog who had transformed into an adult from a puppy overnight when she brought Davie home from the hospital.

The *puppy* had followed her around from room to room wherever she went. The *dog* had parked itself beside Davie's bed and stayed there, night and day … which in the beginning was still right by Jessie's side because she was always by Davie's.

When Jessie'd started spending a night or two upstairs in her own bed, the poor dog didn't quite know what to do, but opted in the end to remain by Davie's side. It was a comfort to know the big black guard dog was watching over him.

She ground her teeth, thinking about the poor thing, locked up in a kennel at Dr. Mitchell Garrison's veterinary hospital. Quarantined. That was the most ridiculous thing she'd ever … she had to let it go. She'd exploded in the beginning, when Mitch told her

Mrs. Pettigrew was demanding he keep Magic locked up until the rabies test results came back. But Mitch had rolled his eyes, said she was better off not to protest. It wouldn't be but three days. He promised to take great care of Magic, and she was sure he would. Still … Magic belonged *here*, with her and Davie.

She paused.

Magic wasn't here. The *guard* dog wasn't here.

Without giving it a lot of thought, she turned to the back door that opened from the kitchen onto the back porch and started to lock it. Then she shook her head at how silly she was being. She didn't think she'd ever gone to sleep in a locked house in her whole life.

The door beside the back-porch door led to the back stairs, which was the shortest route to her bedroom upstairs. But she didn't go up those stairs, she went back through Mama Ruth's room for one final check on her, peeked into Davie's room, then turned and went up the front stairs to her bedroom and got into bed, aware of a twinge of pain from her shoulder as she settled into the soft mattress.

The world dissolved almost immediately

Jessie came awake quickly. Her eyes popped open.

What was that?

She'd heard a sound, some kind of sound. An out-of-place sound. What was it? She lay still, listening.

She heard only the wind brushing a tree branch past her window, and the gentle creaking every old house makes as it sleeps. Relaxing back into the pillow, she began to drift back off—

"… you the porter?"

Mama Ruth's voice from her room carried up the stairwell to the second floor.

"How come that nice fella in the uniform don't come see me no more?"

The "nice fella in the uniform" was the cruise ship's captain, who came to wish her good day every morning, to make sure she didn't need anything.

Goody. Mama Ruth was awake.

Jessie lay still. Sometimes, the old woman awoke, babbled to people she could see but you couldn't, and then drifted back off to sleep.

"C'mere into the light so's I can get a look at you. Why, you're one of Davie's Army buddies, ain't you?"

That was odd.

Jessie sighed and swung her feet off her bed and felt around on the floor for her house shoes. Mama Ruth had imaginary conversations with people all the time, but they were always with people she'd made up in her head — people who didn't exist out in the real world. The ship's captain. The rich woman in the suite down from hers with diamonds all over her fingers. The waiter who made sure Mama Ruth was served before everyone else.

Why would she be talking to an *imaginary* friend of Davie's?

As Jessie stepped out into the upstairs hallway she heard … like another voice almost. Was Mama Ruth making up *both* sides of the conversations now?

"Do you know where my Davie is? I've looked and looked and can't find him nowhere. You seen him?" A pause. "What'd you bring that thing in here for? You know I don't 'low guns in my—"

There was a sound then — maybe a sound, hard to tell, it was so soft — and Mama Ruth stopped talking in mid-sentence.

Jessie opened her mouth to cry out, "Mama Ruth, are you all—?"

She caught herself in time and kept silent.

Was somebody in Mama Ruth's room *with a gun*?

Oh, that was crazy. Mama Ruth was imagining the whole thing.

Oh, surely it was just—

Another sound came from downstairs, like a thump. A movement.

Maybe somebody bumping into something in the dark.

Jessie was suddenly terrified.

Chapter Fifty-Seven

WILLIE RAY MADE Riley say it over and over, made him repeat the story again and again until the words finally carried the meaning into his soul.

Then Willie Ray's legs collapsed out from under him and he was sitting in the floor.

Andy was beside him.

Riley was crouched in front of him on his knees, his hands on Willy Ray's shoulders.

"… the barrel of the RPG … the black hole … I've been dreaming about it for years … and after I hit my head this afternoon …"

He paused, like something had just occurred to him, but he pushed it aside and went on.

"I saw him. I *saw* Jackson McClusky holding that RPG, pointing it at the bunker, at me, at us. I think Davie Monaghan saw him, too."

Willie Ray looked at Andy. He had been standing beside Willie Ray before Willie Ray collapsed, so he had to look up into Andy's face.

It was dark, too dark to see anything. With your eyes, anyway. Anything *real*. Riley was just a shimmering shadow backlit by the moonlight in the front yard. But Andy was clearly visible. Lit up in some way from no source of light that Willie Ray could see. His face was clear, his blue eyes looking solemnly at Willie Ray beneath eyebrows and eyelashes so blond they were almost invisible.

"He wanted to keep us from telling the captain what he did, how he set fire to the Jingle Bell Man," Riley said, and Willie Ray looked back at him.

Riley got to his feet and extended his hand down to Willie Ray.

"Get up. We got work to do."

Willie Ray didn't have to ask what he was talking about. Taking the extended hand, he pulled himself up and was standing beside Andy. Andy, with his chest torn open and his guts hanging out on the floor.

The rage that dawning understanding had built in Willie Ray was not white hot. It was cold. As cold as an Arctic glacier. He would kill Jackson McClusky. Slow. He would stick a knife into his belly and draw it upward slowly, rip him open from his groin to his throat, reach into his body and drag his guts—

"… think about this …" Riley was saying.

"Think about what? Ain't nothing to think about."

Willie Ray wanted to step to the wall switch, turn on the lights, so he could go into his bedroom and put his pants on. But it was easier to look at Andy when the light was dim. In bright light … you could see the blood, how slimy his guts were, shrining—

"… listening to me, Willie Ray?"

Taking a step around Riley, Willie Ray did turn on the lights then, realized for the first time that Riley was in his underwear.

He turned toward Andy, but he was gone. Not clear and detailed in the bright light … gone.

"I said, we can't just grab a gun and go shoot him."

"Copy that. I ain't gonna shoot him. I'm gonna cut him open, drag his guts out," Willie Ray was turning toward the bedroom as he spoke, "slice——"

Riley stepped in front of him, blocked his way.

"I ain't gonna let you spend the rest of your life in jail for murder."

"You think I *care*——?"

"*I* care."

"You saying we ain't gonna kill——?"

"Of course we going to kill him! But I ain't gonna let you rip him apart in front of a dozen witnesses."

"And how you plan to stop me? I'm gonna go find him, and soon's I do——"

"If that's what you're determined to do, I'll help you. I'll watch the lights go out in his eyes right alongside you and then … whatever happens to you happens to me, too."

That gave Willie Ray pause. There was Riley to think of, after all. Riley mattered and what happened to him mattered. Willie Ray could throw his own life away in the killing of Jackson McClusky and glory in the doing of it, cheer at the sheer raging power of it.

But Riley …

"I thought you wanted to kill him slow," Riley said, when Willie Ray paused. "He don't deserve to die quick. He needs to pay."

Some part of Willie Ray realized that Riley was doing what he always did when Willie Ray was drunk. Willie Ray thought of it as steering the ship. He was the ship, that the wind was blowing every which way, and Riley was the ship's captain whose job it was to steer the ship so it didn't crash into anything or go aground.

Willie Ray was being *managed*. And a huge part of him wanted to throw off the restraint and charge off fueled by his bloodlust, wanted to rip into the little McClusky weasel with his bare hands, wanted to …

But he'd spent his whole life letting Riley keep afloat the floundering ship that he so often was, letting him steer Willie Ray away from the jagged teeth of the reef.

Oh, he absolutely knew Riley was right. That Riley was *thinking* while he was only *feeling*, that Riley was being reasonable and sensible while he wanted no tethering lines of any kind. He didn't give a rip what happened to himself after the deed was done. Couldn't see anything out there beyond Jackson McClusky's blood on his hands, *in his teeth where he'd ripped his throat out*. There was nothing on the other side of that but a black void of nothingness.

But there was Riley to think of.

And there was a slow death.

If he went running out of here and found Jackson,

tore him apart with his bare hands, Riley would help him. And Riley would suffer the consequences.

He grabbed hold of himself and found that it was easier to do than he'd thought. Riley always had that effect on him.

"Sounds to me like you got a plan? Do you?"

"If by plan, you mean what we *do*, then no, I don't have a plan. But if by plan, you mean what we *don't* do, yeah … I am all over that."

Willie Ray took a breath, let it out slow and took another.

"Do you even know where to find Jackson?" Riley asked.

Willie Ray had to admit that he didn't.

"I assume he lives with his folks, with Big-un."

He knew Riley was recalling the image of the big man, lumbering into the barn where they had the Colombians tied up.

"Kill 'em!" he'd growled. It was possible that scared the South Americans more than anything else that happened to them.

Big-un had put on that little show because Nate had asked him to. Obviously, those two had some history the others weren't privy to — a McClusky helping out a Hannacker didn't happen every day!

"It ain't like we can go rolling into Big-un McClusky's house hellbent on killing his son," Riley said. "How far you think we'd get?"

"Then what *do* we do?"

"We find out where he is. We plan. We figure out a place where we can take him." Riley ground out the next words through clenched teeth. "Somewhere that *nobody can hear his screams*."

Willie Ray liked the sound of that. He surely did like the sound of that. A *lot*!

He nodded, wondering as he did if Andy would show up for the execution. He suspected his big brother would be there.

"Works for me."

He watched Riley let go of the helm, knowing from experience that he didn't need to steer Willie Ray anymore, that he could maneuver his way between the buoys on his own.

"It wasn't a squirrel hunter this afternoon," Riley said. "This is what that was about."

"I ain't got no idea what you just said."

"Somebody shot at me this afternoon."

"*Shot* at you?"

"Yeah. I was on the tractor and … I'll tell you about it. I just figured it had to be some freak accident, a squirrel hunter. It wasn't. It was Jackson. They hauled him off to prison right after we got back from 'Nam or he probably would have come after me sooner — silence me before I could remember."

Riley stopped then, stood very still.

"If he came after me to silence me … maybe he's gonna go after Davie too. We need to go tell Jessie."

Willie Ray looked at him, ran his eye down his body.

"Might want to put on some pants first."

❧

SHERRY LYNN HEARD the jangle of the telephone. It jarred her awake from an uneasy slumber and she turned to rouse Riley.

He wasn't there.

His side of the bed was cold.

Cold. He'd been gone a long time.

She remembered then that she'd thought she heard him earlier, moaning, making the sounds he made when the nightmares attacked his sleep. He usually thrashed around when that happened. That's usually what woke her up, but he hadn't done that this time.

The phone rang again.

She looked at the alarm clock on the bedside table, the hands and numbers illuminated that pale green florescent color that made them visible. She didn't like that florescent thing, but wouldn't tell Riley that. He'd laugh at her. But wasn't that green-glow stuff made out of radiation? Like atomic-bomb radiation? She'd been going to school to be a radiation technologist, had dropped out to have Drew and never went back. She didn't remember a whole lot about it but did know she had to wear protective clothing. And that the effect of the radiation *accumulated*. So if you forgot to wear that lead apron thing one time, that one time *counted*. It was added onto the next time no matter how long—

The phone rang a third time. The telephone was downstairs in the living room on the table beside the recliner. Nate's was the only bedroom down there — he was the closest to it. Why didn't he answer it? Did he expect her to come all the way downstairs when he was right down the hall? If he didn't get it before it rang again, it might wake Drew up. That child was always grumpy when he woke up — well, except when Riley went to get him in the morning and she could hear Drew giggling.

She heard the soft sound of a voice downstairs and relaxed back into the pillow. Nate had picked up.

So who was calling at this hour of the night? Her grandmother had a saying: "Don't nobody call before the rooster's crowed over the day with *good* news."

And where was Riley? He was probably sitting on the front porch in the dark. He did that sometimes after he had a bad dream. She'd gone to him a couple of times as he sat there, tried to help, asked him to tell her about the dream. But he had slammed the door in her face, didn't want to talk about it, end of discussion.

What part of "he doesn't want to share it with you" didn't she understand? She never bothered to ask anymore.

Sighing, she got out of bed to go down the hall and check on Drew before she went back to sleep.

Chapter Fifty-Eight

SITTING on a log in the dark woods, looking at the brightly lit Monaghan house through the trees, Jackson McClusky felt alive!

Gloriously, incredibly *alive*. And strong. He patted the snub-nosed revolver he'd stuck down in the waistband of his jeans and felt the power of having it there surge through him. He'd remembered the little pistol Wade kept in the top drawer of his dresser. His brother wouldn't move out of his old room until him and Jeanie got back from their honeymoon in Gatlinburg, so the gun was still there — and on an impulse, Jackson had sneaked into the house and gotten it.

Didn't make no difference that he didn't need it, wasn't planning on *shooting* Davie Monaghan, just smothering him. But it felt good to be *packing* and he liked that sensation. Made him feel strong, almost invincible.

The invincible part — and the rest of it too, likely

— was chemically induced, however. And understanding that should have tempered his elation.

It didn't.

But it should have. Jackson shouldn't have done it.

Oh, but it felt so good, so *right.*

One part of him wanted to kick himself all the way to China for the lapse in self-discipline and the other was celebrating the rush the little bit of cocaine he'd sniffed had given him.

He'd been clean, absolutely one hundred percent *clean* ever since he went through withdrawal without benefit of rehab in a cell in solitary in the Jefferson County Jail. Once he got clean, everything in his life turned around. When he got out of prison, he'd stayed clean. The education that prison had been had taught him everything he needed to know about life. And one of those lessons was that your mind had to be clear. Leaders stayed away from drugs because such self-indulgence led to mistakes. And the leader who makes the fewest mistakes wins. Every time.

Since he walked out of the Castle on the Cumberland in February, he had taken nothing more potent than aspirin, got a little buzz on his own weed — to test it, that's all. And only a little now and then. Weed muddied your thinking and judgement but that wasn't even the worst part. It drained away your motivation. He'd seen it in 'Nam and he'd seen it in prison. Might be pot wasn't physically addictive, but the sense of well-being it gave you was psychologically addictive. Smoke pot and you lost your edge. In the same way the horror of war takes away a soldier's give-a-damn, weed sapped your resolve, allowed you to laze around in the warm waters of ... *whatever.*

He had maintained strict control over his consumption of weed, put limits on how much and how often and he'd denied himself every other indulgence. He had a life plan and using drugs was counterproductive to that plan.

Today, though ... he'd *needed* it today. And the need had *overwhelmed* him.

The rollercoaster had been too much for him.

Screwing himself up to killing Riley Hannacker had taken more out of him than he'd imagined it would. Oh, not remorse or regret. It had just ... drained him, left him awash in a sea of relief that he'd dealt with the danger, neutralized it.

Only, maybe he hadn't killed Riley Hannacker after all! And what was he supposed to do about *that*? He had to find out. There might be some reason he hadn't heard about Riley's death, but he had to find out, one way or the other, make a plan from there.

Right now, though, he had bigger fish to fry. The "catch of the day" had literally dropped into his lap. And suddenly, he had a chance, *one* chance, a golden opportunity, to take care of the only other threat to his life plans, not nearly so present and eminent, but a threat nonetheless, a "loose end." Take the chance now, today, *tonight,* in just a few hours ... or miss the chance and perhaps never get another one.

It certainly had never been his plan to kill Riley and Davie on the same day! But a good leader had to be willing to abandon the plan, know when to bob and weave, take advantage of some random chance that came his way.

The certainty was the thing. *Knowing.* That's what the coke had given him. Jackson was *right.* He *would* be able to pull it off. He was *the man.*

He'd had doubts before, questioned not only his plan but the need for it in the first place.

After all, he wasn't even sure Davie Monaghan had seen him.

And he didn't know for sure Davie Monaghan could remember it if he did.

And he wasn't sure Davie could tell anybody about it if he remembered.

And even if he did tell somebody, who'd believe an addlebrained shell-shocked veteran?

But this was an opportunity Jackson would *never get again.*

He had seized it with both hands, and would look back one day to see that it was the best decision he'd ever made.

He'd been clean for too long, though, to fall head-first into euphoria without looking back at his clear-eyed, unmedicated self. *That* was Jackson McClusky. That Jackson hadn't needed coke or anything else to give him the strength and determination to get the job done. That Jackson would chart out a future. He had to *be* that Jackson.

And he would be. He would. As soon as he got this job done, he would foreswear drugs from now on. Make himself a pledge, a solemn oath to walk the straight and narrow. But right now, he *needed* the rush, the certainty, the strength and mental acuity. A need like this wouldn't come up every day to seduce him into backsliding.

He'd quit, just as soon as …

"I'll quit, man, just as soon as …"

That's what all the junkies said. And tomorrow? What about tomorrow's need? He'd have to deal with … whatever had gone wrong with Riley Hannacker's shooting. Wouldn't he *need*—?

The light in the room on the downstairs right, the one with the big picture window, went out.

He sat up, watched, could see a shadow — Jessie — moving behind the drawn shades in the room on the other side. He sat, not holding his breath, but not aware of breathing, either. Three minutes. Five.

Then that room went dark, too, and an internal light came on somewhere that threw just a faint glow through the windows. He'd been inside Ruth Monaghan's house one time — almost two decades ago. He'd been eight years old, maybe, and she and Davie's father had a cookout for all the players on Davie's tee-ball team. Jackson had been invited, of course, though he understood that nobody really wanted him there. He was on the team, though.

The cookout was around the grill in the back yard and he'd gone inside to use the bathroom. The memory was just a ghost after all these years, but this house was built like every other house its age in the county. Same basic layout. Wasn't like no architect come in here and done 'em so every one was unique. They all had kitchens on the back. He'd gone from the kitchen to the bathroom that opened off a hallway to the front of the house. Other rooms were on that hallway, he supposed, but couldn't picture them. He thought he'd glanced down the hallway to the front door, and saw a staircase on the right that went up the wall beside it. He figured the light that'd just come on had been the staircase light. And sure enough, another light came on upstairs right above it, and then the downstairs light was turned off. The light was lit in the upstairs room on the left, a bedroom, and the one next to it — a small window, a bathroom.

Jessie was getting ready to go to bed.

Though he wasn't sure of the layout of the whole house, he did know that what had been gutted when Jessie'd renovated it were the two rooms on the front. One of them was for Davie's mother, Ruth, and the other was for Davie. He figured to slip in the back door, let himself into the kitchen. He would go to the right front room first — hope that was Davie's. If not, he'd go to the other room. He'd do the job and come back out the way he'd come in. He wouldn't be in there five minutes.

And he'd be done!

Exhilaration swelled in his chest. No more wondering and waiting and hoping. He'd get rid of the enemy — strike first, one swift blow with staggering brutality. That'd worked in prison and it would work now. He leaned back against the trunk of the tree and waited for the upstairs light to go out.

Chapter Fifty-Nine

Drew was asleep on the floor under the kitchen table when the phone rang and woke him up. The phone was in the living room. He sat up, dug his fists into his eyes, looked around, and couldn't remember why he'd fallen asleep under the table.

He did that a lot, got out of his bed and went somewhere else in the house to sleep. On the couch, usually, somewhere comfortable. But he sometimes just lay down on the floor and drifted off and he must have done that this time.

Then he remembered why it was he couldn't go to sleep in the first place.

He liked to sleep with his GI Joe doll, the one Pop Pop got him that Mommy didn't like. He'd gone looking for it at bedtime and couldn't find it … then he'd remembered where he'd left it. In his secret room, the storage room in the back that Pop Pop had turned into a war room for him, had got him blocks to build forts out of and a bunch of little GI Joe soldiers, little plastic ones only a couple of inches tall, but they were flat on the bottom so they'd stand up.

The phone rang again.

He wanted to go get the GI Joe doll, but Mommy didn't know about the room and if she found out she would yell at Pop Pop. Not in a loud-voice kinda yelling. In a quiet-voice kind of yelling where she squinted up her eyes real tight and said loud things softly. When she yelled at Pop Pop — which she didn't do very often — she always used that soft, mean voice. She used it to yell at Daddy all the time. But she also used the loud-voice yelling on him, too. He got both kinds.

The phone rang again and he heard Pop Pop coming down the hallway from his bedroom to answer it.

Pop Pop could get his GI Joe doll for him!

Pop Pop was awake and Mommy was asleep so she wouldn't know. He would ask him.

Climbing through the tangle of table legs, Drew went to the door of the living room to wait for Pop Pop to get off the phone so he could ask him to go out to the barn and get his GI Joe doll out of the secret room.

"Drew Hannacker!" Mommy flipped on the light in the kitchen, momentarily blinding him. "What are you doing down here? Were you up wandering around again?"

"I wasn't wandering around," he said. "I was asleep under the table."

"What have I told you about getting out of bed to

go sleep somewhere else?" She took him by the arm and headed with him in tow toward the stairs, flipping the light off behind her. Pop Pop was talking quietly on the phone in the living room and didn't even look up when they went up the stairs. "Beds are for sleeping in. That's why we have beds."

She kept saying stuff but he stopped listening. He didn't listen to what Mommy said when she said dumb things like "beds are for sleeping in." He knew that. Just because that's what a bed was for didn't mean you had to use it. He liked other places better. As Mommy's voice fell unheard on his ears, he looked back over his shoulder at the dark entryway into the living room where Pop Pop was still talking on the phone.

JESSIE THOUGHT HALF a dozen different thoughts at the same time, though her head felt completely empty.

Her mind spun like the Tilt-A-Whirl at the hinky-tinky carnival that came to Brewster every Labor Day when she was a little girl. It had old, rusty equipment — a Ferris wheel that struggled to carry its passengers all the way to the top and a rollercoaster with cars that didn't go a whole lot faster than a riding lawnmower. The merry-go-round had given her nightmares her whole childhood — wild horses frozen in mid-gallop, their glaring eyes wide and horrifying. Their teeth were bared and poles were stabbed right up through the middle of them.

The South Americans? From Colombia, weren't they?

Was that it? Had they somehow found out she was a partner in the Cornbread Mafia? Had they shown up here for payback?

That made absolutely no sense for half a dozen reasons — including, but not limited to, the absurdity of them finding out about her, the ridiculousness of a sneak attack in the middle of the night and ... she couldn't articulate the others.

She was profoundly grateful she hadn't been at Riley's when the drug dealers had ... *attacked*. She could fire an M1 carbine with the best of them, might not have been as good a shot as the soldiers but they'd said the "enemy" had been ducks-in-a-washtub close. It was just that ... a *gunfight?* She'd kept her face expressionless when the guys told her about the battle and what they'd done afterward to convince the Colombians the Cornbread Mafia was a badass operation. She hoped they couldn't see how horrified she was.

Jessie was determined not to justify the infamous *just-a-girl* thing. She'd always hated that kind of condescension from boys, faced it at every turn. She was as strong, smart, capable and tireless as any of them, and over the past few years she'd earned the respect of the three men who were her partners with her dogged determination to work them under the table.

But *guns*.

No, not guns.

Shooting at people? People *shooting back* at you?

No, thank you very much, Jessie would pass.

And the pigsty! She wouldn't have been able to take that part. She'd have thrown up. She'd come home after hearing the description of the Cornbread Mafia One-Day War and had a serious talk with herself. She'd grabbed herself by the shoulders and told herself to get a grip.

You agreed to do this.

Yeah but …

You signed on—

But I didn't know—

A bargain is a bargain.

They'd stacked hands on it.

And so she had swallowed her horror at what'd happened to Ace, Riley, Willie Ray and Nate. Never allowed them to catch so much as a hint of her squeamishness.

They had assured her that they'd never have to do anything like that again, that they'd taught these guys a lesson, established a reputation for the Cornbread Mafia they hoped would spread out like ink through water — set foot on our turf and an *army* of hillbillies will mow you down!

Had the guys been wrong, though? Had the South Americans come back — why *here*?

Well, there was *somebody* down in Mama Ruth's room with a gun.

Two thoughts collided head-on in her mind.

One, her own gun was in the glove box of her truck.

And two, *Davie was down there!*

That thought galvanized her. Davie was helpless. She had to protect him!

How? She didn't have a weapon.

Go down the back stairs, out the back door, get the gun out of her truck?

That would take too long.

Someone was down there *right now* and she had to do something *right now*.

Never take a knife to a gunfight was one of Nate Hannacker's favorite sayings.

But when a knife was all you had … a knife was better than nothing.

There was a butcher-block knife holder on the kitchen counter with half a dozen *big* knives.

And then she was running silently down the hall toward the back stairs.

Chapter Sixty

Jackson almost wet himself when the old woman started talking.

"Are you the porter?" came out of the darkness from the puddle of deeper darkness that was where the bed stood.

He froze, panicked, unsure whether to bolt out the door or—

"How come that nice fella in the uniform don't come see me no more?"

Then he remembered what Phyllis Carter had said Saturday afternoon in the Buy-Low. She'd told Erlene and Edna that Harriet Porter'd said Ruth Monaghan woke up in the middle of the night all the time, babbled for hours, not saying nothing that made sense. That was what she was doing now, right? Still, it would wake Jessie up, wouldn't it? And she'd come down to investigate.

He turned, ready to cut bait and run, when the bedside lamp suddenly came on, casting a dim glow from a dark lampshade over the bed and the woman in it. She was smiling at him.

"C'mere into the light so's I can get a look at you. You one of Davie's army buddies, ain't you?"

Crap. The old lady could *see* him! Could she tell he wasn't some phantom in her imagination? Of course not, she didn't know one from the other, thought all of it was real. But he hadn't heard anything from upstairs. He'd been listening for footfalls on the stairs, was sure they was wooden like the hardwood floors, wouldn't be no stair treads or carpet. The stairs in old houses always made noise when somebody came down 'em. He would hear Jessie coming in time to get away.

"Do you know where my Davie is? I've looked and looked and can't find him nowhere. You seen him?"

Jessie had to be hearing this! Why wasn't she … because she was *ignoring* it! Yeah, Phyllis had said the old lady done it all the time. And if you's ever gonna get any sleep, you'd have to learn to ignore stuff like that, wouldn't you?

Forcing himself to smile at her, he said softly, "Me and Davie's old friends. We was in 'Nam together, but I ain't seen him lately, don't know where he's at."

He eased away from her bed back toward the darkened kitchen he'd just come out of. Obviously, the *other* room was where Davie—

"What'd you bring that thing in here for?"

It took Jackson a second to realize she was talking about the pistol. He'd drawn the pistol out of his belt. *Was holding it!* Why had he done a thing like that?

Didn't even realize he was doing it. Musta just been …
breaking into somebody's house and all …

The old lady was looking right at him, could see
him, knew he had a gun. He had to shut her up.
Without thinking about it, he took two steps and had
the gun raised to whack her with it when he stopped
just in time. He couldn't clock the old lady, leave a
knot or a bruise on her head.

"You know I don't 'low guns in my——"

"Shhhh!" he whispered fiercely, putting his finger
to his lips, and she hushed instantly. "You don't wanna
wake Jessie, do ya?"

She shook her head, put a crooked finger to her
own lips and nodded. He turned toward the kitchen
again, bumped into the side of a chest by the doorway
and it made a loud, thumping sound. He ignored it,
heading for the darkened area on the other side of the
archway. Davie's room.

"Don't go running off now." The old lady whispered, real soft. "I ain't done talking to you yet."

He kept going, was three steps into Davie's room
when she whispered again. It was so soft he barely
heard it.

"Why, looka there, you done tracked mud all over
my clean floor."

Jackson froze and looked down. It was too dark to
see. *Had* he tracked mud into the house? If he had——?
The implications of that were horrifying and his heart
started racing, thumping so loud in his ears he
couldn't think. Were there muddy footprints——? No,

the old lady was imagining it. Hadn't rained since last Monday. It wasn't muddy outside.

Still, he tried to get a look at the kitchen floor he'd just crossed, but the light from her lamp barely reached. There was nothing there … nothing he could see. It was clean. It *was*. He was rattled, though, starting to unravel, coming down off the coke high that had sent him running in here in the middle of the night without thinking the whole thing through.

But he could see Davie on the bed now, only a few feet away. It wouldn't take no time at all, less than a minute probably, to finish the job he'd come here to do.

Stuffing the pistol down into his pants, he went to the bed and pulled the pillow out from under Davie's head, placed it over his face, and leaned into it, holding it tight.

JESSIE'S HEART was hammering so hard and fast she could feel it pulsing in her ears. She slipped soundlessly down the unlighted stairwell she'd traveled hundreds of times to the door that opened into the kitchen. There was a warm glow from the nightlights that lit the downstairs, always reminded Jessie of a jar full of lightning bugs. The one in Mama Ruth's room had the kind of lightbulb used in Christmas lights behind a real shell, so the glow coming through was pink and the veins in the shell were visible.

The light in Davie's room was a plain, unpretentious nightlight. It was plugged into the socket in the far wall, though, on the other side of his bed. So it made a silhouette of his bed backlit in the darkness.

She could tell as soon as she stepped into the kitchen that Mama Ruth had turned on the bedside lamp in her room. It was a dim bulb behind a dark lampshade because harsh artificial light gave her a headache, but it was brighter than Davie's nightlight. His room was still a puddle of darkness.

Why had Mama Ruth suddenly stopped talking? Had somebody …?

There was a light on a pole on the other side of the driveway and it cast streaks of light to stripe the kitchen floor. Jessie moved like a shadow across the room to the block of knives, pulled out the biggest one. It was almost a foot long with a vicious point and razor sharp. Harriet Porter, Davie's day nurse, did most of the cooking now, and she'd asked for nothing special by way of equipment.

"A plain old black skillet will do, and a pressure cooker," she'd said. Jessie had long since replaced the one she'd burned up. "And *sharp* knives. You'll end up cutting your whole thumb off with a dull knife. Gotta keep 'em like razors." Harriet kept them like razors.

Turning toward the archway that opened into the room that now was Davie's, Jessie thought she caught a glimpse of a dark shadow passing in front of the night light.

Was she imagining this whole thing? Somebody in there in the dark with Davie?

Oh, what she wouldn't give for Magic right now. If

there really were any danger to Davie, he'd rip the intruder apart.

She reached for the light switch and stopped short. She had only a knife — she'd have a better chance against someone with a gun in the dark.

Then she saw the outline of a figure clearly. Someone was standing beside Davie's bed. Leaning over him.

Holding something …

He was holding a pillow, pushing it down on Davie's face!

Jessie lunged.

Chapter Sixty-One

HIS MOMMY TUCKED Drew back into his bed, said she wouldn't let him play outside all day tomorrow if he got up again. He wished Daddy had found him instead of Mommy. Daddy wouldn't have been mad at all. He might even have picked Drew up and carried him sleeping back to bed. He did that once when Drew fell asleep on the couch. Drew had pretended he was still asleep and Daddy'd carried him all the way up to his room.

Mommy didn't ever do stuff like that.

After she pecked his cheek with a kiss and left, he rolled over and tried to go to sleep. But he missed his GI Joe doll. It was hard to go to sleep without it snuggled up next to him.

He heard a sound and tensed, listening. It was the sound of the back door opening softly, then the screen door. Pop Pop didn't ever let it slam when he went out. The screen door slamming was one of the things — there were a lot of them — that Mommy said "got on her last nerve." And sometimes Drew let it slam on purpose just to annoy her.

Hopping out of bed, Drew went to the window. He'd seen a full moon when he got out of bed to go sleep under the kitchen table … well, he hadn't intended to do that, just to go downstairs and find somewhere that looked like a good place, and under the table'd looked like a good place. Now that moon was smaller and in a different place. Drew didn't know why the moon did that, but now there wasn't as much moonlight as there'd been before. But even in the dimmer light, he could plainly see his grandfather crossing the open area in front on the barn, heading that way. He watched Pop Pop open the front bay door enough to go inside and then he was gone.

A few moments later, light suddenly shone out through the barn cracks into the darkness around it. Pop Pop had turned on the florescent light bar that hung from the rafters.

Racing out of his bedroom to the hallway, he tiptoed quietly past his parents' room, and edged down the stairs. The third step from the bottom always creaked when you stepped on it. That's how he always won when he played hide-and-seek with Daddy. While Daddy counted to fifty, Drew would hide in the linen closet at the top of the stairs. He'd hear Daddy stop counting, then he'd hear him looking around downstairs, opening and closing doors and cabinets. Then Daddy would try to sneak up the stairs, but that third step squeaked every time so Drew knew he was coming, held his breath while Daddy passed right by the linen closet door. Daddy never thought to look in the linen closet, and as soon as he went into one of the other rooms off the upstairs hallway, Drew would hop out of the closet and run down the stairs to the kitchen table and holler out "Olly olly oxen free!"

And Daddy would come down the stairs shaking his head, saying he couldn't imagine where Drew had been hiding that he always got to the table first.

Drew stepped carefully over the third step to the second, hopped down to the floor, then crossed the kitchen to the back door. Pop Pop had left the door open, and Drew was so little, he didn't have to open the screen but a few inches to squeeze out, not far enough to make the spring squeak.

He almost went in the bay door of the barn after Pop Pop, but then had a better idea. If he went in the outside door of the tack room and then into the storage roof where he played, he could get the doll and go back to the house and even Pop Pop wouldn't know he'd sneaked out of bed. Then Pop Pop wouldn't get in trouble with Mommy for letting Drew do things she didn't like. Drew always hated it when that happened and it happened a lot.

He went around the outside corner of the barn. It was dark there, no light from the barn shone around that corner. The dark space between the corner of the barn and the tack room door looked spooky, but he crept forward. The dark weeds growing up beside the barn were almost as tall as Drew was and when the wind blew and they moved, he almost went back. But the door was just ahead and it was closer than going back, so he ran to it and pulled it open. He didn't have to turn on the light in the tack room. Big cracks between the wall planks would let in light from the barn.

Pop Pop was in the barn talking to somebody, Drew could hear their voices.

He went into the storage room/playroom, looking around on the floor, but he couldn't locate GI Joe. Had he left it somewhere — then he saw it, lying right in a shaft of barn light and he picked it up. Maybe he'd just go out into the barn from the tack room instead of back out into the dark. Pop Pop was in the barn and they could walk back to the house together.

He leaned over and looked through the crack into the barn. There was something blocking part of the crack. Pop Pop was standing not far away, facing the crack, talking to someone, but Drew didn't know who it was.

Pop Pop had a mad face. But he looked scared, too.

Chapter Sixty-Two

DAVIE DIDN'T RESIST at first, but as his oxygen supply was cut off he began to wiggle and squirm, tried to turn his face away from the pillow. Jackson's thoughts were racing, rocketing through his mind so fast he couldn't grab any of them long enough to think it proper.

Davie was more than just a vegetable, alright, if he was fighting back.

If he could fight back, he could think.

If he could think, he could talk, couldn't he? If you can think, you can talk.

If you can think, you can remember, too. Sure you can. And you'd remember the last thing you seen before the lights went out. That made sense. That's what you'd remember before you remembered anything else!

If you could think and remember and talk, you'd tell somebody. You'd—

Jackson could feel panic from his racing thoughts

rise up in his chest, making it hard to breathe. The panic was trying to take over and he fought it, leaning all his weight on the pillow.

Then he heard a sound, a scuttling sound from behind, and felt a blinding pain in his left shoulder. He cried out and turned, striking out blindly with his fist as he did so.

He hit somebody in the head, the face — Jessie! She screamed, falling backward away from him, shrieking.

His legs collapsed out from under him and he buckled, dropped to his knees on the floor. Fumbling the gun out of the front of his pants, he aimed it upwards at whoever — had to be Jessie — was behind him.

"Don't touch him. Don't you *touch* him!" She was shrieking, sounded like a madwoman in an asylum. Sounded crazy. "I'll kill you if you touch him."

He didn't want to shoot, just wanted to get out of here. If he could just make it past her to the door, he'd be gone and she'd never know who he was.

Something silver glinted in the dim light, long and shiny, above him. A knife, plunging down. He dived to the side, leveled the gun, had to fire now.

Suddenly, the world was a blaze of light so bright he was momentarily blinded. There were scuffling sounds on the other side of the room where it opened into the front door entry hall. He turned toward the sounds tracking the gun that way, saw figures, then he felt his gun hand explode in agony, like it'd been struck by lightning. The gun went flying, and then someone was hammering at him with fists, making grunting sounds, not even human. A blow caught him square in the temple and the world went black.

~

WILLIE RAY RACED AT JACKSON, lying on his side on the floor, pointing a gun at Jessie. Flew at him in animal fury. He kicked the pistol out of his hand and before Jackson even had a chance to turn around, he was hitting him with his fists, landing one blow after another. Jackson collapsed in a heap on his belly and Willie Ray kicked him savagely again and again.

He could hear voices, words.

"… enough, Willie Ray …"

That was Riley's voice. He could only hear the sounds, though, was unable to make the sounds into words and make sense out of them. He couldn't see or feel or breathe, he was all white-hot rage that *consumed* him.

He couldn't hit Jackson *hard enough*, couldn't kick him *hard enough*.

The world had turned blood red and blood was all he could see. Blood pooling around Andy as he lay with his belly ripped open on the ground in front of the bunker.

Something slammed into him from the side, knocked him to the floor beside Jackson's limp body, and he felt someone on top of him. Riley straddled his chest and grabbed his hands.

"That's enough," Riley cried. "He's out cold, unconscious."

"Kill him." Willie Ray ground the words out with a rumble from deep in his chest. "Gonna beat him to death with my bare hands." Willie Ray bucked upward, tried to throw Riley off. He heard himself screaming, making grunting noises he'd never heard come from anybody.

Riley slapped him. Slapped him hard, snapping his head to the side and sending blood squirting out of his nose. He slumped onto the floor in shock, but the rage still consumed him.

"What'd you do that—?"

"Willie Ray, you're hysterical. Stop. You're gonna beat him to death."

"Yes, I am, beat him until—"

Riley was suddenly in his face, right down in his face, nose to nose.

"No you're *not.* You're not gonna kill him by yourself. We *all* get a piece of him."

The rage in Riley's voice equaled his own and Willie Ray focused his eyes for the first time and saw his friend's face. The cold menace there turned Riley's whole face to stone.

"You, me, Jessie. We all get a piece."

All the air went out of Willie Ray and he stopped struggling and collapsed on the floor. Riley remained where he was, making sure, then he got up off Willie Ray's chest and stood up.

Willie Ray saw Jessie for the first time behind Riley. Her face was dead white, the face of a corpse that'd bled to death. But her eyes were not the eyes of a dead body. They were twin coals of red-hot fury. They'd come here to tell her what Riley'd remembered, and walked right into Jackson …? What was Jackson doing here?

Trying to kill Davie, of course, but why?

If they hadn't come, if they'd waited until morning …

Then he saw the bloody knife in Jessie's hand. She'd armed herself, had been attacking Jackson with it. She'd have died to protect Davie.

Sitting on the foot of Davie's bed, he saw Andy. The Andy who'd just had his picture taken in his brand new uniform. Crisp and pressed, his hat on just so, his chin tucked, his eyes forward and resolute.

The front of the shirt was ripped open, though, and bloody guts hung out of it, staining the white sheet on Davie's bed.

Chapter Sixty-Three

JESSIE'S HANDS were shaking so violently she couldn't hold the cup of coffee Riley'd handed her. The cup clattered against the table top and he reached over with both hands and helped her hold it, helped her raise it to her lips and drink.

The act of swallowing was soothing, the rhythmic nature of it. The rhythm calmed her gasping breath, slowed it.

She started to set the cup down.

"More," he said, and held the cup to her lips and she obediently drank more. The black liquid burned her tongue and scalded her throat, brought tears to her eyes.

It tasted like road tar.

When she'd taken the second gulping drink, he let her set the cup down on the table, but she still gripped it in both hands, held onto it, had to hold onto something or she would fall off the edge of the world into the black abyss below, the one just behind the edge of where the floor tilted down to meet it.

"… more coffee?"

"Please, no, it's awful," she gasped.

"Sorry."

She tried to focus her eyes on Riley's face then. He was standing next to where she sat but she couldn't manage to maintain eye contact because that felt dangerous, too, like the depth of the blue in his eyes was an ocean and if she looked deeply into it she would drown there.

Willie Ray sat on the other side of the table facing her, his own eyes focused on the doorway leading into Davie's room, where Jackson McClusky lay sprawled unconscious on the floor.

Riley had asked her for duct tape, she'd gotten a roll out of the kitchen drawer, didn't even know what he wanted it for, but her hands had been steady then. When had they started shaking? He'd used the tape to secure Jackson's hands behind his back and he lay on his belly on the hardwood floor, the blood from his crushed nose pooling under his face.

His arm was bleeding, too. No, his shoulder. The left one. Blood was running down that arm. She'd done that, she thought. She'd stabbed him.

Stabbed?

The word banged around inside her skull, refusing to conjure up the memory to go with it, though she clearly remembered seeing Jackson's shape over Davie's bed, running at him with the knife raised.

After that, it all happened fast.

He hit her in the face, she thought.

She reached up and touched her bloodied lip, swiped at her chin and wiped blood off on her palm.

"Put this on it," Riley'd said, handing her something. She'd looked at it without any idea what it was. "It'll keep down the swelling."

It was a dish towel wrapped around something lumpy. Ice. Put ice on it so it won't swell?

Seriously.

She put the towel/ice against her lip, felt the cold and dropped it on the table in front of her.

"Let it swell."

Riley sat down next to Willie Ray across from her then, reached across the table and took both her hands in his and held them, which was a good thing because they were trembling so violently it was positively annoying.

"Why?" She screamed the word but it came out her mouth in a whisper. "Why was he trying to kill Davie?"

"He must have thought he'd seen," Riley said.

"Seen *what*?" She looked from Riley to Willie Ray and back to Riley. "What are you doing here in the middle of the night? Just happened to be driving by and decided to stop off and have a cup of road tar with me?"

The coffee really was that thick and black. Whoever had made it in her coffee pot had used two or three times too much coffee. Maybe on purpose.

"Why are—?" She could hear the sound of incipient hysteria in her words and she fought it. "What's going on?" She did scream that … well, the last word rode a sob out of her throat.

"You want to hear it now? Can you listen?"

She nodded and thought he might have asked her the same question, or something similar, earlier and she'd not given the correct answer.

"Ain't no sense in trying to sugar-coat it, but what I'm about to say's a hard thing. Jessie …" He paused, and she could almost swear he was about to say, "Jessie, *honey,*" but he didn't. "The rocket that was fired into our bunker that night in Tweety Bird, the one that killed Andy and wounded me and Davie … it wasn't fired by the Viet Cong. *Jackson* fired it. Jackson did it. He killed Andy and left Davie …"

He let that dangle. Most people did. They didn't know how to talk about Davie's condition, and she got it. It was an uncomfortable subject, hard for people to deal with so they—

She froze. Understanding had lagged behind Riley's words and when it caught up to them it took her breath away.

"Jackson …? *Jackson?*"

That was as much as she could get out and then she lost her breath.

"Remember, I told you what Jackson did to that civilian, before we got to Tweety Bird that night, how he poured gasoline and—"

"I remember." She didn't want him to describe it again.

"Davie, Ben and I reported it to the sergeant, and all four of us were supposed to have a sit-down about it with the captain the next morning. Jackson was facing a court-martial, brig time, maybe for years. Dishonorable discharge at the very least."

"He didn't even have a gun that night," Willie Ray said, as if that'd just occurred to him. "He was unarmed during the battle, was on house arrest."

"Well, he found one," Riley said, and his words rang as cold as death. "He picked up an RPG, that's a rocket-propelled—"

"I know what it is."

"A Cong soldier had it and got shot. I saw his body lying in the mud. He must have dropped it and Jackson picked it up and fired it into the bunker where Davie, Andy and I ... Ronnie Benson was there, too, in a bunk in the back. I don't even know if he was injured. He was already so burned ..."

Burns over ninety percent of his body. Jessie would hear those words in her nightmares for the rest of her life.

"I saw Jackson do it. Andy had his back turned, but I was looking right out the door into the rain and I saw him." He ground out the words then, *"I saw him!"* and suddenly slammed his fist down on the table so hard all the coffee cups danced in place. "It was a glimpse, just for a second before he pulled the trigger. And when I woke up in the hospital in Japan, I didn't remember, everything that happened that night was all jumbled up in my head. The doctor wasn't surprised, said it happened all the time, head-trauma amnesia. People in a car wreck almost never recall the actual crash."

"And Davie ... saw, too?"

"I don't know. When Andy dived into the bunker, he crashed into Davie and the two of them were tangled up on the floor. I don't know what Davie saw. It was just a split second. Maybe he was looking that way and maybe not."

"Jackson musta *thought* he saw or he wouldn't have tried to kill him," Willie Ray said, but his voice was measured, his rage controlled, like a banked fire threatening to burst back into flame.

"But … it's been *four years.* Jackson was gone for … I don't know how long, in prison. But he's been back home since— I saw him in Brewster, I don't remember when it was, last winter sometime, after Christmas. Why suddenly *right now,* tonight, did he decide to … kill Davie?"

"Wasn't just Davie he tried to kill," Willie Ray said, and nodded his chin toward Riley.

She turned to Riley.

"He shot at me this afternoon."

"*Shot* at you? What, just walked up to you on the street, pulled a gun and—?"

"I was on the tractor and I didn't see him, thought at the time it was an accident, musta been a stray bullet — a squirrel hunter. That was a stretch, but I didn't have any other explanation." He made a grunting sound in his throat. "Wasn't no squirrel hunter. It was Jackson. And he definitely screwed the pooch with that one. I think that's what did it, what made me remember — that gunshot and then banging my head on the ground right after. I think that blew up the log jam in my mind."

"After he shot you——?"

"Shot *at* me. He missed."

"——shot *at* you, you remembered?"

"Not right away. I was dreaming and woke up. I've been having nightmares ever since … I'm sure now that I'd have remembered it on my own eventually. But I think the gunshot——"

"Riley come and told me," Willie Ray interrupted. "Ran through the field from the house in his," he amended the last word, "pajamas. We were on our way here to tell you." Willie Ray shook his head. "The middle of the night, yeah, I know — but we couldn't hold onto it. It was too big to just go back to bed and come by in the morning."

"And we were worried about Davie. If Jackson tried to kill me, then maybe … it's a good thing we walked in on your party."

Jessie shook her head, her thoughts so fragmented they felt like individual pieces of shattered glass.

Davie hadn't been injured in war. It wasn't a random act of violence, like getting hit by a bus crossing a street. He hadn't been wounded by the enemy he'd gone there to fight. He'd been wounded by the enemy he'd brought with him.

It changed nothing — didn't matter what'd put him there, Davie was still lying in a bed smiling at the ceiling. And yet it changed everything. Absolutely *everything*.

She could see the rage on Riley's and Willie Ray's faces. Deadly rage. And she should be just as mad. She could sense that anger down deep inside her, a tiger pacing back and forth in its cage, waiting to be set free. But right now she was so surprised, so shocked … Two hours ago, the most pressing concern in Jessie's life was that pulled muscle in her shoulder. But now—

Yeah, now.

"I hate to sound like a broken record, but I still don't get it — why *now*?"

"That's one of the questions I intend to ask him as soon as he comes around," Riley said.

"Then what?"

Nobody had to ask what she meant. She said it out loud anyway. "What are we going to do about it? About Jackson?"

"That's what we're going to have to decide," Riley said.

Chapter Sixty-Four

BAM!

Sherry Lynn had just drifted back off to sleep when she was jolted violently awake by a sound. It was a gunshot.

She looked around. Riley still hadn't come back to bed. Was he outside somewhere? What could he possibly be shooting at?

Bam!

Another gunshot.

What on earth …?

She got out of bed, put on her house shoes and grabbed her robe off the bed post and went downstairs. She glanced out the window beside the front door. She could see where Riley always sat when he and Nate sat together on the porch at night and Riley wasn't there.

She stepped from the hallway into the kitchen and could see light coming from the barn. A stream of it sliced out across the dirt where one of the bay doors was slightly open. What was Riley shooting at in the barn? A rat? A weasel, maybe? But in the middle of the night?

She turned on the kitchen light, pulled open the kitchen junk drawer, dug around in it until she found a flashlight.

She flipped the switch.

It was dead.

She shouldn't have been surprised, and she really wasn't, but she still felt that sinking feeling of disappointment in her belly that she felt every time her nose was rubbed in Riley's inattention. Her father had always made sure there were fresh batteries in the flashlights. He didn't want her mother to need one and find it dead. He always put gasoline in the car — her mother had probably never bought a gallon in her life. He kept the front walk shoveled on the rare occasions when there was enough snow to shovel, kept the lawn mowed, the bushes trimmed ... and all kinds of other things that didn't have anything to do with living on a farm. Her father *took care of* her mother. Looked after her, made sure she didn't need anything. That's how her father let her mother know he loved her. He would never, *ever* behave in some lovey-dovey, mushy sort of way — she'd seen them hug maybe half a dozen times but never kiss. He was a proud man and proud men were good husbands and fathers and they took care of their wives. It was their job.

Sherry Lynn had expected the same kind of behavior from Riley. In fact, she didn't even realize what she was expecting until she didn't get it. She ran out of gas once on her way into town, was stranded there on the side of the road until she could hitch a ride into town to the Esso Station, and return with a one-gallon metal can filled with gasoline. Riley had driven the car to Cincinnati the day before and hadn't bothered to refill the tank. He mowed the lawn and trimmed the bushes *if she asked*. But she had to ask. And if you had to ask, it didn't count.

She sighed and shoved the drawer shut in irritation. Holding the dead flashlight, she pushed the switch on and off, hoping it would catch. Sometimes it did that, maybe the batteries inside weren't making good contact and if you shook it … She shook it as she went to the back door and noticed that it wasn't closed all the way. Wherever Riley had gone to … do whatever it was he did after one of his nightmares, he'd left the door open behind him. Maybe he always did. Sherry Lynn had never come down to see. He'd never stayed gone this long before. It seemed like long, though she wasn't sure exactly when he'd left. She'd taught herself not to respond to his battles with middle-of-the-night demons. Hey, she'd tried to help, okay, offered a dozen times. Now, she just rolled over and went back to sleep.

Pulling the back door the rest of the way open, she lifted her hand toward the porch light switch and then stopped. If she turned it on, it would light up the porch and yard. But the light would be so bright that when she got out into the darkness between its glow and the barn, she wouldn't be able to see a thing.

It wasn't a totally dark night. The full moon was

high in the sky and there were no clouds. She shoved open the screen door, with its squalling spring, and stepped out onto the back porch without turning on the light, shaking the flashlight — and it suddenly came on, casting a bilious glow on the porch steps. Lighting her way with the faint flashlight beam, she crossed the back yard and continued out into the area in front of the barn, heading toward the bright arrow of light that shone out through the open door.

She was halfway across the dark area when she saw … *something.* Or thought she did. A shadow passed in front of the arrow of light, blocked it for a moment and then was gone. When she looked closer, it seemed that the arrow of light was bigger … like the door was open a little wider now than it had been before. But that was ridiculous.

The doors opened outwards and the one on the left was always harder to open than the one on the right. But it was the left one that stood slightly ajar now. She reached out and took hold of the right-side door and it swung out easily on its oiled hinges wide enough for her to enter.

The barn was empty.

"Riley!" she called out, but no one answered.

Chapter Sixty-Five

RILEY COULD TELL Jessie was shocked by the words that came out her own mouth.

"We decide whether Jackson lives or dies? Is that what you're saying?"

The look of confusion and fear and pain and rage and probably half a dozen other emotions fighting for purchase on Jessie's face broke Riley's heart.

The part of his heart that had not already turned to stone at the memory of Jackson's face and the barrel of the RPG through the rain. Not just stone, granite. No, a single, flawless, impenetrable diamond. That image had filled him with a blind rage like nothing he'd ever experienced, had sent him running out into the night in his underwear.

That fire was no longer blazing. It was banked, red hot coals smoldering, heat rising in undulating waves into the air, and the slightest breeze would bring forth a flame.

Jackson McClusky would die. There was absolutely *nothing* to talk about, nothing to decide. The man's fate was sealed. All that remained was figuring out how to kill him and not get caught.

At least that's what he'd thought until he and Willie Ray pulled up in Jessie's driveway and heard her scream. The image of Jessie in danger had so empowered Riley that he would have knocked down the front door if it had been locked, would have bull-dozed his way through it.

He hit the light switch, took in the scene, could not have been more surprised if she had been fighting off a cougar.

Jackson? *Here?*

Why?

Willie Ray'd been half a step behind Riley, had not paused at the sight of Jessie as Riley had — just rushed forward and kicked the gun out of Jackson's hand while Riley knelt to see to Jessie.

Maybe he should have let Willie Ray beat Jackson to death right then and there, have it over with. But the violence of that … the look on Jessie's face as she watched it happening. He didn't want her to be a party to that.

He knew so many things he wished he didn't know. War had taught him such powerful lessons, and he'd paid dearly for every one of them.

Riley knew that the killing of Jackson would do something to Jessie; violent death always changed a person. He'd watched his tee-ball buddies become hardened men with a look behind their eyes, innocence and a large part of their humanity stolen from them by what was happening around them.

Taking a life, even in a battle, was a thing that would haunt you forever. The first VC soldier he'd killed — up close where it was real — was on the day Ace had saved his life. Before that, he'd picked them off at a distance — it was just like shooting wild turkeys back home, but then one broke through. Riley had shoved a bayonet into a VC's belly, a man *who was trying to kill him*. Still … the doing of that deed, however justified and necessary, had taken a hunk out of Riley's humanity. Every death he'd inflicted had done the same.

Killing Jackson would do that to Jessie. And yet she had a right to be here. What Jackson'd done to Davie had purchased her seat at the table. He had to answer to *all three of them*.

But Riley'd do anything he could to shield Jessie's heart from the damage the doing of it would cause.

"We ain't got to decide *if* he lives or dies—" Willie Ray began.

"Yes, we do," Riley said. "We all have to be *equally* responsible for killing him."

"Okay, then … I say we kill him. What do you two say?" He looked at Jessie, who nodded her head like a woman in a dream.

"Not like this," Riley said. "We vote. Proper. Rocks-in-a-box."

"Why in the world go through that kind of charade—"

"Because we're *all* going to have to live with this."

Riley cut his eyes to Jessie when he said "all," hoped Willie Ray caught the gesture and maybe he did. "Not just today when we're full of rage and blood lust, but tomorrow and next week and next year. We got to look ourselves in the mirror every morning for the rest of our lives. We got to *own* it, equal responsibility, nobody thinking later we shoulda done something different."

The other two were silent.

"And it's gotta be a private thing. Each one of us gets to decide on our own, for ourselves, no pressure from the others. With the rocks-in-the-box, none of us will ever know who voted which way."

"Three black rocks and Jackson McClusky is a dead man," Willie Ray said.

Jessie said nothing. Riley prayed Willie Ray wouldn't ask what they'd do if there were only two black rocks — maybe just *one*, or all *white* — because he didn't have an answer. Jackson *had* to die, they couldn't let him go, let him walk out of here after he killed Andy, and tried to kill Riley and Davie. But Willie Ray didn't ask and when Riley looked at Jessie, there wasn't a whole lot of *there* there. She wasn't tracking everything that was going on. He understood. She was in shock. You couldn't have a madman come into your house in the middle of the night and try to kill your bedridden husband, and then find out the madman was the reason your husband was in that condition in the first place, and still have all your oars in the water.

He was sure she wasn't even aware that her cheek

was turning an ugly purple shade and her eye was beginning to swell shut where Jackson had punched her.

Jackson had *punched* her.

The thought came very close to releasing the pent-up rage in Riley's chest. If it broke free, it would wash away everything in its path, roar out of his body and he'd be powerless to control it. Then *he* would beat Jackson McClusky to death with his bare hands.

Willie Ray got to his feet, not looking at either Jessie or Riley.

"Fine, then. I'll go get the box." He looked toward Davie's bedroom where Jackson was unconscious on the floor. "What'll we do with the sack of garbage?"

Jessie stared straight ahead, like maybe she hadn't even heard. Riley looked around, saw the door to the utility room that held the washer, dryer and hot water heater.

"In there," he said. He got up then and went to get Jackson, didn't trust Willie Ray to touch him. Grabbing him by the back of his shirt collar, Riley dragged Jackson's limp body across the kitchen floor, leaving a bloody snail trail in his wake. He had a nasty cut somewhere, his shoulder maybe. Blood from it had run down his arm and was puddling on the floor. He wouldn't bleed to death, though. That was too easy.

So what wasn't too easy? *How* would they kill him? He shook it off. One step at a time. He dumped Jackson on the floor, kicked his legs out of the way and closed the door.

Willie Ray banged out the back door on his way to his truck. It wasn't far to the tobacco barn where they kept the box. He'd be back in a few minutes. Between now and then, what could Riley possibly do to prepare Jessie for what came next?

Chapter Sixty-Six

THE WHOLE THING WAS SURREAL. Jessie's face throbbed, her eye was swelling shut. She could hear Mama Ruth's nonsense babble from her room. The commotion had brought the old lady fully awake — wasn't any way to sleep through *that* — and now she was prattling on about high-heeled shoes, and how they hurt her feet, but she couldn't wear flats to the royal wedding!

The room seemed to be filled with fog and Jessie saw everything in it as though looking through mist, the figures blurred around the edges, no sharp angles.

Yet somehow it was crisp in her mind what Riley was doing, *why* he was demanding they vote with the rocks in the box. That was as clear as a spring morning. He was doing it for *her,* trying to help *her,* trying to make things easier on *her.*

In this extreme moment in his life, he had set his own feelings aside and brought all his attention to bear on making things easier for Jessie.

She didn't have anywhere in her mind to put that revelation, though once it stood there in the spotlight on center stage, she had to admit it wasn't really a stranger. It wasn't like she hadn't seen the edges of it before. The care and concern. Since that first day in the barn when she'd been real and raw about how desperate her situation was, she'd known there was nothing she couldn't ask of him.

In fact, she didn't even have to ask. He had joined his fortunes to hers, partnered with her and Willie Ray in the harrowing journey into they knew not where. And in truth, he'd been the one who led her out of that dark tunnel into the light.

The night that storm had blown through, knocking out the electricity, tearing limbs off trees and slamming them into the side of the house. She was at home with Mama Ruth, the two of them trying to figure out if they needed to get Davie to safety … somewhere. In the storm cellar? How could the two of them get Davie to the storm cellar in the dark—?

Then Riley appeared on her porch, the hood of his wet rain slicker casting his face in shadow but the light of his lantern was bright. Had they heard that a twister'd taken the roof off that little Baptist church out on Crocker Lane? All over now, though. Did they know half the county was without power? He'd got his family squared away … would they like for him to stay until the power came back on?

They would.

The day Mama Ruth had had her stroke. Jessie'd

been on the tractor, on the tobacco setter. Nate was driving and Riley was sitting beside her on the other seat, the two of them feeding the seedlings one at a time into the setter and watching the line of little green cadets line up behind them.

They'd been laughing, just like she and Davie used to do, at how neat the little soldiers stood there in line. And it'd felt good to laugh about that again, felt good to have somebody to laugh at it with.

Willie Ray had come to get her, told her Mama Ruth had collapsed. Jessie hadn't known what to do. She had to get there, be with Mama Ruth, of course, but who'd stay with Davie while—

Riley'd taken over and she didn't even remember now what it was he'd done exactly, how he'd worked it all out. But he had, had lined up her brothers and others to get the farm work done so she could stay with her mother-in-law while she was hospitalized.

Of course, he'd done all that. He was Davie's best friend, after all.

He was Davie's Army buddy.

He had suffered as Davie'd suffered, understood the magnitude of the horror.

That was why. Of course that was why.

Except it wasn't.

Why was this one thing lit in bright light when everything else was so vague?

Riley Hannacker had been the rock-solid foundation of her life ever since he got back from Vietnam. And what he was doing for her now, what he'd been

doing for her for years, was not motivated by his feelings for Davie.

It was motivated by his feelings for *her*.

And what on earth was she supposed to do with
that?

~

DREW HEARD MOMMY'S VOICE. But she wasn't
calling for him. She was calling Daddy. Drew could
hear her voice where he was hiding behind the pile of
old blankets in the corner of the tack room. He could
crawl *under* the blankets if he had to, and then nobody
could find him ever.

The mad person with the gun would never find
him if he hid there.

And neither would Mommy, who'd be mad, too, if
she knew he had gotten out of the bed when she told
him to stay there.

"Riley!" his mother called again. She was looking
for Daddy, but Daddy wasn't in the barn. Only Pop
Pop was in the barn. Drew knew Pop Pop was here
because he had seen.

He had looked through the crack in the wall of his
playroom into the barn and he had *seen.*

The image of his grandfather formed in his mind
— but it wasn't his smiling face, the one he always
wore when he looked at Drew. It was his face the way
he'd looked after the *Bam* sound. The first one.

Surprised and sad and hurt.

He had looked down at the front of his shirt where he was bleeding because he'd been shot and then he fell down.

And Drew could see the person who'd been blocking his view, the person with the gun who went to Pop Pop and — Riley shook his head, shook it so hard that he shook the tears off his cheeks.

No!

Drew didn't see that. He didn't.

He didn't see anything. He wasn't even here in the barn. He was in his bed. He *was.* That's where he was supposed to be.

Drew Hannacker was in his bed where he didn't see anything at all.

"IT WON'T TAKE Willie Ray long to get the box," Riley said, "but I could make coffee — want some?"

Coffee? More road tar?

"You really ought to put ice on—"

"Stop it!" She hadn't meant to shout but she wasn't in control of anything right now as pedestrian as the decibel level of her speech.

"I'm sorry, Jessie, I—"

"And stop that, too. Stop all of it!"

"All of what?"

Yeah, all of *what?* What exactly was it that she wanted Riley Hannacker to stop doing? It wasn't really as simple and straightforward as wanting him to chuck the chipper cocktail-party prattle that seemed so damnably inappropriate to what was going on.

It was something way more basic than that.

Jessie wanted Riley to stop …

To stop caring.

She wanted him to stop … if she *thought* the words *being in love with her,* even thought the words, she would start screaming and scream nonstop until the end of time.

But he had to stop that!

And why did he have to stop?

Before she even had a chance to haul out the laundry list of his wife and her husband and the absolute horror of … of … she had a flash of insight that struck her like a lightning bolt.

She didn't want him to stop that at all.

The lightning strike had strobed the air a brilliant white in the room, in her mind, had fried the little dust motes that were still settling out of the air from the exploding of her world. Had cast everything and everybody in harsh relief.

You look at a chess board and the pieces are arranged on it the way they'd been when you'd stopped playing.

You blink and the same chess board has the same pieces as it'd had a millisecond ago, but now they're in different places entirely.

Some have moved up, some have moved back. Some are out of the game entirely, lying on their sides beside the game board. And now it's an entirely different game that requires moves you hadn't planned on having to make. The stakes were different, too.

Now everything in life was up for grabs, on the line for the taking.

Might be you needed to turn and run and get out of the game entirely.

Might be you needed to engage on all fronts.

Might be you needed to *win.*

She was standing, though she didn't remember getting to her feet.

"Air," she gasped. "I need air." She turned toward the back door and sensed him starting to go with her.

"I need to be *alone* right now. Please." Then she fled out into the cricket warmth and familiarity of her back yard, amid the blinking fireflies, under the canopy of icebergs sailing in the cold black sea.

And she wandered around without seeing or feeling or thinking. Either she managed to totally empty her mind of all thought and emotion, or the lightning strike had burned all thought away.

She was still wandering around, orbiting in a loose circle when the twin sabers of Willie Ray's headlights stabbed through the night.

He got out of the pickup without speaking and she walked with him in silence back into the house. Riley was sitting where she'd left him at the table, just sitting. The house was quiet. Apparently, Mama Ruth had finally gone back to sleep.

Setting the little box on the table, Willie Ray lifted up the lid and dumped out the voting rocks. Eight of them. They made a clacking sound on the table. Four dark ones. Four light ones. He moved one of each color to the side – Nate wasn't here, wouldn't be casting his rock-vote – and looked at Riley.

"You said you wanted to vote, well, let's get to it." Reaching out wordlessly, Willie Ray picked up one black rock and one white one and closed them both up tight in his palm.

Chapter Sixty-Seven

THE TRIP to the tobacco barn to fetch the box didn't happen, there was only the trip back. Willie Ray had exploded like a rocket out of Jessie's kitchen, fueled by inestimable rage, and the rocket had propelled the truck to the barn in a nanosecond. He didn't have to drive there. He was just there.

But when he got back into the truck with the box …

He should have sent Riley, should have stayed in the house with Davie and Jessie, should not have allowed himself to be *alone.*

The truck would not move on its own now. He would have to start the engine, turn the wheel, put his foot on the accelerator. As soon as he shut the truck door and reached for the ignition key — desperate to roar away down the field road from the tobacco barn back to the house — the world changed.

All the boundaries of reality vanished.

He had … *come apart* after 'Nam. Literally. He hadn't been a whole being after that, just a pile of little pieces no longer attached to each other. He spent months in the VA Hospital putting those pieces back together, like trying to assemble a three-dimensional rag rug that'd been ripped to shreds. The pieces didn't fit right, of course. They were tattered and damaged. He didn't even know where some of the pieces were supposed to go. And what was finally assembled in the end was only William Raymond Taggart on the outside, like the pattern of a rug. From the inside, you could see what lay beneath the pattern, the snarls and knots and tangles, the dangling and unraveled fabric.

That "re-assembled" Willie Ray was fragile, barely held together in the beginning by tiny filaments of thread that stitched the pieces to each other, little strings that were at once as strong as catgut and as delicate as a spiderweb. Over time, the threads thickened, grew tougher.

But now …

Now it was all coming apart again. Sitting there in his pickup truck in front of the Cornbread Mafia's clubhouse in Jessie Monaghan's barn, the threads began to dissolve and the pieces began to float away. The world was too big. He could feel nothing solid holding the contents of his humanity inside him anymore. The black emptiness — as vast as the black infinity of space — beyond everything that was Willie Ray Taggart was a gaping maw waiting to absorb him.

He was coming apart now as he had done before, completely apart. But this time, there'd be no pile of pieces. They would be scattered to the four winds. He would cease to be. He would—

"It's okay, bro."

He turned toward the words and found Andy sitting in the front seat beside him. He'd been seeing Andy for years, in every conceivable circumstance, and Andy in every conceivable state of being — from Andy-the-blond-haired-little-boy to Andy-the-ripped-open-soldier. But Andy had never before spoken to him.

Over the years, his intellectual understanding that Andy wasn't *really* there had finally surrendered, run up the white flag and left the battlefield in defeat. Maybe Andy wasn't really there — but oh yes he was, too! His presence was on a deeper level of reality than most people understood, that's all.

Every time Andy showed up, Willie Ray withered inside, grew smaller, became somehow less than he'd been before, though he couldn't have explained how that was or even what it meant. When you came right down to it, Andy was in charge of Willie Ray's life. As long as he was a part of it, Willie Ray would never be whole, he'd remain forever pieces stitched together with slender thread.

Discovering tonight that Jackson McClusky, not some VC soldier, had really killed Andy had detonated a nuclear explosion in Willie Ray Taggart's soul, released a dragon of rage. If Riley hadn't pulled him off Jackson, the dragon would have eaten Jackson alive. Now, for the first time ever, there could be *retribution*. Raging against the indiscriminate violence of war was futile, it was battling smoke and shadows, nothing substantial. But now, Willie Ray could vent his rage on something *real*. Some*one* real. The real killer.

Would it matter? Would Jackson's death put the disparate pieces of Willie Ray's soul back together somehow, cement them in place so he would no longer be a straw-man, his humanity stitched together? Would it perhaps dispel Andy's spirit forever?

"What's … okay?" Willie Ray asked Andy. It was the Andy in bloody combat fatigues with his guts hanging out who had appeared at the foot of Willie Ray's bed for the first time when Willie Ray woke up in the hospital after the corpsmen had drugged him to get him on the evac chopper.

"All of it," Andy said. "It doesn't matter anymore."

And then Willie Ray was back at Jessie's house, as unaware of driving back there from the barn as he'd been of driving to the barn in the first place.

He sat behind the wheel staring at the brother who wasn't there.

"All of what?" he asked. "What doesn't matter anymore?"

But Andy said nothing else, just looked at him.

When Willie Ray opened the door of the pickup to get out, Andy was standing in the yard waiting for him. He walked with Willie Ray up toward the house.

When Jessie came out to walk beside Willie Ray, Andy disappeared. But when Willie Ray opened the door, Andy was sitting in a chair next to Riley.

Willie Ray dumped the rocks out on Jessie's kitchen table — four black rocks, four white. He shoved Nate's two voting rocks to the side and set the box on the table. They each picked up two, one of each color.

What happened next mattered to Andy. Willie Ray knew it did. He'd stayed here to see it through. He was watching Willie Ray pick up the two rocks and hold them in his hand.

Which one did Andy want Willie Ray to drop into the box?

JESSIE'D SUGGESTED once that if they planned to continue to make rock-box decisions, maybe they should buy some black and white marbles. They didn't. The "white" and "black" rocks Willie Ray had picked up off the ground that day in front of Jessie's barn worked fine.

Riley picked up the box Andy Taggart had made in shop class. He handed it to Jessie. She took it, turned her back on him and put into the hole on the top of the box one of the rocks she was holding. She turned back around and gave the box to Willie Ray. He did what Jessie'd done. Then so did Riley.

IT WAS TIME. Jessie held her two rocks tight and felt a great weight pressing down on her chest, the weight of knowing what Jackson had done. Of knowing and understanding.

The whole world had exploded in her face tonight and the dust hadn't even yet settled out of the air. Blown apart was everything she thought was true, all that she'd spent years learning to *accept*. Davie'd been wounded in a war. She'd processed her way through the grief of his condition — the way everyone did, one stage at a time, denial, anger, bargaining — and she didn't know the names of the other parts. She'd read it in a magazine once somewhere. But at the foundation of all the devastating reality was the immutable fact of *war*.

War happened. Men were wounded. Men died. You could rail against it all you wanted, and she had railed, but it was rock solid, permanent, an unchangeable reality of life.

Now, she knew Davie hadn't been wounded in war after all. He'd been ambushed. He'd been the victim of evil incarnate, a monstrous creature in a human-being suit called Jackson McClusky.

What was she supposed to do with that understanding? How did she integrate it into waking up every morning and brushing her teeth and plowing a field and digging in the garden?

If it hadn't been for Jackson McClusky, Davie would be fine! *Not a mark on me.* She and Davie could have floated out there into the future on a magic carpet, awash in their love.

Because of Jackson, Davie was incapable of love.

Davie didn't even recognize her.

And he never would.

Somehow that realization had shaken loose when the world exploded, seemed obvious on the surface of it now, but she had managed not to see it for four years. Davie's condition might improve a little. He might regain some function. And he might not. But either way, Davie would never again be the man she'd married.

That part was over. Forever.

Davie Monaghan had *died* in that bunker.

Andy Taggart had died in that bunker, too.

Jackson McClusky had killed them both.

She reached out and dropped one of the rocks into the box.

RILEY HELD THE TWO ROCKS, though in his mind there was nothing to vote on. Nothing for *him* to vote on. It'd just been a ruse to take the pressure off Jessie, let her get a grip.

Riley Hannacker knew Jackson McClusky had to die. Here. Tonight. At their hands. His whole being knew that. The only unknowns here now were: would Jessie be able to vote to kill him, and if she did, what affect would his death have on her?

And, of course, what would he and Willie Ray do if they found a white rock in the box?

It wouldn't matter. They'd kill him anyway. They

absolutely would. He and Willie Ray could not draw breath on the earth so long as Jackson McClusky breathed there, too.

All Riley could hope for was that the voting had somehow lifted off Jessie some of the responsibility for what was about to happen. She had a choice. She could vote no. She could put a white rock in the box. And when Riley and Willie Ray executed Jackson anyway, surely that gesture would matter to her — Jackson's death was not her fault. She had done what she could to save him.

Beyond that rock box lay other considerations Riley'd put off until he had to think about them, and in a few moments he would have to.

How would they put Jackson to death? His rage wanted to rip Jackson apart — literally. Tear him to pieces. But some rational part of him realized that an act of such singular brutality — whether Jessie voted yay or nay — would not make the world right again.

It wouldn't make Davie whole.

It wouldn't bring Andy back.

It would satisfy some animal lust inside Riley, but he thought maybe it might just take a hunk out of his soul bigger than he could afford to lose.

Would the satisfaction be worth it?

And what would ripping Jackson McClusky to pieces do to Willie Ray? His best friend balanced every day on an invisible tightrope of sanity. Riley understood that better than anybody, certainly better than Willie Ray did himself. Would Jackson's death put Willie Ray's feet once again on solid ground? Or would it tip him off the tightrope to fall down into the dark abyss below?

Chapter Sixty-Eight

SHERRY LYNN CALLED OUT AGAIN, "RILEY!"

Still there was no answer.

The shadow she'd seen flash in front of the light … had it been Riley, leaving the barn? Now that she thought about it, that's what it'd looked like — somebody leaving. Why would Riley slip out the barn door and … what? Run away?

That didn't make any sense.

But Riley must have been in the barn. Where else would he be? He was shooting at something, and you couldn't see anything out there in the dark well enough to shoot at it, so he had to be in here.

Except he wasn't.

She had taken a few steps into the barn, and now she began to edge backwards. Suddenly, the hair on the back of her neck started to stand up and she wanted out of here. She needed to be gone from this place, *had to be* somewhere on the planet that was not this barn at this moment. Anywhere that was not *here*.

She didn't turn and run, though. She wanted to, yearned to, ached to. But she couldn't. For some reason, she *could not* turn her back. And so she edged backward, one step, then another.

The flashlight had gone dead again. When she opened the barn door, it went out, would not provide even a pallid glow, was a dead weight in her hand.

Then it suddenly came back on again. This time, the glow wasn't yellowish and dim. It was a beam of light so bright it startled her and she jumped, making it dance across the barn floor casting bizarre shapes on the walls. It flickered over something in the shadows and then danced away. What was that something? Sherry Lynn gripped the cold metal with both hands, steadied and focused the beam and the light burned away the darkness, illuminating the something. She couldn't at first tell what it was.

A pair of overalls?

She started toward it and only got a few steps before she realized exactly what she was looking at.

Nate Hannacker lay on his back on the barn floor. The whole front of his overalls was dark, but that's not the image that burned itself into her consciousness, the image she'd see in nightmares for the rest of her life.

There was a bullet hole right in the middle of Nate's forehead.

Sherry Lynn started screaming.

∽

WHEN RILEY TURNED BACK AROUND, he was holding in his hands the will of the three of them, individually and cumulatively. Jessie was looking at him, her face expressionless. He saw Willie Ray's eyes shift sideways, as if he were looking at somebody, then he returned his gaze to Riley.

Riley held the box out over the table, turned it upside down and dumped out the contents.

They stood together then — Riley, Willie Ray and Jessie — saying nothing, looking at the three black rocks on the table.

All the considerations about how to kill Jackson McClusky and where to do the deed and how to keep from getting caught came crashing down on all three of them as their gazes shifted from the rocks on the table to each other's faces and back to the rocks.

Riley hadn't realized how much it mattered to him that the three of them were united. He saw the rocks lying there on the table and a lump rose briefly in his throat. He shook off the emotional response, needed to think clearly, plan. What mattered most to him was making sure they didn't get caught, that *Jessie* didn't get caught.

All the unknowns he hadn't considered jumped out at him now and yelled, "Boo!"

Where could they put Jackson until … some place other than in Jessie's utility room? Did Jackson tell anybody he was coming here tonight?

"You reckon he told anybody he was coming here?" Willie Ray asked, as always an echo of Riley's own thoughts.

"No way to know," Jessie said. "I can't imagine that he did — who would he tell and what would he say? *I'm going over to the Monaghans' tonight to kill Davie?*"

"It'd be better if he didn't tell anybody," Riley said, "but whether he did or not, we have to erase every trace that he's been here."

Something to do now.

"We have to find wherever he put his truck," Willie Ray said. "And … do what with it?"

"Hide it for now. We can figure out where to get rid of it later. I'm sure it's not out in the open. He hid it somewhere, didn't want to be seen sneaking around."

A flash of rage washed over Riley, brief but energizing. It warmed him, and he hadn't realized how chilled he'd been.

Jessie looked at the door leading to the utility room, where they'd thrown Jackson on the floor … what? Half an hour ago. "What are we going to do with him?"

That was, indeed, the first order of business.

"Let's see if he's come to, can walk," Riley said and Jessie took an involuntary step back away from the door. "Why don't you get something and start cleaning up the mess in that bedroom," Riley told her, knowing she'd be grateful for a task, something to do so she could hover on the edge of what the other two were doing.

Riley sized Willie Ray up, made sure he wouldn't see Jackson and … do something stupid. He seemed to be in control. Riley reached over to the counter and picked up the roll of tape he'd used to bind Jackson's arms behind his back. "I'll be ready with some tape to tape his mouth shut if he starts making noise."

Jessie went to the sink and opened the cabinet below it, took out a plastic tub and cleaning cloths. Willie Ray went to the door of the utility room, with Riley a step behind him in case he needed to silence Jackson.

Willie Ray opened the door.

The room was empty.

Jackson was gone.

Chapter Sixty-Nine

Jackson ran, flat out, crashing through the woods in a blind panic unlike anything he'd felt since 'Nam. He had no control over his flight, just *away*, and he didn't stop running for miles. Tripped and fell, was scraped and scratched, tumbled down hillsides, splashed through creeks, propelled forward by a great primal fear in his chest that threatened to consume him. It was magnified by all the years of dread, a boil growing bigger and more painful until it finally burst.

They would kill him. Of course they would! But not outright. He could see it in the loathing hatred in their eyes. They would kill him slowly, painfully, torture him until he was begging to die.

When he tripped over a tree root hidden in shadow and went tumbling down a rocky hillside, the pain of banging into the rocks was cold water splashing in his face and brought back sanity.

He lay gasping in the dirt, hurting all over, until his heart was no longer thundering like a freight train in his chest. But when he tried to roll over, a jolt of agony from his left elbow to his fingertips focused the all-over pain into one spot, informed him that he'd broken his wrist. Moaning, he eased himself slowly onto his right side, wanting to scream from the agony but still so terrified he didn't dare make a sound. He lay there for ten minutes, maybe half an hour, without moving a muscle, just listening, a frightened doe in the bushes, trying to hear the approach of the hunters.

And they would hunt him down!

Perhaps they were in the woods even now — three of them to spread out, searching, maybe even following a trail. Did he leave a trail? Of course he did. He'd charged like a bull elephant through the undergrowth, leaving a path of broken limbs and bent twigs you didn't have to be Tonto to follow. Struggling against the agony, a lightning strike of white light in his brain that burned away every other thought, Jackson fought for reason.

He had to think!

The others would come after him, yes, but they'd need daylight to track him proper and dawn was still hours away.

Flashlights! They could use flashlights …

An image of flashlights behind him, blades of light stretching like fingers into the woods, coming from three directions—

No, they'd lose the trail if they tried that. And besides, he didn't know if they had even yet discovered he was missing.

It wasn't until then that he actually felt the fiery

agony on his whole left arm, fingertips to shoulder. It screamed like it'd done for months after 'Nam. That's when he'd got addicted to narcotics, but he'd managed to keep the addiction under control — for a while.

The burning sensation shrieked at him now just like before. The whole top layer of the skin on his left arm had been burned away when he'd tried to put out the flames on the Jingle Bell Man. The doctors'd had to graft skin — dozens of skin grafts — onto his arm to replace the skin that'd burned, leaving behind the smooth, white scars the doctors said were not the same as regular skin. The scars didn't have the same blood vessels as before, or the same nerves. The scars were "fragile" and he had almost no feeling there. Or he'd thought he had no feeling! The burned places on his arm were screaming in pain now. Why …? And then he knew. The skin on the top of the scars had *peeled away with the duct tape!*

The scars had saved him! The ugly, twisted scar tissue was smooth and slick and tight. That had to be it, how he'd got the tape off — the combination of blood and scars. And desperation.

He'd pretended to be unconscious when they dragged him into the laundry room and dumped him on the floor. He'd rolled over as soon as they left, struggling frantically to get free — wild to get away. He'd rolled around and around in his own blood on the floor in total panic for a time, soaking his upper body, then pulled his taped-together hands under his butt and around in front of him. He looked around for something, anything to cut the tape. There was nothing. So he'd sat down with his back against the dryer, braced both feet against the tape and used the strength of his legs to peel the tape off.

It came away slowly, agonizingly, *peeling the scared flesh off his arm* with it.

He had a head start — maybe a big one, maybe not — but he was out front and if he allowed himself to be herded along in a panic, heedless of where he was going, no plan of any kind in mind, they would catch up with him eventually.

Moving with infinite care, he managed to pull himself up into a sitting position leaned against a rock, cradling his agonizing broken wrist in his lap, walling off the burning sensation all up and down his arm. Think. He had to think. He had to have a plan.

He looked around — like he'd see something he recognized and know where he was. Riiiiight. He was totally lost, had no clue whatsoever where he was. He'd run north from Jessie's house in a mostly straight line, didn't turn aside or veer off that he could remember. So what was north of Jessie Monaghan's farm? Woods!

But if he stayed on course, he'd come out somewhere along Sanderson Pike or maybe Gopher Hill Road. They both branched off Blandford Lane about fifteen miles east of from Brewster.

Who lived on Sanderson Pike? The Wheatleys — Jeb and Alice and their kids. Maybe Buzz Watters or Neal Purdom. Squirrel Hansford used to live on Gopher Hill but …

Bottom line, he couldn't think of a soul anywhere

near who'd help him. He wasn't in the McClusky part of the county, where there were a considerable number of relatives, aunts, uncles or cousins. As his mind settled and he managed to retreat into himself as best he could from the agony in his arm, shoulder and wrist, it occurred to him that even if he knew someone who'd help, he didn't know where he was going and figuring that out was the first item of business.

Where?

Home?

What for?

He hadn't exactly been welcomed with open arms when he'd returned from prison. His father let him know quick that his presence was tolerated. Jackson could see the contempt in the big man's eyes and wasn't surprised by it. He'd never measured up to whatever standard Big-un had for his oldest son. His size had doomed him from birth. Though his mother was a big, stout woman, most of her kin, the Crockers, were small-boned and slender, and Jackson had taken after that side of the family. His brother Wade was two years younger, but by first grade Jackson was wearing clothes his brother'd outgrown. His twin brothers, Angus and Archie, would never be the size of their father, but at twelve now both were taller than Jackson — who topped out at five feet, four inches and never grew another inch. Even his sixteen-year-old sister, Linda, was taller. Fourteen-year-old Sarah soon would be, too, if she wasn't already.

His outcast status had shaped who Jackson McClusky was in every way that mattered. He was too small to fight for what he wanted, so he got what was his by any other means available, stole what he fancied, and if he couldn't have it — like that harmonica Wade had got for Christmas one year — he destroyed it so couldn't nobody else have it either.

In reality, Jackson had always been on his own. Had no family, no backup. It was just official now.

If not home, then where?

Somewhere outside Callison County.

With something like a tinge of loss he realized he had burned all his bridges and there was no way back. He had to leave. If Willie Ray Taggart, Riley Hannacker or Jessie Monaghan ever set eyes on him again, they'd kill him. And before long, word would spread among the whole Taggart/Hannacker network. He was a marked man and he wouldn't dare show his face to anybody.

He had to make his way out in the wide world on his own. Well, so be it. He could take care of himself. He'd had a plan for his future all mapped out, and he didn't intend to abandon it now. He'd just have to rearrange it, that's all, set up his business enterprise with his South American friends before he was ready to do it, unprepared. Fine. He'd manage somehow. But he did need one thing to pull it off.

Marijuana seeds.

The seeds from which he'd grown this year's crop of seedlings — a crop he'd never be able to harvest — were in three coffee cans hidden under a pile of brush next to the tobacco barn where his crop was to dry. He'd have to send somebody to fetch them, though.

That was for later. Right now his first priority, his only priority, was getting out of Callison County alive.

Scooting to a standing position by bracing his back against the rock and sliding upward, he cradled his injured wrist in his other hand, used the piece of tape that still clung to his left arm to form something like a sling, and then he began to make his way through the trees.

Chapter Seventy

Pieces of duct tape lay on the blood-slathered floor of Jessie's utility room. The window sill below the open window had blood smeared on it, too.

Willie Ray and Riley were struck momentarily speechless. From behind them, Jessie croaked out a single word, "No!"

Willie Ray ran to the window, Riley almost knocked Jessie down running past her and out the back door and around the house, searching the side yard like maybe Jackson was actually still there.

Willie Ray looked out the window at Riley, turning first this way and then that, trying to see into the dark trees.

The moon was high and cast a faint glow, but Riley'd been in the brightly lit kitchen and his eyes weren't adjusted to the darkness. He couldn't see a thing.

Willie Ray went running out the back door then with a flashlight, turned it on and lit up the wall beneath the window. It was smeared with blood. But beyond that …

You could see where Jackson'd landed when he'd jumped out the window, the grass was mashed down there and maybe there was blood on it, hard to see in the glow of a flashlight. But beyond that … he could have taken off in any direction — certainly into the nearby woods, but he might have gone through the cornfield instead, or down the road to his truck, or …

Riley looked at his watch and groaned, realizing for the first time how long it'd been since they'd dumped Jackson in the utility room. If he'd gotten free quickly, he could be … *anywhere* by now.

Willie Ray threw the flashlight on the ground and started yelling, "Where are you, Jackson?" Then he spewed out a string of expletives the like of which Riley hadn't heard since they were in the military. "Come back here, you—"

Come back?

Not likely.

But how had Jackson gotten away in the first place? Riley had bound him with *duct tape.* The tensile strength of duct tape was … Riley didn't know exactly, but he'd wager you could hold a tank together with it. Nobody was strong enough to tear duct tape, certainly not a little wimp like Jackson.

He ran back into the house, into the utility room, and found Jessie standing there, holding up a piece of bloody duct tape between her finger and thumb the way you'd hold a dead mouse by the tail.

"There's … *skin* on it," she said, indicating the

tape. "At least I think that's skin. He pulled … how'd he …?"

It took them a while to calm down enough to think, and once they did, they pieced the grim reality together, figured out how he'd escaped.

"It was them scars on his arm," Willie Ray said. "That's what done it."

The scars Jackson had gotten not as a battle wound, though he'd been awarded a purple heart based on his injuries. He'd been badly burned when he'd tried to put out the flames from the fire he'd started with gasoline poured on the Jingle Bell Man.

The scarred, skin-grafted flesh on his arm … Riley hadn't even looked at it. That was the arm Jessie's stabbed and it'd been covered in blood.

It had been wet, slick, and he'd been able to …

Jessie was right. That was skin stuck on the duct tape. Skin he'd peeled off his arm to get away. Riley thought about traps he'd set for foxes in the woods, where he'd find a paw they'd gnawed off to get free.

"What do we do now?" Jessie asked.

"We find him," Willie Ray said. "Ain't likely he's gonna tell the whole world what he done tonight, what happened to him."

"He'll hide for a while, try to, anyway," Riley said. "But he can't hide forever."

"We *will* find him," Willie Ray said, his voice oddly calm. "I don't care if it takes a month, a year, a decade, a lifetime. I will find Jackson McClusky one day. And when I do, I'm gonna kill him."

Chapter Seventy-One

THE DAWN WAS TURNING the eastern sky shades of pink and yellow, but the red glow Riley Hannacker could see as he turned into Hickory Stump Hollow and started toward his house was in the west. What in the world——? Flashing red lights. Police. Fire truck. *Ambulance.*

Terror clutched at Riley's chest, grabbed hold and squeezed so tight he couldn't breathe.

Drew!

Something had happened to Drew!

And then he was leaping out of his truck, left the door open, the engine running.

He didn't remember any of the drive to get to his driveway, to get up to his house, winding his way around the official vehicles. Three police cars, the sheriff's car, a deputy and a Kentucky State Police cruiser. And the ambulance sitting behind the house.

All with lights flashing.

Drew!

Please, God, no. Don't let anything hap—

He was running then, his eyes raking over the people standing around. In uniforms, the view of them a smear. His heart hammering—

She was there, he saw her coming toward him, wearing that ratty white bathrobe, her hair wild, her eyes wild.

Sherry Lynn.

"Drew!" he cried as they collided, him running to her and her to him. "Where is he? What happened?"

"Oh, Riley. Thank God you're finally home. Where have—"

He grabbed her by the shoulders and shook her, watched her head snap back on her neck.

"Where's *Drew*?"

"Daddy." He heard the cry with his heart. No, with his ears. He let go of Sherry Lynn, looking around frantically.

"Daddy!" And then a small bundle of warmth crashed into his legs, grabbed him and held tight, repeating over and over again, "Daddy! Daddy!"

Riley dropped to his knees and gathered the child into his arms. The boy was shaking like a frightened puppy, his breath hitching in and out the way a child breathes when he's been crying hard for a long time. He crushed the boy to his chest, his eyes squeezed shut. Relief washing over him, washing through the hole the fear had opened in his belly. He felt the wet of tears on Drew's cheeks, knew he was squeezing too hard but couldn't help it.

He let go suddenly and pulled Drew out away from him where he could look at him, his eyes devouring the child, checking for injury or illness. The boy was fine, but his face was a mask of utter desolation, and he started crying again, launched himself into Riley's arms, his arms squeezing tight around Riley's neck.

Riley looked up then at Sherry Lynn standing beside him. Her face was lit on one side by the hard glare of headlights from a car pulling up the lane and the harshness of white light and shadow made her look like a witch, some kind of harpy, a monster. The headlights went out and the image vanished and he saw a mix of emotions on her face — fear the most obvious.

It only occurred to him then, that if all this wasn't about Drew, or Sherry Lynn, then—?

He had to peel Drew off him to stand up, and the child immediately reattached himself to Riley's leg, sobbing hard. Fear flooded back in then, the sense that a horrible black wrecking ball had just swung out all the way to the end of the rope and it hung there, the forces pulling it and pushing it equal for a millisecond, and then it would come crashing back down on him, slam into him—

"Where's Papa?"

"Oh, Riley, honey." The words rode sobs out of her throat. "I'm so sorry—"

"About what?" He was shouting and he couldn't seem to stop. "Sorry about what? What's going on?"

She turned and looked toward the barn and he

saw then that the place was lit up like a circus. The big searchlights on the top of the nearby ambulance were focused on the open bay doors and the interior was lit up—

"Nate," Sherry Lynn gasped.

The word was the wrecking ball, slamming into Riley, knocking his soul out of his body to wander in dark places, where there was no light anywhere.

Shoving Drew at Sherry Lynn, he ran toward the barn — the nightmare vision of running as fast as you can toward something but no matter how fast you run, the something remains a uniform distance away, just out of your grasp.

Someone in a uniform stepped in front of him.

"I'm sorry. You can't—"

He shoved the uniformed man out of his way and saw other uniforms behind him. A huddle of them, gathered around something on the ground.

"Riley!" The voice was LeRoy Taggart's voice and Willie Ray's father was suddenly standing in front of him, holding his arm. "Riley, you need to listen to me. You—"

He brushed LeRoy off, like swatting away a fly, refusing to look into his face, not meeting his eyes, and barreled ahead.

Hands grabbed at him.

"Let me go!" he cried.

"You can't—"

"This is a crime scene, you—"

Crime scene?

With a surge of superhuman strength he threw off

the holds of who knew how many men, intent now on reaching whatever it was that the officers were gathered around.

"Let him go," somebody said, a familiar voice. "Just let him go."

Those trying to block his path moved away, in unison, like it was the rehearsed, choreographed move of a dance troop. And everyone else parted like the Red Sea as he rushed forward to— what was on the ground. He could see now it was a body, somebody was lying there, but he wouldn't let himself know that until he was too close to deny it.

The overalls covered only a tee shirt, and the front was a dark red.

His eyes moved upward from the red stain and his legs buckled, wouldn't hold him upright and he was suddenly on his knees.

Papa.

Papa was stretched out on his back, a small puddle of dark red in a perfect circle around the back of his head, shining, sparkling in the light.

There was a bullet hole in the center of his forehead.

Riley was frozen by the sight as solid as a glacier. Not breathing or moving or feeling or hearing. He only saw, his eyes were all that functioned and he saw.

He saw!

Tilting his head back, he cried out, some kind of primal scream of anguish and grief, a cry that ripped out of his very soul, that tore through his heart on its way, tore through it and left it in tatters, the pieces dangling in the cold wind.

Someone knelt beside him. LeRoy.

"He's gone, son," LeRoy said, his voice thick with emotion. He put his hand on Riley's shoulder. "Nate's gone."

Chapter Seventy-Two

"WHO DID IT?"

Speaking hurt his throat and he didn't say the words to anybody in particular. A question for the universe. Who did it? Who cut short this life force of such power and strength the world itself was unstable without it?

"I don't think they know," LeRoy said, indicating the group of law enforcement officers who'd gathered near the barn door, who had backed up to give Riley some space. Riley looked that way and saw Sherry Lynn standing off by herself, just standing there in a bathrobe with a sobbing child clinging to her legs.

"What—?"

That's all he could say, but it was plenty.

"I got a call from Sherry Lynn. She was hysterical, wasn't making no sense whatsoever, screaming about finding Nate …" He paused, gulped more air. "I come right over but by the time I got here the law was in."

"Who called—?"

"She did, I reckon."

A wave of irrational rage washed over Riley, that the police should be here, now, defiling everything they touched. That *she* would call them.

"Called the ambulance, maybe, and they called the law. I ain't sure. All's I know is when I got here, all them po-lice officers was strutting around, every last one of them determined to look like they was the one that crowed and all the rest just laid eggs. "

Riley saw a man approach Sherry Lynn and Drew and for a moment his mind refused to identify the familiar face. He'd taken two steps in their direction before it registered that the man was Callison County Sheriff Clyde McClusky. He was writing in a little notebook as Sherry Lynn spoke.

"Like I told you before, I don't—"

Riley crossed to where his wife and son were standing, shoved the sheriff out of the way and spoke to Sherry Lynn.

"What happened?"

"I was just telling Uncle Clyde—"

Uncle Clyde. *Uncle!* The word made Riley so angry and sick his stomach rolled.

"Don't tell him, tell *me!*" He could hear the anger in his voice, knew he was spewing it all over her and she didn't deserve it, but couldn't strain it out.

"Now you listen here, Hannacker." That's as far as the sheriff got before Riley turned on him, shoved him so hard he stumbled backward and almost fell. He came back at Riley ready to fight, but somebody grabbed him and held his arm.

"Let him be," said the man holding his arm. The man was Kentucky State Police Detective Booth Graham. "It's his grandpa."

And that was a kind thing to do, a compassionate thing, taking up for the grief-stricken relative — except it wasn't. The words and the action were contradicted by the face. When Riley looked at the detective, his face was a mask — literally a mask. Like it was Halloween and he'd put on a Booth Graham mask to go trick-or-treating. Missing from it were the expressions that would have accompanied such an act. There was no expression of any kind on that frozen face. That face of stone.

But the eyes. The expression in the eyes.

Ah, there was, indeed, expression there. Riley could see it and read it — he was meant to see it and read it, was meant to receive the message those eyes were transmitting. Unbridled *delight*. The vicious, wicked joy in those eyes shone out like a barge light through thick fog. Riley leapt at him, but he was ready, knew Riley'd react to what he could see that maybe others couldn't. He was coiled to strike. Stepping to the side, he grabbed Riley's arm and twisted it up behind his back.

Sherry Lynn cried out and tried to intervene but her uncle pushed her away. Out of the corner of his eye, Riley saw LeRoy Taggart approaching like a storm off the sea.

"Don't you hurt my Daddy," cried a little voice, and they all looked to see the child who'd been clinging to his mother pounding his fists on the detective's legs. "Let him go! Let him go! *Da-deeee!"*

That froze everybody, took all the fight out of them. Shamed them.

Graham released Riley, having made his point, then he leaned close so only Riley heard.

"I'll tell you what I told your grandfather a long time ago when you were off playing soldier in Vietnam. 'One day it will be payback time.' Well, it looks like Christmas came early this year."

He shoved Riley forward and Riley stumbled. What Graham said to him next was loud enough for everybody to hear.

"I don't know who killed Nate Hannacker, but I'd like to find him … and *shake his hand.*"

Drew crashed into Riley again, like he had before, only even more upset.

"Daddy, I want Pop Pop!"

Riley scooped the little boy up into his arms, held him as he cried, great, gulping sobs that seemed to tear his whole body. Riley discovered he was crying, too, must have been because his cheeks were wet. But he wasn't aware of crying, not aware of grief, even. That would come later, he supposed. Right now all he could feel was an emptiness inside that was bigger than he was. The vast, open nothing, the *hole* in his soul was beyond comprehending. He couldn't see the outside edges. It went on and on and on …

And he understood, though he understood little

else that day, that the hole was un-fillable. That nothing he would ever put there in the weeks and months and years ahead would be big enough, that the wind would blow its mournful song through the caverns of that empty space for all eternity.

Chapter Seventy-Three

SCENES, images, words, feelings swirled in a frenetic dance around Riley as he stood holding Sherry Lynn's hand — she'd grabbed him and wouldn't let go — while the rescue squad loaded up his grandfather's body to take it to Mattingly's Funeral Home. Sidney Mattingly was the only mortician in town.

They waited, just *waited,* for hours, everything drawn out as excruciatingly slow as possible, maximum pain and damage. The police took their pictures and talked their talk and tried to act like they were accomplishing something, which they weren't, tried to act like they knew what they were doing, but they didn't.

Riley tried to piece it all together. Somebody had called the house in the middle of the night. Sherry Lynn heard the phone ring, but Papa answered it and she rolled over and went back to sleep. Well, after she went to check on Drew and found him AWOL from his bed. She'd gone looking for him and found him under the dining room table, had dragged him up to his bed before she went back to hers.

Then a loud noise had awakened her. She didn't know what it was, though it was a familiar, and then she heard another gunshot, knew it was a gunshot then.

Riley wasn't there … she'd said that part with accusation, even tonight, even now. So she'd gotten up, gotten a flashlight in the kitchen and went to see what was going on. Assumed, of course, that it was Riley in the barn. He wasn't in the house, after all, so he had to be somewhere. But he'd fired a gun for some reason, which was odd.

She was confused, and the flashlight didn't work because Riley'd never put in fresh batteries, but she finally got it to turn on with a faint beam and she stepped out on the porch, called for Riley but he didn't answer. It looked like the bay door of the barn opened slightly wider then and someone came out. Sherry Lynn wasn't sure at the time it was even a person. It was just a shadow. But instead of coming toward the house, the dark shape darted out into the inky blackness around the barn and was gone.

"Then I started getting frightened. I mean, Drew and I were here and you were *gone* …"

She might have waited for that to elicit some sympathy, and when it didn't she went on.

So she'd gotten the flashlight to work, went out to the barn, opened the door and found …

She'd teared up then, sincere tears and he did feel

some pangs of sympathy for her then, alone at night, going out into the barn and finding—

And she did care for Papa. She really did.

Riley's head was spinning.

Sometime later — still morning, before noon — Willie Ray showed up with Jessie.

It was such a double-edged sword to see her there, her face full of concern. As soon as Sherry Lynn spotted her, she literally tackled Jessie. Collapsing into Jessie's arms, she sobbed in renewed hysteria, had finally found an audience for her performance — too loud, too grief-stricken to be real. Riley turned away.

Willie Ray'd spoken to his father before he approached Riley so he knew what'd happened. They exchanged a look. What was there to say? About any of it? Besides, the two of them had stopped using words to communicate the important things a long time ago. Willie Ray put his hand on Riley's shoulder. That was all. He shook his head then, and Riley even knew why without asking. The sheer magnitude of it defied logic. All that'd happened *in less than twenty-four hours* was staggering.

From finding a bullet hole in his cap through standing together on Jessie's porch, pledging to find and kill Jackson McClusky, no matter what they had to do, no matter how long it took. And then ... *this.*

Riley asked Willie Ray, "You tell your Pa what I remembered?"

"No, and I ain't gonna. No need dragging him into this, he's done been through enough." He paused.

"'Sides, he don't need to be a party to what comes after. That there's just the three of us."

Willie Ray, Riley and Jessie would execute Jackson McClusky.

Execute.

That's what'd happened to Papa. And it'd happened while Riley was at Jessie's last night dealing with Jackson. It occurred to Riley that if he'd been home … then maybe …

But he was honest enough with himself to admit it likely wouldn't have mattered. Papa's bedroom was downstairs. The phone was downstairs. Papa would have answered it, whether Riley was home or not. And after he went out into that barn, Riley's presence wouldn't have mattered then either.

Someone had set Papa up.

Someone had lured Papa out into the barn. How? What possible excuse could somebody come up with to get Papa …?

He'd gone out there willingly, though.

Why?

Most important of all, of course, was why somebody'd … killed him.

Murdered him.

Riley rolled the word around in his mind, mixed it with *dead* into a macabre sauce to pour over reality so he could taste it and feel it, the realness of his loss. Right now that realness kept slipping out of his grasp, there and then gone again. But he couldn't hang onto it for long. Not yet, anyway. That part would come, though. It would come. His grandfather was the most important person in Riley's world. Papa and Drew. Papa had been a part of just about every moment that mattered in Riley's whole life, had guided him, taught him, shaped and formed him, made him a man.

And somebody had shot Papa down in cold blood. Murder. Premeditated. Planned and plotted out. Shot him in the chest, and then …

Just like Ike had shot Johnny and Joe after the wreck. Papa had described so often and so well what'd happened that day when Nathaniel Hannacker had been just sixteen years old that Riley felt like he'd lived it, too.

… in the forehead.

Was there some significance to that?

Chapter Seventy-Four

JACKSON MCCLUSKY LEANED against the wall of the boxcar.

It bumped and swayed, the wheels clickity-clacking along the track as the train lumbered toward Louisville. He watched the landscape fly by the six-inch slit where the sliding door of the cattle car was ajar. He tried to keep his focus there, because if he looked down at the screeching agony of his broken wrist he would be sick. It was huge, had swole up three times normal size, had turned an ugly shade of blue-black.

But might be the swelling would keep the bones in place until he could get it seen to. Maybe. It sounded reasonable anyway and right now that was enough.

Weak from exertion, dehydration and constant pain, his head lolled on his shoulders, his mind somewhere between sleeping, waking and unconsciousness.

His own fault. All of it had been his own fault.

Everything that'd happened was because he'd screwed up. He had to own that. Them as laid everything off on somebody else, saying nothing was their fault, they never got anywhere. If ain't nothing your fault, then you ain't got no control over nothing, you just a leaf in a stream, bouncing off rocks. If you take responsibility for what happens to you — you got power. You got control, because the onliest thing in life you got any say over whatsoever is your own self. Change yourself and you change your destiny.

He'd seen the threat of Riley remembering and done what he knew to do — strike first, unexpected, and hard. That hadn't been a bad decision. But in his haste, he'd gone off half-cocked. He'd ought to have waited to take Riley out until he had a proper rifle to do it with. He hadn't fired that .22 in years — maybe the shots pulled one direction or another — he didn't know. And that's the thing — he *should* have known. You don't try to kill somebody with a gun you can't depend on. You don't try to kill somebody with the wrong gun in the first place! A .22? Seriously? He needed a .30-06 with a scope. Lie in wait like he was hunting a deer. Put a bullet through Riley Hannacker's forehead and blow the whole back of his head off. *That's* what he shoulda done. He'd used the .22 because it was all he had, couldn't get no better weapon. Now see, there's where the fault lay. It wasn't that he *couldn't*. It was that he *didn't*. It woulda been real hard to lay his hands on the weapon he needed, but he didn't even try, just took what was easy. He'd been in too big a hurry.

Scared. Yeah, he'd been scared. Had let fear pilot the ship. Well, he would learn from that. He would never again let fear take control and determine what he did. He'd think things all the way through to the end from now on, plan for every possible outcome.

And Davie.

The fault there was drugs.

He'd given in for the first time to the urge and his weakness had come within a hair of getting him kilt. He shouldn't never have gone after Davie like he done — just hightail it over there, his judgement clouded and his courage fueled by coke. He'd seen a chance he might never get again, a tiny window of opportunity open up, and went diving headlong into it like he was bulletproof. Coke made you feel like that — that was the draw, the power of that feeling was seductive. Trouble was, coke didn't make you bulletproof, it just made you think you were. He'd learn from that mistake, too.

Jackson's understanding about the need to plan and the destructive power of drugs had come at a high price. It had cost him *everything* — home, future, wealth and very nearly his life.

He'd paid a staggering price ... so what he'd bought with it had to be worth what he spent. What was it his granny used to say — the juice had better be worth the squeeze. He would *never* make those mistakes again. To be worth the price he'd paid, what he had learned from his mistakes had to change the whole trajectory of his life. He would see that it did.

Then the tenor of the train's wheels changed to a different sound, higher and lighter. The train was passing over a bridge, crossing the Rolling Fork River out of Callison County and into Nelson County.

Enduring the agony to sit up straighter, Jackson gazed at his six-inch slit of reality, flashes of sunlight bouncing off the bright river water below.

And he made himself a promise, a sacred vow. He would be back someday. Oh, my yes, indeedy, Jackson McClusky would be *back*!

The End

Epilogue

"I's real sorry to hear about your grandfather."

"I doubt that."

Mama Bert's head snapped up. She wasn't used to being talked to that way. Like Riley cared.

"I assume you come to talk about us being business partners."

"We ain't partners."

"You telling me you ain't gonna honor your grandpa's word about—"

"Honor?" He made a hump sound in his throat. "They ain't no honor here. Papa wouldn't never have gone into business with you if you hadn't blackmailed him. Now he's dead and you ain't got nothing to hold over me so they ain't no business arrangement."

"Now see, that ain't entirely true."

"How you figure?"

"The part about your grandpa wouldn't never have gone into business with me. True fact is him and me was partners long 'fore he got into the weed business. I was the silent partner in a chop shop operation. You didn't know that, didja?"

"I knew. That's why I'm here."

"I'm listening."

"I come to make my own arrangement with you. New contract, new terms. You got something I want, and I got something you want and I'm here to trade."

"What is it I got you want?"

"Information."

"About what?"

"About what you was holding over my grandpa to blackmail him."

"He didn't tell you?"

"If he had, chances are I wouldn't be here asking you, now would I." Riley didn't even try to hide the sarcasm. He was long past caring about offending Mama Bert.

Either she didn't notice, didn't care, or cared too much to let her reaction show. Her face was immobile.

"And if I's to provide that information, you …?"

"We'll cut a deal. I sell you weed to—"

"Why would I agree to buy—?"

"Because you ain't got no idea how big this is. You're thinking small-time. I ain't. I can grow more weed than you could ever hope to sell. I'll guarantee you a set amount and a price that's two-thirds the current market value. And I'll guarantee a better quality weed than your customers can get anywhere else. For five growing seasons. After that, we're quits."

"Son, you's the one don't know how big this is. I got customers—"

"Weed sells by the ounce on the street, by the pound to dealers — you got distribution to move it by the *ton?*"

That stopped her.

"How much do you know about marijuana?" Then he waved her off before she could answer. "You can get roughly a pound and a half of weed from a single mature marijuana plant. If it's righteous weed, that is." He smiled and her face remained impassive. "And mine will be righteous. You can grow between three and six thousand plants on an acre of land. Takes about nine square feet per plant and an acre's 43,560 square feet. By next year, I'll have the seed and the land to grow ten, maybe fifteen *acres* of it."

She said nothing. Neither did he.

"You serious, ain't ya?"

"As a heart attack."

"And you can pull that off?"

"Lot of variables. One of 'em's the law. They'll get some fields. But with a *safe* place to process the crop," he let that hang in the air for a beat, "most all of it'll make it to market."

"Uh huh," she said and just nodded.

"You get more bang for your buck as time goes by. My weed's gonna become the gold standard — THC level so high, won't take but half what it used to take to get high."

"Pretty sure of you self, ain't you, son."

"I ain't your son." He didn't say it hateful or snide or mean. Matter-of-fact as pass the mashed potatoes. Just like Papa woulda said it. "And the proof's in the pudding. You'll find out soon enough if I'm ... *blowing smoke.*"

"So how much weed can you guarantee—?"

"We ain't got a business arrangement until you tell me what I come to find out."

She took his measure and nodded.

"All right. You and them others was in Vietnam, and you wasn't likely paying much attention to what was going on back home. I believe it was on the same day of that big battle — July fifth. Shep McClusky was kilt in a wreck that day and his daddy Parker disappeared. Ain't nobody seen hide nor hair of him since."

Oh, Riley remembered all right. Not the event, but Papa telling him about it when he was still in the hospital at Ft. Knox.

PAPA STANDS beside his bed and Riley thinks he looks old. He couldn't have put his finger on why that was, what specifically had changed about the man, hard to describe when somebody just ages, all of them, body and soul, but that's what Papa had done.

Hadn't even been a year since he saw him last, but he seems to be a decade older. Riley suspects he looks a decade older, too. Maybe more than that. Except Riley's aging is on the inside, not anywhere you can see it. His soul. Riley Hannacker's soul has become an old man.

Papa mentions being in jail with Big-un McClusky, calls Big-un his "partner in crime." The phrase sickens Riley, and he snaps at Papa for getting involved with a McClusky.

Nate is quiet for half a minute, then says softly, "I'm sure you ain't heard, but Parker McClusky disappeared. His boy Shep was killed … in a car wreck, you know, and after that, Parker was just … gone. They've looked and looked but can't nobody find him anywhere." He catches Riley's gaze and holds it. *"He just,"* Nate whispers the last word, *"vanished."*

RILEY HAD NEVER ASKED his grandfather what he'd meant by that.

"I went partners with your grandfather because I knew I could trust him." She gave Riley a sideways look. "Knew he was a honorable man. The fella I'd been working with was Shep McClusky and he didn't take kindly to your grandfather replacing him. 'Parently, neither did Shep's daddy, Parker.

"Me and your grandfather'd agreed we would try out the partner thing for six months, see did it suit us, and the six months was up on the Fourth of July. I ain't total sure what exactly happened, just put it together from what I seen. Your grandfather took a sports car, a red Corvette Stingray, out for a spin, and when he got back to the shop, Shep was there, high as the Goodyear Blimp. He shot the fella working there and took out after Nate in his own sports car, chasing him, shooting at him." She paused there, let that much sink in.

"And a few minutes after that, Shep was in a … traffic *accident*. He run off the road and through a guardrail and was kilt. I wasn't right sure what'd happened 'tween your grandpa and Shep, but that wreck wasn't no convenient coincidence. If I could figure that out, might be some other McClusky who knew Shep was mad at your grandfather could, too."

She stopped.

"You do know what Nate and Big-un McClusky done to Oliver Morris on the Fourth of July — doncha?"

Riley nodded. Papa had told him the whole story one night as they sat together on the front porch, listening to crickets and watching fireflies. Riley could hear the smile in his grandfather's voice when he described how Big-un had grabbed Morris by the lapels and yanked him out of his chair, could still see the rings of cigarette smoke coming out of the darkness.

"I know."

"After what him and Big-un done, if something was to happen to your grandfather, the law wouldn't look no farther than Oliver Morris. Seemed to me that kinda get-out-of-jail-free card would be a powerful temptation for somebody wantin' to settle a score with your grandpa. So I called Nate, tole him he'd best watch his back.

"Later on that same morning — a couple of hours, maybe — I get a call from Nate. He told me he had a 1969 Grand Prix Pontiac, black over silver that he had to get rid of, told me to cut it up into little bitty pieces. Shep's *daddy*, Parker McClusky, drove away in a car just like that and nobody ever seen him again."

Riley's head was reeling.

"When Nate took that red Corvette back to the shop, it was full of bullet holes."

Shep McClusky had tried to kill Papa and Papa had … what? Well, duh, run him off the road. It wouldn't be the first time. And when Parker came gunning for Papa … Papa had killed him, too.

His mind finally arrived at the question Mama Bert was clearly sitting there waiting for him to ask.

"But how could you … *blackmail*——"

"Let's just say I always plan for the future, hang onto all kinda stuff for a rainy day. Things like bullets … a car with the original Vin number …"

Riley was still confused. So she kept those things — how did they *prove* …? He let it go. It didn't matter. The only thing that mattered was that Papa wanted her to keep silent. Wanted it so bad he was willing to strike a bargain with her to shut her up.

"Who else knew about all this?"

"Nobody but me."

Of course she'd say that.

Somebody'd cut that car up. Somebody'd dug those bullets out of the Corvette. Who was that person and who had that person told?

Because if some other McClusky had found out/figured out that Papa was responsible for the deaths of Shep and Parker McClusky, then yeah, that'd be a pretty powerful motive for murder.

And there was another salient fact here to file away for a later time. Mama Bert kept the "evidence" in case she ever needed it. She had it plotted out years ago — kept an ace in the hole to hold over Papa's head. So who else was she holding an ace on? Who and what else was Mama Bert controlling through blackmail?

Papa'd trusted her. He shouldn't have. Riley wouldn't make the same mistake. He remembered the parable from childhood about the snake who got a ride across a river, then bit the man who'd helped. When the man asked why, the snake had said, "You knew I was a snake before you took me in."

Mama Bert was a snake. Riley would never forget that.

"You satisfied?"

He nodded.

"Then let's talk business."

"They ain't nothing to talk about. I told you my terms. It's take it or leave it. You can't blackmail me to get what you want. I ain't give you nothing you can hold over my head." He paused. "And I never will."

Her face turned to stone.

"We do need to talk about Land's End, though. When can we move in and set up shop there? I got a weed crop needs harvesting. "

Want to know what happens next? The saga of the *Cornbread Mafia* continues in Book 3 *Ridin' For A Fall*.

Get Ridin' For A Fall today.

A Note from the Author

Thank you for reading *Blowin' Up A Storm*.

If you enjoyed this book, please consider writing a review on your favorite bookselling site so other readers might enjoy it too. Just a couple of sentences would mean a lot to me.

Thank you!

Ninie Hammon

Ninie Hammon (rhymes with shiny, not skinny) grew up in Muleshoe, Texas, got a BA in English and theatre from Texas Tech University and snagged a job as a newspaper reporter. She didn't know a thing about journalism, but her editor said if she could write he could teach her the rest of it and if she couldn't write the rest of it didn't matter. She hung in there for a 25-year career as a journalist. As soon as she figured out that making up the facts was a whole lot more fun than reporting them, she turned to fiction and never looked back.

Ninie now writes suspense--every flavor except pistachio: psychological suspense, inspirational suspense, suspense thrillers, paranormal suspense, suspense mysteries.

In every book she keeps this promise to her Loyal Reader: "I will tell you a story in a distinctive voice you'll always recognize, about people as ordinary as you are--people who have been slammed by something they didn't sign on for, and now they must fight for their lives. Then smack in the middle of their everyday worlds, those people encounter the unexplainable--and it's always the game-changer."

The Taken

The Changed

The Hidden

The Saved

The Unexplainable Collection

Five Days in May

Black Sunshine

The Based on True Stories Collection

Home Grown

Sudan

When Butterflies Cry

The Knowing Series

The Knowing

The Deceiving

The Reckoning

The Fault

Stand-alone Psychological Thrillers

The Memory Closet

The Last Safe Place

9 781629 551494